ADVANCE PRAISE FOR CHARLOTTE HUBBARD AND *A PATCHWORK FAMILY*!

"Heartwarming characters, a moving story…
A Patchwork Family is a magical book."
—BOBBI SMITH
New York Times Bestselling Author

"*A Patchwork Family* confirms the power of
love. Charlotte Hubbard is a wonderful writer."

—EVAN MARSHALL
Author of *The Marshall Plan*

LOVING MERCY

Judd brushed her cheek with a kiss. "What does the Lord require of us, Mercedes?" he whispered.

Mercy focused on the top button of his shirt. The verse from Micah was as familiar as her own home, for she'd stitched it into a sampler that hung in the front room. Still, her husband was evading the issue! Quoting Scripture, rather than caring how she felt about a decision that would alter their lives so suddenly. So drastically.

"To seek justice, to love mercy, and to walk humbly with our God," he replied softly. He pulled her closer so she couldn't wiggle out of this conversation. "Now—I already love Mercy more than life itself, more than I ever dreamed possible when I married her. And Lord knows you've had to walk humbly, since you left your family to homestead out here, for me.

"But where's the justice for these children, if we don't help them? Malloy's done all he can to find their mother. Maybe God's chosen us to be their caretakers, knowing what a very special, loving woman you are. Knowing that we feed the hungry and clothe the naked—like we did Nathaniel and Asa—rather than just giving lip service to our faith."

Why did Judd have to be so eloquent, and so absolutely right? Why did her own selfish wishes— her already busy life—seem more important than the welfare of children who'd done nothing to deserve abandonment?

Still, there was only so much time and love to go around. Wasn't there?

A Patchwork Family

CHARLOTTE HUBBARD

LEISURE BOOKS NEW YORK CITY

A LEISURE BOOK®

July 2005

Published by

Dorchester Publishing Co., Inc.
200 Madison Avenue
New York, NY 10016

ISBN 0-8439-5551-1

Printed in the United States of America.

Visit us on the web at www.dorchesterpub.com.

"All I am or ever hope to be, I owe to my mother."
—Abraham Lincoln

*In memory of my mom, who told me I could
be and do whatever I really wanted. So here I am.*

*And with much love and many thanks to Neal,
who never stops believing I can write my books.
Happy 30th anniversary!*

*Many thanks as well to my agent,
Evan Marshall, for his guidance and enthusiasm!
And to my editor, Alicia Condon, for her contagious
sense of excitement as we begin this journey together.*

AUTHOR'S NOTE

The characters in my "Angels of Mercy" series discuss Negroes and colored men and Indians, because in the 1800s such terminology wasn't derogatory or demeaning. It simply was. The Monroes and Malloys pray and discuss their faith in public, too, because a strong belief in God was the foundation these homesteaders built their lives upon.

So, at the risk of writing a politically incorrect story, I have told a more authentic, historically accurate one. I applaud my editor, Alicia Condon, for supporting me in this.

A good wife who can find?
She is far more precious than jewels.
The heart of her husband trusts in her,
and he will have no lack of gain.
She does him good and not harm,
all the days of her life.

She opens her hand to the poor,
and reaches out her hands to the needy.

Her children rise up and call her blessed;
Her husband also, and he praises her:
"Many women have done excellently,
but you surpass them all."
Charm is deceitful, and beauty is vain,
but a woman who fears the Lord is to be praised.
Give her the fruit of her hands,
And let her works praise her in the gates.

—**Proverbs 31**

Chapter One

July 1866

"Stagecoach a-comin'! Stagecoach a-comin'!"

At the sound of Asa's spirited cry, Mercedes Monroe stepped out of her steamy kitchen to witness the event that never ceased to amaze her. In the distance, a cloud of dust hovered above the Kansas prairie, creeping closer until she could just make out the boxy shape of the coach and the rumbling of the horses' hooves. The driver, Mike Malloy, had a flair for showmanship, so he always urged his team into a final dash before he brought his passengers to a spectacular stop.

Mercy had no more time to watch him, however. In minutes, her front room would be filled with peevish, ravenous passengers jostling for seats around the long trestle table set for their dinner.

She rolled her calico sleeves higher above her elbows and dished up food from pots on her cookstove.

1

Today she was serving sausages, which had split their casings to season fresh cabbage wedges floating in fragrant broth. Three prairie chickens, browned to perfection, fell quickly into serving pieces as she wielded her knife. As Mercy carried these platters to the table, she heard her husband, Judd, instructing the two colored hands.

"Be quick about trading those teams, now—but check the wagon axles and harness leather, too! If stages break down, or word gets out that we provide poor horseflesh, we're out of business."

Mercy smiled. Judd's warning was more to inspire Nathaniel and Asa than to express real concern. His reputation on the Holladay stage route remained solid because he raised the sturdy Morgans the drivers depended upon—and because his wife served up the best meals between Atchison and Denver. Mr. Holladay had told her so himself.

She checked the sideboard, where five apple pies waited alongside baskets of fresh cornbread. Coffeepots and pitchers of lemonade sat on the table, with butter and peach preserves she'd made last fall. They collected a dollar and a half for each meal—more, when well-heeled passengers were favorably impressed—so Mercy proudly presented her morning's efforts as her part in supporting Judd's ranch.

As she carried out bowls of corn pudding and gravy, the stage pulled to a halt out front. Malloy's jubilant cry of, "Whoa, there! Easy does it, now! Everybody out!" rang around the yard, and as the dust settled, Asa rushed to open the stage door. Three stalwart young men who'd ridden atop the coach clambered down like monkeys, but passengers who'd been cramped inside for the past few hours accepted Judd's help.

"The basins and privies are that way," he announced, gesturing toward the side of the house. "And if the aroma's any indication, my wife's cooked up a fine spread. Please hand her your money as you go inside."

Mercy opened the door, smiling at the assortment of humanity headed toward the washbasins. The young bachelors who would each devour enough for three people—probably westward bound, to seek their fortunes in California. Two enormous matrons, apparently sisters, who would criticize every bite, yet slip the last of the cornbread into their skirt pockets if they saw the chance.

Others walked stiffly to the privies, and then Mercy's gaze riveted on the last two to disembark, a girl of perhaps twelve and her younger brother. Both sported flame-red hair and dusty, worried faces. Malloy spoke to them with a kind smile, pointing toward the basins. Then he took Judd aside.

Mercy frowned. Something was amiss with these children. Passengers were now greeting her, however, so she welcomed them and took their money. When one of the young men speared a sausage before his backside had even met the bench, she cleared her throat.

"Excuse me, sir!" she called out. "But in this house, we wait for everyone to be seated and the food to be blessed. Otherwise, the women and children wouldn't have a fair chance at it, would they?"

His dark eyes challenged hers, but he dropped the meat fork.

"Thank you," she replied graciously. "And I'd be obliged if you gentlemen would pour the coffee and lemonade. Those who arrive first must be the servants of all, you see."

The young man gaped at her, until his cohorts snick-

3

ered and reached for the pitchers. The other passengers had washed and were urging those in front of them to be seated quickly, so they could maintain the coach's schedule. Again her eyes were drawn to the two children, who fidgeted in front of Mike Malloy as though they would rather have remained in the coach.

"I hope you like chicken and cornbread and apple pie," Mercy said to entice them. She longed for the day when children of her own would sit around their table, so she always greeted young travelers with enthusiasm.

This pair, however, seemed anything but happy to be here. The girl turned her slender face away as though she were tongue-tied, while her brother glanced doubtfully up at Mike and Judd.

"Eat up, kids," their driver encouraged. "Those two places on the end'll be fine, and I'll cover your tab. Mr. and Mrs. Monroe wouldn't let anybody go hungry, believe me."

Mercy shot her husband a questioning glance as Mike guided the two redheads to the table. Judd brushed his black hair back from blue eyes that caught hers in a serious gaze. "After grace, Malloy wants to talk. I'm not sure what it's about, but by the looks of his two charges, we'd better be ready for anything."

What on earth did he mean by that? Her heart lurched in her chest, and the brief caress of his callused hand did nothing to quell the uproar inside her.

Mercy stole another look at the waifs who perched nervously on the wooden bench. Like the others, they were caked with the grit that drifted though the coach windows onto their sweaty clothes. The girl's dress was taffeta, but a size too small. The boy's shirt was patched, and the seat of his britches shone slick from wear.

4

"Shall we return thanks?" Judd invited in his low, steady voice. He stood with his hands clasped at the end of the table. "Dear Lord, for the privilege and opportunity of another day, we thank Thee—"

Mercy peered through the slits of her eyelids. The children sat with their heads bowed, as though accustomed to prayer at home. The boy kicked his legs back and forth, a sign that he was never still.

"—ask Your blessing upon those around this table, who journey to new horizons and—"

Where were these two bound? And why did they appear to be running from something, instead of to the new opportunities Judd mentioned in his prayers? Mercy shifted, eager for the blessing to be over so she could hear Mike's answers to the questions whirling in her head.

"—for we ask these things in the name of Your Son, the giver of life and salvation. Amen."

The clatter of forks filled the room as passengers stabbed the biggest pieces of meat before passing the platters. It had taken most of her morning to prepare this food, so it seemed a pity these folks had to eat so fast. In about ten minutes, she would be left with only crumbs and grease and a mountain of dirty dishes.

Malloy nodded toward the door, and the three of them stepped outside. The hot breeze offered relief from the close quarters of the front room, yet Mercy felt herself growing warmer, bursting with curiosity. Ordinarily, Michael Malloy was an outgoing young man who swaggered in with their mail—because Judd was the postmaster for these parts—and news from around Dickinson County. Today, however, his hazel eyes carried a much more serious message. He stroked his sandy mustache as they stopped a few yards from the house.

"This is a mighty big favor to ask," he began, looking from Mercy to her husband, "and a tough decision to make in a matter of minutes. Those kids were abandoned by their ma, back in Leavenworth. Billy says she rode off in a surrey, with a man in a checkered suit, while he and Christine used the privy."

"How could a mother do that?" Mercy blurted.

Draping his arm around her shoulders, Judd leaned into the conversation. "And how could they have come this far west without her? Why were they even allowed to board the stage after she left?"

"That was *my* question." Malloy slapped his dusty hat against his thigh in disgust. "They say the driver was taking on mail and loading luggage, so he didn't notice anything unusual. Billy caught sight of the surrey as it was hurrying down a side street, and by the time Christine came out of the privy, their ma was long gone.

"I'm thinking Mrs. Bristol arranged all this beforehand," he continued in a low voice. "Folks in Missouri are desperate these days, but not even a destitute woman would disappear with a total stranger. The father died in a skirmish with a group called the Border Ruffians, after the war. They have no kin left in Richmond, and the kids' fares are paid through to Denver."

"Maybe she plans to meet them there," Mercy piped up.

Judd looked doubtful. "Sounds to me like the man in the suit paid their fares to get rid of them. They'd be excess baggage to the sort of man who'd meet a woman on the sly."

"That's my guess," the wiry driver agreed, "and I'm betting he paid that express office manager—and maybe the driver—to look the other way. Any man with a conscience would've chased that surrey down or kept the kids himself, until their ma was found. But the war's changed things."

Judd pondered the story for a moment, glancing toward the house. "So they've ridden nearly two hundred miles, and nobody's taken them in?"

"I—I was hoping you folks would," Michael said urgently. "The Barstows don't have the room, but since you were kind enough to take Asa and Nathaniel under your wing, I thought maybe—"

"I don't believe what I'm hearing." Sweat dribbled down Mercy's spine, but the summer heat was nothing compared to the apprehension that made her cheeks prickle. The story was so sketchy. So many questions would probably never be answered about these children and their wayward mother. "Judd and I really need to talk about this. We—"

"Of course you do," Malloy said. "I'm hoping it'll be a temporary situation. When the next driver out of Leavenworth heard about this, he sent word along the stage line, and to the authorities there, hoping somebody might catch sight of Mrs. Bristol and her gentleman friend."

"But if they don't leave town, or if they go east, they're not likely to be found," Judd speculated.

The driver nodded. "I also sent a message back to Richmond, to see if any neighbors might take the kids. Might be a few days before we hear back, though."

"*If* you do," Mercy mumbled. She glanced over her shoulder, hoping the adults were seeing that the chil-

7

dren ate enough. Mike's story explained their worn clothing and haunted expressions, but how could she and Judd assume such a responsibility on such short notice?

"You folks talk it over," Malloy suggested quietly. "Don't mean to rush you, but those two old biddies've been pestering me about meeting their connecting stage in Denver. So the sooner I eat and leave, the sooner another driver gets the pleasure of their company!"

A smile withered on Mercy's lips as Malloy hurried toward the house and whatever scraps might be left. As though sensing they'd be heard from the front window, Judd steered her toward the back of the house. The two hired men were now leading a fresh team of Morgans toward the stagecoach, but the animals' beauty was lost on her.

"How can he expect us to . . . it's one thing to take on two colored hands who help keep the ranch running—no matter how the neighbors object," Mercy muttered. "But two children! What if their mother never comes for them?"

"That's a distinct possibility," her husband said with a sigh. "But where else can Billy and Christine go? What a horrible sight it must've been for that boy, to watch his mother take off. To realize she'd planned to leave them."

Mercedes swallowed hard. Judd was calling them by name, worrying about them, as though he sincerely cared about their welfare. She did, too, of course. But a man never considered the extra cooking, the laundry and sewing, the emotional investment these poor vagabonds would require. It was work she would take on in addition to picking and preserving their vegetables, and preparing for the stage passengers, and—

"They could be a big help, you know," Judd said quietly. "The girl's old enough to assume duties in the kitchen, or—"

"Or to make more work, if she's mad at her mother. What if they don't want to stay? They'll be nothing but trouble!"

Judd frowned. "It's not like you to be so uncharitable, Mercy. They're casualties of the war, and if solid folks like us don't open our homes, how far will they have to go? The streets of Denver are no place for them to end up."

"So you've already decided? What about *our* children, Judd?"

He rested his hands on her shoulders, sensing that the real issue had surfaced now. Tendrils of Mercy's chestnut hair had worked loose and were clinging to the sides of her damp face; her huge brown eyes shone with unshed tears as she gazed up with a challenging yet tremulous expression. Five years of an otherwise satisfying marriage had brought them no babies, and the subject was becoming difficult to discuss. She wanted children so badly. And he understood why a woman would prefer to raise her own, rather than taking another mother's castoffs.

But there was no time to repeat the reassurances he comforted her with when she lay awake at night, wondering why God hadn't granted her fondest wish. The stage left in five minutes. He had to make her see reason without upsetting her further, or those two kids would ride on to more rejections instead of finding the home he felt so compelled to give them.

Judd brushed her cheek with a kiss. "What does the Lord require of us, Mercedes?" he whispered.

She focused on the top button of his shirt. The verse

from Micah was as familiar as her own home, for she'd stitched it into a sampler that hung in the front room. Still, her husband was evading the issue! Quoting Scripture, rather than caring how she felt about a decision that would alter their lives so suddenly. So drastically.

"To seek justice, to love mercy, and to walk humbly with our God," he said softly. He pulled her closer so she couldn't wiggle out of this conversation. "Now—I already love Mercy more than life itself, more than I ever dreamed possible when I married her. And Lord knows you've had to walk humbly, since you left your family to homestead out here with me.

"But where's the justice for these children if we don't help them? Malloy's done all he can to find their mother. Maybe God has chosen us to be their caretakers, knowing what a very special, loving woman you are. Knowing that we feed the hungry and clothe the naked—like we did Nathaniel and Asa—rather than just giving lip service to our faith."

Why did Judd have to be so eloquent, and so absolutely right? Why did her own selfish wishes—her already busy life—seem more important than the welfare of children who'd done nothing to deserve abandonment?

Still, there was only so much time and love to go around. *Wasn't* there?

The scraping of benches against the floor signaled the end of the meal. Mercy's heart pounded, torn between what she wanted and what she ought to do. She turned toward the open back door to see a taffeta flounce and a dusty red braid disappear into the kitchen.

10

"That little . . . she was eavesdropping!"

"In her situation, wouldn't you?" Judd teased.

He knew not to press for an answer, knew his wife needed a few moments to make this difficult decision. As the wind whipped her faded blue dress around her slender frame, Judd wondered if Mercy ever regretted marrying him, and he wished he could provide the comforts she'd been accustomed to in Philadelphia. Life on the plains was difficult, and he prayed he hadn't asked more of his loyal, compassionate woman than she could agree to this time.

He entered the kitchen a few steps behind her. Judd had felt responsible for Billy and Christine the moment he heard their story—and so had his wife. Yet she wavered for very human, very understandable reasons.

And if Mercedes said no, he wouldn't argue. A man was the head of his household, but out here where the endless days of drudgery made a wife an equal partner, Judd knew not to push too far. He couldn't possibly manage this ranch and the way station alone.

He heard voices heading out the front door, eager to press on now that appetites were satisfied. When a small, redheaded figure appeared in the kitchen doorway, Judd held his breath. The boy's question was written all over his face. So young he was, to beg for the home and affection that should have been his birthright.

Mercy stood near the stove, looking down at the dusty, bedraggled stranger. Her back remained gracefully straight, but the loose knot of hair at her nape quivered with her indecision. Judd wanted to smile at the boy from over her shoulder, to say something encouraging. But this moment and this choice belonged to the woman he loved.

Billy Bristol glanced at the departing passengers behind him, curling the brim of his hat in his hands. His sister lingered in the front room, pretending to study the stitched samplers on the wall. The house was so quiet that when the boy cleared his throat, the sound filled the little kitchen, amplifying the tensions he'd caused a dozen times in the past two hundred miles.

"I . . . that was the best dang pie, Mrs. Monroe! And since there ain't but two pieces left, I was wonderin' if I could wrap 'em up for me and my sister," he said in a tumble of words. "We don't know how far it might be before . . . before we set down to another feed like you fixed us."

Mercy stifled a sob. What a brave young man, to think ahead and provide for his sister! She crouched to get a better look at him, realizing that he might be small for his age. Billy focused eyes the color of cornflowers on her, eyes that blazed with his determination not to cry. His gritty face, lined with a telltale track on each cheek, gave only a hint of the agony he must have felt since he saw that surrey whisking his mother away.

"Judd and the hands and I haven't eaten our dinner yet," she said in a tight voice. "So maybe—"

"Oh." He let out a forlorn sigh. "Guess you'll be needin' that pie, then. We better be gettin' back onto the—"

"So maybe you can sit and talk to us while we eat," she heard herself continue. Her hands went to his shoulders, and for this boy her heart found the words she couldn't give to Judd. "I always save our share back . . . and the pie on this windowsill is peach. So if

12

you and your sister want to stay with us awhile, there'll be plenty to go around, Billy."

His mouth dropped open. "You mean it?"

She nodded, blinking rapidly, feeling Judd's strength and approval as he stepped up beside her.

"We've got tickets to keep going—clear to Denver," Christine challenged from the other room. "So it's not like we have to stay."

"No, but we'd like you to," Judd replied firmly. He smiled at her, respecting the fear behind her defiant pride. "If you'd rather ride another four hundred miles with those two old ladies, though . . . I bet they snore something awful, and take up an entire seat."

Christine giggled nervously. And when she realized her arduous ride could be over, she ran through the door, hollering, "Mr. Malloy, wait! We need our trunks!"

"I gotta go help!" Billy rasped. He wiggled out of Mercy's grasp, his voice joining his sister's outside.

"You certainly have a way with women, Judd Monroe."

Mercy rose on shaky legs. Her husband's arm steadied her, and his lingering kiss spoke of a love come down from God, a love she would have to trust more completely in the days ahead. Not since she'd left her family and friends back East had she made a decision that scared her this way.

In the time it took to eat a meal, their four lives had changed forever.

Chapter Two

"Mama just weren't the same after they killed Daddy and kidnapped my brother Wesley," Billy remarked with a doleful shake of his head.

"*Wasn't* the same," his sister corrected. "But she had no excuse to dump us like unwanted puppies! She's got some tall explaining to do when she passes through here. And believe me, I'll be waiting for her."

Christine glared across the table at Billy, as a warning not to air the family's dirty laundry. The little boy who looked so much like her returned her scowl, as though he intended to have his say despite her embarrassment.

"We left Topeka 'cause you said she weren't never comin' for us! So—"

"I changed my mind, all right?" she snapped. "It only makes sense that Mama would head west to pursue those business opportunities she mentioned. And to get to Denver, she has to ride the stagecoach through here. Right?"

14

Piercing green eyes brought Mercy out of her wool-gathering. She'd been so intent on listening between the lines of this conversation that her dinner remained untouched on her plate, and Christine's question caught her by surprise. The girl wasn't telling everything she knew, perhaps because the truth was too painful. Or because she enjoyed toying with Billy.

"She could head west in her own wagon," Judd reasoned, "but given the Indian troubles we're having, I hope she's not that foolish. Do you have relatives in Denver, or—"

"No! It—it just seemed like a good place for us to start fresh," the girl answered quickly. "Billy's right. Ever since we lost Daddy and Wesley, Mama has acted very confused. Who knows what she had in mind when she packed us all up and bought those stagecoach tickets?"

Christine was dodging the issue, which was understandable: she sat at a strange family's table, where two colored hands stole glances at her as they ate and the man and his wife asked a lot of questions. Christine Bristol was young enough to be extremely upset by the drastic changes in her life since the war, yet old enough—proud enough—to pretend she and her brother could get by on their own.

Seeing how Billy's eyes lingered on their food, Mercy set a slice of peach pie in front of him. "So the Border Ruffians took your brother, and you've never seen him again? How awful."

"Yes, ma'am. Wesley was my twin," he clarified, brightening at the first taste of the pie. " 'Cept he was bigger and ornerier than me. He was out in the corrals with Daddy that night, drivin' the horses into the barns before a storm blew in. Next thing we knowed, a

15

gang of bushwhackers with torches and shotguns come thunderin' in, demandin' fresh mounts. Daddy said they could pay for 'em, same as everybody else. We had us a fine breedin' farm, with registered stock, you see."

He plied his fork slowly through his pie, as though recalling these events had put him into a trance. "But they was in no mood to argue. They shot Daddy down and then lassoed themselves each a horse. Left the gates open and shooed out the rest of the herd before throwin' their torches into the barns.

"That's when they spotted Wesley runnin' down the lane to get help," he continued in a tighter voice. "They rode right at him, and one man just scooped him up off the ground. Mama run out of the house, screamin' at 'em to bring her boy back, but—but they just kept ridin' into the night."

Mercy's eyes went wet. Any woman could lose her mind after witnessing such events. She could picture the family they must have made: Christine and her mother in their stylish gowns; Wesley and William, two redheaded boys with devilish grins; a strong, hard-working father who ran the ranch. And within minutes, this portrait—their life—was forever shattered by a shotgun blast and then burned beyond recognition. It would be horrible enough to bury a husband and lose the family's livelihood, but perhaps worse to wonder if Wesley was dead or alive.

"I'm so sorry," Mercy murmured. "I didn't mean to upset you, Billy. Didn't mean to pry."

He shrugged, still appearing removed from the harsh realities he'd described. "The neighbors returned what horses they found wanderin' loose, but

16

there wasn't enough to keep the farm from goin' broke, even when we sold 'em."

"And hardly a week after Daddy was in the ground, Mr. Massena paid us a call," Christine chimed in bitterly. "He said a payment was due, knowing full well Mama didn't have the money—and wouldn't, what with the horses and barns being gone. He reminded me of a vulture in his black frock coat, staring down at Mama with those beady eyes and that beak of a nose."

"The bank foreclosed on her?" Judd's blue eyes blazed as he considered this. News often reached them about corrupt bankers and politicians seizing the farms in war-torn Missouri, but it took a truly despicable man to turn a widow and her children out of their home. Knowing how long and hard he'd worked to establish his own breeding stock here, Judd felt a special sympathy for these innocent victims who now sat at his table.

Christine nodded, playing with the end of her rust-colored braid. "Mama pleaded with him to give her a little more time, until the hay could be cut and sold. But he'd have no part of that. A couple weeks later, he came by to introduce a Mr. Wyndham as a possible buyer for the place."

"He did?" Billy's next bite of pie stopped short of his mouth as he shot his sister an accusing look.

Christine's smile was catlike. "I was on the upstairs landing when they arrived, so I couldn't help hearing their conversation. Mr. Wyndham was an Englishman, looking to invest in a country estate—very dapper in his pinstripe suit. He wore his waxed mustache curved up like a wicked grin," she added smugly. "But he wasn't interested in the property. Said it required too many improvements."

Mercy wanted to slap Christine for baiting her little brother with information she'd been withholding—information embroidered by an eavesdropper's active imagination, perhaps. But this was no time for discipline that might further alienate the girl.

"That's a shame," she remarked as she stood to stack the dirty plates. "I wish your mother could've received something for the place, even from a foreigner who might pay less than it was worth. But you and Billy are here now, and we're pleased to have you. We'll pray she's finding another way to support her family, and that she'll come for you as soon as she can."

Was she giving them false hopes? Did she sound sincere, to children who'd been abandoned by the woman they loved and depended upon most?

As she carried the dishes to the kitchen, Mercy ran the fragments of their story through her mind. Billy appeared thunderstruck by some of his sister's statements—betrayed, because he hadn't been privy to information that he, acting as man of the family, deserved to know. Her heart went out to them both, even as she shook her head over Mrs. Bristol's unmotherly deeds.

She was inclined to believe Mike Malloy's version of the story, about how the man in the checkered suit had paid the children's way, as well as bribing the express office manager to get rid of them. After all, how would Mrs. Bristol have scraped together more than three hundred dollars for their stagecoach fares?

Judd was apparently interested in this angle, too, because when she returned to the front room he was encouraging the children to recount the events at the Holladay depot. "What can you tell us about the driver

18

and the man in charge of the stage stop in Leavenworth? They might help us locate your mother," he
added with a kind smile.

Christine rolled her eyes, pointing across the table.
"Ask *him!* I was using the necessary, and when I came
out, Billy was babbling about Mama riding off in a surrey, with some man in a suit. If *Wesley* had been with
us, he would've chased them down!"

"If you didn't take so long in the—I couldn't just
leave you there to—"

"Scaredy-cat! If you weren't such a baby—"

"Enough!" Judd smacked the table to silence them.
"I know you're tired and upset, and we're asking you
questions about a very difficult situation, but squabbling with each other won't solve anything. Billy, did
you get a good look at that man with your mama?"

"No, sir. We'd spent most of the night in the stage
comin' from home, and I had to use the privy, too." He
studied the crust of his pie. "When we went runnin'
back to the coach, the clerk handed us our tickets like
he knowed who we was. He told us we was to ride on
ahead. Said Mama had run across an old friend, and
she'd be along a stage or two later."

"I informed him our mother would do no such
thing!" Christine put in. "And I said we'd best wait for
her there at the depot. I told him to get our bags out of
the boot, but he refused—and showed us that Mama's
two trunks were still on board. Then he gave me
money for our meals and a hotel room in Denver.
Mama had told him we'd be obedient, capable children, and that I was to be in charge and Billy was to
quit sniveling and mind his sister. It . . . that's just
what she would've said, you see."

Judd exchanged glances with his wife, noting the suspicious rise of her eyebrow. "Is that how you recall it, Billy?"

"Yup." He sighed, resting his head forlornly on his fist. "The man told us to hurry up, that we was makin' the stage late. I just couldn't believe Mama would send us ahead—not after the way she carried on when Wesley got snatched. But when I caught sight of her, ridin' away with that man, she weren't lookin' back, neither."

"And as we rode to the next couple of stops, we talked about how Mama didn't have any friends in Kansas," his sister said. Her voice faltered, and she took a moment to compose herself. "And if she did, she'd want them to meet us, wouldn't she? We—we thought she might've had one of her spells when she's not thinking quite right, so we got off at Topeka. Stayed there two days and nights, watching for her when every stagecoach passed through. Hoping it was just one of her silly mistakes."

Mercy had stepped up beside her seated husband to listen to this tale, and she gripped his sturdy shoulders. All cockiness had gone from Christine's voice as she slumped dejectedly on the bench. The girl's agony clutched at Mercy. How horrible it must have been, to realize her mother had taken off without a backward glance, without any warning. Probably on purpose.

Billy cleared his throat. "We asked the man in Topeka to telegraph Leavenworth, to check the passenger lists for Mama's name. When the reply come back, it said they'd never heard of no Virgilia Bristol nor her children. It was a lie, but what could we do about it?"

"We do have our fares to Denver," Christine asserted with an upward tilt of her chin. "So we've decided to find a new life for ourselves, somewhere we can keep an eye out for Mama. Mr. Malloy took a shine to Billy—even let him ride up on the driver's seat. So of course Billy spilled out the story about—"

"He was a nice man," her brother protested. "He wanted us to be safe, so he asked the station managers along the way if they had a place for us."

"And we do," Mercy said firmly. Now that she'd heard the details from the children's point of view, she couldn't possibly begrudge them bed and board. "Back when the stages first started running, we built the upstairs onto the house to lodge travelers who needed a night's rest. Those two rooms are yours now, for as long as you want them."

Judd's hand found hers, making her heart swell. "We'll expect you to help us out, of course," he told them. "Since you grew up on a horse farm, you know what it takes to keep such a place running. And you can see how much work Mercy puts into feeding stage passengers each week. So as long as you're agreeable to those terms—to pulling your weight, just like you did at home—we'll be happy to have you."

A slow grin lit Billy's face. "I'm small, but I'm real good with horses."

"And how old are you, son?" Judd asked. He liked the boy's honesty, the toughness he'd displayed in the face of such betrayal and loss.

"Ten, sir."

"And you?"

He smiled at the carrot-haired girl, who would try their patience at every turn. But badgering her brother and pretending to be so independent were her ways of surviving, when the only life she'd known had been stripped away by bushwhackers, bankers, and a mother whose treachery defied description.

"I'm thirteen," she replied crisply. "I was at the top of my class in school, before the war, and I can quilt and embroider with the tiniest stitches you ever saw. Right now, though, I want clean clothes and a bath. I doubt we'll stay here long, but it'll be a relief to stop eating and wearing the dust of the road."

"Do you think they'll stay?" Despite the relentless heat, Mercedes sat close to Judd on the back stoop, as they did every evening before bedtime.

"Time'll tell," he replied in a low voice. He wove her small, sturdy fingers between his own. "We can't force them to live here. And as long as Christine has those tickets, she'll be inclined to use them."

"Do you believe what she told us?"

"As far as it goes, yes." Judd brushed loose tendrils of hair back from her damp cheek, studying her moonlit face. His wife had done him proud today, taking on a responsibility she hadn't wanted at first. The boy was easy to like—so eager to please them—but his sister was cut from stiffer cloth.

Christine had shown disgust at having the two colored hands eat with them, and her dislike of their log house, as well as utter disdain for chores performed by servants at home—all before she'd been there for three hours. Mercy's faith and patience would be severely tested, just tolerating such a thorny rose, much less giving her the care and compassion she so badly needed from another woman.

"Like Billy pointed out, she keeps changing her story," he went on. "Partly to bully him, and partly to keep a distance from folks she'd rather not reveal herself to. It's her way of maintaining some control over her life, now that she's lost both parents and her home, I suppose. I can't believe such a comely girl's been a prickly pear all her life."

Mercy smiled ruefully. "I hate to judge their mother, after all the horrible things that have happened to that family. But I doubt Virgilia Bristol will come for them."

"Me, too. She may have spells when she behaves unpredictably, but the way Billy and Christine were whisked out of Leavenworth smacks of a plan. A woman who's grieving for a kidnapped son wouldn't send her other two kids west alone, unless she had some very strong incentive."

"And someone else's money backing her."

"My thoughts exactly." He slipped his arm loosely around her, aware of the heat her calico dress held in. Ordinarily, Mercy sat here nights in only her shift, but the children's presence was already affecting their private moments.

"Could be the man in the checkered suit paid their way to Kansas and made her decisions for her—taking advantage of her financial and emotional state," Judd speculated. "Plenty of women have fallen into that trap of late. A man with such a flair for fashion must've appeared very dapper to Mrs. Bristol, in her loneliness. Judging from the girl's looks, her mother's an attractive woman. Ripe for the picking and ready to fall."

Mercy's fingertip found the single dimple beneath the corner of his lips; the distinctive mark that made this burly man look boyishly endearing. "Makes me awfully glad I fell for *you*, Judd."

He settled his mouth over hers, in a satisfying kiss only longtime lovers could share. "I love you, too," he whispered, plucking out pins until her warm hair cascaded down her back, over his arm. "Shall we go to bed? We've had an eventful day, and another one awaits us tomorrow."

Chapter Three

Christine stepped away from the open window. The Monroes' talk enraged her: they were probably right about Mama, and she hated them for it. Small triumph that a handsome man like Judd found her pretty, when he expected her to work like a slave for the privilege of staying here.

The upstairs room felt airless despite its two windows. Cloying odors of cabbage and sausages lingered in the heat, and she fluttered the hem of her cotton shift to cool herself. Everything about this place grated on her nerves: the log walls with their yellowed chinking, the prairie that stretched endlessly in all directions, the faded clothing these people wore. She'd peeked into their curtained-off room, appalled to see only muslin and calico hanging in their armoire, and underthings made from flour sacks in their drawers.

This house could never be home, and she refused to stay here.

But they'd taken a shine to Billy, like everyone did. Bristling with envy, Christine tiptoed across the hallway to pester her brother. If the Monroes considered her such a prickly pear, she'd live up to that description and make them all sorry before she left.

Yet the sight of Billy sleeping turned her anger to sadness. He looked almost angelic, bathed in moonlight that cast a glow around his bed. For the first time in weeks, he seemed at peace. At this moment, Christine resented his childlike resilience and charm more than ever, but she didn't have the heart to waken him just out of meanness.

Besides, this was her first chance to look through Mama's things without him gawking over her shoulder, asking pesky questions.

Christine returned to her room. The two large camelback trunks sat beneath the lowest part of the slanted, unfinished ceiling. It seemed providential that Mama had entrusted the keys to her when they'd left home—in case she suffered one of her spells on the way to Denver. As Christine unlocked the trunks, however, she sensed the Monroes were right: Mama had been in league with the man from Leavenworth all along. He'd probably paid their three stagecoach fares, luring Mama with the flash of his money. And when forced to choose, Virgilia Bristol had forsaken her children for a man who drove a fancy surrey and dressed like a dandy.

Bitterness welled up inside her. She understood that Mama had been lonely, distraught after losing Daddy and Wesley and her way of life, all in one fateful hour. Ripe and ready to fall, as Judd had put it. But didn't her two remaining children count for anything?

I hope you go straight to hell for this, Mama, Christine thought. A hot tear dribbled down each cheek as she removed the wooden tray from the first trunk. *Did you fool that man? Does he know what a spineless ninny he's latched on to? By the time I find you, he'll probably have thrown you out—tired of your crying and clinginess. I'll have a good laugh then, won't I?*

Christine lifted one folded gown after another from the trunk, recalling how pretty Mama had looked at each of the special occasions they were made for. Most of them hadn't been out of her armoire for months— since before Daddy got shot—and as Christine laid them around her on the floor, their colors shone like a rainbow in the light from her candle. Mama had dyed all her everyday dresses black, so these pretty satins and brocades brought happier times to mind—holiday balls and summer receptions on the lawn, which Mama had gloried in hostessing.

After seeing how her mother had brightened during Mr. Wyndham's visit, Christine could easily imagine Virgilia Bristol adorning herself in these gowns to attract an attentive man. However . . .

Christine fingered the delicate Brussels lace around the collar of a deep green gown Mama wore last Christmas. If she'd planned all along to run off with that man in Leavenworth, why had she left all her clothes on the stagecoach? Lacy silk underthings covered the bottom of the trunk, a testimony to Daddy's indulgence of her exquisite taste. Hard to believe that any woman would send these personal items down the road with the children she no longer wanted.

Christine opened the other trunk, vowing to sort through it before she dissolved in tears. She couldn't believe that Mama had abandoned her without so much as a whispered good-bye, or a hint of her intentions. Harder still to think she'd left her precious Billy behind. Because he was small and had an agreeable nature, the boy had been Mama's favorite since the day he was born.

Fueled by resentment, Christine tossed hats, gloves, handkerchiefs, and shoes to the floor, heedless of their clatter. Beneath the clothing she found the monogrammed comb and brush set that had graced Mama's dressing table. Velvet-covered photograph albums thumped to the floor beside her, the sole mementoes of their home and family before the war.

She glanced at a few framed likenesses—one of herself with Mama on the verandah; one of her twin brothers, dressed in new riding suits, posed with their favorite ponies, Mavis and Maureen. Wesley's mischievous grin made her swallow hard. She'd never told Mama or Billy, but she believed that Wesley was dead. Feisty and clever as he was, he would've escaped his kidnappers long ago if he were still alive.

She found a tin of money, most of it worthless Confederate paper. Assorted fans and buttonhooks and the heavy leather-bound Bible lay at the bottom of the trunk.

Christine smirked. Religion was the furthest thing from Mama's mind these days. Indeed, they hadn't attended a single service since Daddy's funeral. Perhaps Mama's guilty conscience kept her from entering a church, for fear that God would send the roof tumbling down around her. How long had she been planning to deceive her children? To send them away, on a wild-goose chase west?

When she shoved her mother's embroidery bag

aside, her breath caught. Here lay the small diary Mama had kept in her nightstand, locked, so curious eyes couldn't enter Virgilia Bristol's private world.

Christine paused. After all that had happened this week, she had every right to read the secrets recorded between these red velvet covers. A few seconds and a hairpin opened Mama's innermost soul to her, and then she scanned the pages of neatly looped script, eagerly searching for the answers her heart craved.

Entries from last January gave a glowing account of Daddy's surprise birthday party and Mama's crafty ways of keeping it a secret. These paragraphs seemed much too cheerful to be of any use right now, so she skipped forward.

Late February revealed the stark terror that held them captive after the Border Ruffians stole so much more than their horses. Here Mama's penmanship faltered, and details were sketchy. So many things Christine vividly remembered about that stormy night had gone unrecorded, and then days passed when Mama wrote nothing at all. Not surprising, considering how their mother hadn't dressed or left her room for nearly a week following Daddy's funeral.

Brief mention was made of Leland Massena's visit, and Christine scowled. Had the old buzzard given them half a chance to rally, she wouldn't be stuck here in this godforsaken place with two do-gooders who expected her to feel grateful for the chores she was to perform! A page later Mr. Wyndham appeared, dressed in pinstripes with his jaunty hat and handlebar mustache, just as she recalled from peering through the upstairs railing.

Mama's tone radiated hope, and the ink splotches and shaky strokes disappeared from her writing.

Richard Wyndham provided pure delight to-day when he stopped by unexpectedly. I must've looked a fright in my widow's weeds, muddied by my work in the garden . . .

Christine sucked in her breath. Mama hadn't breathed a word about this visit, nor about the ones mentioned on the next few pages! Her eyes devoured the paragraphs, racing through descriptions of his British accent, his genteel manner, the picnic he brought one afternoon. Richard this, and Richard that!

She rocked in a crouch, thunderstruck. Mama was in love with this Englishman—only weeks after she buried Daddy! And Mr. Wyndham had disregarded the conventions of mourning as eagerly as she did.

So why had they left Missouri? Even if this Englishman had found their property in need of too many repairs, he could have acquired another place the bank had foreclosed on. That Mama would have said yes to a marriage proposal was painfully evident on these pages. Yet when she'd explained why they'd be starting fresh in Denver, she spoke only of business opportunities rather than romance.

Christine frowned. What on earth did her fanciful mother know—or care—about business? That should have been the first clue that something was amiss, when they made such feverish preparations for taking the stagecoach to Denver. Forgetting the room's oppressive heat, she plunged back into Mama's narrative, so close to the answers, her heartbeat raced in anticipation.

"Whatcha doin'?"

Christine fell back on her bottom with a gasp and glared toward the doorway. There stood Billy, his hair standing in auburn tufts like ruffled chicken feathers, his drawers drooping from their drawstring waist.

"Nothing! I—" She slammed the diary shut, cursing her brother's uncanny sense of timing. "What're you doing up? Last time I looked, you were dead asleep."

"Heard a funny noise. Then I got to thinkin' about Mama and couldn't drift off again." He took a few steps into the room, taking in the two featherbeds and the washstand with its plain pitcher and bowl, before focusing on the items scattered on the floor.

"Forget about her, Billy. Mama's long gone."

Her brother blinked, looking sleepy and confused. "Then why'd you let on at the table like she was comin' by here to—"

"Shhh!" Christine pointed to the floor, a signal that the Monroes' bedroom was directly below this one. "These people don't want us as part of their family," she went on in an ominous whisper. "They plan to work us like slaves, same as they keep that monstrous big darkie to train their horses—"

"Nathaniel? He is big—and mean-lookin'," Billy agreed, "but he sure has them yearlin's takin' to the bit. Maybe he'll let me help him, after a while."

"—and that little old Asa's not fit to be more than a house boy! Yet they've got him out in the hot sun, working just as hard!" She paused, wondering what ploy would convince Billy they should leave as soon as possible. Since he'd been so close to Mama, perhaps some of her ideas would persuade him.

"Mercy and Judd come on like fine Christian folks, Billy," she said in a low voice, "but they didn't take us in out of the kindness of their hearts. They'll be driving us like slaves before long, and we weren't raised to

31

be anyone's servants. Mama always said we Bristols should never stoop so low."

Billy scowled sleepily. "Daddy gave us chores, Sis. Can't see no harm in helpin' out, after the way they let us have these rooms. Mrs. Monroe makes a fine pie, and—"

"*Shhh!*" Christine hissed. "There's more to life than pie! And you know darn well we'll have to share these rooms when travelers pass through!"

Her brother was obviously too young—or too stupid—to understand the degradation and toil that would be their lot if they remained under this roof, so reasoning with him would get her nowhere.

"Do you want to look at these log walls and wear homespun every day? No, thank you!" she said in a sibilant whisper. "We have our tickets, and when the next stage passes through, we ought to be on it.

"But don't you let on!" she warned, pointing a finger at him. "If they suspect we're short-timers, they'll lock us up here at night, so we can't escape."

Billy didn't look the least bit fazed. In fact, he shuffled slowly around their mother's gowns and belongings, wearing a wistful yet wary expression. "And what about Mama? Are you writin' her off, after only three days?"

"I intend to find her, Billy! She owes us an apology for humiliating us in Leavenworth. For forcing us to scrape and bow for people's pity!"

The heat and her exasperation almost pushed her too far; it wouldn't do to admit she'd listened in on the Monroes, because Billy would tattle on her. If he thought she was innately wise to the ways of women, however, maybe he'd realize she was right—and leave her alone with Mama's diary.

She stroked its crimson cover, continuing in a furtive voice. "She and that man are too smart to follow the stage route, knowing we could spot them. But I bet they head west anyway. I was just reading Mama's account of Mr. Wyndham's enterprises in—"

"How'd you unlock that?"

"Shhh!" Christine shot him a catlike smile. "With a hairpin, silly. Now scat, so I can figure out where they're going. I doubt they'll stay in Leavenworth long, so we've got no time to waste."

Billy didn't take the hint. He stood as though rooted to the floor, pondering what she'd just told him. "You think that was Mr. Wyndham driving the surrey?"

"I do. Mama wouldn't take off with a stranger, you know—and from what I've read, she spent quite a lot of time with him that we didn't know about. Out by the garden, in the gazebo, down around the spring house . . ."

As angry as she was at her mother, Christine couldn't help smiling about her secret rendezvous. "I bet she told him when we'd be working on our lessons with Miss Bryce, so he'd come over when we couldn't spy on them."

Billy's brow puckered. "Why didn't you tell me there was a man lookin' to buy the farm?" he demanded. "I shoulda been there, to show him how we'd reseeded the pastures and painted the outbuildings—things Mama didn't know nothin' about! Maybe he would've let us stay on to run the place for him when he went back to England."

"I'm not sure it was the land he wanted, Billy," she said with a sad sigh. "Now get back to bed. We need to be rested, so we can formulate a plan to leave this awful place."

But again, he seemed deaf to her suggestion. "It really ain't so bad here," he said in a faraway voice. "Better'n bein' squeezed into a stagecoach, gettin' stared at and bein' asked all them nosy questions. Better'n not knowin' what we might find for ourselves in Denver, or—"

Christine rose swiftly to her feet. "Do you know why the Monroes don't have any children?" she demanded in a tense whisper. Her face remained only inches from his while she awaited his answer. "It's because God doesn't think they're good enough, that's why! Do you want to live with wicked people who'll make you eat with slaves and work until you drop? Do you want to be around when God punishes Mercy and Judd for their sins?"

"What about Mama's sins?"

"*Shhhh!* It's not right to speak ill of Mama, Billy. She's not herself."

"But *you* do! You've been accusin' her of—"

Christine grabbed both his bare shoulders and peered into his wide eyes. "I want to track her down to remind her of her responsibilities. To—to keep her from straying down the path of—unrighteousness— before it's too late. It's our duty to save her, Billy. We're all she has."

As he considered this, his expression wavered between a disapproving scowl and utter dejection. "If she can't be the same Mama we had before we lost Daddy, then there's nothin' left worth savin'."

Her jaw dropped. "Billy, that's—"

"It's the truth, and you know it," he insisted bitterly. Tears clung to his eyelashes, but he made no effort to wipe them away. "What kind of mother skedaddles down the street while her children use the privy? And

34

never looks back! And what kind of woman don't lift a finger to save the farm—the home our daddy worked all his life for?"

Christine saw her own pain burning in Billy's blue eyes and couldn't respond. She'd never expected Mama's favorite child to denounce their errant parent so soundly, in a tone that sounded so final.

But as Billy ambled across the hall, she was more determined than ever to hear the answers they needed, from Mama herself. With or without her little brother.

Chapter Four

Billy padded down the wooden stairway barefoot so he wouldn't waken his sister. At the bottom, the door opened to a summer morning that shimmered in the sunrise, revealing the dusty yard, Mercy's garden, the stables and corrals, and an ocean of tall, green cornstalks beyond the trees that lined the river. Chickens pecked nearby, and low grunts told him Nathaniel was slopping some hogs. A milk cow, tethered beside the barn, absently chewed her cud as she glanced at him.

Billy lingered in the doorway, drinking it all in. This separate entrance allowed the Monroes their privacy when travelers stayed over, but it would take more than an extra doorway to keep Christine from nosing around where she didn't belong. Her behavior appalled him. Sometimes he wondered how much of her information she made up, just to string him along.

The smell of bacon and fresh bread lured him to the open kitchen door, where he paused to watch the woman who'd taken them in. Her brown hair was pulled back into a neat knot, and she wore an apron made from a flour sack over her yellow checked dress. She sang as she bustled between the cookstove and her worktable, a vision of sunshine and cheer. Mama had rarely risen before ten, and even then, she pecked at everyone like a discontented hen until nearly noon.

Mercy dribbled hot water from her kettle into a large crockery bowl, stirring its sweet-smelling contents. Intrigued by the lower voice that now harmonized with hers, Billy peered inside to see if Judd was helping her. He seemed too ruggedly masculine—just too big—to fit himself into a woman's kitchen routine.

When he saw Asa with his sleeves folded to his elbows, wielding a rolling pin, Billy gasped.

Mercy and the colored man grinned at him. "So now you know the secret behind my pies!" she chirped. "Sit down for some breakfast, Billy. I hope you like bacon and mush with honey."

"Yes, ma'am. Thank you."

Billy edged up onto the stool beside the table, where Asa trimmed excess dough from around a pie. "You made them pies we had yesterday?"

"Yessir, I did." The old fellow beamed as his knife flew around another pan. "Before the war, I was a chef at a sugar plantation, down 'round Atlanta. Made pies out of pee-cans and buttermilk custard, and biscuits that would please a queen."

Billy cut into his crusty square of cornmeal mush, his eyes wide. "But they let you go when Mr. Lincoln freed the slaves?"

Asa smiled wistfully. "No, Mr. Billy. When General Sherman marched through, we got burned out. Like hell opened up and swallowed us whole, it was. The family moved in with a sister up the coast, but they didn't have the wherewithal to keep the help. So we were on our own."

Billy nodded, wishing he hadn't spoiled the fine mood with his question. Maybe Christine was right: this old man was best suited to household chores. But it seemed clear that the Monroes respected him as a friend and appreciated whatever work he could do.

Glancing around the cramped kitchen, Billy noted half a dozen pies already on the windowsill. Huge bowls of dough rose on the back of the stove. The aroma of sugar and cinnamon mingled with the saltier scents of bacon and coffee, and he soaked up the homeyness of this room. He hadn't been allowed in their kitchen while Beulah Mae was cooking, so it was a treat to watch this white woman and her chocolate-skinned assistant work together. Mercy poured the filling—thick, sweet cherry now—while Asa crimped the crusts and cut designs in the tops.

"Stage comin' through today?" Billy asked. "You got enough food here for an army."

Mercy laughed. "No, we're making ready for our party tomorrow. Our nearest neighbors and folks who manage other way stations will be here for Sunday services, followed by a big picnic and some music. It's an all-day event! Everyone brings food so we can visit until after supper."

"You pitch horseshoes, son?" Asa asked. "We menfolk generally get up a game while the ladies quilt."

"No, sir, I haven't had much practice at it." Delighted to be part of the menfolk, Billy didn't admit that Mama hadn't let him play after one of Wesley's wildly tossed horseshoes hit him in the head.

Asa crimped another pie crust. "Maybe this evening

Mr. Judd and I can give you some pointers, after we get everything set up outside. Lots to do today. Work for every size hand we can find."

Billy nodded eagerly. As he savored his third strip of bacon, he wondered why Christine thought it was so awful to associate with Negroes. Asa's wrinkles and gray-sprigged hair suggested advanced years, yet the sparkle in his coffee-brown eyes told of joy in work well done—an ageless quality that went beyond race and color.

Billy turned to see his sister standing in the doorway. His enthusiasm withered. Christine's peevish pucker suggested she'd been poking into Mama's diary all night, and that she'd sour the pleasant talk he'd been sharing.

"Good morning, Miss Christine!" the colored man greeted her.

Mercy turned to smile at her, too. "Pull up a stool and I'll fix you a plate, dear. We're in the middle of party preparations, so the table's a mess."

Billy felt her condescension as his sister took in the log-walled room that was so much smaller and darker than their own kitchen. They'd eaten in the dining room since they'd been old enough to behave properly, so he hoped Christine wouldn't launch into an unflattering comparison between Mercy's household and Mama's.

She looked at her mush with an exaggerated sigh.

"Asa was sayin' there'll be games tomorrow—and quiltin'," Billy added, hoping to lift her spirits. "There'll be church, and everybody's bringin' food, and we'll have music and singin'. Just like the lawn parties back home!"

His sister scowled. "Sounds like a lot of bother. We won't know a soul."

Mercy set the last four pies in the oven as Asa handed them to her. "Folks along the stage line gather here because our house is the largest, and we have a barn in case the weather takes a bad turn. You'll meet a lot of new friends, Christine. People who've stood by each other through the hard times of homesteading."

"And with all of us helpin', it won't be much bother to get it all ready." Billy grinned, even though he knew that cheerfulness was wasted on the killjoy beside him. "And I'm gonna play horseshoes! Asa and Mr. Monroe are gonna help me polish up my game tonight."

Christine's scowl could have curdled his milk. She looked ready to tell Mama that he was about to live dangerously—to have *fun*—and he enjoyed the fact that she couldn't. As she picked at her food, however, she was working up to something that would put him in his place again.

"So why don't you have any children, Mrs. Monroe?" she demanded. "It seems you have plenty for *little hands* to do around this place."

Billy wanted the floor to open up and swallow him. As Mercy straightened, flushing at his sister's rudeness, he hoped she wouldn't load them both onto the next stagecoach that came through.

Gazing at the girl, Mercy prayed for the wisdom to nip Christine's impertinence in the bud. If the girl sensed this issue was a source of constant torment to her, there would be no controlling such a cruel tongue.

"Children arrive in their own good time," she said softly. "If you recall your Bible stories, Abraham was a hundred and his wife Sarah more than ninety when God announced they would have a son. And this began the lineage King David and Christ Himself came from. Samson's parents were childless for years, too. Good things come to those who wait."

She took a deep breath, to allow her words to sink in.

Christine smiled smugly. She remained silent, so Mercy would have to plead her case.

But Mercy thought of an approach that might appeal to a girl of the Bristols' background. "I know you find our home lacking, compared to what you're used to," she began, "so it's to your advantage that Judd and I don't have children, Christine. This way, when we go to town, the money for shoes and yard goods will be spent on you and Billy."

The girl let out a snort. "Save your money, Mrs. Monroe. I wouldn't be caught dead in calico."

"I wouldn't push my luck, young lady."

The kitchen went silent as Judd's burly frame filled the doorway. His raven hair fell around his face in unruly waves, while his shirt clung to a broad body already damp from a hot morning's work.

"I won't have the people under my roof at odds. And I won't tolerate a thankless child who berates my wife," he stated. He stepped into the room slowly, casting a long shadow across the table.

"You miss your parents terribly, I know—even though your mother deserted you," he went on in a low voice. "But you'd be hard-pressed to find a kinder woman in all of Kansas to care for you, Christine. Your mama would be appalled at the way you've badgered Mercy, and you know it."

Billy shriveled in shame, even though Judd's words weren't directed at him. Clearly Mr. Monroe was the head of this house and his wife didn't wheedle or pout to get what she wanted, like at home. A sense of respect bound them together, apparent in the way he draped an arm around his wife's shoulders as he awaited Christine's response.

His sister had sense enough not to sass back. Her knuckles went white from gripping her fork, though, and he could feel the rage coming off her in waves. The only sound in the room was the rapid tattoo of his own heart.

"When you've finished eating, you'll do whatever Mercy asks of you," Judd instructed. "And if our way of life doesn't suit you, feel free to use that stagecoach ticket you keep telling us about, come Monday.

"But I'll warn you, Miss Bristol," he went on with blue fire in his eyes. "Folks west of here live in soddies and dugouts, where the floors, the walls—even the ceilings—are made of dirt. It crumbles down into your plate while you eat. It lands in your face while you're sleeping, and snakes like to slither inside during a rainstorm. We live in a two-story log house with puncheon floors because Mercy's dowry bought us plenty of homesteading supplies."

His expression relaxed, but his voice remained firm. "Proverbs tells us that the wise woman builds her house, but the foolish one plucks it down with her hands. You're no fool, Christine. We expect you to behave accordingly. Come outside when you're finished eating, Billy."

"Yessir. I'm on my way."

He followed Judd from the kitchen, glad to leave the tension behind him. Sunlight pierced his eyes when he stepped outside, and he had to walk double-time to keep up with the man's longer stride. They were heading toward the corrals when Billy looked up to find Judd smiling at him.

"We have to let the women work that out between themselves," he said.

"Uh-huh. Daddy always did that, too."

"I bet you were his right-hand man, and had a real struggle after he was gone," Judd continued. "You probably had hired men, but he gave you your own responsibilities, didn't he?"

Billy brightened. "Yessir, Wesley and me kept the horses fed and watered, and put down fresh straw after we mucked out the stalls. And after trainin' sessions, I walked the horses around the paddock to cool 'em down."

"What breed did you raise, son?"

"Mostly Belgians, for field work, and quarter horses. But we had Arabians for pleasure ridin', too," he added proudly. "Our trainer was the best in the business. Folks paid top dollar, knowin' their wives and daughters could trust a mount they bought from the Bristols."

He was shielding his eyes with his hand, squinting up as he spoke, when Judd stepped sideways to block the intense sunlight for him. Billy grinned, grateful that this mountain of a man didn't crouch down to his level like most adults. His face resembled leather, from years in the sun. His blue eyes sparkled beneath long black lashes, but Billy sensed that nobody called Judd a sissy because of them!

"If you could do the same chores here that you did at home, I'd be grateful. That way, Nathaniel and I can get the platform ready for tomorrow, and set out the benches and tables. Other days, it'll allow us more time to work the yearlings and expand the corrals."

"Yessir, I could do that!"

A huge hand came to rest alongside his face, gently brushing his hair back.

Billy held his breath. His father hadn't touched him much; felt such coddling was for girls. So this unexpected contact with Judd Monroe felt like a blessing, a benediction. A welcome into the family.

"Your daddy would be proud of how you're carrying your family name through troubled times, Billy," he said. "I'll show you around now. I know you'll take care of these Morgans like they were your own."

After a noon meal marked by Christine's sullen silence, Billy ran outside again. His arms ached from hauling pails of water from the creek behind the barn, but he felt a wondrous sense of freedom. Nobody watched him like a hawk. Nobody treated him as though he were fragile—or teased him mercilessly about being the runt, like Wesley had. He thought about his brother a lot as he worked, wishing he could know the fate of the companion and rival who'd shared his every activity.

Yet it wouldn't be the same if his twin were here. Wesley would complain about the heat and sneak off to the tree-lined river to catch frogs, leaving the work to him and then taking the credit for it. Billy secretly admired his brother's knack for bending Mama's rules and defying Daddy's authority. He wished he had the same courage to speak out when things bothered him.

But being in charge of the horses—being his own man—felt mighty fine, now that the burden of overseeing a bankrupt ranch wasn't on his shoulders. When Billy finished scooping grain into the wooden troughs, he stood back to admire the sleek coats and sturdy conformation of Judd's Morgans.

He'd missed being around horses. He loved their

earthy smell and their soulful eyes; their quiet whick-
erings when they greeted him. Horses would come up
to him when they knew his voice and his way of moving, and he looked forward to that day.

When he passed through the shadowy barn into the
yard, he saw that Asa had joined the other two men.
They were arranging wooden benches in semicircles
that faced a platform, preparing for the worship service. Billy had never gone to church outdoors, except
for Easter sunrise services, because Mama and Christine fretted about bugs crawling up their skirts. Judging from the number of seats, Judd expected quite a
crowd.

"Did you say Mercy's dowry helped you settle this
place?" he asked as he grabbed the end of a bench.
Then he flushed. His question could be considered just
as offensive as Christine's query about children.

Nathaniel regarded him with an unreadable expression, but Asa chuckled. "Mr. Judd's the only man I
know who'll admit his wife helped set him up. Some
are too proud, you see."

Judd laughed, tugging the platform into its usual
grooves in the ground. "You'll find this hard to believe, but my wife came from a wealthy family in
Philadelphia. When we got engaged, her father offered
me a position managing one of his carriage factories.
But I didn't feel suited to the work."

"And you didn't want to be beholden to Mercy's
dad?" Billy asked.

The big man chuckled again. "You hit the nail
on the head, boy. My own father farmed—quite
prosperously—but he had too many sons and too little
land to support us all. So Mercy's parents gave us a

generous endowment to buy land of our own. They nearly shot me when they learned we were going to Kansas to homestead."

Billy scowled. "Why? Didn't they like you?"

"Oh, they tolerated me all right, but I was taking Mercy where savages still roamed and towns weren't settled yet. They were afraid they'd never see their daughter again."

Billy thought for a moment, letting the breeze lift his hair from his collar. "Did her folks live in a big house? With servants and runnin' water and a ballroom?"

"Yes—and they still do. Mercy gave up a privileged life and then invested her entire dowry in supplies so we could stake our claim here. That's why I love her so much."

In Judd Monroe's smile, Billy saw pride of accomplishment, as well as fierce loyalty to his wife. He felt honored that this man would share such feelings with him. And he understood why Judd wouldn't tolerate his sister's insolence.

"We lived in a big house, too. With flower gardens, and a white plank fence around the paddocks, and servants to do the housework," Billy said in a faraway voice. "That's why Christine's bein' so hateful. She ain't used to folks tellin' her what to do."

Judd nodded. "It must've been hard to lose all that. I'd like to think your mother went off with a wealthy man to regain that way of life—for all of you."

Billy's eyes prickled, but his agony had subsided. He felt good here. He had no further worries about food, shelter, or security, and he sensed he could be happy in this untamed land with the Monroes as long as he wanted.

But it was different for Christine. And for Mama.

"You may be right," he murmured. He gazed across the vast, grassy plains, marked only by the ruts of stagecoach and wagon wheels headed west. "But Mama's not strong—leastways, not the way Mercy is. I don't look for her to come after us any time soon."

The next morning, when he was too excited about the party to sleep, Billy heard Mrs. Monroe working downstairs long before dawn. He pulled on his britches and padded outside to fetch a pail of dried buffalo chips from the pile out by the barn. Her smile made his stomach flutter as he filled the bin beside the cookstove.

"Thank you, Billy! What a thoughtful young man you are."

He shrugged, basking in her compliment. "Judd showed me where things was yesterday. I s'pose you'll be needin' some water hauled? Or things brought in from the springhouse?"

By the time he filled the water barrel outside the kitchen door and made his last trip from the little shed where the creek kept their butter and milk cold, wagonloads of neighbors were arriving. Asa and Nathaniel emerged from their quarters in the barn, dressed in fresh muslin shirts and clean pants, to help the guests unhitch their horses. Billy laid the cool food on the kitchen table and hurried upstairs to change.

"Christine! Folks're comin' for the party!"

He peeked into her room, where she was still a large lump beneath the sheet. "Rise and shine!" he crowed, mimicking Beulah Mae's morning ritual. "You's gonna be late, missy, and yo' mama be plumb disgusted with you!"

She raised her head to scowl at him. "I'll be down when I'm good and ready. Not one second sooner."

47

He knew better than to bait her. Felt too fine to waste his good mood on a sister who might rise but would never shine much before noon.

Once he'd donned his better pants and his only clean shirt, Billy glanced out the window. His confidence wavered. These people with picnic hampers would soon find out he and Christine were staying here, after being politely turned away from some of their homes. Would they talk behind their hands? Would they stare at two kids who didn't belong anywhere anymore?

Billy had the urge to burrow beneath the sheets, too, but Mercy would come looking for him. Better to face the neighbors, grateful for the Monroes' hospitality, than to cower behind the unfortunate story that brought them here. How would he defend himself against comments about Mama? Such remarks would always hurt, even though most folks meant well.

But when he reached the kitchen, Mercy steered him toward the yard with a bright smile that made her eyes dance. Her excitement was contagious, and the slender hand on his shoulder transferred some of her strength and energy to him.

"Good morning! Good to see you!" she hailed their guests. "Billy Bristol and his sister are staying with us, so I hope you'll make them welcome."

Billy was immediately surrounded by smiling men and women who shook his hand. Names flew by him in a blur, yet he felt as if Mercy had worked some sort of magic. Just days ago these people had eyed him doubtfully, shaking their heads. Now they seemed glad for him—as though he were a prodigal come home!

Billy blinked. He supposed this tingly feeling, as if

angel dust drifted around him, might be a religious experience. He looked around to see if Christine noticed it, too, but she hadn't come downstairs yet.

She showed herself just as Judd was urging everyone to sit down on the wooden benches. The preacher was making his way toward the platform when she slid in beside Billy, dressed in a frilly blue dress and matching kid slippers.

"Goodness, that man's skinny!" she whispered. "Do you suppose that's his big brother's frock coat he's wearing?"

Billy sighed. She and Mama had prided themselves on being the best-dressed in church, so at least his sister was in a good mood now, seated like a queen among commoners. "He's a circuit rider, Miss Priss. Can't carry many clothes in his saddlebags, you know."

Mercy leaned forward on the other side of him. "Good morning, Christine. How pretty you look."

"Thank you." Her demure reply was counterpointed by a sharp flick of her fan.

Billy wondered what people thought as the scent of Mama's favorite perfume wafted from Christine. The other women and girls wore cotton or homespun, without much trimming. The men favored light, collarless shirts and denim pants, and they removed their straw hats as they sat down. Everyone looked clean—wholesome, Mama would've called it—but many of them had probably given up their finery to farm out here, just as Mercy had.

It wasn't a time to ponder appearances, however. Reverend Larsen was flipping through a leatherbound Bible, and then he handed it to Judd, who stood beside him.

"It's good to greet you on this fine summer morning," the preacher proclaimed in an accented sing-song, "and always good to gather here with the Monroes. Judd has offered to share the thirty-first chapter of Proverbs today. Let us listen to the word of God."

Judd paused a moment, smiled at his wife, and began reading in a voice that carried easily over the crowd. " 'Who can find a virtuous woman? For her price is far above rubies. The heart of her husband doth safely trust in her. She will do him good and not evil, all the days of her life.' "

The woman on Billy's left sat straighter, and he shared in her pleasure. He didn't understand much about females, but this passage fit Mercy like a glove. Since he couldn't imagine anyone dedicating these verses to Mama, he was again struck by the depth of Judd's devotion to his wife.

" 'Strength and honor are her clothing, and she shall rejoice in the time to come,' " he read on. " 'She openeth her mouth with wisdom, and in her tongue is the law of kindness. She looketh well to the ways of her household, and eateth not of the bread of idleness.' "

Billy noticed Christine's fan fluttering like an agitated butterfly. She studied the backs in front of them, silently judging the home-sewn clothing.

" 'Her children rise up and call her blessed; her husband also, and he praiseth her: "Many daughters have done virtuously, but thou excellest them all." Favor is deceitful and beauty is vain, but a woman that feareth the Lord, she shall be praised.' "

Christine let out a petulant sigh, glaring straight ahead. Billy was struck by how much she resembled Mama; the red hair and fair skin had been passed along by nature, but she'd taken on that tilt of her chin by choice. She shone like a jewel among lumps of clay, and here on the Kansas plains she seemed just useless.

Billy prayed hard for her while Reverend Larsen droned on. As the grace gave way to their picnic, he stayed beside her, because no matter how many people Mercy and Judd introduced her to, Christine didn't want to know them. Didn't want to belong.

He stuffed himself with buffalo stew and beans sweetened with molasses. He sampled foods he'd never seen at home, products of the prairie and creative cooks. Then he topped it all off with a wedge of Asa's cherry pie.

He grinned at the colored man, raising his plate in salute. Asa winked at him. He and Nathaniel sat off to one side of the benches, the way Beulah Mae and the help at home had always done. When Billy saw how his sister dawdled over her food, he decided to leave her be. No sense in letting one of her moods ruin his whole day.

"I'm fetchin' some more of that pie. You want anything?"

Christine shook her head listlessly.

"I'll be back in a bit, then."

"Go on and have your fun. I—I can take care of myself."

He wanted to smack her and tell her that acting so pathetic wouldn't win her any favor from these people. But she didn't want to hear that.

So Billy walked over to the long tables and gleefully dished up the last slice of Asa's pie. These guests had better taste than Christine gave them credit for! And now that he was out from under her cloud of self-imposed misery, he wandered among the neighbors to get to know them.

His eyes sought Mercy out. She was talking to a stout, dark-haired woman—Nell Fergus, he recalled—as though they had a lot of catching up to do. Both women's hands fluttered as they talked, side by side on a bench, erupting into laughter.

Billy went warm inside: it was good to see Mercy enjoying herself. Her face radiated kindness as she listened to her friend. And when her gaze met his, she raised her eyebrow in a question.

He gave her a little wave so she wouldn't leave her conversation to ask after him. Judd stood over by the corrals, talking horses to a few neighbors. The Barstows, whom he remembered from the home station east of here, were bending the preacher's ear. Around their legs, four little towheads clamored for attention, so he could understand why they had no room for him and Christine.

The voices rose and fell around him in a pleasant cadence. At gatherings like these, he enjoyed watching facial expressions, hearing scraps of gossip, and seeing the men spit streams of tobacco juice off to the side. Except for their simpler clothes, they reminded him of people who'd attended parties back home.

This realization startled him, because he'd always heard how uncivilized Kansas was. He was trying to recall what Daddy had said, about how Indians waited for the white men to let down their guard and then attacked, on painted ponies! But a hand jostled him out of his thoughts.

"Hey there, Billy Bristol."

He turned to see a girl about his own age, a little taller and heavier than he was. She smiled shyly, so he smiled back. "Hey there, yourself."

"You gonna stay here awhile, or you fixin' to get on the stage tomorrow?"

"Reckon I'll stay. The Monroes told us we could."

Her straw-colored hair glinted with gold when the sunlight caught it. "They're nice that way. I like comin' here, seein' their big house and walkin' down by the creek. I'm Emma Clark. We farm the next spread to the west."

Billy nodded. She had the face of a fairy princess, yet her sturdy, tanned arms and bare feet told him Emma was no sissy. Indeed, as her face took on a sly smile like Wesley's, he liked her immediately.

"You wanna see my . . . secret place, Billy?"

He stepped back, slack-jawed. The last time a girl asked him that, he'd gotten his bottom blistered because Jewel Mayhew had lifted her dress. They were only five at the time, but the incident had stayed with him.

"What're you gawkin' at? I thought you liked me, Billy."

"I—I don't know. I—"

"Well, you can stand here lookin' like you swallowed a frog, or you can help me find some," she said, turning on her heel. "Just tryin' to be neighborly. Never showed anybody else that cave down past the creek."

Billy let out a sheepish laugh. The women were clearing the tables and the men were choosing teams for horseshoes. He didn't see Christine anywhere. The prospect of viewing a cave only Emma Clark knew about suddenly seemed like the best offer he'd ever heard.

He trotted up alongside her. "I thought you was gonna try the same trick a little girl back home did.

53

She dropped her drawers, and I got my butt beat for lookin'."

"Well, I should hope so!" Emma's eyes sparkled, as blue and dewy as the hydrangeas in Mama's garden. "Let's you and me make a pact, Billy Bristol. We gotta promise to never take off our clothes or touch each other, 'cause it's a sin. And I don't intend to burn in Hell for the likes of you!"

She stopped at the edge of the cottonwood grove along the river and solemnly extended her hands. Billy took them, and a single, hard shake sealed the bargain.

He grinned at her. Emma Clark didn't seem the type to lie or tattle or make a fool of him. She was his sworn friend now, and he felt better than he had in weeks.

Behind them, he heard the clang of horseshoes hitting iron posts, but he didn't look back. The two of them spent the afternoon watching dragonflies skim the stream, and laughing at frogs that hit the water when they approached. The trees formed a canopy over their path, shading them from the harsh summer sun. And when Emma motioned for him to hunker down and enter an opening in the hillside, Billy could hardly contain himself.

"Outlaws like Jesse James use the caves around home for hideouts," he announced.

"You know Jesse James?" Emma whispered over her shoulder. "Ever met William Quantrill or Bloody Bill Anderson?"

Her awe made him feel important, until reality sank in. "No. Frank and Jesse lived out our way, on their mama's farm, but I can't say I really knowed 'em. But it was a gang like theirs—the Border Ruffians—that snatched my twin brother, Wesley."

She nodded, and Billy thanked her silently for not

asking any questions. He and Emma sat cross-legged in the cool shadows, trading stories as the time slipped by. It was nearly dusk when they emerged from the cave, and the jubilant squeal of a fiddle made them hurry along the creek bank.

"That's Iry Barstow playin'," Emma said as they ran. "Let's go listen!"

When they entered the yard, the music beckoned them from in front of the house. Rhythmic clapping accompanied the catchy tune, and lanterns lit the area where the wiry fiddler played, along with Nathaniel, who strummed a guitar. Emma spotted her parents, and Billy followed her to where they stood.

He grinned up at them, tapping his foot as the music sped up to a breathtaking pace. Mr. Barstow's fiddling inspired big smiles all around, and Billy laughed as he tried to outclap Emma. He looked around, expecting to see Judd and Mercy enjoying the music, too.

But the big man stood near the front door, scanning the crowd.

Billy frowned. It wasn't like him to look so deadly serious, unless something was wrong.

When Mercy appeared in the doorway, her pale face made Billy shove through the crowd. As he ran closer, his worst fears were confirmed.

"She's gone, Judd! Said she felt peaked, and went upstairs a while ago," Mercy said in a stricken whisper. "When I checked on her, I found a sideboard drawer open and a napkin on the floor. She must've wrapped food in some of them, but—but she took the supply money that was in there, too! Nearly forty dollars!"

Chapter Five

The blood drained from Billy's face. He ducked into the shadow of the house, too mortified to face the Monroes. Not only had Christine run off without letting on to him, but she was a thief, as well!

"She can't have gotten far," Judd speculated in a worried voice. "Couldn't have left until everyone was on this side of the house, after the music started. I'll get a few men together and look for her."

Billy desperately wanted to go with him, but his feet seemed rooted to the ground. Would Mercy and Judd hate him now? Figure he was part of Christine's plot and send him on his way? He sucked on a grubby knuckle, wondering what to do next.

As though Judd could hear his thudding heart, the big man turned in mid-stride to address him. "Help us saddle some horses, son. Then I want you to help these folks hitch up when they're ready to leave. I'm taking

Asa and Nathaniel, because they know the lay of the land."

"Yessir. I—" He stepped away from the rough log wall, into the light of Judd's lantern. "She went after Mama, I just know it! Spent all night readin' her diary. Told me how that Wyndham fellow'd come over to see Mama when we was recitin' our lessons."

"Any idea which way she went?"

Billy shook his head, wishing he'd pressed Christine for more details last night. "She said—she said it was our Christian duty to find Mama, 'fore she wandered off the path of righteousness. You just gotta find Christine, Mr. Monroe! I—I heard wolves howlin' last night."

Judd smiled at him. "Chances are she'll come right back, Billy. It's dark out on the road, and those animal cries will scare some sense into her."

Billy hoped he was right. Christine had never been the adventurous sort.

But a few minutes later, when the lanterns that Judd, the two hands, and the preacher carried had bobbed out of sight, he began to worry. They'd discovered that his sister had taken off on Reverend Larsen's horse, so she could have covered more distance than they'd originally thought.

"Good night, now. Thanks for coming." Mercy's voice carried over the yard as guests headed to their wagons. She tried to sound confident, thanking the friends who promised to keep an eye out for Christine as they traveled the dark road home.

But Billy heard the same tightness in her throat that he felt in his own. Folks were being especially kind as they said good night to him, but no amount of encouragement could raise his sinking spirits. It was after nine o'clock, and his sister was out there alone, on a prairie as dark and fathomless as death itself.

Emma lingered beside him while her parents loaded their hampers into the wagon. "I sure hope your sis ain't run into trouble, Billy."

"My sister *is* trouble," he muttered. But he immediately regretted it.

"See ya again sometime." She clambered up onto the wagon's wheel and then over the side. Her hair shone like a halo in the lantern light when she turned for a last look at him. "I'm glad you was here tonight, Billy."

"Yeah. Me, too."

He watched the Clarks pull out of the yard, feeling swallowed up by the night now that the last guests had gone. As soon as everyone had heard Christine was missing, the party broke up, as though folks knew that Mercy felt embarrassed about it. The horizon on all sides of him showed no sign of the search lights. A mournful howl broke the silence, and although it was off in the distance, Billy shivered and shuffled toward the house.

Mercy was placing candles in all the windows. She waited until the tiny flames cast a steady, funereal glow over the front room, and then looked at him. "I'm sorry this happened, Billy. I know you had nothing to do with it."

He swallowed hard, nodding. Her sympathy struck a soft spot that nobody else had found, and before he could catch himself, he burst into tears. Appalled at his girlish behavior, Billy turned toward the door, but two arms caught him before he could stumble up the stairs.

"This is no time for either of us to sit alone," Mercy whispered. "Hold on to me, Billy. We'll both feel better for it."

She sat down on the stoop and he crawled into her lap. His arms twined around her neck, and then Billy broke down. Fear and anger drove him into a mindless state; he cried so hard he couldn't even think. When his daddy died, he had to be brave for Mama. When Wesley didn't come home, he had to be the man and deny an even deeper loss. Mama's abandonment stung him like a fresh wound. And now his sister had left him, too.

Mercy rocked him, amazed that one small body could generate such heat. She closed her eyes to savor the moment, because she hadn't held a child this way since she'd left nieces and nephews behind in Philadelphia—and she sensed that Billy would never succumb to his tears again. Her heart ached for this lonely little boy, and as she peered over his shoulder into the vast darkness, she prayed that God would watch over Christine and bring her back—if only because her little brother needed her.

When Billy's sobs turned to sniffles, she loosened her hold on him. He rested, silent and spent, with his face pressed against her damp shoulder.

Billy let out a long breath, drained. He couldn't recall the last time he'd sat this way. Mama had favored him with such affection long after Wesley wiggled out of her embrace, yet he'd sensed it wasn't a manly thing to do. Mercy Monroe smelled of dust and supper and the evening's heat, an earthy combination that soothed him because it was so much like his own scent. Plain. Natural.

59

With a sigh, he slipped out of her lap. Then he squinted west, toward where the Clark farm would be. "That a firefly or a lantern?" he mumbled.

Mercy followed the direction of his gaze. "Someone's heading back. And there's another light, coming from the river. Why don't you fill the washbasins while I see what's left of the lemonade. They'll be hot and tired."

He nodded, glad for the chance to splash his own face before the men arrived.

They came back without Christine.

"We'll tell Malloy to put the word out along the stage line tomorrow," Judd said quietly. His face was lined with exhaustion, and he looked older. "I can't think she'd stray far from the road—which would be the logical place to look for her mother, anyway. I don't suppose she left that diary behind?"

"If she did, it's locked in a trunk," Mercy replied.

Billy listened glumly. Christine had hung those keys on a little chain beneath her clothes, and he had no doubt they were still there.

"Let's turn in and try again tomorrow. Gregor, you can have her room tonight. We'd all rest better if you led us in prayer."

Billy bowed his head, but the preacher's words didn't fill the emptiness inside him. He said his good nights quickly and went upstairs. Asa and Nathaniel talked quietly on their way to the barn. Reverend Larsen entered the room across the hall. And then the creaking and settling of beds faded into the night.

Staring out his window, he saw an infinite blackness broken only by the stars and a small patch of light below him, where a candle burned in a window. He wished Christine Godspeed while hunting for Mama, and prayed for their safe return.

But when a wolf wailed in the distance, Billy wondered if he'd ever see either one of them again.

Christine had watched the men's lanterns disappear in different directions, while the glow of candles came into each window. As she'd figured, the search party had kept close to the road. This cottonwood grove due north of the house—which she'd spotted from her room—had made the perfect place to wait until they'd gone the other way and the guests were headed home.

Everything had fallen into place so perfectly! She felt bad about leaving Billy, but he was better off with the Monroes. His wheedling and stalling would only slow her down.

"Come on, you old nag," she muttered to the preacher's horse.

She'd had plenty of nicer animals to choose from, but the neighbors' draft horses looked too large to saddle. And Judd's Morgans usually hauled stagecoaches at breakneck speed, so she wasn't sure she could handle one. She figured Reverend Larsen's horse was used to walking a long way without much to eat, and the saddle resting on the partition beside him had seemed like a lucky omen.

Christine mounted awkwardly, clinging to the animal's neck. The dark prairie loomed endlessly in every direction. It occurred to her that if she fell off the horse and the wolves got her, it might be days before anyone found her remains.

But she nudged the horse anyway. If she caved in now, she'd look like a fool. A sneaking, thieving fool.

She had money, and fresh cornbread wrapped in napkins, and a passage from Mama's diary to spur her on: *Richard says we'll take a few days in Leavenworth, to get better acquainted and plan our trip west.* If she waited any longer, she'd miss them.

Christine settled herself in the worn saddle. This tributary of the river roughly followed the stage route, and would also provide the cover of the trees along its banks. By tomorrow, Mike Malloy would know she was missing and spread the word, so it was best to avoid the main road.

She smiled, thinking about the note she'd mail to Billy when she found Mama. Thinking about how he and the Monroes and Mr. Malloy would have to admit she was pretty smart, for a girl.

A mournful howl made her shiver. Those wolves sounded closer. She'd read how a pack of these vile creatures would surround its prey and then close in, lunging when the victim fell, scared and helpless, to the ground.

The coppery taste of fear filled her mouth. Christine licked her lips and glanced over her shoulder at the house, a dimming beacon in the distance.

But she couldn't turn back, and she'd never forgive herself if she allowed her mother to run off with Richard Wyndham. She didn't know much about men—or the Bible—but she recognized that smooth-talker in the checkered suit as the very same snake who'd corrupted Eve in the Garden.

At dawn Billy stopped tossing in his bed and got up. He scanned the horizon from his window, desperate for a sign of his sister. But Christine was gone. He slipped into his overalls and went down the stairs, hearing the reverend's lusty snores from across the hall.

The chickens pecked at the corn Judd had tossed them. The cow bawled as Nathaniel milked her. The corn crop swayed in the wind, tall and proud and green. He smelled sugar and cinnamon and roasting meat, signs that Mercy and Asa were preparing dinner for the stagecoach passengers who would arrive later.

How could everything seem so normal—so peaceful—when he felt so agitated and alone? How could he possibly get through this day, not knowing where his sister was or what trouble might have found her in the night?

Billy blinked hard. Before anyone could catch him crying, he walked to the washbasin and splashed his face. He should be helping Judd move those benches back into the barn, or fetching buffalo chips for Mercy's cookstove, but he just couldn't face the Monroes yet. The sympathy in their smiles would only make him more miserable.

So he stood with his eyes shut, letting the cool water drip down his face. If Wesley or Christine saw him this way, their catcalls would brand him a sissy. Right now that didn't matter, though. When he thought about either of them, his heart turned into a big, aching knot.

He was about to slip around the side of the house where he could cry unnoticed, when a hand closed over his bare shoulder. Billy opened his eyes to see Reverend Larsen smiling kindly at him. His sandy waves were wild from sleep, and he looked like anything but a preacher without his shirt, yet his presence was comforting.

"Your sister impresses me as a . . . resourceful girl,"

he said quietly. His voice had a foreign lilt that made Billy smile in spite of his agony. "We'll have to have faith that between Christine's pluck and God's purpose, some good will come of her little adventure."

Billy sighed, nodding. He'd never seen a preacher half naked, and it fascinated him that Gregor Larsen's narrow chest sported the same coarse hair his daddy's had.

"And she took the best horse for the trip, you know," he added. "Moses stops at every house he sees, hoping to be fed. Won't be long before some homesteader recognizes him and brings Christine back."

"Prob'ly so," Billy mumbled.

"Meanwhile, you've chosen the wiser path. You've accepted the Monroes' hospitality—the love they long to lavish upon children—and this gift of yourself is marvelous in God's eyes. You and Mercy and Judd will all be blessed because you stayed here."

Billy didn't completely understand these words, but they made him feel better—like maybe he was giving as much as he got in this awkward situation. When he stepped into the kitchen, the greetings confirmed this.

"There's our boy!" Asa called out from a corner of the table. Pies were lined up in front of him—apple today—for the oven.

Mercy, too, gave him a warm smile. The circles under her eyes betrayed her sleepless night. It touched him that she cared enough about his runaway sister to lie awake worrying about her.

"I could use some butter and cream from the springhouse," she said. "And on your way back, tell Judd and Nathaniel to come eat. I'm sure Reverend Larsen wants to be on his way."

Billy nodded, glad for the diversion. He was hungrier than he realized when they all gathered around the table for biscuits and bacon and stewed apples left from the pie-making. As they bowed their heads, Mercy's hand found his under the table. The reverend prayed for Christine's safety, and for their faith in her return before he blessed their breakfast.

Nobody speculated about his sister's motives or mentioned the things she'd stolen, for which Billy was grateful. In Judd's eyes he saw compassion rather than pity. They all had their separate tasks in order to prepare for today's stagecoach, yet he sensed a unity in the room. A strength born of concern and love and hope, as voiced in the preacher's prayer.

Billy wasn't surprised that Gregor Larsen rode off on a fine Monroe Morgan, with clothing of Judd's and a quilt from Mercy's cedar chest, to replace what Christine had taken with her. Mercy wrapped the remaining biscuits, a chunk of cheese, and a small jar of jam in a cloth bag for him, too.

As the preacher rode toward the rutted road, Billy realized that he sat in one of only two saddles from the barn—yet another toll Christine's escape had taken on the Monroes' precious possessions. It would take weeks of serving meals to recover what his sister had ridden off with, yet nowhere did he see signs of anger or malice. Judd and Mercy were discussing what needed to be done before noon, when Mike Malloy would pull in with his passengers.

The more Billy thought about it, the heavier their kindness weighed upon him. "I—I promise I'll pay back every single thing you had to provide for that preacher!" he blurted. "We Bristols honor our debts. Daddy always said so."

Judd's tanned face creased with a smile. "I've never

65

doubted your integrity, son—or your intentions. For now, though, you carry a heavy enough load just worrying about your mother and Christine. But comes a time when I can use some extra effort, I'll let you know, all right?"

"Yessir. I'll be right here."

Chapter Six

For the next few days, Mercy watched Billy struggle valiantly with the absence of his entire family. They'd done all they could to find Christine. At Billy's suggestion, Mercy had opened Mrs. Bristol's trunks with a key from her own luggage, but his sister had taken the diary with her. The boy repacked his mother's things with great sadness, placing all he'd ever loved about his former home in a casket and then closing the lid on it. How young he was to grapple with such a profound loss!

Judd broke the news of Christine's disappearance to Mike Malloy, while his passengers washed and crowded around the table.

The driver sighed as though he'd anticipated this. "I'll send word along the stage line. Maybe look for her myself, after I finish this run."

"I'd be forever grateful," Judd replied quietly. "I'd go after her myself, but with other stages stopping, and

67

the Indian trouble they've had farther west, I don't want to leave the place for that long."

"It'll be like hunting a needle in a haystack," Malloy agreed. "I don't like to think about what might happen to a girl alone on the prairie. I doubt she's got much sense of direction, or the know-how to protect herself."

"She ain't much of a rider, neither," Billy mumbled.

Mike rested his hand on the boy's auburn hair, his hazel eyes narrowing in concern. "Can you recall anything else about this Wyndham fellow? Or about what Christine said before she slipped away?"

"Nope. Mama's diary made it sound like she and him was better friends than we thought. Like maybe they'd been plannin' to head west for quite a little while." Billy considered this glumly. "That would explain why he didn't wanna buy our place, wouldn't it?"

Mercy glanced at the two men. "Christine's sharper than we think, if she managed to sneak off during a gathering of nearly forty people. Let's assume her determination will make up for any lack of experience, and hope for the best. We just have to leave the whole matter in God's hands now."

She said this to make Billy feel better, and to convince herself his sister would be all right. Her cooking, washing clothes at the river, and tending the garden at its midsummer peak couldn't come to a halt so she could fret over a runaway. Miss Bristol had feigned illness and then stolen from her with the finesse of a professional hustler. She would no doubt prove herself a worthy match for whatever might come her way.

But that was small comfort as the days went by without any word from her. Billy buried himself in chores, mucking out the barn with a vengeance, as though shoveling out all the loneliness and heartache heaped upon him by his mother and sister. He didn't have much to say, and his blue eyes remained clouded with concern.

A note from Reverend Larsen came on the next stagecoach.

My horse Moses has returned home, the squared lettering announced. *He was saddled, but Christine wasn't on him. Nor were any clothes or food. My prayers continue for Billy as we all keep watch.*

Billy gazed at the paper as though his whole life resided in those few lines. "Guess she's makin' her way back to Missouri, then. Or back to where Mama took out with that English fella," he said quietly. "Much as you folks tried to make her welcome, she just didn't take to the dust and the hard work and the wide open spaces."

"Understandable, for a girl," Judd reassured him.

"It's a good sign if the saddlebags were empty," Mercy said around the lump in her throat. "It means she found a place to stay, or a faster way to travel. And she still has the money."

An uneasy silence surrounded them. It went unsaid that she could have met up with Indians, or shiftless men on the trail who'd relieved her of her belongings.

Billy nodded, as though convincing himself that the better options were true. "She made her own choices, didn't she? I couldn't never convince her to see things my way, even before we lost Daddy," he recalled with a halfhearted grin, "so I gotta stop worryin' over it. Worry won't change *nothin'* about Christine."

Little they could do would console him, so Mercy

and Judd kept their conversations to the tasks at hand whenever Billy was around. Even references to his life before the war, before his daddy's death and his twin's kidnapping, brought pain to his slender face. Billy spent the next several evenings flipping through the padded velvet photo albums, as though committing each image from his past to memory. Neither Mercy nor Judd could imagine the loneliness he suffered, the losses he'd borne at such a tender age. The degradation of knowing that his mother and sister had chosen to leave him behind.

Asa brought the boy out of his misery by telling tales of his childhood in the South. He'd been a favorite with his master's family, and showed an early aptitude for learning—enough that he sat in on lessons with his owner's children. Desperate for something to occupy himself, Billy asked the colored hand to continue his schooling. Mercy was happy to provide a slate and some books she'd used in school, so she and the boy and the black man could do lessons in the evenings.

"Billy's no slouch," Judd commented as he sat with Mercy on the back stoop one night in early August. "Listen to him! He's reciting his multiplication tables without a second's hesitation."

"You should hear him spell," Mercy added proudly. "He can recite the countries of Europe and their capitals, and then rattle off the letters in those foreign names as though he were spelling his own."

"Can better grammar be far behind?" her husband teased, and for the first time in days they laughed.

The sound was sweet to Mercy's ears. She delighted in Judd's kisses, and the sparkle in his deep blue eyes, and his whispered endearments as the dusk fell around

70

them. The stars came out to a chorus of katydids, like diamonds dancing in a velvet sky.

The peacefulness of the prairie settled over her, as though the Lord were sending His reassurance that everything would be all right. As she and Judd came in for the night, the lingering scents of roasted beef and buttery corn settled her soul; the sight of her familiar furnishings in the cozy lamplight restored the warmth Christine had taken away on the reverend's horse. Knowing better than to kiss Billy—for the boy would be mortified if Judd saw—Mercy just brushed his hair back from his brow.

"You're a blessing, Billy Bristol," she whispered. "Sleep tight tonight. I have all faith that your sister is safe, and sleeping soundly herself."

Christine awoke with a jolt from her fitful nap. The train was hissing its way toward the station as the conductor entered her car.

"End of the line, folks! All out for Atchison!" he cried, plucking tickets from the clips above each seat. "Gather up all your belongings, and watch your step getting out!"

He was a tall man with gray hair curling around his dark blue hat, and a smile she found far too pleasant. "Best wishes for your mother's recovery, Miss Bristol. I'm sure she'll feel better fast, now that you'll be home with her."

She flashed him a tearful grin, eager to join the other passengers clambering down to the platform. It wasn't the first fib she'd told to get this far; her story became more elaborate each day, with details that compelled everyone she met to help her.

She'd first tried her tale of woe on the O'Tooles, who'd driven her to the train station in Junction City after that stupid nag insisted on stopping at their door. It didn't hurt that she looked bedraggled and dusty, clutching the letter that summoned her to her mother's deathbed. Not only had they fed her and wrapped up fresh biscuits and cheese, they'd given her a carpetbag and two simple dresses their deceased daughter had worn.

But this was Atchison, not Leavenworth!

As Christine entered the station, the travelers around her faded into a haze of exhaustion. How many days had she been running now? And after all the clever ways she'd devised to get home—avoiding the stage route, where the way-station families already knew her—how on earth had she boarded the wrong train?

If Billy were here, he'd say God was getting back at her for sneaking off with Mercy's money and stealing the reverend's sorry excuse for a horse. But that was claptrap. If God had been paying any attention at all, Daddy would still be alive and Wesley would be home on the farm where they all belonged. So He couldn't care less about her little lies. They were small potatoes, compared to the whoppers Mama had obviously told.

It was this thought that kept her walking. No use crying over all the stories she'd believed—all the trust her mother had betrayed—and no sense in fretting over Billy. He'd found a home, and now she would, too. Right after she figured out which train went to Leavenworth. Right after she ate some real food and slept in a real bed. If she was going to catch up to Mama and Richard Wyndham, she had to keep looking ahead, like a horse wearing blinders. No distractions. No more mistakes made because she was so tired.

Compared to that spot in the Kansas prairie they called Abilene, Atchison was alive and thriving. Wagons were parked all along Commercial Street, which was lined on both sides with brick and board buildings—real stores and restaurants! Why, if Mama and that Englishman were smart, they'd settle *here* rather than heading west, where only rutted dirt roads and the endless prairie awaited them.

Christine paused in front of a plate-glass window, where red lettering announced Aunt Amanda's Cafe and the scents of frying meat and coffee beckoned. Her stomach growled, but she walked on, wanting to get a feel for this main street before the sun went down. She compared the room rates posted at two hotels, and calculated what she'd have left for a train ticket after she bought a meal. Clutching her carpetbag, she moved on.

Should've taken more than forty dollars, she chided herself as she ambled along the wooden sidewalk. *Could've taken things easier to sell than those monogrammed napkins, too*.

She passed a furniture store and then noticed a photographer's front window, cleverly painted to look like it was framed. Christine gazed wistfully at the people who'd posed for this man's camera, for she dearly loved having her picture made. How else did a girl remember last year's Easter frock, and smile over how much she'd grown up since then?

Here, however, she saw a pair of curly-haired twins in sailor suits, posing with their mastiff between them—a young lady whose hair cascaded down her back like a river as she glanced coyly over her shoulder, and an adventurous sort wearing only an artfully arranged silk sash that barely covered the unmentionable parts of her body. And then there was a couple, perhaps newly married—

Christine's heart stopped. A man wearing a derby and a houndstooth suit with leathered lapels smiled from behind his waxed mustache, as though he had the answers to her every question.

And indeed he did. For the woman standing behind him was none other than her mother, Virgilia Bristol. Her arms were wound around his shoulders, and a delighted smile lit up her face. She had the gall to be gazing directly at the camera. Directly at the daughter she'd left behind!

Christine caught her breath, calmed the pulse that pounded in her ears, and got control of the knees that trembled with shock and exhaustion. Perhaps it was no accident that she'd taken the northbound train. Perhaps God Himself had guided her here, and was about to reveal her future!

Christine grabbed the door handle and walked inside the photograph shop. There was no time to waste!

Chapter Seven

A bell tinkled merrily above her head. The shop was empty, except for the framed faces on the walls and a desk where orders were taken. The floors were plain but clean, and the acidic scent of chemicals tickled her nose. One entire wall displayed awe-inspiring spectacles of nature from the West—the Grand Canyon and other places she'd read about in schoolbooks.

"Help me! Can somebody please help me?" Christine cried in a tone that always got people's attention.

Then she felt a pair of eyes peering at her from behind the curtained doorway that divided this front room from the studio in back. A bright flash and a *poof* of gunpowder told her the photographer—one Tucker Trudeau, according to the lettering on his door—was busy with a customer.

The wizened woman who came out looked right through Christine, apparently assuming the waif wanted a favor she couldn't pay for. Dressed in motley prints of many colors, the woman seemed quaintly European. Her manner seemed suspicious. Reminiscent of a Gypsy—or what Christine imagined a Gypsy to be like.

"Oui? Que voulez-vous, ma'amselle?"

It was a form of French, Christine realized, but it left her textbook learning far behind. The heavily accented voice sounded centuries old, and as those obsidian eyes widened, she wondered if she was being hexed.

Christine let out the breath she'd been holding. "I— I must look a fright, because I just got off the train after days of—"

But her tragic tale wouldn't sway this old crone. Better to try another tactic.

"You have a certain—very fine—photograph in your window," she began in a more sophisticated voice, "and I'd like to ask Mr. Trudeau about it. When he has time, of course. I could come back later—"

"Qui est-ce, Maman? Je ne crois—well, now. Hello, *ma princesse.* There is something I can do for you?"

A sable-haired man stepped out from behind the studio curtain to tower above his scowling mother. His close-cropped beard, broad, muscled shoulders, and plaid shirt suggested a lumberjack, yet the fingers he combed through his hair looked too long and pale to belong to an outdoorsman.

Christine gave him her finest smile. *Now* her mission would be accomplished. Mr. Trudeau was perhaps twenty-three, and he was certainly drinking her in with those eyes—eyes the color of a springtime sky, which sparkled with an energy she felt from across the room.

Standing taller, brushing the dust from her skirt,

Christine smiled at him again. "My name is Christine. Bristol," she added, in case he'd heard of her family's horse farm. "I just arrived in town, and—it's God's providence! I'm looking for my mother, and you have her picture in your window!"

The blue-eyed giant blinked and then remembered his manners. "Tucker Trudeau, *à votre service*," he said as he came around the desk. He reached for her hand, so Christine offered it coyly.

She had him now. Had him mystified and curious about why a girl her age had come alone, telling such a tale. God's providence, indeed.

"And which portrait would that be?" he asked. He gestured toward his front window display, assessing her as though he wanted to make *her* picture, perhaps.

"The one with—the man in the houndstooth suit."

Christine swallowed hard, appalled that a lump had risen into her throat and her eyes were getting wet. After all this time—all these miles—it wouldn't do to dissolve in tears like some ninny who couldn't withstand a little torment.

Or would it?

"You know him, this fellow?" Tucker retrieved the large frame from the window display. The cadence of his accent played in her ear, and he moved with a restless grace—like the thoroughbreds they'd raised. "These two, they came in just last week for this wedding picture. Said they were heading west to start a new life. Denver, I think."

She swallowed hard again. Nothing he said struck her as a surprise, but it was still hard to hear an uninvolved party confirm it so casually. And soon this man would know her secret fears. Her utter humiliation.

"They make a pretty pair, *non*?" he remarked. He focused those eyes on her, assessing her reaction as he turned the portrait so she could see it.

"Well, they might be pretty, but by God, they left my little brother and me at the stage depot in Leavenworth!" she blurted out. "Mama sent us west, saying she'd catch up to us—but that was before she *married* Richard Wyndham! Of all the . . ."

She pivoted, wiping tears from her dusty face. It was one thing to play upon people's pity, but unwise to air the family's dirty linen before she knew how these strangers might react. Or use her weakness to their own advantage.

A large, warm hand settled on her shoulder. A blue bandana dangled in front of her face, and she snatched it. Blew her nose loudly, and then felt mortified by the grit and grime she'd wiped from her face.

"Nearly time to close up shop," Mr. Trudeau said from behind her. His voice sounded kind and unhurried now. "We'll go to the house to talk about this, *oui*? You can freshen up. Eat some supper, maybe get some sleep."

Christine turned slowly, blinking at his sudden kindness. "Thank you," she breathed. "I'd like that very much."

Mother and son exchanged a glance that spoke volumes: while Tucker wished to accommodate her needs, his mother smelled a rat. The old woman left with a swish of her skirts and dangling gold earrings. It was plain she was planning on getting her licks in once it was time to talk about Christine's unusual family situation.

When the door had closed behind her, Tucker smiled. "Don't mind *Maman*. She refuses to speak

English—but understands most of it—and her second sight scares people sometimes."

Second sight? Wasn't that like being a witch?

"She sees beyond a person's surface—and usually *knows* if the truth is in them," he continued in a warier voice. "And you *are* young to travel alone, Miss Bristol. And to say this woman is your mother—after *Maman* met her, and had the impression—"

Christine snatched the portrait and held it up beside her face. "Tell me I don't look like her! And then tell me where they were going—what they were planning to do—and I'll be out of your way," she pleaded. "No need to inconvenience your mother, if she doesn't believe me. I—I have a hotel room, anyway."

The photographer glanced at her carpetbag, stroking his beard. He was indeed noting the resemblance . . . gently turning her chin so the angle of her face matched the woman's in the photograph.

"*Désolé, chérie*. Forgive me for doubting your story."

He let out a puzzled sigh as he looked at the portrait again. "This—Richard Wyndham, you call him? He was a fast talker, big ideas. Introduced himself as Dick Witmer, and the lady he called Veronique—and that's *Maman*'s name! Not common here, like in the bayou country. And *Maman*, she whispered to me that this man was not the marrying kind. That he—how do you say? He talks from both sides of his mouth."

Christine drank in these details like a girl parched from a trip across the Kansas prairie. It fit, every bit of it. What if they *weren't* married? What if Wyndham really *was* leading Mama down a primrose path to perdition—just as she'd suggested to Billy a few nights ago—and they were living in sin?

79

"You're probably right," she breathed, gazing up at him. "So I'm sure you understand my concerns, Mr. Trudeau. We suspect Richard Wyndham paid our stagecoach fares to get rid of Billy and me, so he could . . . well, we don't *know* what he had in mind."

Her agitation would eat her alive if she didn't control it. She must display just enough that this man with the musical accent and mischievous eyes would see her side and help her. This was no time to act like Mama, since Tucker Trudeau had already seen the warped cloth *she* was cut from!

"We only know that Mr. Wyndham—or whatever his real name is—was feigning an interest in our horse farm. He had to realize Mama was still lost in grief after Daddy got shot," she went on, dabbing her eyes with his bandana. "She—Mama—was never the most *astute* woman, you see. And in her vulnerable state, well, who *knows* what wicked intent that man might carry out?"

Thank goodness Tucker nodded, and when he'd put the Closed sign in the window, he ushered her out the door. The sidewalks of Atchison still hummed with people attending to their business at the end of the workday, and she felt their curious gazes as they greeted the large man strolling beside her.

But it didn't matter. She was walking toward a hot meal and information that might lead her to Mama. Not bad for a day that began on the wrong train.

Christine swirled her spoon through broth with a layer of grease that nearly gagged her, as had the chunks of smelly old cabbage and stringy meat she'd gingerly picked out of it. Or she *thought* it was meat. The little kitchen was so dark and dank-smelling, she wasn't sure what might be swimming in that oily mess before her. Tucker and his mother were spooning it down as though it were the ambrosia of the gods, so she hoped they wouldn't notice how little she had eaten. She took another bite of bread so stale it took a good bit of chewing before she could swallow it.

She felt those dark, feral eyes from across the tiny table . . . eyes like the ones she'd seen peering at her from the bushes along the riverbank at night while she traveled on Gregor Larsen's old horse. Mrs. Trudeau was so quiet, Christine wondered if she'd only imagined the old crone could talk. There was no mistaking the woman's dislike of her, however: it came across the table in waves almost as noxious as the odor of her soup.

Tucker swiped the back of his hand across his face, letting out a satisfied sigh. Then, with a little grin at Christine, he plucked the napkin from his lap—just for her, she sensed—and patted at his beard. It framed lips now pink from the heat of his dinner, and she wondered if it felt as soft as that unruly mop on his head looked.

"Now then—what about yourself, Miss Bristol?" he asked with an enticing smile. "You would be what age?"

"Sixteen—going on seventeen!" she piped up. "I'd nearly finished my schooling when . . . when Daddy got killed. Things have been pretty horrible since then. When those same outlaws kidnapped my younger brother Wesley, Mama lost a part of herself. Which explains why a dandy like Richard Wyndham could just sashay into her life and convince her to abandon her children!"

The man nodded, glancing at the gnarled woman who sat at his other side. He spoke to her in rapid-fire French, as though translating what he'd just heard, pointing to the dapper man in the photograph.

But Mrs. Trudeau only narrowed her eyes, like a witch putting a hex on her. She looked thoroughly unconvinced.

Tucker smiled gently. "*Maman* says so little. Didn't really want to come north, and it's been difficult for her to learn new ways. But we all do what we must, eh?"

Nodding, Christine wondered where this thread of conversation might lead. If she found a graceful way to escape this shack, she'd walk to that hotel nearest the depot. But for now she hung on, ignoring everything she found repugnant in order to clutch at the straws this man offered . . . any information he might have about Mama's whereabouts.

"My mother was very sociable. Talked *too* much sometimes," she replied with a sigh. She turned the photograph so she could see it again, while Tucker steadied it between his hands. "She hasn't looked this happy since . . . long before Daddy passed on. I can only wonder what this man must've enticed her with. Lord knows she was ripe for the picking."

"You're not far wrong about him, *chérie*." Tucker glanced at the man in question, as though considering how much he wanted to share. "They had this likeness made—the minute they came from the justice of the peace, he said—but they never came back for it. I found out yesterday there's no bank account for the check he wrote. So no money in it."

Christine's eyes widened. "So he *is* crooked! I knew it! I just knew—"

The darkening gaze from across the table stifled

her. But she had a right to know these things! She would not be intimidated by some old witchy woman!

"Did they say what they would be doing?" she asked breathlessly. "Time is of the essence, Mr. Trudeau. Once they get much farther west than Abilene, there'll be no finding them! They could get lost out there on the prairie if they ride alone. Or Indians could attack them! Or even if Richard—or Dick, or whoever he is—finds his way to Denver, they might disguise themselves so they *can't* be found!"

She fought for control again, wishing his mother would leave the room and take those silent, interrogating eyes with her.

"And then, well—I'll get a job and make out all right," she continued in a softer tone, "but my little brother Billy will be heartbroken. He's too young to understand such things."

The man beside her listened carefully, focusing his full attention on her as though she were a woman of the world who knew precisely whereof she spoke. Christine sat straighter, so her chest would stick out.

Tucker looked more closely at the photograph. "She's very pretty, your mama. You and your brother must miss her, even after the way she's behaved, *non?* So I want you to have this."

He eased the frame into her hands, closing his fingers around hers.

Her eyes went wet, and despite the rage Richard Wyndham's oil slick of a smile inspired, she hugged the picture to her chest. "I don't know what to . . . Thank you," she murmured. "Thank you so much for understanding."

"We'll hope it's not the last time you see her, Christine. Although she'll be showing up in your own mirror as the years go by."

He leaned toward her, his gaze more speculative. "I'd help you more, but the only thing Wyndham really mentioned was land speculation. 'Invest in the Kansas Pacific Railroad,' he told me. Like he was letting me in on a big secret."

"May I have your address? And I'll give you mine— in case you hear something about them?" she gushed. It meant he'd have to send any letters in care of Judd Monroe, but it was a way to stay in touch with this fascinating man.

"My paper and pencils are at the studio. We should get you a bed ready—"

"I—I have a room," she reminded him, flashing her best grown-up smile. "It's close to the depot—so I can catch the first train bound for Denver. And I'd hate to trouble your mother, Mr. Trudeau. If we could stop by your studio on the way to the hotel . . ."

Tucker's grin made him look boyish, yet aware of her wiles. And she liked it.

"That's best, perhaps, *oui*?" he agreed. "*Maman* is a fitful sleeper. Tends to wander the house at night. Especially if the spirits are restless."

Spirits? As Tucker turned to address his mother in that breakneck French, Christine felt an immense relief. The sooner she left this dreary little shack and its odious aromas—and those ghosts—the better! Mrs. Trudeau's knowing, animal-like eyes would no doubt glow in the dark all night, watching her. Such bad dreams might haunt her forever, and she already had enough on her mind. She said her polite good-byes and wasted no time in walking out the front door toward civilization again. Toward Mama, she hoped.

The moon shone like a beacon in the clear night sky, and a warm breeze stirred her skirts as they walked. Tucker strode beside her, shortening his strides to match hers as he carried her carpetbag and the photograph. It felt exhilarating, having such a nice man walking close enough that his boots occasionally brushed the hem of her skirt—even though he was far too old to be seen in a romantic light. Far too old.

But then, Papa had been several years older than Mama. And Judd looked at least five years older than Mercy. Most men established themselves in some line of work before they went after a woman, and from the looks of Tucker Trudeau's photography shop, he was well on his way to being a prosperous businessman here in Atchison. After all, what family didn't want to have its portrait made on important occasions?

And as she paused at the plate-glass window while he unlocked the front door, she was also aware—even in the dusk—of the skill required to capture the grandeur of those Western landscapes . . . the silent, somber dignity of soldiers come home from the war . . . the unabashed glee of those twins with their mastiff.

She followed him through the unlit waiting room, watching his quick, efficient movements as he lit the lantern and wrote out his name and address. His boldly looped penmanship showed a flair for the artistic, too. And when he handed her paper and pencil, Christine forgot why. She was lost in his smile.

Had he really let his fingertips linger on hers just now? Or was her imagination running away, like Mama's had, at the first sign of interest from a handsome stranger?

She quickly wrote her name, followed by Judd Monroe's, in Abilene, Kansas. "This is where we're staying for now, watching for Mama on westbound coaches," she explained. "How much do I owe you for this picture? I can't believe Wyndham cheated you—"

"Not a thing. The pleasure, is mine, Miss Christine. I'll pray your search is successful."

This time there was no question—he squeezed her hand! And as he escorted her toward the hotel, she couldn't hide her smile in the fineness of the summer night. It was a moment—a triumph!—she would remember forever.

"Thank you so very much for your help, Mr. Trudeau," she said as they reached the steps of the hotel. "I'll be forever indebted—"

The brush of his lips across her knuckles sent her heart skittering up into her throat.

"A great pleasure it's been, Miss Bristol," he said, gazing at her with azure eyes that twinkled like stars. "I so much admire your efforts, and I hope you find your mother soon. *Maman*, she can be difficult, but I can't imagine my life without her. *Au revoir*, Christine."

Until I see you again.

She nearly stumbled up the stairs, and then turned to watch him go, waving when Tucker looked back at her from up the street.

So excited she couldn't count—didn't care what it cost—Christine laid out some money for the man at the hotel's front desk. Her simple room felt like Heaven after so many days and nights on the road: she had clean sheets, painted walls that didn't move, and the privacy to review her amazing afternoon—when she wasn't gazing at that photograph.

"I've got you now, Mama," she whispered to it.

Christine fell into a deep sleep on a feather mattress that wrapped around her like her mother's arms once had. Visions of a male face framed in a close-cropped sable beard played in her mind, and she awoke smiling.

In the morning, she felt refreshed and had a new sense of purpose: she would head west as far as the Kansas Pacific would take her, and then use the stage-coach ticket in her carpetbag to get to Denver. When the coach stopped at the Monroes' way station, she wouldn't go into the house. The sooner she followed Mama's trail, the better chance she had of finding her and that scalawag who'd suckered her into some nefarious scheme.

She poured water from the pretty pitcher into its bowl, washed, and then smoothed her hair back into a crumpled lace cap. Her dress from the O'Tooles' was dusty, but so what? She would never see these people again. And she'd certainly have better dresses along the next time she met Tucker Trudeau!

Head held high, she thanked the man at the counter for a lovely night's stay and sashayed to the train station. What a difference a day made! How fine it felt to have someone believe in her purpose, rather than trying to talk her out of it.

"And how may I help you, young lady?" the railway agent behind the ticket window asked.

She smiled up at him as she dug out her money. "I'll be traveling west to Denver, and I'd like a ticket on the next westbound—"

A hand clapped heavily upon her shoulder.

"No, Miss Bristol, I believe you'll be traveling with me instead."

Chapter Eight

"Somebody's a-comin' down the road!"

Elbow-deep in dishwater after the stagecoach's departure, Billy lit up at the hopeful tone in Nathaniel's announcement. It was an occasion when someone came along, and even though nearly two weeks had passed since his sister had disappeared, he looked for her to return at any moment. He simply couldn't believe Christine had fallen into the wrong hands. She was too feisty for that.

"Why don't you see who it is?" Mercy wiped sweat from her brow on this especially hot August day, and then brought another stack of plates to the sink. "Might be somebody needing Judd's help. Considering what that new stage driver said about those Cheyenne raids, we might need to prepare ourselves."

With dripping hands, Billy ran out the back door, past the pecking chickens, to where Nathaniel and Judd were cutting new sections of corral fence. Sure enough, a distant dust cloud in the east foretold a visitor. Somebody in a wagon, rather than a coach as big as the Holladay stage that had pulled out minutes ago.

His feet took off without his head telling them to. Out here on the plains, with only the growing corn crop to whisper secrets to him, an approaching wagon was too exciting a thing to let go by—even if he only stood by the road to wave as it clattered past. Shielding his eyes from the midday sun, Billy could make out a slender fellow driving—effortlessly, considering how dang fast that pair of Morgans was coming at him. It was an open buckboard wagon like most families hereabouts owned, and—

His heartbeat raced like the horses' hooves. That figure beside the driver had rust-colored hair waving wildly in the wind, and looked no bigger than a minute sitting there beside—

"It's Mike Malloy!" he hollered over his shoulder. His bare feet slapped against the hard-packed road, while his mind raced with possibilities. Maybe his prayers were about to be answered!

A loud *creeeak* of the brakes rang around him. The wagon kicked up a whirlwind of dust as it slowed to approach the farmyard. Billy cried out before he even knew what he was saying.

"Christine! Christine—is it really you?"

With a leap and a whoop, Billy vaulted up over the wheel and onto the bench seat before the buckboard came to a full stop. Lordy, but he couldn't hug her hard enough—couldn't dare to believe that she'd really—

"No, silly, I'm your sister's ghost. Now let me down from here before I die from all this dust."

For just a moment, she let down her guard and hugged him back. The embrace told him she'd missed some meals—and maybe missed him. And for just a moment, he buried his head against her neck and allowed himself a single sigh of relief.

Then, of course, she became the Christine whose peevishness put him in his place again. He eased away, blinking to see her more clearly.

She widened her eyes—as though he should know what came next.

"*Well*, are you going to just *sit* here?" she asked archly. "I see you had cherry pie for dinner and got it all over your shirt, like always. My bag's in the back—"

"I missed you, too, Miss Priss," Billy countered, sticking out his tongue.

He then turned to the driver with a huge grin. "I knew you'd find her, Mr. Malloy. Yep, she weren't near as smart as she figgered, and I'm dang glad of it!"

Mike clapped him on the back, happy to see someone who appreciated his efforts. "We've got lots to talk about, but it all turned out for the best, Billy. And how's everybody here on the Monroe spread? Good to see you folks."

Judd and Nathaniel had dropped their saws to hurry over. Asa had left the pail of scraps he was taking to the pigs, and Mercy was trotting out of the house, drying her hands on a flour sack. Her tied-back hair came loose in the hot wind, and her red calico dress blew tight against her slender frame as she hurried toward them. But it was the expression on her face that Billy knew he'd never forget.

"Christine Bristol!" she hollered, half an accusation and half a greeting that resounded with her relief. "If you knew how worried we've . . . how hard and often we've prayed you'd be . . ."

She stopped beside the buckboard, struggling to

catch her breath, wiping her tear-streaked cheek with the flour sack. "Next time you plan to run off, young lady, I'll help you *pack*, understand me?" she demanded. "That way you won't have to steal the napkins my grandma embroidered for my—"

"What she's saying," Judd interrupted in a low, purposeful voice, "is that we've been worried sick about you. If that means nothing to you—if you don't care that you tore your brother's heart out—well, you can just keep on riding, Miss Bristol. You've got a ticket to Denver, as I recall. The stagecoach is only a couple miles out. Mike'll have no trouble catching up—or I'll drive you myself."

Only the next gust of wind interrupted the tight silence.

Billy's heart ached with the finality of Judd Monroe's edict. But he understood it. This whole family had spent sleepless nights since his sister had run off, and they had no time or energy to spare for such foolishness.

At least Christine had sense enough not to sass back. Her green eyes widened in a pale face caked with dust. She shuddered once, before finding that core of control and incorrigible pigheadedness that always determined her next move.

"I found what I was looking for," she replied with a lift of her chin. "And though I intended to travel to Denver in search of my mother—until Mr. Malloy here changed my plans—I now realize what a waste of time that might be. I—I had no idea anyone would be upset by my absence. I'm sorry if I caused any inconvenience."

Another painful silence had Billy holding his breath, searching the earnest faces around them. A deaf man could have heard the self-righteous edge in Christine's sorry attempt at an apology, as if she thought nobody here wanted her in the first place. Girls were too proud that way. His sister became as standoffish as a cat when folks told her what to do.

Luckily the Monroes saw through her. While Judd helped Christine to the ground, Nathaniel reached behind the seat for her carpetbag. Billy exhaled, aware of the sweat trickling down his spine.

With a grateful smile, Billy turned to Mike. "Just so happens we've got us a cherry pie, and some fried-up prairie chicken and biscuits," he chirped. "Betcha could use some lemonade to wash that down. I'll go set your plates out."

Malloy's bronzed face creased in a grin. "Best offer I've had in days, Mr. Bristol."

Billy sprang from the wagon, and with a parting swat at his sister's backside, he sprinted toward the house. His feet felt light, like he was bouncing on clouds. She was back! She didn't much like it, but just maybe she'd learned her lesson. And she said she'd found what she went after—whatever *that* meant. What if she'd seen Mama? And caught up to that trickster, Richard Wyndham?

He hung on Christine's every revelation at the table, between her bites of chicken and gravy-laden biscuits she would have turned up her dainty nose at before.

"—and after I got off the train in Atchison, I got myself a room at the hotel—"

"Money comes in handy, doesn't it?" Mercy murmured, glancing across the table at Judd.

"—and lo and behold, as I strolled down the sidewalk I came to a photographer's shop," Christine continued, her eyes lighting up like green fires. "And there, for God and everybody to see, was a picture of *Mama*. Right there in the front window! So of course I went in—"

"Lemme see it."

Billy had half a mind to tell her this whole made-up story was wearing him thin. She hadn't said a thing about how she'd found her way to Atchison, except to hint that it was all a part of her *plan* for tracking down their mother. She wasn't *that* good at getting around.

Christine glared at him, looking tired and then peeved. As if he'd forced her into a corner she hadn't figured on getting trapped in. And when she realized that Mercy, Judd, and even Mike now expected her to back up her tale with this evidence, she licked the thin line of her lips.

"Like I was saying," she went on, her voice a notch higher, "the photographer—his name was Tucker Trudeau, and he spoke with some sort of a Frenchie accent, and he had black hair and a beard that hugged—"

"Lemme *see* it!" Billy grabbed her elbow, forcing his sister to look at him. "She's my mama, too, dang it! You're just stringin' us all along, with your muckety-muck about this Tucker fella!"

Her eyes narrowed in that superior, feline way he knew so well. She jerked her arm free. "Patience is a virtue, William," she cooed, "and I can see you're still lacking in it."

The heat in the room increased with the silence. Expectant gazes awaited whatever she'd found. Christine looked like a cornered animal for a moment, and then slowly rose to fetch her carpetbag.

"I can see no one believes me," she muttered, yanking it open. "You all think I'm too stupid to find my way across this godforsaken prairie, just because I'm a girl. Well, here! See for yourself what I found!"

She brought out a framed picture, thrusting it at whoever wanted it first,

Billy sprang up from the bench seat to grab the other end of it. And when he caught a glimpse of that smiling woman with her arms around a very dapper, satisfied-looking man, he wished he hadn't.

"Mama," he murmured. It was all he could do not to bawl in front of everybody.

Then he challenged his sister with a glare. "You sure this is the same fella Mama talked about in her diary? The one who—"

"You saw him, too! Stop making it look like this is all my fault!"

She let go, and he'd been pulling just enough that the frame flew backwards out of his hand. It hit the floor with a sickening tinkle of glass.

Christine looked so hateful, he thought she'd slap him into Kingdom Come. But before she could accuse him of being ignorant and stupid and clumsy, Mike Malloy rose from the end of the bench to pick up the picture.

The man who'd fetched Christine straightened to his full height as he studied the likeness. The lines of his face grew tight, and Billy thought this man—who could deftly handle six horses at a full gallop across the rutted stage trail—might just crumple up, as sad as he looked.

He gently handed the picture to Billy, but his words were for Christine. "Honey, I know you've gone to a lot of trouble to find your ma," he said softly. "Heading to Denver from Atchison—and I bet you'd've made it, too.

"But you're better off to just leave it be," he went on

with a sigh. "A man like Wyndham can make himself as invisible as the wind, and your mother's chosen to go with him. Probably best to remember her as the dear, sweet woman you loved before all that trouble found your family. I'm thinking that gang of Border Ruffians stole her soul as sure as they took your daddy's life and your other brother."

Christine's eyes got as wide as her plate, and looked just as empty. Then she blinked, defiance shining in her unshed tears. "We'll see about that, Mr. Malloy," she replied tartly. "I thank you for your concern and for the ride back."

"It'll be the *last* one," Mike countered just as sharply. "Mr. Holladay was good enough to give me time off to go after you when we got Reverend Larsen's note about how you abandoned his horse. You grew up in a privileged home, Miss Bristol, and I'm sorry you lost all that. But folks in these parts have problems just as worrisome as yours. You'll be wise to remember that, if you get the itch to take off again."

His somber warning brought the meal to an end, and when he stood up, Mercy and Judd followed him out to his buckboard.

"Can't thank you enough for all your time and effort," Judd said. And in a voice low enough not to carry back to the house he added, "I know it was a thankless job, bringing her back against her will."

Mike shrugged, but then he shook the big hand extended toward him. "I felt responsible—to you folks, as much as for Christine. Knew she'd be a handful when I left her here, and I never intended—"

"She's got a mind of her own," Mercy reminded him, "and at thirteen, she thinks nothing bad can happen to her."

He chuckled then, deepening dimples she'd never seen in his tanned cheeks. His hazel eyes shone like polished stones in his dusty face, and even with his hat-matted hair and gritty mustache, he struck her as a fine-looking fellow. A lot younger than she'd figured before. In his many comings and goings, while she was busy dishing up dinner for a dozen passengers, Mike Malloy's boyish features had gotten past her.

"She's older than you think," he remarked, "and I don't doubt for a minute that she'll try this again. Too feisty to leave it alone. But then, if it was my mother caught up with the likes of Richard Wyndham, I guess I'd be chasing her down, too."

Judd's dark eyebrows went up. "Did you hear anything about—"

"Nah, she's keeping all that to herself, like a big, juicy secret—if she really learned anything," he replied. "You can tell by looking at him that Wyndham's got a story for every occasion, and he probably changes names like you and I change our shirts. The war's brought his type out to play, and good honest folks are the ones who'll pay for it."

He smiled at Nathaniel as the tall, dark man brought two fresh horses to hitch to his wagon. Again Mercy was struck by his integrity, his *concern* about a runaway and those she left in her wake. Many of Holladay's drivers had a wild and woolly reputation for consuming all the liquor and women that came their way, so it was pure pleasure to meet a young man with values and principles. A man they could call a true friend.

She grabbed his muscled hand between hers. "Thank you again," she said in a voice that shook more than she anticipated. "If there's ever anything we can do for . . . She had us mighty worried, even if she *is* too big for her lacy little britches, and—"

The hitch in her voice brought the tears that had threatened to fall ever since she'd come running from the house. Mike was kind enough to squeeze her hand and keep smiling.

"Mrs. Monroe," he said when she'd gotten herself together, "after a long drive's behind me and I'm fed up with the dust and the cranky passengers and the threat of those Indians, thinking about your dinners gives me a reason to hop on that stage and do it all again. You and Judd are fine folks, and I'm glad I've come to know you."

As though his sentiment had caught him off guard, Mike hopped onto his bench and laced the reins between his fingers. With a tight nod and a "giddap!" to his horses, he was off.

"Good luck with that Bristol girl!" he called back to them. He drove off in a billowing cloud of dust.

Mercy leaned into her husband as he slung an arm over her shoulders. "You certainly have a way with the menfolk, Mrs. Monroe," he quipped, and then he kissed her soundly. "Good thing I found you first."

Mercy flushed with the warmth of his humor, reveling in the strength of the bond between them, as solid as this man's body. Her mind was already at a canter, like those horses Nathaniel had provided in place of Mike's tired ones.

"I know that look. What's going on inside that pretty head of yours?"

Chuckling, Mercy laced her fingers between Judd's as they walked back toward the house. "I just thought of the perfect antidote to Miss Christine's penchant for turning everyone's lives upside down on a whim. At least it worked on me when *I* was her age."

Judd's blue eyes caught the sparkle of the afternoon sun. "You going to share this with me—or do you keep deep, dark secrets like our little flame-haired angel does? Of course, who would believe Miss Mercedes ever *needed* an antidote for her perfection?"

Mercy's laughter bubbled up inside her, itself the perfect antidote to the worries she'd prayed about these past few weeks.

"Aunt Agatha Vanderbilt," she replied smugly. "Otherwise known as the headmistress of Miss Vanderbilt's Academy for Young Ladies."

Chapter Nine

Christine awoke the next morning with the glow of sunlight on her face muted by muslin curtains. Stretching like a languid cat, she reveled in the way the feather mattress wrapped around her, in a house that smelled like fresh bread and bacon rather than rancid cabbage. It felt so good to be *clean* again, and to have the tangles combed out of her hair. She was even glad to be back with Billy, although her wild-goose chase to find Mama had taught her a valuable lesson in trusting herself and her own instincts. Oh, the Monroes were good people, and *maybe* they wanted the best for her.

But this would never be home.

Propping herself on her elbows, Christine gazed around the humble room with its dark log walls and chinking the color of the muslin at the window. The fabric seemed to vibrate with the light of the sun— why, it must be nearly noon! And they'd let her sleep undisturbed.

She snickered. *That* would never happen again! And as the images from her dreams resurfaced, she envisioned a pleasant face framed with unruly black waves; cheeks defined by a coal-colored beard as thick as the bristles in Daddy's shaving brush.

Tucker Trudeau. She could still hear the roll of his accent and feel the grip of his fingers, and these memories felt so clear, so distinct, it was as if he'd joined her here, filling a void in her heart like the sunlight enlivened this room.

Did he like what he'd seen in her? Or had he only seen through the stories of a lonely girl who hungered for her mother's love again? Maybe she was just one more waif in the aftermath of the war, and her rumpled clothes and dirty face had inspired his pity rather than a spark of potential affection.

Maybe she would never hear from him again.

This thought jarred her from the bed to fetch the photograph of Mama and that slippery Wyndham— which she'd locked in a trunk so Billy wouldn't sneak in and get it. Without its glass, the likeness shone less with Mama's newfound brightness and took on an earthier tone.

But it was hers. Perhaps the last memento of her mother she'd ever have. Thank goodness Tucker had been kind enough to let her keep it.

Furtive footfalls on the stairs made her hold her breath. She braced herself for when Billy would burst through the door to rail at her for still being in bed, her mind racing over the details she might reveal and those she refused to share. She held the portrait to her breast like a shield, her most intimidating expression in place.

Yet when Billy peered through the crack, as though afraid to approach her, Christine softened. He was just a kid. He'd been Mama's favorite, so he felt her abandonment much more acutely than anyone else would. His loyalty to the Monroes was his way of shoring himself up for whatever might lie ahead, now that everyone they'd loved had left them.

"Come on in, Billy. I just woke up."

He looked a little taller than she remembered, but his walk had lost its happy-go-lucky spring. When his gaze fell to the photograph, she lowered it so he could at least see it upside down.

Billy eyed the likeness somberly, letting one finger drift alongside Mama's smile. "So what'd you find out? Did that photographer fella—"

"His name is Tucker. Tucker Trudeau."

"—hazard a guess as to where they was headed? What they was gonna do together?" her brother asked in a voice edged with pain. "She looks purty again, don't she? Too happy to be thinkin' about the farm. Or findin' *us*."

Christine closed her eyes. How could she explain, without wounding him further? "Tucker said Richard Wyndham wrote him a worthless check on a bank account that didn't even exist—and then never came back to claim this picture. Probably just sat for it to stifle Mama's whining. Tucker said they'd just come from the justice of the peace. Wanted a wedding picture."

"Mama?" Billy whimpered. "Already got herself married again? And she didn't want us there with her?"

His mouth opened and closed a couple times. Then he focused his pale blue eyes on her. "You're not pullin' my leg, are ya? This is the God's honest truth, and there ain't nothin' we can do about it? And Daddy not dead six months yet."

"That's about all I know, yes. Tucker was nice enough to—"

"Tucker this and Tucker that!" Billy jeered—and then he leaned in close to stare straight into her eyes. "*You* didn't get yourself hitched, didja? Just because Mama—"

"What if I did? Who'll I ever find out here in this wasteland?"

Christine shoved him away, all compassion for him gone now. Marrying Tucker Trudeau had certainly occurred to her these past few days, but *that* dream was something she knew better than to share with anyone!

"If you're going to talk crazy like that, get out of my room! Get out anyway!" she amended curtly. "Make yourself useful and fix me something to eat while I dress."

Billy planted his fists on his hips as though to challenge her, but then he turned on his bare heel and stalked out. The silence he left behind rang with unspoken accusations—or was that her conscience prickling? After all, if she kept pushing him away and hurting his feelings, who would do her bidding? It was pointless to be a princess if she had no one to step and fetch for her.

Christine smiled as she got out of bed. In her mind, Tucker Trudeau was flashing a winsome grin at her, grabbing her hand to show her the lot he'd just purchased as he described the fine house he intended to build her. It sounded a lot like her home in Missouri, but grander—more like the pillared mansion on the manicured estate owned by Leland Massena, the banker.

She plucked the folded paper from her carpetbag

and held his handwritten address to her lips. She'd write him a letter soon. To thank him for Mama's portrait, of course.

Mercy looked up from the large camelback trunk in the curtained-off room where she and Judd slept. She silently thanked Billy for being enough of a thorn in his sister's side to make her squeal; make her reveal her girlish imaginings more in what she didn't say than in what she admitted. And thanks to the round metal grates that allowed heat from a winter fire to rise into the rooms upstairs, she'd heard every word. But that would be *her* secret!

Her plan for the fanciful, pampered Christine was falling into place nicely, and not a moment too soon. And Billy, bless him, had sprinted outside to help the men rather than bowing to his sister's breakfast wishes.

So now was her best chance for some girl talk. Time to plant seeds that would bear fruit for both of them before Miss Bristol took a notion to do something foolish. Like claiming to go after her mother again, when it was a certain man in Atchison she'd really rather see.

"Good morning, Christine. Did you rest well?" she called out cheerfully. Miss Bristol wasn't the only female here who knew a little about leading people in her own direction. "I'd like your opinion about some new dresses, when you've got a moment."

A hand pushed the red calico curtain aside and her unwitting victim peeked in. Mercy looked up from the beautiful gowns she'd spread across her bed in a rainbow of satins and taffeta, praying for the words that would bring Christine closer . . . tempt her to take the bait before she realized any ulterior motives were hidden in it.

Those green eyes widened. Like a moth to the flame, Christine walked toward the fine dresses with her fingers extended to touch them, not even realizing how much she revealed in the simple, universal gesture of a woman who enjoys pretty things. Mercy saw the yearning in the girl's eyes and felt it in her own soul, as well; she truly understood how difficult it was to go from riches to rags, if appearance was the way one measured success.

"You know, I've been keeping these dresses packed away—realizing, of course, that fancy balls and evenings at the theater aren't likely to happen any time soon for us homesteaders in—"

"These are yours?" Christine's face lit up with amazed curiosity. It hadn't occurred to her that Mercy had lived a different life before coming west four years ago to help claim this land.

"Oh, yes! Philadelphia was an exciting place to grow up," Mercy said with a smile. "You probably think I'm hopelessly *old*, but it wasn't that long ago when I had my coming out. Lawn parties and holiday balls were the highlight of my life then. I loved to dance and play the piano and gossip with my friends about which young men we wanted to—"

"And you married Judd?" Christine blurted. "I mean—he's a very fine—"

"He was the handsomest thing you ever saw in a suit," Mercy confided, "even if it took him a while to realize what a wonderful wife I'd make him. Papa's money frightened him, you see."

She paused to let these details sink in. "But I knew he was the right man for me when he insisted on making his own way, rather than following in our family's financial footsteps. Why, managing one of those huge carriage factories in the city would've been as poor a fit for Judd Monroe as trying to squeeze his feet into my kid slippers."

Christine's face lit up with interest in the secrets being shared.

"So I married him!" Mercy continued with a girlish grin. "It was such a beautiful day, with a church full of my family and friends. And thanks to Mother's prodding, Papa saw fit to give us the money for more homesteading supplies than most folks out here could ever dream of. This log house, the barn, and the corrals were my dowry, Christine. But it was Judd's sweat and effort that built them."

Her little lecture wasn't entirely a lure; she hadn't forgotten her parents' reservations about the life she and Judd would lead on the untamed prairie. Judd's dream had never been the same as theirs, and each winter when the wind howled around this little house, driving snow inside through cracks in the logs, she recalled the comforts she'd given up.

"Were you ever . . . sorry?" the girl asked, her gaze drifting to the finery spread before her.

Mercy let out a little laugh. "I can't say it's been easy. You know very well how difficult it is to lose a life of luxury and the friends who were a part of it. You probably think I'm a heartless shrew who's been so dried out by the Kansas wind she's forgotten about *fun* and—"

"No," Christine interrupted pensively. "I just don't understand why you'd *choose* to live this way. I mean—it's not that I—"

"Believe me, Christine, there are days when I wonder about that, too," Mercy replied quietly. "It certainly wasn't the life I prepared myself for, much less dreamed about when I was your age. So I'm thinking we should send you to a reputable school—perhaps the one I attended in St. Louis. You'd have to board there full-time, of course. Abilene will someday be civilized enough to have its own schools and churches, but I can't think you'll be happy here."

The flaring of those bright green eyes told Mercy she'd set the right hook. It was tempting to weave in a little homily about God's providence and the rewards to be had in working the soil rather than making another needlepoint sampler, but Christine didn't want to hear that. At thirteen, nobody did.

"You'd—you'd send me to school? Even though I'm not your daughter?"

"Miss Vanderbilt's Academy for Young Ladies is the ideal place for a girl of your abilities and station in life," Mercy continued with enthusiasm. "You should know how to manage a household and the staff who maintain it. Along with such social graces, Miss Vanderbilt insists her students excel in literature, geography, French, and art, as well as useful skills like cooking and sewing.

"And," she went on in a lowered, more confidential tone, "it's the best place to meet girls whose brothers might become suitable matches someday. I've found out you're *quite* capable of thinking—and acting—independently, Christine. But I doubt you want to be a woman alone."

The girl's lips twitched with a secret: Christine was adept at holding her cards close, and playing her aces at just the right time. Those catlike green eyes narrowed as she caressed the dresses.

"Why are you doing this for me?" she asked warily. "You obviously can't afford to—"

It was the perfect occasion to recall the story of how

Jesus encouraged His disciples to feed the hungry and clothe the naked, but Mercy refrained. The last thing this willful young lady wanted to be was a charity case. She would turn a deaf ear—and turn away from a plan that would keep them both sane.

"We would be remiss if we didn't help you become a personal and social success," Mercy began, focusing directly on her charge's freckled face. "My family firmly believes that girls should be educated. If I ever have a daughter of my own and circumstances would separate us, I hope someone would do the same for her.

"And while I'm willing to remake these dresses for the social events you'll be attending, you'll earn part of your tuition by taking on jobs at Miss Vanderbilt's academy—just like the other girls who attend," she stated. "But won't that be better than living in isolation here with us?"

Christine blinked with sudden awareness. "Miss Vanderbilt . . . you mean the millionaire Vanderbilts who built the university?"

Mercy nodded, keeping her smile under control. She, too, knew when to play her aces.

"But with a fortune like that, why is she running a school? Why, she could be living in a mansion—"

"Indeed she does. But the palatial home Agatha Vanderbilt inherited is more of a nuisance than a boon to a woman who never married. So she's made it her mission to instruct girls in how to lead useful, purposeful lives."

Mercy couldn't conceal her grin as she recalled the forthright, opinionated headmistress she'd butted heads with more than once. "Matter of fact, she moved from the social circles in Philadelphia to live in St. Louis because back then that city on the Mississippi was considered too rough and rowdy for an unmarried lady of her station. Never let it be said that Miss Vanderbilt doesn't appreciate—and invite!—adventure."

A grin lit Christine's face, giving a hint of the happy child she'd been before the war. She turned her attention to the gowns, fashioned from rich brocaded silks and satins, tulle and taffeta that rustled seductively at her touch. They glimmered like jewels in the light from the little window.

Then her brow wrinkled. "But what if Mama comes back? What if she needs—"

"We'll see she's taken care of, dear. Or we'll see that she gets to St. Louis, to be with you."

Mercy held up the lavender satin gown at the edge of the bed, smiling fondly. "I wore this to a spring cotillion, Christine—back when I was the belle of the ball. 'Making over and making do' is something we women tolerate now because the war has forced us to. But I believe your mother would be pleased that you were attending such a respected school. I'm sure she had that in mind for you once you outgrew Miss Bryce's expertise."

Holding the gown against the girl's slender shoulders, she assessed the alterations that would be needed. "If we took out these sleeves and nipped in the side seams . . . you're a bit thinner than I was, but a few tucks in the front would—"

"And we could cover those adjustments by stitching the lace—"

"You know, if we bought a copy of *Godey's Lady's Book* next time we're in town—"

"I can do these alterations myself, you know!" Christine piped up. She had pinched the dress to her waist and was looking down to check its length. "And if you had a sewing machine . . ."

Their eyes met, and they burst into laughter that filled the room as joyously as it warmed their hearts. For the first time, they shared a passion. A mission.

"Look behind you," Mercy whispered.

Waves the color of honeyed flame whirled in a circle when Christine pivoted. "Why, it's just like the one Beulah Mae and Mama taught me on! You see, I've been sewing for years now, so—" She turned, comprehension dawning in her bright eyes. "And so have you? Even though you grew up in a well-to-do family?"

"That treadle machine was my gift from Miss Vanderbilt when I graduated at the head of my class," Mercy replied proudly. "I'm sure it'll welcome the chance to stitch silk and satin again, rather than calico. So if you're certain you'd like to attend the academy—"

"Oh, yes, please!" Christine gushed. Then, with a sheepish grin, she added, "And thank you, Mrs. Monroe."

And thank you, God! Mercy thought as she clasped two slender hands in hers. "I'm pleased to do this for you—but here it is August already, so we haven't much time to prepare you! You'll be wanting new underthings, but right now I don't have the money. Judd needs lumber for more stalls in the barn, and—"

"I—I—" Christine's skin turned pink beneath her freckles, and she bolted from the room and up the stairs.

Mercy smiled: the young runaway had a conscience after all.

Moments later, the girl's steps descended in a quick

rhythm and Miss Bristol burst through the curtain with a conciliatory expression on her face. "Twenty dollars of what I took from . . . I'm sorry, I never should've . . . my train fare and that night in the hotel . . ."

She thrust the money into Mercy's hand, shifting from one foot to the other in her agitation. "And I can wear the underthings I found at the bottom of Mama's trunk. Why—I can alter some of *her* dresses, too!"

Struck with this sudden idea, Christine settled herself. "That—that's only fair, since you're sacrificing your own nice frocks . . . out of the kindness of your heart. Because—well, there hasn't been much kindness in mine, has there?"

Mercy longed to hug this girl, but she was as skittish as a new foal from owning up to her thievery and deciding to go away to school—all within the past few minutes. She placed her hands on those slender shoulders and felt her smile fill her whole face.

"Apology accepted," she said softly. "If my mother had disappeared, I'd be acting distracted, and chasing halfway across Kansas for her, too.

"Now," Mercy went on, while the fragile bond between them still held, "we'll need to go into town soon—to send a letter to Miss Vanderbilt, so she'll make you a place in her fall session, and to get the latest issue of—"

"*Godey's Lady's Book*!" Christine chimed in.

"Yes, and meanwhile I'll write out my shopping list. We'll gather more eggs, and churn the milk into butter—so we can trade those things for flour and sugar, and sturdy fabric to make shirts and pants for Billy—"

"He's shot up like a weed," his sister said with a roll of her eyes, "and come winter, his shoes won't fit."

"Ah. Lots to do, so we'd best get busy."

As Mercy lovingly draped her frocks over the sewing machine, a deep sense of satisfaction filled her: they'd bridged a wide chasm during this little chat! And when she thought about how Aunt Agatha would handle this headstrong little princess, it was all she could do not to laugh. She couldn't *wait* to release Christine into the legendary disciplinarian's care! But she also had her mother's sister to thank for the practical skills, poise, and confidence she herself had developed at the academy.

"How soon will we be going into Abilene?"

Mercy turned toward the girl, who wore a hopeful, utterly lovely expression on her face. For a moment Mercy became thirteen again, eager for new dresses, a shopping trip, and a new school year. *Where would any of us be without something to look forward to? A purpose—and meaningful work*, she pondered. "How soon can you make that butter?"

Christine's mouth dropped open. But with amazing aplomb, she grinned and dashed out the back door.

"Billy! Billy!" she cried. "You go fetch that bucket of milk from the springhouse while I find the churn!"

Chapter Ten

As the buckboard headed into the sunrise, Mercy settled herself beside Judd for the ride into town. Behind them, Billy and Christine talked in low voices. The girl kept touching the pocket of her skirt. Mercy had noticed the flickering of candlelight through the grating in the ceiling, so she suspected that Christine had written a letter late into the night.

Was it to her wayward mother? Or to that man in Atchison who'd given her the picture? Perhaps she'd also brought the money from her mother's trunk, along with big ideas for how to spend it.

For whatever reason, Miss Bristol couldn't sit still and seemed very eager to reach Abilene, such as it was. The little settlement still boasted fewer than fifty residents—the population of Dickinson County tallied at less than five hundred—so their limited shopping wouldn't take nearly as long as the trip there and back.

She talked quietly with Judd, reviewing what they needed before Holladay's next supply wagon passed through. The peaceful countryside rolled along, with farmsteads on their right and the Smoky Hill River with its maples and cottonwoods on their left.

"Almost there," she said over her shoulder. Glancing sideways to catch Judd's eye, she awaited the reaction from the back.

"Almost where?" Christine stood up to scan the land ahead, to be sure she wasn't missing anything. "I thought Abilene would be a *town*, instead of just a few little buildings. Why, Atchison was—"

"Established a while back, and became the terminus for the railroad and the stage line," Judd pointed out.

He pulled the horses to a halt beside a log cabin with a sign that said FRONTIER STORE. "Most folks out this way came to homestead rather than to open up shop, so we make do with Doc Moon's merchandise. You're used to better—and so were we, back East. But for day-to-day survival, this little place gets us by."

While the Bristols hopped down from the back, Mercy waited for Judd to come around. She never tired of the look in his sky-blue eyes as he reached up for her; reveled in the strength of his muscled arms as he lowered her to the ground so effortlessly. Would he forgo their habitual kiss because they had two red-haired observers?

Ah, no. Her husband's hands spanned her waist as he lowered his lips to hers. Judd kissed her as though he could make those kids wait a week . . . as though he'd forgotten about them altogether and could only focus on her.

When he raised his head, Mercy giggled with the sensations his kiss always caused. She turned toward the door, but he held her until she looked up at him again.

"I love you, Mercedes," he murmured. "You're the best thing that ever happened to me."

"I love you, too, Judd." She held his gaze a moment longer, noting long, black lashes lowered just enough to say he'd been moved by their kiss, as well. "And where would I be without you?"

They often repeated this conversation, simple, yet rich in its familiarity. But today Judd burst out laughing. "Probably shopping in a fine Philadelphia store, with a mother whose hobby is spending your father's money. Who ever thought we'd end up here in denim and calico, with two kids looking at us like we're crazy?"

He grinned at Billy and Christine. When he opened the door, they hurried inside as though witnessing affection between man and wife had embarrassed them a little. The boy hung back, surveying the log interior and long aisles of merchandise, waiting to tag along with Judd. Christine was off like a shot, to the table where bolts of yard goods awaited her eager eyes and fingers.

"Here it is! A new *Godey's Lady's Book*!" came her excited cry.

The other folks milling about looked up with understanding smiles.

"How about if Billy and I see to the nails and lumber while you ladies take your time with finer things?" Judd suggested, waving to Ira Barstow across the store. "You'll need to remind her that money doesn't blow in with the wind, even when you're spending it to help somebody else."

Mercy nodded, spotting her friend Elizabeth as she started down the narrow aisle of cooking pots and crockery bowls. The youngest Barstow, a towheaded girl, rode her hip while a boy with the same fair features toddled along, gripping her skirt. It was a picture of motherhood that made Mercy nip her lip with envy.

"Well, hello there, Miz Monroe!" her neighbor sang out. "And what brings you to Doc's store on this fine summer morning?"

It was good to see a familiar face, after long days of labor on their isolated farm, so Mercy overlooked Elizabeth's speculative expression when she glanced toward Christine. "Judd needed supplies to enlarge the corrals. And we're making over some dresses to get Miss Christine ready for school in St. Louis come—"

"Well, why on earth would you do that? It's not like she's kin!"

Everyone in the little store stopped talking.

Mercy felt a surge of protectiveness. Hadn't the Bristol children already endured rejection from most of these people? It wasn't as if she and Judd expected anyone's help! They might as well hear this story firsthand, so they'd have all the facts when they gossiped about it later.

Mercy smiled at Elizabeth, standing taller. She might be wearing calico, but she begged for no one's approval. "When will *I* ever need those gowns?" she asked with a shrug. "Lord knows I'll never see twenty-two again—or the figure I had before I married Judd. And what a waste, to let those pretty fabrics fade by keeping them packed away."

She smiled at Christine, who was bustling up the aisle with an open book and a face lit up like a summer sunrise. "Miss Bristol is a skilled seamstress, so she's doing the alterations herself," she said so everyone

115

could hear. "I think that's very commendable, for a girl of thirteen."

"Look at this pattern, Mercy! Wouldn't that lavender gown look splendid if we made it over this way?" the young redhead exclaimed. "Just like you said, with tucks at the waist and the lace trim coming down in this vee, to cover them!"

"And hello to you, too, missy!" Elizabeth jiggled the baby on her hip, her curiosity a-simmer. "Goodness me! The Monroes took you in like a stray cat, and then took you back after you ran off—and now they're sending you away to school? Aren't *you* just the fine and fancy princess?"

Mercy cringed. Doc Moon and everyone in his store were pretending to go about their business, but they were hanging on every word of this escalating exchange.

Christine glanced at Mercy, flummoxed. Then she squared her shoulders and forced an ingratiating smile, to face their neighbor with all the presence of a princess, indeed. "Thank you for noticing, Mrs. Barstow," she replied politely. "How very nice to see you again."

With that, she turned back to Mercy. "You know, there's a green taffeta gown in Mama's trunk that could look just like this one if we—"

"You're sure you want to alter your mother's dresses? What if she comes back, as we talked about before?" Mercy asked.

"When will she wear them again?" Christine's eyes betrayed a painful truth, but she didn't back away from it. "And if *you've* been kind enough to sacrifice in my behalf, my mother wouldn't begrudge me a few dresses. It's not like she'll be throwing any more lawn parties back home, is it?"

Mercy's throat tightened with admiration. She smiled at this waif's determination—a mature acceptance, mixed with enough spunk to disarm whatever Elizabeth might challenge them with next. In fact, her friend's broad face was turning a deep shade of rose— and then the baby made a splattering sound in its diaper. Perhaps from being squeezed too hard.

"Nice to see you again," Mrs. Barstow muttered. Then she pivoted, knocking into the shy son who still gripped her skirts. As the trio made for the door, the boy's wail filled the little store and then the baby joined in. It was a noisy duet that had everyone returning to their business with quiet chuckles.

"Nicely done," Mercy said with a wink. "Catty, but called for."

"Why was she on such a high horse? I thought she was your friend."

Mercy wondered about that herself. "Maybe she's having a bad day, or she's in a peevish mood. Lord knows we all take our turn at that, don't we?"

She grinned broadly at the girl, but Christine missed her point. "Why don't you find a couple lengths of modestly priced lace for those dresses, and pick out some cloth for Billy's pants? I'll get the groceries and put my note to Miss Vanderbilt in Doc's mailbag."

Christine reached into her skirt pocket. "Would you please post this letter for me, and I'll pay you for the stamp?" she asked coyly. "I thought it only proper to thank Mr. Trudeau for that likeness of Mama."

It was a very thick thank-you note, written on fine

vellum Virgilia Bristol must have carried in her trunk. But Mercy let the girl have her pride. Christine would be as comely as her mother, and would entertain a bevy of beaux when she was old enough to be romanced. By then, the young man in Atchison would have found someone his own age—if he hadn't already. So what harm would it do to let Christine pour out her lonely heart on paper?

"Of course. I'll be back in a few minutes."

When she got to the counter where Doc handled the mail, Mercy stood to one side to reread her letter. It was far too short, considering all the details her aunt would enjoy reading, but it served her purpose.

Dearest Aunt Agatha,

Have I got a challenge for you! Christine Bristol is thirteen. She and her brother Billy were abandoned at a stagecoach depot, and are staying with us now—a long story. I hope you have room for her in your academy courses this fall, as she's a bright girl who needs guidance and a purpose at this precarious point in her life.

We're doing well, but the days never have enough hours for the tasks at hand. I'll write more soon, and I look forward to your reply.

With love,

Mercedes

P.S. THANK YOU for teaching me patience and the art of conversational strategy!

After tallying the postage, Mercy had Doc bring the items on her list to his counter: flour, coffee, dry beans, sorghum molasses, salt, and tins of fruit for pies. As she was returning to the yard-goods table, she spotted Billy struggling beneath a bulging bag of grass seed, followed closely by her husband, who carried an ax, two spades, and some packets of nails. From the other side of the store came Christine, clutching bobbins of lace trim in the crook of one elbow as she waved a card of colored hair ribbons at her brother.

"Look at these!" she crowed. "And we got you some denim for pants, and some thread and trims for my dresses, and—"

Judd's supplies landed on Doc's counter with a *whump,* beside the food Mercy had ordered. When he glanced in the girl's direction, Mercy saw it coming: reality and dreams were about to collide. And she already knew which one would win.

She fished the pitifully limp coin purse from her skirt pocket, assessing what the "princess" had picked out in her absence . . . at least four types of lace, plus those pretty ribbons and her book of patterns. They hadn't even looked at shoes for Billy.

The hopeful glow on Christine's face took her back to her own girlhood. And why *wouldn't* she be excited about almost-new dresses for a new school? The pale yellow one she wore today pulled too snugly over her budding breasts. And what girl, riding high on a moment of social success, hadn't pushed her luck and tried to get just a little more than she'd been allowed?

Judd saw things differently, of course. Even though he'd be fair, Christine would never appreciate his priorities.

"We'll get you that book, and the fabric for Billy's pants," he said in a low voice.

"But Mercy told me I could—"

"No fuss, young lady."

"But I brought my own money—"

"I really don't need no new pants," Billy piped up in a husky voice. "Why, those horses don't give one hoot about how I look!"

"We'll discuss it later. Keep the fabric and put the other things back."

Judd's tone brooked no argument, and once again the little store rang with an interested silence. "Will you please help your brother bring in the butter and eggs from the wagon?"

Everything about the girl sagged. Mercy's heart went out to her, even as her hand closed around her pitifully small purse. She'd felt the pinch of their financial situation herself. It was no easy thing to accept, when necessities had to come before the niceties a girl had grown used to.

But then, it was no treat to come up short when it came time to settle up with Doc Moon, either.

During the ride home, the parching wind was nothing compared to the powerful waves of anger coming from behind the wagon seat. Mercy talked with Judd about what needed doing in the next day or so, while thinking about what to serve for dinner after their day away. By the time they rolled into their yard, she knew Christine's temper was about to cut loose like a Kansas tornado.

The girl clambered down from the wagon, reaching impatiently for the packages Billy handed her: the very small, flat one for her, and the bulkier roll of denim for her brother's pants. She ran to the house—probably so no one else could lecture her, or ask her to help carry things—and by the time they all sat down to supper, Christine's expression could have curdled their milk.

"Christine, will you return thanks for us tonight?" Judd asked.

Billy began swinging his legs, as though he wanted to hit the floor running before the storm blew in.

"Give *thanks?*" his sister snapped. "For what? Why couldn't I buy that lace trim—*with my own money!*— when Mercy herself told me—"

Her fiery hair quivered around a face growing pink with agitation. Then those green eyes narrowed at Mercy. "And why didn't you say one word to him in the store, Mrs. Monroe? It was fine and dandy to put that snooty Mrs. Barstow in her place—and didn't I help with that? Mama always said it was the woman who really runs the family. And it was *you* who had the money in your pocket—"

"And it was you who ran off with forty dollars of it." Judd's face remained composed, his voice low and controlled. But those eyes were alight with a powerful blue flame.

"While we understand that you're upset about your mother, and that the money was for your provisions while you went after her, you stole it rather than asking for our help," he went on. "It's time you learned that no matter how good your intentions were—how urgent your mission—you'll face the consequences of your actions. Because, believe me, the rest of us are."

The little room got so quiet that their breathing was the only sound for several seconds. Asa and Nathaniel gazed at their empty plates, knowing not to eat before anyone else. Billy's face got tight with worry, while his legs kicked up a breeze beneath the table. Mercy gripped her hands in her lap. She'd known this matter would raise its ugly head again,

121

and Judd was right: Christine had stolen money, and she should face up to it.

Judd cleared his throat. "You probably don't realize this, but that money you snatched would've bought nearly a month's food, to tide us over until Mr. Holladay's supply wagon comes around. I had to ask for credit today, to buy enough to feed us and our stage guests, and I *detest* being beholden to Mr. Moon. He's not just a storekeeper, Christine. He's my friend.

"And what if Doc hadn't agreed to run a tab for me?" he went on. "Mercy would have to feed those passengers just the vegetables from her garden and whatever we can trap for meat. No biscuits, no coffee, no pies. Other women along the stage route would see nothing wrong with that, but you *know* Mercy would feel she's shorting Mr. Holladay's passengers."

Christine sat with her shoulders hunched, gazing at the tabletop. Her tightly pressed lips bespoke the wish for this lecture to end—the wish that the floorboards would open up and swallow her whole, so she'd have no more of Judd's lecture to endure.

But he wasn't finished.

"And then there's the matter of Reverend Larsen's horse. You apparently abandoned him on your way—"

"He kept stopping!" the girl blurted. "And when I saw he was heading for a little log hut with a cross on it—"

"—east, which means we had to give the circuit rider one of our Morgans and a saddle, and clothes to replace what was in his saddlebags," Judd continued. His shirt was tugging damply across his shoulders with the evening's heat. He brushed his black hair from his brow and leaned in for the final stroke.

"And last but certainly not least, young lady, you took napkins that Mercy's granny embroidered for us as a wedding present," he said in the lowest, most insistent tone he'd used yet. "That dear old lady died last year, so there'll be no replacing them."

He let this settle in; let the girl stew in her own nervousness while his gaze provided the flame for a few moments more.

"So when I heard Mrs. Barstow's surprise because we were sending you to school—in Mercy's remade party dresses—I had to question the wisdom of that myself," he pressed on. "Not because you're not kin, but because you have no remorse for the trouble you've caused. No real understanding of the sacrifices we've all made on your behalf."

A tear trickled down each of Billy's freckled cheeks. He'd gone very still, again acting far sorrier than his sister for sins he didn't commit. Yet she, too, finally bowed her head as though she could no longer stand up to Judd's accusations.

"I'm asking you again, Christine," Judd said quietly. "Will you please say grace for us this evening? Because if you won't, you can go right on upstairs. I won't have a thankless child at my table."

The girl cleared her throat, and then sniffled. Her cinnamon waves had worked loose to hang like a curtain around her face, and she spoke very softly. "Our Father, who art in heaven, hallowed be Thy name—"

"Thy kingdom come, Thy will be done," everyone else joined in. And as the familiar prayer continued, the voices around the table rose with conviction—and relief. They ate the simple meal more quietly than usual, and after Christine picked at her food she asked to be excused.

When she was out of the room, Billy's face went tight with boyish worry.

"That girls' school in St. Louis must cost a heap, and—and I know it's the best thing for Christine, 'cause she was nearly as smart as Miss Bryce! We was doin' our lessons at home, after renegades burned down the school, you see." His words rushed out in a tumble, and his eyes blazed blue. "I promise you on my good name I'll pay you back every cent of her schoolin' someday—just for puttin' up with that *sass*—"

Mercy slipped her arm around his shoulders, thankful for this boy with a heart as big as he was. "What an angel you are to care for your sister that way, Billy," she said in a shaky voice. "Your parents would be very proud of the man you've become. But there's no need for you to worry about that expense. I wouldn't send her to Miss Vanderbilt's school if we couldn't afford it."

"And, comes a time *you* want an education," Judd joined in, "we'll see that you get it. I've heard you firing off your multiplication tables—"

"And I'm having to study up to stay ahead of him in geography," Asa said with a wide, white grin.

"—and if a profession besides farming or raising horses appeals to you, that's fine, too."

Billy's smile brightened. "That's right nice of you folks. Can't thank you enough for takin' us in." His gaze wandered across the table, to the round pan beside Nathaniel's elbow. "But I *can* lay into a piece of that apple pie, if you don't mind!"

Mercy laughed and got up to fetch a knife. Above her, she heard muffled sounds coming from the corner where Christine had set her mother's trunks. The girl was licking her wounds, perhaps salving her injured dignity by studying those pretty gowns, envisioning how they'd look when she redesigned them.

If she were packing to run off again, surely she'd wait until dark. Wouldn't she?

Mercy set aside this thought and returned to the front room, where plates were scraped clean and awaiting a wedge of her tart, sweet dessert. On impulse, she slid in beside Billy again and spoke near his ear, so her voice wouldn't drift up to his sister.

"Can you keep a secret?" she asked, deftly sectioning the pie.

He nodded, his eyes glancing toward the ceiling as though this particular treat was all for him.

"This Miss Vanderbilt who runs the academy? Well, she was *my* teacher—not so many years ago!" she added with a grin. "And she nearly expelled me once, because I had a sassy mouth *almost* as bad as your sister's."

Billy's eyes got as round as marbles. "Go on, now—*you*?" he replied with a laugh. "What in tarnation did you say, Miss Mercy?"

The memory put a conspiratorial smile on her lips, and the three men leaned in to catch every word.

"I spread the rumor among the other girls that our headmistress was always so strict and cross because she was laced up too tight. And if that wasn't enough," she confided with raised eyebrows, "I went on to speculate that Miss Vanderbilt could die sitting in her chair and no one would know it for days, because all that starch in her drawers would hold her upright."

Billy's eyes twinkled. This was mischief he could understand! "And she heard about it?"

"Of course she did! Teachers have eyes in the back of their heads and ears that hear every little thing. And in a huge houseful of girls, there's bound to be a few who can't keep their mouths shut." She placed the largest slice of pie on Billy's plate, grinning to emphasize her point. "And I'm sure Miss Vanderbilt's only gotten older and crankier since then."

The boy let out a snicker, shoving a large bite of pie into his mouth. "Sounds like Christine's about to meet her match."

Chapter Eleven

The next morning Mercy found a folded note on her kitchen table, and her heart went into a spin. Had that foolish girl run off again, unable to handle Judd's reprimand? How would Billy possibly weather another emotional storm on top of his other losses?

But when she picked up the page, money fell out: almost thirty dollars, in old worn bills. She read the dainty, precise script twice, nipping her lip.

Mercy and Judd,

Please accept my apologies for the trouble I've caused. This is all the money I have left from what I took, plus some that Mama had stashed in her trunk. I promise to behave myself, and to be worthy of the schooling and dresses you've provided for me. Not everyone would take in two strangers and treat them like family, the way you have.

> *Yours sincerely,*
> *Christine Bristol*

For the next few weeks, the girl was as good as her word. She helped in the kitchen and washed dishes *almost* without complaint after the stagecoaches passed through.

And when she wasn't performing chores, the quiet, steady rhythm of the treadle sewing machine hummed beneath the other sounds in the house. Mercy offered assistance only when Christine asked, for it was clear the girl had a talent for envisioning the gowns in more current designs, and then remaking them according to the fashion dictates in her dog-eared copy of *Godey's Lady's Book*.

As she finished each one, she gently washed it, hung it to dry in her room, out of the dusty wind, and then pressed it meticulously with a flatiron. By the middle of September, Judd and Billy were fastening new pegs along the upstairs wall so she could hang all her dresses to keep them fresh.

"Wouldja look at these colors!" Billy said when his sister hung the final gown in her room. Then he approached a dress of sage-green silk with flounces of a coordinating paisley print, fingering it reverently. "Mama wore this at her birthday party, right before Daddy got shot. You're gonna look just like her when you put it on, Sis."

Christine blinked at his revelation, while Judd studied a magenta dress with ribbons of deep rose satin sewn into a flower pattern on one shoulder.

"And Mercy wore this one to a nephew's christening, right before we got married. You did a fine job of covering that spot where the baby's breakfast landed on her."

The girl flushed with pleasure. Despite the stern way he'd lectured about her misdeeds, Christine purred like a cat at his compliments.

"I know! I know! We need to see her wearin' these dresses—like one of them fancy parades of ladies comin' to church on Easter Sunday!" Billy exclaimed. He whirled around to face her, his face lit with the joy of his suggestion.

"Oh, I don't think—"

"But it's the only way we'll get to see 'em! *Please*, Christine?"

Then he got quiet, following the display of gowns from one wall over to the next. "That way I can think about how you'll look goin' to all them parties and dances and such. And maybe I won't miss you and Mama quite so much."

"I think that's a wonderful idea," Mercy agreed. "These gowns were made to be seen in, and you're just the girl to show them off. I hope you're proud of what you've accomplished, dear."

Christine stood looking at all of them, pleased with their compliments. Yet she'd soon be leaving Billy behind, for months at a time.

"All right," she murmured. "After supper. And if you see loose threads, or hems not hanging straight—anything that needs fixing—I can take care of it tomorrow. Do—do you think we'll be hearing from Miss Vanderbilt soon?"

"I'm sure her response to my note is in the mail by

now," Mercy said. "You'll have plenty of places to wear these pretty gowns, Christine. And she'll be pleased to have you at the academy."

During their evening meal of corn cakes with creamed prairie chicken, Christine hardly tasted a bite. She'd tried the dresses on, of course. But with only the clouded mirror on Mercy's vanity to go by, she had no idea if the gowns truly became her, or if she looked like an abandoned girl making do with her mother's hand-me-downs. If the other students wore newer, prettier gowns and recognized hers as makeovers, she'd be doomed—like a little kid who could only press her nose against the candy-store window.

How she hated these days of making over and making do! They had to end soon or she'd go insane for wanting something fresh—something that wasn't years behind the trends now that the war was over. And if Miss Vanderbilt made one condescending remark about her wardrobe, well—she'd just board the next train!

These thoughts whirled in her mind as she carefully dropped the skirt of the first gown over her head. She'd remade Mercy's lavender dress in two pieces to preserve the lines of lace trim at its hem when she shortened it—and so she could dress without assistance. The top half was now a fitted jacket, boasting rows of repositioned lace that pointed just below her slender waist, like ivory arrows from each shoulder.

She adjusted the crinoline so it felt evenly balanced, smoothed her hair into a simple chignon, and took a deep breath. If she could negotiate these narrow, dim stairs in this belled skirt, she could handle anything in the palatial home of her future headmistress.

When she stepped through the kitchen, she saw that

Judd had moved the long table along the side wall of the front room. There they all sat on the benches—even Asa and Nathaniel—looking toward her with anticipation shining in their eyes.

"Now, *there's* a picture!" the wiry little colored man sang out. Lo and behold, he began to clap. And the others applauded, as well.

"Oh, Christine, let me see what you've done!"

Mercy hopped up from her seat, and her expression made Christine's pulse race with exhilaration.

"Why, you've shortened the gown at the waist, rather than . . . and made a separate jacket that buttons in the front. It's perfect for you!"

The woman deftly smoothed the fine satin at Christine's shoulders, and then she came around to face her. The awed light in those brown eyes was priceless. "I wouldn't ordinarily admit it, for this lavender gown was one of my favorites, but I believe you look even lovelier in it than I did."

Christine sucked in her breath, holding Mercy's gaze for several seconds. She'd been sewing for years, helping Beulah Mae with most of the family's clothes. But never had she received a compliment that made her float a foot from the floor.

"Thank you," she whispered. "It was wonderful to work with such fine fabric again—like all your gowns were made from. I'd better try on the next one or we'll be here all night!"

The smiles that followed her from the room felt warm and encouraging. Her feet barely touched the stairs, and as she carefully rehung the gown, she considered her next choice. Something of Mama's, to see how Billy would react.

As she entered the front room again, the taffeta of

the sage-green gown rustled provocatively when she walked. Her little brother's mouth dropped open. His eyes widened until she thought he might cry.

"Lord a-mercy, if you was wearin' that little hat with the peacock feather, I'd swear you was Mama," he gasped.

It hurt to smile, but she managed. A proper young lady rose above her difficult emotions when more than family were gathered around. She'd needed practice at that lately.

"Your mama's eyes were green, too, weren't they?" Judd murmured. "It suits you, honey. Makes you look all grown up."

Christine's heart pounded. Could he see the gown's delicate bodice fluttering from the force of it?

When he wasn't putting her in her place, Judd Monroe was a man whose approval she yearned for; a man whose open affection for his wife made her want the same thing when she grew up. Recalling the way he'd kissed Mercy at the Frontier Store made her cheeks tingle. And having Mercy circling her again, admiring her handiwork, was a sign she'd earned high marks on this dress, as well.

"I don't know that I've ever seen such a pretty print in a lace trim," Mercy mused, fingering the layers of paisley silk. "The gold and sage certainly complement your complexion, dear. When Miss Vanderbilt takes you on outings to meet influential people around town, you should wear this gown."

"I wanna see that purty turquoise one," Billy piped up. "The one Mercy said belonged to a princess."

Christine rolled her eyes. "It's a princess gown because that's what Mr. Worth, the designer, called it," she corrected. "And because that was one of my fa-

132

vorite ones to work with, I—I hope you won't mind that I took a few more liberties with it."

Mercy's smile flickered with interest, and she sat back down on the bench to await the showing.

Christine bustled up the stairs, unfastening green button loops as she went. She could tell *no* one that when she'd spied the dark aqua gown, her thoughts had gone immediately to Tucker Trudeau—imagining how he would gaze at the silk, which made her skin glow with its richness. The unusual color would set her apart from a roomful of young ladies by calling attention to her auburn hair. Never mind that it also reminded her of his unusual, sparkling eyes!

And when she slipped it on, she felt privileged—no, she felt *beautiful*, in ways she'd never known before. She'd spent untold hours folding and hand-sewing the row of aqua roses along the line of Chantilly lace from one of Mama's chemises—lace that made the daring dip of her new neckline a bit more modest. If Judd or Mercy said anything about the gown being too revealing—

Well, what could they say? She'd sewn it to suit herself, and no one else could wear it now!

Christine patted her hair into place again. She descended the stairs slowly—to let them anticipate her entry, and so she wouldn't gasp unbecomingly when she reached the front room. How had Mama and Mercy endured such tight corsets anyway?

Their expressions made her pulse gallop. Mercy's hand went to her throat. Billy sucked air. Asa and Nathaniel stood up as though the Queen of England had entered the little log room.

Judd looked her up and down, a remark ready to spring from his lips. She hoped it was more praise

133

from the stalwart head of the Monroe family . . . so different from her own rather henpecked daddy.

"You're too young to be showing so much—"

"And aren't you the belle of the ball already?" Mercy exclaimed over her husband's criticism. She stood again, taking in the new seams at the waist and the lace-trimmed silk roses that camouflaged them. "My goodness, with your hair swept up in a—"

"Somebody comin'," Nathaniel grunted as he rose to peer out the front window. The slanting rays of the sunset made enough glare that he opened the door and stepped outside. "Looks like Mr. Mike. 'Cept he's on horseback."

The distant hoofbeats grew gradually louder, and moments later halted near the door. Judd, Billy, and Asa went outside, looking concerned as the horse whickered and snorted with its exertion.

Mercy remained beside Christine, smoothing the folds of silk that draped gracefully from the gown's fitted bodice.

"We'll let the men tend to their business," she said as their low voices drifted inside. "I can't tell you how proud I am, Christine. You've given these gowns a whole new life. Let's light the lamps, so we can see them better when everyone's here again."

Christine grinned. The glow of Mercy's match made the glass lamp globes shine the way *she* was doing. And when Mike Malloy stepped through the doorway, staring as though he were witnessing a miracle, she knew she was indeed a social success. Or at least looked the part.

"My goodness, Miss Bristol, you can't be the same ornery, pouting little spitfire I hauled back from Atchison," he said, rolling the brim of his hat in his hand.

"Yep, she is!" Billy spouted cheerfully. "Just changin' into a silk purse from a sow's ear, is all!"

Her tongue shot out at her brother before she thought about it, but she regained her ladylike composure when she saw the two envelopes in Mike's hand. "Thank you, Mr. Malloy. It's good to see you again. I hope that's not bad news you've brought us tonight."

His mustache lifted with his grin as he handed Mercy the smaller envelope. "Found this on the floor of the coach. Probably fell out of the mail bag a while back," he said. "When I saw it was from—"

"Aunt—Miss Vanderbilt's academy!" Mercy popped the wax seal quickly, as though her own future depended upon the letter's contents.

"And this one caught my eye when I was helping sort the week's letters today," he continued, handing the letter to Christine. "Thought it might be news about your mama, so I brought it right out."

"Thank you! Thank you so much!"

A little squeal almost escaped her. That was Tucker Trudeau's handwriting! He hadn't forgotten her! Her first inclination was to rush to her room to read his letter.

But Mercy's surprised "Oh, my!" kept her pinned in place.

"Listen to this!" she went on, smoothing the folds of a page displaying neat, regular script. "'It will be my pleasure to welcome Miss Bristol to the Academy. I have often thought of traveling west to see our country's newly expanded borders—and to visit your homestead, Mercedes—'" she read with a lilt in her voice, "'so I'll be taking the train and then the stagecoach to Abilene for a brief visit, before escorting Christine back to St. Louis for the fall term. If the itineraries are correct, I should arrive on or about September twenty-second.' "

The front room rang with an excited silence.

"Why, that's tomorrow!" Asa chirped.

"C'mon, Christine. What'd he say?"

She lay as still as death in her bed, pretending to be asleep. That letter from Tucker Trudeau was *hers*, and the words she'd lingered over three times before she snuffed her candle rolled through her mind with the lilt of his French accent. *Such a pleasure it was, to meet a young lady whose concern for her mother—*

"I know you're awake, dang it!" Billy's whisper sliced through the darkness again. "If he said somethin' about Mama, I've got a right to know!"

Squeezing her eyes tighter against his intrusion, Christine weighed her options. Maybe if she told him just that little tidbit, he'd leave her alone. If Miss Vanderbilt was to arrive on the stagecoach tomorrow, she didn't want dark circles under her eyes. Didn't want to be peevish from lack of sleep.

Still, she'd never gotten a letter from a man before. Was it so wrong to keep those sweet words all to herself?

"I ain't leavin' you alone 'til you answer me, Sis. I betcha that letter's stuffed under the mattress, right there where you're layin'—"

"All right, you little pest—yes!" she hissed. "He saw Mama when she came back to his shop to fetch that picture."

Her brother's gasp sounded so satisfying. But that wasn't enough, was it? Here he came, tiptoeing across her floor.

"If you step on the things I've laid out to pack, I

136

won't say one more word!" she warned in an ominous whisper. "Now stop right there! You'll step on my packets of pins and needles!"

He let out a mewling whimper.

She raised herself up in bed to peer at him in the dimness, chuckling at the way he stood with one foot on top of the other, as though her underthings were snakes that might slither up his leg.

"Was she all right?" he wheezed. "Was Mr. Wyndham with her?"

His worried voice tempered her irritation—but she refused to tell him any more than she had to. "Yes, they both looked fine, he said. And they seemed *quite* surprised that I had been there hunting for Mama," she added smugly. "He told them to come back the next day and he'd have another print of the picture ready for them. Now scoot! That's absolutely *all*, Billy!"

For a few moments more he stood like a stork, his earnest eyes focused on her in the darkness. Christine plopped down on the feather mattress and turned her back toward him. Only after he padded back across the hallway did she relax again, but sleep eluded her.

The lines of Tucker's handwriting kept running through her mind, and when she finally slipped into a fitful sleep, she was back in Atchison, strolling down Commercial Street by his side. . . .

Chapter Twelve

"Stagecoach a-comin'! Stagecoach a-comin'!" Asa sang out with his usual excitement.

Today the little man's voice had a more urgent ring to it as Christine scurried to the table with a steaming bowl of cabbage wedges cooked with sausages, and a pan of sweet-smelling baked beans. Billy followed close behind with a platter of sliced ham, and when Mercy set down biscuits, a little pitcher of sorghum, and then a large pan of apple-raisin crisp, their day's offering was complete.

The thunder of approaching hoofbeats made her smooth back her hair, wishing it weren't so wavy and unruly today; wishing she weren't so hot and sticky from working in the kitchen. Mercy brushed her apron with nervous excitement, and went to stand in the doorway. Then she turned around.

"If Miss Vanderbilt's on this stagecoach, just be yourself, Christine," she said with a kind smile. "She has a reputation as an exacting headmistress who demands the best from all her girls, but there's no finer woman on the face of this earth. I owe her a great deal for all she taught me."

Christine nodded, glancing anxiously toward the red Concord coach trimmed with gold as it pulled to a dramatic halt out front. This driver, Vance VanBuren, called out instructions to his passengers in a clipped, rather brusque voice that hinted at a hair-trigger temper. Billy ran out to help Nathaniel unhitch the snorting, wet team of Morgans while Judd directed the passengers toward the basins and privies, as he always did.

A large man with shocks of black hair that swayed like snakes waddled out first, followed by a young couple who gripped each other's hands, looking around the house and corrals with a delighted air of adventure. Three men in dusty suits clambered down from their perch on the coach's roof, joking about how the rough ride was keeping them awake enough to watch for Indians.

And then a lone woman paused at the stage door, sticking her head out so she could survey the yard and the plains beyond before looking toward the doorway. Her face creased with a grin, and she waived daintily before giving her hand to Vance.

Christine's heart sank. Miss Vanderbilt was older than Moses.

And as the spry little woman's dove-gray traveling suit and matching hat caught the hot wind, she even *looked* like Moses as he was portrayed in the tinted prints in Mama's Bible: stern, with a commanding presence, despite her slight stature and slender frame. Her hair was pulled back tight and matched the white, lace-trimmed collar encircling her neck. And as Mercy hurried toward her, she stood primly in place, making the younger woman close the distance between them.

Christine felt the sweat trickling down her back. This didn't look promising at all.

"Aunt Agatha! It's been too long—"

"Goodness, Mercedes, you're as brown as a bean! Where's your bonnet?"

Forcing a smile, Christine took money from the other passengers as they entered the front room. That high-pitched voice could grate on a person's nerves . . . and she was Mercy's *aunt*? Why did it suddenly feel as if the Monroes had set her up for a prison sentence under the guise of giving her an education?

Judd greeted the old lady with a quick hello, and then entered the house behind the bulky man with the swaying hair. He smiled at Christine, squeezing her shoulder. "Be ready for anything," he teased in a low voice. "You never know what'll come out of Agatha Vanderbilt's mouth."

His remark was intended to help her relax, but as Mercy steered the headmistress toward the door, toward the inevitable introduction, Christine stiffened. Her things were all laid out upstairs. Some of them could be easily crammed into her carpetbag for a quick getaway in the night—

"And this is Christine Bristol," Mercy's voice cut through her frantic thoughts. "She's a very talented seamstress, and I'll certainly miss her help with these dinners. Christine, may I present Miss Agatha Vanderbilt, your new teacher."

The woman's bright, beady eyes looked right through her, assessing and astute.

"Good afternoon, Miss Vanderbilt," Christine rasped.

"It—it's truly an onerous—I mean, truly an *honor* to meet you at last."

"Time will tell which one proves correct," the headmistress said with a wry smile. Then she stepped inside, to find the rest of the passengers glaring at her as Judd held them in abeyance to say grace.

With the elegance of a swan, Miss Vanderbilt took the last vacant place at the end of a bench, inclining her head toward the rest of them.

Like a queen bestowing her blessing upon peons, Christine thought. *And now she thinks I'm a tongue-tied fool.*

"Shall we return thanks?" Judd said from the end of the table. He bowed his head and began in a reverent, resonant voice. "Dear Lord, we thank You for this day and the opportunities it brings. We ask Your blessing upon all these folks as they travel to their destinations. We give our special thanks for the arrival of Miss Agatha—"

"For cryin' out loud, can we just *eat* already?!"

Everyone in the room drew a startled breath as the man with the crazed hair stabbed a slice of ham with his fork. Perhaps because he took up the space of two normal people, he felt he had the right—the might—to do as he pleased. Christine saw a frightening shine in his piggy eyes.

Like a lightning strike, Miss Vanderbilt rose to smack the back of his hand with her folded fan. "I've only had to tolerate your rudeness since I boarded in Topeka, Mr. Barco, but I've had quite enough of it!" she stated. "Your mother would be appalled! Our distance from civilization is no excuse for leaving it behind!"

The man's hair swayed with his agitation, and for a

moment Christine wondered if the two of them would come to blows as they faced each other across the table. Her money was on Miss Vanderbilt.

"She's right, you know," the young woman with the handsome husband chimed in. "You've done nothing but complain and make the rest of us miserable listening to it!"

"Yeah! Sit down so we can finish our prayer and eat!" one of the men who'd ridden on the roof insisted. "We'll have the driver set you out at the side of the road to wait for the next stage! You're a hazard to our sanity!"

By now Mr. Barco's hair looked like an angry nest of snakes coiling to strike, and his fleshy face had turned as red as a radish. It was this man's sanity that seemed in question, and as the seconds ticked by, they awaited his response.

Miss Vanderbilt hadn't backed down—not a lick. If anything, she was leaning farther over the table, her fan still on his hand. Christine could well imagine the evil eye she was focusing on her contrary opponent.

He sat down with a heavy wheeze, pursing his pudgy lips. Everyone exchanged relieved looks, and Miss Vanderbilt retracted her fan.

"Thank you, Mr. Barco," she said crisply. "And thank you to our host, Judd Monroe, for invoking the presence of the Lord at this table. Lord knows we need it."

Judd smiled at her, waited for everyone to get settled, and continued his prayer. "And for the food we are about to receive, God our Father, we give You thanks. Bless the hands that prepared it, and bless us all to the carrying out of Your will here on earth. Amen."

"Amen!" came the unanimous echo, followed by the rapid reaching for plates.

It still amazed Christine how quickly a morning's

work got gobbled up by people who had no time to linger over this meal. Even those dreadful wedges of cabbage disappeared like magic as the passengers bolted their food and gulped glasses of water as fast as she could refill them.

Vance VanBuren hunched over his plate like a buzzard, his shaggy hair brushing his shoulders as he forked down his food. "Thanks, Missus Monroe," he grunted as he rose to go outside. It was a reminder to his passengers not to dally; a chance to stretch his legs and check the fresh team Asa and Nathaniel had hitched to the stagecoach.

Within minutes, the others were expressing their appreciation, too, and as they boarded the coach, Miss Vanderbilt went to the door to watch them. With a dramatic "Hyahhh, there!" and a smart crack of his long whip above the Morgans' backs, Vance barreled away at full speed, leaving a thick cloud of dust in his wake.

The little woman let out a ladylike "Hmph!" and returned to the table. "Just like a man, to put on a show for the folks at home. Now that he's out of our vision, he's already slowed the team to a trot that barely stirs the breeze inside that coach."

"Saves the horses from wearing out too fast or hurting themselves," Mercy remarked. "Take your time eating, Aunt Agatha. We'll clear away these other plates and join you."

"It's downright sinful, the way those poor souls had to bolt this meal you prepared, Mercedes. I hope they pay you well for it?"

"Well enough. The money we receive for being way-station employees is insurance against a poor crop, and gets us through the winter with more supplies than we'd have otherwise."

She glanced at the older woman's plate, noting how she drizzled a thin stream of sorghum over her split biscuit. "Christine made the biscuits this morning. She's been a tremendous help since she's been here."

From the kitchen, where she'd taken an armload of greasy plates, Christine watched the headmistress cut a small bite with her fork and raise it to her lips with a gentility she hadn't seen since Mama's last garden party. She told herself she didn't *care* what that old lady thought of her cooking, yet she had to know . . . had to see exactly what she was getting into, before she spent several hours on the stage and train with this woman. Not to mention months at a time in a faraway city, where no one knew her family or would take her in if she ran away from the academy.

Miss Vanderbilt closed her eyes to savor the tiny bite. "Passable. Perhaps in the oven a minute too long."

Passable? Christine fumed. This from a rich old relic who no doubt had a chef to prepare her private meals. She should challenge the headmistress to make *better* biscuits with this cranky old cookstove that burned buffalo chips for fuel!

"And you say the girl and her brother were abandoned? What on earth possessed their parents to send them west into Indian territory alone?"

Mercy balanced one last bowl on her tray. "That's a question we've all speculated about, and perhaps Christine should be the one to answer it. Bring out our plates, dear," she said in a louder, more purposeful voice, "so you and Aunt Agatha can get better acquainted."

Christine closed her eyes against a prickly chill that ran up her backbone. Why did this little spinster in-

144

timidate her so? Why couldn't she save such a conversation for the long ride to St. Louis?

She was ready to excuse herself to the privy, when Billy burst through the back door to get a good look at their visitor. Christine shoved the stack of clean plates into his arms and steered him into the front room ahead of her.

"Miss Vanderbilt, I'd like to introduce my little brother, Billy," she said, smiling sweetly. "Billy, this is my new headmistress, Miss Agatha Vanderbilt."

The moment he opened his mouth, Christine regretted her decision to let him do the talking.

"It's right nice to meetcha!" he said. He set the stack of plates on the table to give her a courtly little bow—which looked utterly ridiculous, with his bare feet sticking out below his patched overalls and a rusty-red cowlick bobbing at his crown like a rooster's tail. "Me an' Sis had us a tutor back home in Missouri 'fore the war—"

"Did you, now?" the white-haired woman asked wryly.

"—but now that Daddy's dead, and my twin brother Wesley's been took by the Border Ruffians, and Mama's done run off with a fellow named Richard Wyndham," he continued, barely pausing for breath, "why, it's a blessin' like you wouldn't believe, livin' here with Judd and Miss Mercy. The Monroes are true saints, seein' that Christine gets the schoolin'—and enough starch in her drawers—to become an upstandin' pillar of society."

Billy, so help me, when I get ahold of you—

Miss Vanderbilt's brows had knit in concern at his account of their postwar tribulations; she'd nodded her accord when he called the Monroes saints. But the reference to starch in unmentionables made the head-mistress turn pink—and turn to Mercy as though some family secret had been revealed.

"Young man," she finally said—although she seemed to be shaking with suppressed laughter—"I'll consider it my highest mission—my gift to your war-torn family—to see that your sister receives the finest education my academy can provide."

As Judd and the hands came to the table, Christine shot poisoned-arrow looks at the brother who ran off at the mouth, yet managed to charm everyone he met. Who else could talk about underthings at the table, within arm's reach of the venerable Miss Vanderbilt, and not get whacked with her fan?

She found herself sitting so straight and stiff, she could hardly taste her food—except for that disgusting cabbage, which she only took to avoid getting quizzed. And of course, she'd be expected to clear the table without slopping anything out of the bowls. She might as well paste a smile on her face, because ladies were expected to perform household duties as though they were privileged to have a home.

It came as quite a surprise when Miss Vanderbilt thanked Mercy for the delightful meal and then removed her jacket and plumed hat. She rolled up the sleeves of her blindingly white blouse, and began washing the dishes with a vengeance that had Billy and Christine drying double-time to keep up with her, while Mercy put things away. When the kitchen was set to rights again, their guest—looking as dry and un-splattered as when she'd arrived—stepped out the back door to catch some air.

"The prairie just rolls on forever, doesn't it?" she

mused aloud. As she buttoned the cuffs of her blouse, she took in the corrals and the cornfields ready for harvest. "This is a vastly different life from what you're accustomed to, isn't it, Christine?"

"Yes, ma'am," she replied, wondering how the little biddy even knew she was standing behind her. "Back home we had hills and woods, and a row of sugar maples lining the driveway to the house."

"And a household staff?"

"Oh, yes! We had Beulah Mae to cook and clean for us, and Daddy kept hands to tend and train our stock, and we had a man for the lawn and gardens," she replied wistfully. "We bred and raised registered horses, you see. We'd still be there if it hadn't been for those blasted outlaws shooting everything up and killing Daddy."

"Maybe. And maybe not."

The headmistress stepped back into the shadow of the house, shading her face with her hand. "Even in places where battles weren't fought and homes weren't ransacked, there's no going back, Miss Bristol. We have to rebuild our country and rethink our priorities now. And I'm guessing the plains of Kansas aren't your choice for starting afresh."

Christine let out a little snort before she could catch herself. "I don't know how Mercy stands it," she replied in a more apologetic tone. "And she says she's from a privileged family in Philadelphia—"

"Where her parents' home covers half a city block, and her mother manages a staff of two maids, a cook, a butler, and a groundskeeper," the little woman affirmed. "But Mercedes wanted more than a life spent changing gowns several times a day to sip tea in drawing rooms while her friends twittered about the latest neighborhood scandal. And now that I'm here, I understand why."

Swallowing a retort, Christine waited for her new headmistress to continue. She could not imagine Miss Agatha Vanderbilt living in this log house! If the smell of the manure didn't offend her, the hot, dusty wind would send her running for cover to protect her precious complexion.

The woman turned to assess her, and Christine was amazed at how smooth and unfurrowed her face looked. Why, the headmistress glowed with the vigor of a woman half her age! She radiated an excitement Mama had never displayed—at least not until Richard Wyndham waltzed into her life.

"Most everything can be looked at like the proverbial glass that's either half full or half empty," Miss Vanderbilt remarked. "Homesteading on the prairie can represent either isolation and hardship, or freedom and opportunity that are unavailable to women back East.

"And while I understand your youthful view of their situation," she continued in that crisp chirp of a voice, "I can't tell you how *proud* I am that my niece married a working man like Judd Monroe. They grabbed this opportunity by the horns to make the most of all the Lord has provided them! It shows *backbone*, and a sense of purpose. That's what I try to instill in all my girls, and Mercedes exemplifies my highest ideals."

"Even though I could never set a formal table to suit her and I often got sent to my room for improper conversation at dinner," came a voice from behind them.

A hand rested on Christine's shoulder, and for once it didn't feel as if Mrs. Monroe was trying to keep her from running off.

"But thank you, Aunt Agatha. This isn't the life I was

born to, but I couldn't have survived out here without your encouragement—no, your *prodding*—to find my true purpose. I'm hoping Christine will find hers, too."

It was higher-minded talk than Christine was used to, yet as evening fell and they lit the lamps, she gleaned a lot from listening to the two women catch up on family from back East. Were Miss Vanderbilt's hands never still? As she conversed, her tatting shuttle flew between her fingers, and the ivory thread produced a delicate floral pattern of lace—and she wasn't even reading a pattern! Mercy sat at the table with a basket of colorful fabric scraps, tracing around a template.

"Those are the leftover pieces from Mama's dresses. And yours." Christine went over to observe, and sure enough, the rich silks and shiny satins were being cut to use every scrap to best advantage, probably for a quilt.

Billy came up beside her, running a fingertip along a piece of sage-green taffeta he recognized from happier days. "Sure ain't for my bed—"

"*Isn't*," his sister corrected.

"—'cause I'd get it dirty just lookin' at it. Don't reckon I've ever seen a quilt pieced from such fancy, purty fabric."

Mercy smiled as though she were keeping a secret. "Maybe it won't be for a bed. I haven't decided yet. With winter coming soon, I thought it'd be nice to work with these bright colors—to remind us of those beautiful gowns Christine will be wearing while she's away.

"You'll be impressed, Aunt Agatha," she remarked to the woman sharing her lamplight. "Christine has a true talent for redesigning clothes."

"I can't wait to see them in full daylight. But meanwhile . . ."

The snowy-haired woman clipped her thread and

pressed her lace flat to the tabletop, letting the heat from her hands smooth it into a symmetrical crescent arrangement of flowers and leaves. "Here's a pretty collar to pin on your calico dresses, Mercedes. A little touch of elegance goes a long way toward refining rough days and ways, don't you think?"

The look on Mercy's face stopped Christine's heart. Such a simple gift, yet it seemed as though Miss Vanderbilt had handed her niece the keys to the kingdom. In fact, the breathless way she said her thank-you—the intensity of her gratitude—touched Christine so deeply she had to back away from the table.

"I—I think I'll go on up to bed now," she said awkwardly. "Probably do some more packing. Good night, everyone."

Billy's scowl challenged her early retreat, but she kept walking toward the staircase. He was just a kid—a boy, as well—so he would never understand why the exchange between those two women had upset her so.

What she didn't need was another reminder that Mama would probably never embroider any more handkerchiefs or knit any more shawls for her. Just as *she* would never be able to say how much those mementos meant to her now. She'd stuffed most of them into the drawer with hair ornaments and stockings she seldom wore, thinking them silly—either not to her liking or not suiting her mood. They were still there, in that abandoned house in Missouri.

Another part of the life she'd left behind.

Christine sighed, realizing what a waste it was, to be going to the esteemed Academy for Young Ladies, when she already knew her life's purpose was to catch up to Mama and bring her back. So they could all go home.

And Miss Vanderbilt, the eternal optimist, would never convince her otherwise.

Chapter Thirteen

"No, Billy, I am *not* leaving Mama's diary here for you."

Christine tucked the little book, bound in cherry-red velvet, beneath those pretty remade dresses she'd folded into their mother's trunk.

"But surely I could have *somethin'* of Mama's." He sat cross-legged on the floor of her room, amongst the treasures she was taking away tomorrow. If only he could shrink down enough to hide in her luggage! "You know dang well she ain't comin' through here—"

"*Isn't* coming, Billy!" she snapped. "How many times do I have to—"

"—so why do you get to keep *all* her secrets?" he protested. "What else is there to know, 'cept that she met up with that Wyndham fella? Why can't you leave me that likeness of her? If that Tucker fella in Atchison is so sweet on you, why, he'd surely send you another print."

"*Sweet* on me?" She fixed her fists on her hips to

152

glare at him. "What would *you* know about such things, Billy? If you're going to be such a bother—"

"Maybe you'll miss your brother, there in a strange city surrounded by girls you don't know yet," a voice suggested from the doorway. "Maybe you'll wish—as we all do at some time—that you'd spared him a little memento of your mother. He might repay the favor someday."

Miss Vanderbilt's crow's-feet crinkled when she smiled, and her brown eyes sparkled a lot like Mercy's.

It took all of Christine's effort not to toss her head like a mare with a dead mouse in her grain. But danged if she didn't look around—just to sweeten up her new teacher, of course—and pluck something from a hat she hadn't packed yet.

"Here! Satisfied?"

Billy snatched it before she changed her mind. And when the light from the window caught its swirls of blue, purple, and green, he knew he'd find a special place for Mama's peacock feather. Recalling how grand she'd looked in that green hat made his toes wiggle.

"Thanks, Sis!" He hopped up to hug her, and then dashed to the door. "I'll put it where I'll see it every—"

Billy stopped short in the doorway to his room, where Miss Vanderbilt was staying. The white-haired woman smiled, waving him in. "Put it wherever you like, dear. It'll remind you to keep your sister—and your mother—in your prayers until you see them both again. Because I truly believe you will."

What made her so sure? Why couldn't he have this same faith in the mother who'd loved him—a woman Miss Vanderbilt had never even met?

Billy smiled at her; decided he had nothing to lose by believing what she said. He stuck the peacock feather in a crack near the window, where it would shimmer in the light like it had when Mama wore it to church.

Then he returned to his sister's door, chuckling at the sight of her backside pointed toward the ceiling. Once upon a time he'd have given her a shove and then closed the trunk on her.

Wesley still would. The thought came out of nowhere, along with the memory of his brother's ornery grin, and it saddened him.

"I'll miss ya, Sis," he murmured. "If I see Wesley, I'll say 'hey' for ya, if you'll do the same with Mama. Double-dog deal?"

The old phrase from their childhood made his sister turn to gaze at him sadly. "Double-dog deal, Billy."

The next day, Billy felt itchy, as if he'd picked blackberries without a shirt. He knew it was best for Christine to go away to school, but he dreaded being left behind. Again.

Never would he forget the sight of that surrey hurrying away from the station in Leavenworth, when Mama never once looked back. He'd survived those weeks his sister was off on her wild-goose chase all right, but he didn't like the idea of being the only Bristol on this homestead. Judd and Mercy couldn't possibly treat him any better, but he was only here because he wasn't brave enough—or brazen enough—to leave, the way Mama and his sister had.

The stagecoach rolled to a dusty, dramatic halt in the yard just before noon. When Vance VanBuren hollered for the passengers to eat and be quick about it, Billy focused on the bowl of golden corn on the cob he carried to the table, inhaling its sweet, buttery aroma. Christine looked fine indeed, in a traveling suit she'd made from one of Mercy's plainer gowns. It was the color of the dust they would wear all the way to the station in Topeka, with a watermark pattern that shimmered as she carried in the basket of biscuits she'd made that morning.

None of them had slept much, so the meal and the front room were ready early. Mercy carried a pitcher of lemonade in each hand, followed by her aunt, who bore a large platter of salt pork in red-eye gravy. How did that little woman work in the kitchen without splattering a drop on her crisp gray dress? Billy was already anticipating her next visit, because Mercy enjoyed her company so much.

"We'll see ya again at Christmastime, then?" he asked, wishing his voice didn't sound so high-pitched and childish when he was upset.

"I'm looking forward to it!" Miss Vanderbilt gave him a nod as crisp as her starched collar.

Her upswept hair was arranged in rows of tight white curls at her forehead; if she were fatter and wore a red hat, she'd look like Santa's wife! Billy grinned at the thought. It seemed reason enough to keep believing in Saint Nick, when everyone else was leaving him.

But then his sister pointed an ominous finger at him. "Whatever you're thinking about," she warned, "*don't*! There's no time to change my clothes before the—"

Mercy nudged her toward the door to take money, while he filled the passengers' water glasses. Moments later, they all bowed their heads and Judd's low voice filled the room.

"For all You've given us, dear Lord, make us ever mindful and truly thankful," he began. "We pray for Your hand to guide this coach safely to its destination, and ask Your special blessing on our Christine as she begins her studies at Miss Agatha's academy. May this food nourish our bodies as Your abiding love strengthens our hearts and souls. In Jesus' dear name we pray, amen."

"Amen," came the echo. From there, the meal proceeded at its usual harried pace.

Billy was fetching more water while his sister and Miss Vanderbilt ate, but all too soon VanBuren rose from the bench: it was time for them to leave. And danged if Christine didn't slip out ahead of the others while he was in the kitchen! And danged if he didn't get knocked aside by two big men hurrying to climb to the coach's roof.

His heartbeat sounded so loud it was as if those Morgans were already a galloping off. He suddenly needed just one more look at his sister—even if she made one of those girl faces that told him he was lower than dirt.

"Christine! Hey, don't fergit to write me when—"

"I'll see to it, Billy," Miss Vanderbilt assured him. And then she winked at him. "And we'll see you at Christmas."

Color rushed into his cheeks, and in his best attempt at courtliness, he handed the headmistress up into the crowded coach. He was straining for a glimpse of his sister when it occurred to him—

"Her trunks! We didn't get them two—"

"Mr. Judd and Nathaniel saw to it," Asa assured him. As the kindly hired man pulled him back from the coach door, Billy realized that Mercy and Judd had come out, as well.

How much had gotten by him in these past frantic

156

moments? His chest tightened with a familiar dread—that same awful ache that clenched every muscle of his body when he awoke in the night and realized, all over again, that his daddy, his twin, and his mama were gone.

Only Judd's large, warm hand on his shoulder kept him from springing up into the driver's seat beside Vance. Even that rough-cut fellow would understand why he had to go along—wouldn't he? Surely in a houseful of girls there was work for a willing boy—

"Giddap!" VanBuren hollered. And with a showy snap of his nine-foot whip above the horses' backs, the overland coach sped off in a cloud of dust.

Billy ducked from under Judd's hand and ran like his life depended on it.

"Christine!" he cried, his bare feet pounding the ground. "If you find out where Mama is, you tell me, and I'll chase her down for ya! Hear me? Ya hear me, Christine?"

He ran until his lungs caught fire, until he stumbled in the rutted road. But he was just a kid, and those powerful Morgans would carry out their driver's need for speed—until they were out of sight of the way station, anyway. Gasping for air, his eyes fixed on the swaying backside of the Concord coach, Billy watched until it was only a tiny speck on the horizon.

When he could see no more, do no more, think no more, he ambled back toward the house. The men had returned to their chores, which gave him a few minutes to compose himself. Maybe splash his face in the basin before he joined them.

But the lone figure in brown calico showed no inclination to go inside. The hot wind whipped the chestnut hair around her face, flattening her skirt against her legs.

Mercy saw two wet trails cutting the dust on Billy's cheeks, and her eyes, too, filled with tears.

"Why'd she do that?" Billy rasped. "I didn't get to say good-bye to—"

Mercy held him until those bony shoulders stopped shuddering, wondering why a boy so small had been called upon to bear such a burden.

"She didn't want you to see her cry, Billy. Christine's plucky, but she's not nearly as brave as you are."

Chapter Fourteen

When Billy saw Judd, Nathaniel, and Asa hauling the long wooden benches from the barn, his heart beat faster. "Time for another one of them Sunday socials?" he asked. He steadied the end of a bench, helping the wiry colored man settle it into the grooves that remained from previous meetings.

"Yessir, in a couple days Mr. Holladay's clerk'll come 'round, and then folks from along the stage route'll be here for some preachin', some catchin' up on chat, and some mighty fine eats," Asa replied happily. "Hardly seems possible it's almost October. Used to roll my eyes at Grandpappy when he said time flew by faster, the older he got. But by golly, he was right!"

"It's almost October?" Billy considered this, and got fluttery inside. "Then it's almost my birthday. Wesley and me'll be eleven, come the third. I keep believin' he's alive, 'cause when I think about him maybe bein' dead, it just don't set right."

"Not a bad way to look at it," Judd replied. His tanned face lit up with a smile that made Billy feel good from the inside out. "More times than not, our intuitions prove right—and faith in God's providence is never wasted, son. Just a couple more benches and we'll be ready to haul out the platform. You're mighty good help, you know that?"

"Thank you, sir. You're mighty good help to me, too."

He shaded his face from the sun, which shone at a more intense angle these days. "So what kind of pies you makin', Asa?"

The old cook's grin flashed white. "Depends on what we find for fillin's. We've used the last tin of Miss Mercy's cherries, but the supply wagon always has dried apples. Sometimes dried peaches and raisins. Or," he added with a tantalizing rise in his voice, "we've got some nice pumpkins in the garden. And there's always eggs and milk for custard. What's your favorite, Billy?"

Thinking back to the sweets Beulah Mae used to bake especially for Sundays, he let out a wistful sigh. "Been a long, long time since I tasted raisin pie. Or punkin, with lots of spice in it," he mused aloud. "Our cook back home made her punkin pie about three inches thick, and it set up so solid and sweet you could lift up a wedge and eat it without a fork. 'Course, we didn't let Mama catch us at it."

The memory made him grin. "Once, me and Wesley snatched a pie apiece and snuck 'em into our room the night before we's to have the preacher's family over to Sunday dinner. Bettin' each other we could eat a whole pie, you see."

Judd's eyes twinkled. "Who won?"

"Well, we both got sicker'n dogs. But Wes felt it comin' on, so he hightailed it out behind the barn,"

Billy recounted with a shake of his head. "He was always smarter'n me that way. Once I was done throwin' up, Daddy marched me outside to cut my own willow switch, and I had to clean up my mess."

"Your brother didn't get punished?"

"Oh, Beulah Mae was madder'n a wet cat about them pies bein' gone. Turned Wesley over her knee before he knew what hit 'im, and he didn't sit down all week!" The memory of his twin's red face—and matching backside—had him feeling better than he had since his sister left. "He had to explain to Reverend Searcy why there weren't no dessert, too."

"Ate humble pie for a while, did he?" Asa teased.

The male chuckles around Billy made him feel accepted . . . maybe even loved like a son the Monroes wished they had.

And Sunday, when the folks who'd passed him up in July began rolling in with their baskets of food, it was as though he'd always been here on the Monroe homestead.

"Why, Billy, I believe you've grown a foot taller!" Mrs. Clark crowed as she handed him her basket. "If you'd put that on the table for me, I'll see if Mercy needs any help."

"Yes, ma'am. Smells awful good."

"Take mine, too, Billy!" A stout, pleasant woman he recalled from last time—Nell Fergus, he thought—wedged a basket into the crook of his other arm. "Don't let those beans slosh out, now!"

He was easing these warm, weighty hampers onto the table when somebody swatted his right shoulder. He jerked his head that way, only to hear a familiar giggle from his left side. "Hey there, Billy Bristol! You gonna dance with me this afternoon?"

"Well, hey there, Emma! I—I dunno—"

"Well, you darn well better eat with me," she said, arching her brows, "or you won't hear my story about Injuns."

Fast as a field mouse, she scampered off. Billy watched her blond ringlets bounce down the back of her pink gingham dress, which made her look frillier than he recalled. He wasn't sure what that meant. But maybe her Injun story could save him from admitting he'd been the clumsiest boy in Mrs. Rayburn's dance classes back home.

He wasn't sure who that skinny kid in the spectacles was, either, but when Emma grabbed the boy's hand to show him around the yard and corrals, Billy frowned. Who did she think she was, taking the boy inside to meet Mercy? As though she had no intention of spending time with *him*—or letting him size up this other boy face-to-face!

But here came the Barstow family, with cotton-haired kids spilling out of the wagon in every direction. Then Reverend Larsen arrived in his threadbare frock coat, riding Moses and leading the Morgan he'd borrowed after Christine ran off. With so many wagons to be parked and horses to be corralled, Billy and Judd and the two hands had all they could do to keep up.

Enough chill nipped the air that shawls and autumn bonnets graced some of the ladies, while their men sported heavier shirts. As though on cue, when the last family had arrived and the circuit rider was stepping up to his platform, the sun broke through the puffy, pearl-gray clouds. The sunbeams glowed with God's own glory. When the breeze caught the cottonwoods along the creek, their leaves shimmered like gold coins.

Billy slipped onto the end of a bench beside Mercy, sighing with satisfaction. He couldn't see where Emma was sitting. And at this moment, happily anticipating the church service and a big dinner, he didn't rightly care if she was holding that other kid's hand or not.

"Friends, it's good to gather here once again," the preacher said in his Scandinavian cadence, "and it's kind of the Monroes to offer their hospitality. Before Judd begins with the Scripture reading, though, he has a very special announcement."

Billy smiled, for Judd Monroe was a man among men, broad and tall and strong—like the tinted picture of King David in Mama's Bible. Respected by every neighbor here. And when those deep blue eyes met his, Billy's heart skittered up into his throat.

"You might've heard that Christine Bristol is now attending a girls' academy in St. Louis," he began, his rich voice carrying above the crowd. "And while we ask your prayers for her success, we'd also like you to help us celebrate Billy's birthday! He'll be eleven tomorrow. And as you could see when you came in, he's a young man we'd hate to be without."

A movement caught Billy's eye, and here came Emma Clark and her friend, carrying a large, round pan between them. They walked carefully, so the big candle in the center wouldn't blow out . . . came right at him . . . although Emma was focused on the other boy as though they shared a secret. Maybe something Billy didn't want to know.

But he caught the aroma of cinnamon and spice, and saw glazed white letters that said HAPPY BIRTHDAY, BILLY. His jaw dropped, and he sprang from his seat.

"Why, that's the biggest dang . . . Asa, did you make

163

me this fine punkin pie?" he piped up. "If you're lookin' to outdo Beulah Mae, well, you done did it!"

Asa, who was standing over beside the corral, tipped his hat, and everyone began clapping.

"Make your wish, Billy," Mercy encouraged from beside him. "Make it a special one before you blow out that candle."

Possibilities raced through his mind, but most of them—about life returning to the way it used to be—weren't really possible. So he squeezed his eyes shut, letting images of Daddy, Mama, Wesley, and Christine linger for a moment . . .

And then it came to him: *I wanna be like Judd and Mercy—good enough to be their son now. Good enough to be family.*

When he leaned toward the candle, the new boy's lenses reflected the flame—and that flash took Billy back to when Wesley would blind him with Mama's little needlework magnifier. Wes pestered anybody he considered a runt, and more times than he cared to recall, Billy had been the object of his attentions.

He blinked; took in this kid's worn suspenders and baggy britches, and the way he chewed his lip as he waited for this birthday tribute to be over. That big pan of pie wobbled between the kid and Emma when he shifted his skinny legs, nervous-like. No doubt he'd been teased and called Four-Eyes on account of those specs. So as Billy aimed and blew, he tacked a new ending onto his wish: *I wanna be this kid's friend.*

"Don't guess I know ya," he said as the applause rose around them. "I'm Billy Bristol. Lost my home and a lot of my family after the war, but I like it here now. How 'bout you?"

Emma grinned over the pie at him. "This here's my

cousin Gabriel Getty from out in Colorado. He's come to live with us—but that's part of my Injun story, and we'd better go set down. Happy birthday, Billy!"

He barely heard a word of Judd's reading; caught only an occasional phrase of Gregor Larsen's sermon. As he sat close enough to Mercy to appreciate the warmth of her soul—and the way she blocked that breeze from the north—Billy felt strangely, wonderfully settled. But more than that, he felt he was about to walk down a whole new path.

Had it appeared as part of his wish? Or had it always been there, and he could see it now because he was turning eleven?

"Amen!" rose around him, and then everyone stood up. The men lingered to chat, but the women hurried toward the baskets they'd brought. While they clucked like hens who arranged their eggs to best advantage, Billy ambled through the crowd toward the Clark family.

Now that he was paying attention, Gabriel did resemble Emma's lanky mother, Rachel: same straight brown hair hanging limply over his ears, same gaunt, studious look about him—which those round, wire-rimmed spectacles seemed to magnify. There was something else about the boy, something Billy couldn't put his finger on. Until he got close enough to look Gabe Getty in the eye.

This kid, who seemed a little older and stood taller than he, wouldn't return his smile. Wouldn't even focus on him.

"Let's fix our plates 'fore everybody else gets all the good stuff! Then we gotta cut ourselves a huge slice of that pie," Emma declared. Her blue eyes sparkled as she grabbed her cousin's hand and then latched onto

Billy's, too. She was leading them toward the tables as though Gabe's behavior was perfectly normal.

"Yep. If I'd knowed it was your birthday, Billy, I'd've brung you a snake to tease your sister with," she went on brightly. "Now that it's colder, they're movin' slow enough I can catch 'em. But then, I guess Christine went off to school, huh?"

"St. Louis," Billy replied, pleased that he could say it in a stronger voice now, without the pang he usually got. "And I'm guessin' Mercy's Aunt Agatha'll put that girl through her paces, too. You got a sister, Gabe?"

He was just making conversation, but as soon as the words were out, he wanted to kick himself. The kid's agonized expression was Billy's punishment for his stupidity: If he *had* a sister, she'd be here, too, wouldn't she? "What I mean is—"

"That's part of the Injun story I gotta tell ya," Emma said, her expression none too cheerful. When she jerked her head toward the corrals, Billy followed her away from the folks filling their plates at the tables.

"Out in Colorado a few years back, there was a Sand Creek massacree, where a buncha Colonel Chivington's soldiers attacked a tribe of peaceable Injuns. So all the tribes banded together, and they've been fightin' back ever since," Emma related in a low voice. She was still holding Gabriel's hand, trying to get this part of the story over with.

"Mama's brother and his family ran a little tradin' post, with supplies for trappers and gold miners and such," she continued. "Them Southern Cheyenne're still peeved about the massacree, and the way whites is settlin' their land and killin' off their buffalo. So they attacked the store and the cabin, ridin' around on their horses shootin' fiery arrows. Gabriel here was the only one they didn't find. The soldier who brung him to us thinks he seen 'em kill his ma and pa and three little sisters, but we can't be sure."

Emma's voice had fallen to a sympathetic whisper, and her eyes glistened like wet blue plates. "They found him huddlin' in the root cellar behind a bin of turnips. He's only eight, Billy. Ain't said a word since it all happened. Ain't that just the sorriest thing you ever heard?"

Billy looked up at Gabriel again—and then looked away so the poor kid wouldn't think he was staring. Stories about Indians had always intrigued him, and small groups of them passed this place now and again—squaws walking with papooses on their backs, following men on painted ponies. He'd never known a victim of an Indian attack, but he sure knew how it felt to be victimized. He'd watched men on horseback destroy his home and family, too.

Clapping Gabriel gently on the back, and noting how bony he felt, Billy smiled. "You and me got a lot in common, ya know it?" he offered awkwardly. What should he say to a boy who looked too lost in his fears to answer?

"One of these days I'll tell ya 'bout how Border Ruffians done the same nasty stuff to my family. But right now, you got some catchin' up to do at the table, Gabe." Billy started toward the food again, glad the silent boy went wherever Emma led him. "And since it's my birthday, I'm thinkin' we should start with dessert! Ain't nobody brought anything half as good as Asa's punkin' pie, so I'm gonna cut you a big piece, all right?"

Was that a flicker of a grin? Or had the poor kid's specs slipped down his nose?

Suddenly feeling very fortunate, Billy led the way to that wheel-sized concoction of pumpkin and sugar and eggs. HAPPY BIRTHDAY, BILLY, it said in Mercy's pretty script—and he realized that she and Asa must have stayed up half the night baking it so it'd be a surprise.

The knife left a well-defined groove in the pie, just the way he knew it would. Without regard for the niceties of size or shape, he carved out three blocks that accounted for nearly half the pie.

"Here ya go," he said, lifting up the first chunk with a pie server. He sighed with sheer joy: it was a full three inches deep, with a sweet, spicy-smelling middle that stood proud and firm when he offered it to his new friend.

"See there? We don't even need no plates!" he crowed as Gabriel took it between his hands. "Now, that's *pie!*"

Chapter Fifteen

Dear Billy,

Be glad you're not a student at Miss Vanderbilt's Academy for Young Ladies, because that white-haired battle-ax who took such a shine to YOU can't find enough ways to torture ME! To earn part of my tuition, I'm sewing school uniforms, and they're so ugly I refuse to wear them in public: plain brown jumpers with butternut blouses. First thing I did when I arrived was suggest a new color and design, and all the girls agreed with me!

Miss Vanderbilt, as you can imagine, is reluctant to change her school's sacred tradition. She says a uniform keeps everyone equal. Well, why would I settle for being equal, when Mama raised me to reign from several rungs above my peers?

But yes, it's better than living in that dim, dis-

gusting log house out in the middle of nowhere. At least we have running water and a real furnace.

I'm making friends, and tomorrow we'll be attending a charity event, la-dee-dah: if you call serving up soup at the Friends of the Homeless Mission an event. No, I'll not be splattering any of Mama's pretty made-over gowns there.

I've heard no more about Mama from Tucker Trudeau. This puzzles me, as I've sent him a note with my new school address. If Mike Malloy brings any mail for me to the Monroes' house, you keep it safe for me! Mercy appears to be a very dedicated woman, but I believe she sent me to her maiden aunt's academy as much for spite as for my education.

BUT DON'T BREATHE A WORD OF THIS, UNDERSTAND ME?

I'll see you at Christmas. Try to behave.
Your dear sister,
Christine

Billy read the small, flowery script again, and again, and then he chuckled out loud. "Don't sound like Christine and your Aunt Agatha's gettin' along too good," he remarked. "But then, that's Sis for ya."

Mercy looked up from the quilt she was piecing from those pretty party-gown scraps, her face aglow in the lamplight.

"I didn't send her to the academy to become good friends with the headmistress, now did I?" she asked mischievously. "Does she sound all right, otherwise? Her letter to me didn't say a lot—and I certainly recall being required to write home on Sunday afternoons while I was a student there!"

He smiled, folding the pretty sheet of parchment into his pocket. No sense in hurting Mercy's feelings. "Yes, ma'am, she sounds just fine. Curious as to why she ain't heard any more from that Tucker fella, though."

Her eyes narrowed as she considered this. "She thinks I'm hiding his letters, doesn't she?"

Billy's jaw dropped. He'd never mentioned his sister's suspicions, yet Mercy knew enough about Christine to guess at them.

"Do *you* think I'm keeping back her mail—or yours, Billy?"

"No, ma'am! You wouldn't never do that," he protested. "You understand how much she wants to hear something—any little thing—about Mama."

Mercy nodded and focused on her quilting again. "Your sister has to learn about trust again. Not an easy lesson, considering how your mother has behaved—and how Christine has compromised our trust in *her.* None of us can make her believe or do anything, Billy."

Didn't he know that! He also knew how his sister made herself out to be suffering so, when—especially compared to Gabriel Getty—Christine didn't know how lucky she was. Billy had thought about that sad, silent boy a lot since the party, and though he missed his sister something fierce, her letter reminded him that some things about her would never change.

She would always be Mama's daughter. And even as he yearned for the sound of his mother's voice again, and the way she smiled when he'd done something well, Billy knew that his time here with the Monroes was remolding his expectations.

It felt good to be a giver now, as well as a receiver.

* * *

171

Hard work and a satisfying sameness turned the days into weeks when autumn came to the Kansas prairie. There were horses to tend and stalls to shovel, butter to churn and eggs to fetch, covered wagons headed west and people to feed each time a stagecoach passed through. Billy spent every possible moment observing how Judd and Nathaniel trained the Morgans that made this way station such an important stop along the Smoky Hill trail.

He collected dried buffalo and cow chips for the stove, aware that winter winds would soon whistle through the cracks in the log walls. Mercy kept newspapers stacked in a corner, and one day they soaked them in water to form a pulpy wallpaper coating on the inside of the house. Not pretty, but practical.

With Asa's help, they gathered the pumpkins and squash, dug the potatoes and turnips and carrots, and then stored them in the root cellar beneath Judd and Mercy's bedroom. A large rag rug covered the trapdoor in the floor, and when Billy clambered down the rope ladder into the earthen cave, he wondered what it would be like to hide from Indians down here for days at a time, like Gabe had done. Would he get so scared he couldn't talk?

Onions hung in bunches along the walls, along with pungent bundles of drying peppermint and medicinal herbs. Their vegetables filled several bins, and a shelf held glass jars of green beans, corn, and jellies Mercy had preserved over the summer. Store-bought tins of peaches and tomatoes sat on the floor, too. A barrel of salt pork filled one corner.

"Never had this much stuff in our cellar back home," Billy remarked as he emptied potatoes into their bin.

"You were closer to town," Mercy reminded him. "And you weren't feeding coachloads of people each week. We'll need to make another trip to the Frontier Store soon, for staples to see us through the winter. Christmas will be here before we know it!"

Along with Christine, the sparkle in her eyes implied.

Billy perked up at the prospect of presents, and a decorated tree, and the aromas of his favorite holiday foods—and yes, he longed to see his sister again. Yet he suspected the Queen Bee's homecoming would be more jarring than joyous: Christine was accustomed to fine gifts that the Monroes couldn't afford.

The quilt Mercy worked on late into the evenings excited his eyes with its bright, shining colors. And knowing whom those clothes had belonged to was a real comfort to him.

But his sister would see it as a collection of scraps and rags that were good for nothing else. To Christine, it was just another example of how Mercy made things over, and made do with what she had—no matter how much love and artistry held her quilt together.

As Christmas got closer, Billy hoped this good woman wouldn't regret the efforts she and Judd had made on his sister's behalf. But he suspected that even Miss Vanderbilt's best lessons wouldn't teach Christine to appreciate the gifts the Monroes gave from their hearts.

"Stagecoach a-comin'! Stagecoach a-comin'!"

Billy set baskets of corn fritters on the table and then dashed outside without a coat. Even though she only had to ride the last eighty miles on that rough, rocking stagecoach—because the train took folks clear to Topeka now—Christine would be peevish after her long trip. Her letters were proof she'd been sharpening that catty tongue, with the help of her snooty new friends.

But dang it, he hadn't seen her since September! Surely she'd missed him a *little*.

As the red Concord coach approached in the swirling snow, he waved high and wide at Mike. The driver had six sets of reins woven between his fingers, so he could only jerk his head in response. Billy yearned to take those reins himself someday, to sit there as unruffled as Mr. Malloy did while controlling six magnificent Morgans. He made it look effortless, but the man's skill and precision came from years of experience—and the respect he had for his horses and passengers.

Once he could read the WELLS FARGO lettering on the side—for Ben Holladay had sold out last month—Billy trotted alongside the rolling vehicle to escort it into the yard, his excitement running high.

"Afternoon, Mr. Bristol!" Mike called out as he set the brake.

"Afternoon to you, Mr. Malloy! You bring my sister this time? And Miss Vanderbilt?"

"Sure did, son! And more trunks for those two gals than for all the other passengers combined." As he hopped down on muscular legs, with his buckskin duster blowing in the wind, Malloy cut an impressive figure. "Why do you suppose that is, Billy?"

" 'Cause they're girls?" he guessed.

"Give that man a cigar! If you'll help the folks get out, I'll fetch the ladies' luggage from the boot."

Billy reached toward the coach door, but it swung open so hard it banged against the vehicle's side. A

174

matronly woman in a maroon cape grabbed his hand to step down. Her distressed expression needed no words to identify the problem.

"Privies are right over there, ma'am," Billy said, pointing the way. "Glad you could make it. Merry Christmas to you."

Though he knew that nine passengers could ride inside, Billy swore he handed down half the population of Abilene before there was a break in the parade.

And then, there stood Christine.

Or was it Mama? Bundled in a heavy woolen coat, with a hat lined in rabbit pelt like the muff she carried, this princess looked like *somebody!*

"I can step down myself, Billy. You're too little to—"

He grabbed her at the waist, whirling her around in his glee while her single long ringlet flew out behind her. Christine's whoops joined his in childlike delight for a moment, but then she remembered where she was. Who she was.

"Put me down, Billy! *Please* put me down!" she amended as Miss Vanderbilt appeared at the doorway. "Who do you think you are, to—"

"I'm that little brother you left in your dust without so much as a fare-thee-well!" he replied. "But I'm not so little anymore, am I? Not the runt you and Wesley could pick on any old time you pleased!"

Where had that come from? Billy set her down, as surprised at his outburst as his sister was.

But it was true, wasn't it? He *had* picked her up without even thinking about it. And danged if he hadn't *shut* her up for a minute, too!

"You've obviously been hard at work with the horses and the harvest, young man," Miss Vanderbilt remarked crisply. She put her dainty gloved hand in his, grinning as she stepped to the ground. "This homesteading life agrees with you, Billy Bristol. And there's nothing wrong with that! Now let's help Mercy get this meal on so these other travelers can be on their way."

Like a little cyclone she approached, all bluster and business beneath her stylish red cloak and plumed hat. Mercy rushed out to hug her, realizing just how much she missed her family in Philadelphia; pleased that this Christmas, Aunt Agatha and Billy's sister would be with them. As the other passengers quickly hung their wraps on pegs and seated themselves, Aunt Agatha assessed the steaming bowls of food.

"How do you do it, Mercedes?" she said with a proud chuckle. "You, who could barely boil water when you were Christine's age! Why, that platter of beef and braised vegetables rivals anything I've seen in a St. Louis restaurant."

"Thank you, Aunt Agatha," Mercy replied. "Actually, Judd and Billy put most of this meal on the table."

Her aunt's eyebrows rose as she filled water glasses for the others. "You're not telling me Billy cooked—"

"No, but he dug the potatoes and carrots," Mercy replied, smiling as her husband and his red-haired shadow stomped the snow from their boots. "And Judd shot and butchered the buffalo."

Had she really left Aunt Agatha speechless? Christine's reaction was easier to read: she'd started to sit down, too hungry to wait for the others, but then stood by the sideboard instead.

Buffalo? she mouthed at her brother.

Billy grinned. "I field dressed it myself, mostly. And I'm learnin' how to butcher, too."

"And shall we give thanks for these gifts?" Judd spoke above the passengers' chatter. When Mike Malloy stepped in and shut the door against the snow, Judd began. "Most blessed Lord who provides all we have, and all we need, we thank You now for the bounty on this table. May it nourish these, Your people, and remind us of the many gifts You give us each day. Make us especially mindful this season of Your precious and perfect Son, the greatest gift of all. Amen."

"Amen!" came the echo, and hands shot out to pass the platters.

When the meat came around to Mike, he was chuckling. "Awfully nice of you folks to leave me so much of this buffalo roast," he said, heaping his plate. "You might think such a wild, ugly beast is not to your liking, but Mercy cooks it real slow—"

"All night," she chimed in, "with buttermilk, onions, and sliced apples, to take out the gamey taste."

"—and as you can see, it falls apart when I put my fork to it." He took a large mouthful, closing his eyes ecstatically as he chewed. "Judd Monroe, if you ever tire of this woman's ways in the kitchen, I'll be taking her off your hands, sir."

"Don't count on it," came the good-natured reply.

With the next passing of the platter, the last slice of buffalo disappeared. Potatoes got slathered with butter, corn fritters held gems of jelly on their way to open mouths, and as ginger snaps and cut-out sugar cookies got dunked in cups of hot coffee, the room filled with satisfied sighs.

"Well, folks, looks like more snow ahead, so we'd better get rolling." Mike Malloy slipped into his duster, warming them all with his grin. "Merry Christmas to you Monroes. And to you two Bristols—and to you, too, Miss Vanderbilt. Have a wonderful holiday together."

As he rounded up his passengers like a shepherd herding a flock, Mercy again felt grateful for this young man's friendship. While some drivers gossiped of dirty dealing and dubious financial management on Ben Holladay's part, Mike Malloy took up the reins for Wells Fargo with the same integrity and levelheadedness he'd displayed under the stage line's former owner. His Christmas wishes lingered as the seven of them ate, and Mercy hoped this was an omen about how the entire visit would go.

Christine seemed reserved, however. Or was she just tired from the trip? Perhaps better behaved, after the months of Miss Vanderbilt's guidance?

Indeed, Aunt Agatha was recounting the girl's advances in language and domestic skills, and complimenting the way she helped other girls remake their mothers' gowns.

"She wants to create a new uniform for the school!" the headmistress raved. "And with the big-city garment factories producing so much ready-to-wear clothing now, Christine could design herself quite a nice career."

The young lady in question smiled politely at this, but seconds later she was rolling her eyes at Billy.

Billy covered his snicker by eating a ginger snap before the headmistress could catch on to their exchange.

"Thank you for taking such an interest in our girl," Judd remarked. "Sounds like she's figuring herself out now. Finding more possibilities than we can offer out here on the plains."

He, too, gave Christine an encouraging smile, but her response was less than enthusiastic.

Mercy chalked this up to the fact that young girls didn't know how to receive compliments graciously, and to Miss Bristol's sullen nature in general.

But Mercy couldn't allow that to dampen her Christmas spirit; she had family gathered around her! The gifts she'd made needed a tree, even if it was just a chubby little cedar seedling from the riverbank. They could string popcorn, and unpack the ornaments she'd brought from back East, and display the crèche that had belonged to Judd's grandmother.

Her buoyant mood sank soon after Christine went upstairs to change, however. The men had gone outside to do stable chores, and Mercy was stacking the dirty dishes, when Aunt Agatha returned to the kitchen with a small bundle of envelopes tied with string.

"I'm assuming you don't know about this," she began in a low voice, "but Christine has apparently been encouraging a man's attentions. Someone from Atchison named—"

Tucker Trudeau, Mercy filled in with a silent sigh.

"—who is helping her locate her mother. Since she has no way of knowing anyone from there, I have to think she read a newspaper advertisement during her trip west. You know how rosy those hucksters make everything sound, from land acquisition schemes to mail-order brides."

The woman's expression sharpened, yet she was sincerely worried. "My immediate concern was that he was swindling money from her, by acting far too interested in her personally to be . . . *proper* for a man of his age."

Mercy's heart sank as her well-meaning aunt pressed the bundle into her hands. There were probably half a

179

dozen envelopes. Only one had been opened. Apparently, Miss Vanderbilt had taken it upon herself to withhold most of the letters from Christine.

"I . . . thank you for telling me, Aunt Agatha, but—"

"It's my duty to keep my students on the straight and narrow," she replied in her shrill headmistress voice, "because most are so far from home, and the reputation of my school depends upon it. I sensed from the start that Miss Bristol would try our patience at every turn, Mercedes. You've taken on quite a responsibility for these abandoned children, and I want to help."

Chapter Sixteen

What could she say to this? Mercy slipped the letters into her apron pocket and picked up a towel. Her aunt, with crisp white sleeves rolled above her elbows, was attacking the dirty dishes with the zeal of a preacher who'd baptized a dozen new converts. Although she understood the headmistress's desire to remove such temptations from the fanciful Christine—to nip Mr. Trudeau's attentions in the bud—this turn of events caught her smack in the middle.

If she showed Christine those letters, the girl would assume *she* had opened that first one. The moody Miss Bristol would despise her *and* the headmistress, which might lead to her running away from school or finding herself constantly on Aunt Agatha's bad side.

Letting Christine have the letters would also undermine Miss Vanderbilt's authority and best intentions. Mercy hated to do that, since her aunt had graciously agreed to reduce the tuition, and had taken Christine on a moment's notice.

But what if Tucker Trudeau had news of Virgilia Bristol? Didn't Christine and Billy have a right to know if their mother had come to her senses? Or if she and that Wyndham character had settled in Atchison?

Mercy didn't want to prevent the reuniting of this war-torn family—nor did she wish to alienate Christine by withholding news from a man who'd captured her fancy. In writing to her, Tucker may just be helping a pretty young girl who'd won his sympathies, rather than pursuing any romantic angles. By Mercy's estimation, he must be at least ten years older than Christine. Probably had a sweetheart or two the starry-eyed girl didn't know about.

"So you're really going to let Christine create a new academy uniform?" she asked. But this was only small talk. Mercy didn't wish to appear critical of her aunt's actions, and she didn't know how to respond to them yet.

As they unwrapped the precious pieces of the Nativity set that evening, Mercy prayed for guidance. She let Billy position the open stable on the sideboard in the front room, a sturdy piece Judd had carved to look humbly rustic. Out of crinkled tissue paper came the porcelain figures of Joseph and Mary, and the manger where the Christ child would lie.

"In our family, we wait for Christmas morning to place the baby in the manger," she explained as she lovingly laid that little figure in the top drawer. "But for now, the ox and the donkey and sheep will look on."

Judd was thumbing through the Bible, locating the familiar passage from Luke they always shared when the crèche came out. He raised the wick on the lamp and smiled at Christine. "We'd be honored if you'd read our Scripture for this evening, honey. It'll be good to hear your voice again."

The toss of her head sent that single ringlet flying. "Billy really needs the practice at reading aloud, don't you think?" she replied tartly.

Judd looked ready to challenge the girl's sass, but Billy took the book from his hands, rather than let the fine mood be shattered by a confrontation. He scanned the fine print until he found the place.

"The Gospel of Luke, chapter two," he began in a solemn little voice. "'And it came to pass in those days, that there went out a decree from Caesar Augustus that all the world should be taxed. And . . . Joseph also went up from the city of Galilea . . .'"

The quiet pride on Judd's face stirred Mercy. She sat absolutely still, letting Billy's raspy, sometimes halting rendition touch her as the familiar story unfolded once again. The lamp brought out highlights in his hair that would *almost* pass for a halo, and she smiled at this notion.

"'. . . And lo, the angel of the Lord came upon them, and the glory of the Lord shone round about them, and they were sore afraid. . . .'"

Mercy certainly understood that part, for as she glanced at Christine, those letters seemed to smolder in her pocket. The girl felt lonely for her mother, upset because Billy was the only kin she had left to celebrate Christmas with. Mercy vividly recalled her first holiday in this log house, away from those she loved, and her heart went out to these children. If she were to give the letters to Christine later, would they mend the hole in her heart?

" '. . . And suddenly there was with the angel a multitude of the heavenly host' "—Billy's voice rose with excitement—" 'praising God and saying, Glory to God in the highest, and on earth peace, and goodwill toward men. . . .' "

Peace and goodwill. Hallmarks of this holy season; a reminder to all of them what their calling should be. But how could she bring this about? Aunt Agatha sat silently, mouthing the verses along with Billy, satisfied that she'd done the right thing by keeping those letters from Christine. The last thing Mercy wanted was to defy this woman's wisdom, and yet . . .

" '. . . But Mary kept all these things, and pondered them in her heart.' " Billy looked at them with a beatific smile only a freckle-faced boy could muster.

Judd stood up and hugged him. "That was a fine job, son. You read in a way that renewed us all, and shed new light on a favorite old story."

Mary had the right idea, Mercy realized as they all said their good nights a little later. Until the right time and the right words came to her, she would keep Christine's letters and her thoughts to herself. A matter like this required some pondering, so the still, small voice of God could tell her when His purpose would best be accomplished.

She hoped it would happen during this Christmas visit.

As Billy held the lopsided cedar tree steady inside a bucket, Judd dropped in the last of the small rocks that would hold it upright. He poured in some water, and then they stood back to admire their work.

"It's not much, compared to the grand fir trees we decorated in Philadelphia," Mercy remarked wistfully, "but it'll give this room some Christmas spirit—and give us a place to put presents."

A fire crackled in the fireplace, popcorn lifted the lid of the long-handled skillet Aunt Agatha held, and they could see light, powdery snow through the window. Christmas Eve at last. Christine sat stringing the puffy popped kernels with cranberries they'd brought from St. Louis, while Mercy unpacked the corn-husk angels and crocheted snowflakes she'd made in years past, and the box of glass ornaments that had survived their trek west. Billy was sticking needle and thread through sugar cookies shaped like holly leaves, candles, and stars—although he was eating almost as many as he managed to hang on the tree.

Mercy knew the true reason for the season, yet she still got as giddy as a girl awaiting Santa when they placed their presents beneath the tree. Some were large and bulky, some were small and neat. Some had simple wrappings of fabric or flour sacking, while a few glistened with printed paper and pretty ribbons. And some were for her!

When she looked into Billy's eyes—for where else would the season's excitement be shining as brightly?—she saw a forlorn pain that tore at her heart. It was a rude reminder that for the Bristol children, the angels' proclamation of peace on earth and goodwill toward men rang false this year.

Mercy sat down on the floor beside the cross-legged little boy. "It's just not the same, is it? No matter how much you believe in the Bible stories you've read us these past evenings, they don't fill in the blanks where your parents and Wesley used to be," she sympathized. "Would a cup of chocolate help? Or singing some carols?"

Christine let out a mirthless chuckle. "You've obviously never heard Billy sing. He'd need more than that bucket the tree's in, to carry a tune."

"Would not, Miss Smarty Britches!" he shot back.

"Would, too, Mr. Patchy Pants!"

"Would—"

"It's time for Jesus to arrive," Judd's voice cut through their squabbling. He carefully removed the crinkled tissue paper that had preserved this little figurine for all the years and miles they'd had it.

Once the porcelain baby with the chipped toes and faded halo looked out at them from his manger of painted hay, the scene was complete—in that stable, and in the house itself. And with that completion came some semblance of peace in the front room, and goodwill between siblings. At least for the moment.

Then Billy leaned heavily against her. "Mercy, it just ain't right that there's presents under that tree for me, when I've got nothin' to give—"

"Oh, how can you say that?" Her heart thumped hard at the utter dejection in his voice. "You've read our Scripture these past few nights, and you've helped us in so many ways since you've been here."

"And you've certainly made *me* smile, young man," Aunt Agatha chimed in. "The best gifts don't come wrapped in—"

"I know all that, dang it!" Billy sprang up with the poignant grace of a boy who understood adult realities yet yearned for the sweet beliefs of his childhood. "But I've watched ever'body else stealin' away to finish the things they've been makin', smilin' 'cause they can't wait to see how the others'll like their presents. And I ain't done *none* of that!

"I'm sorry to be such a killjoy, 'cause you're doin'

your dangedest to make things extra nice," he added, backing toward the kitchen, "but Wesley had it right that Christmas he told me there ain't no Santy Claus."

He was out the back door before any of them knew what to say.

Asa rose from where he'd been sipping his sassafras tea. "I'll talk to him, Miss Mercy. Nobody knows the trouble that boy's seen, and nothin' but time and love can make it go any better for him."

Time and love. As Mercy let down her hair and the house settled into silence around them, the tears she'd held back finally dribbled down her cheeks. "I didn't know what to say, Judd," she whispered. "We should've had better answers tonight—"

"Nobody can know all the answers, honey."

"—and we should've anticipated this! Should've known he'd be too shy—or too proud—to ask for our help in making gifts."

Judd's chuckle rumbled in the darkness as he cuddled up to her. "Now, if you were Billy, would you want the folks who took you in to find out what you were giving them?"

"Surely each of his parents helped make the other's gift—"

"But they're not here now." Judd's sigh feathered the hair at the nape of her neck. "I feel bad about this, too, Mercy. But we're too late to make amends. We have to trust that God'll work things out. A little help from Santa wouldn't hurt, either."

Chapter Seventeen

Mercy awoke and sat straight up. Had she left a candle burning in the front room, too close to the tree? Had the wind blown down the chimney, to send that heavy aroma of half-burned buffalo chips into the house? She threw aside the curtain that closed off their little room and stumbled toward the kitchen.

"Don'tcha be bargin' in here, now!" a boyish voice ordered. Billy blocked the doorway, his eyes sparkling with a challenge. "Me 'n' Asa're cookin' up your Christmas presents! Now be a good little girl and git back in bed, or Santa won't come for *nobody*. You don't want him to leave a big ole lump of buffalo dung in your stockin', do ya?"

A wild giggle bubbled up inside her. Mercy clapped her hand over her mouth, shaking with the night's chill and sheer childlike joy. The change in Billy was a Christmas miracle, and as she sent her thanks to that baby in the manger, she vowed to see that the Santa with the chocolate skin and heart of gold knew she appreciated him, too.

She slipped back into bed, straining to hear those secretive sounds above Judd's deep, even breathing. Billy and Asa were as quiet as midnight snowfall in there: an occasional rattle of a pan . . . stealthy footsteps, and then whispering in the front room over by the fireplace . . . the muffled clatter of—plates and silverware being set out? She certainly recognized *that* sound, but why—?

The scents of warm sugar and cinnamon drifted from the kitchen. Bacon sizzled and popped. And then everything got very, very quiet.

Sheer curiosity had her wiggling out of Judd's embrace. By the light of her bedside candle, Mercy slipped into the red calico dress she'd kept clean for today, and tied her hair back with a twisted length of red and green ribbon.

Footsteps above told her Aunt Agatha was awake, and when she stepped out into the front room, Nathaniel was lighting the lamps. He'd gotten the fire going, and the flames crackled happily in greeting.

"Merry Christmas, missus," the burly hand said with a big grin. "Hope you don't mind us three cookin' up a little magic so early this mornin'."

"The look on Billy's face has already been my favorite gift, Nathaniel. Merry Christmas! And thank you so much for helping our boy."

And here he came, grinning broadly over a platter of bacon and ham, which he placed in the center of the table they'd set. She opened her arms and he rushed into them. It was an embrace to savor, even though she suspected he had his mama in mind as he clung to her.

"Merry Christmas, sweetheart," she whispered.

When she opened her eyes, she found they were being watched by the two who'd slipped downstairs. "And Merry Christmas, Christine and Aunt Agatha! We're so glad you're here to celebrate with us."

Asa set a large plate of raisin biscuits beside the meat platter, while Nathaniel brought out a bowl of stewed apples spicy with cinnamon, and a pitcher of steaming mulled cider.

Judd stepped from behind the curtain, smiling. "Looks like we'd better enjoy this fine feast while it's hot. Santa's helpers must've worked through the night to get it all ready."

"It was Billy's idea, and we were pleased to help," Asa replied happily. "And on this special Christmas mornin', I'd like to offer thanks."

They stood behind the benches with bowed heads as the old Negro began. "Dear Lord, we ask Your blessin' on this food and Your special blessin' on the children in our home this day. For it was *Your* child who came to save us all. Help us to be Your angels on this earth until we earn our wings in Your heavenly multitude. Amen."

Aunt Agatha poured hot cider for everyone from the end of the table, looking regal in her cherry-red dress. "What a joy to be with you all on Christmas Day," she chirped, handing around the cups on their saucers. "I've spent many a holiday with those unfortunate girls who couldn't get home. It's also a pleasure to give presents," she added with a chuckle. "I hope I've chosen well."

Mercy's heart swelled as the Bristol children opened their gifts from Aunt Agatha first. Billy lit up over a book of Edgar Allan Poe stories and two adventures by

Jules Verne. His sister's eyes widened with delight at a pair of white gloves trimmed in seed pearls, and two *Harper's Bazaar* catalogs of dress designs.

"Oh, thank you, Miss Vanderbilt!" Christine breathed. "These are the very latest fashions!"

"And well you deserve them," her headmistress said with an approving nod. "The other girls didn't receive any gifts, however, so you'd best not mention these. But then, no one else had the vision or the pluck to create a new school uniform. The yard goods for those should arrive in a few weeks, and you may begin making them as soon as you wish, Christine."

The girl looked happier than Mercy had ever seen her, flipping the pages of her magazine as she envisioned the finery she would sew for herself.

Her brother elbowed her. "Thought she was an old battle-ax," he murmured.

Christine's glare could've scorched his shirt. "I don't know where you heard that," she muttered, "but I'll thank you to keep your mouth—"

"Well, would you look at this!" Judd exclaimed over their whispered bickering. "A fine new hat. Thank you, Aunt Agatha."

"And—oh, my word, I—" Mercy stood up to unfold the contents of her large, bulky box. The scarlet brocaded skirt and matching jacket rustled with the seduction of stylish new clothes—sweet music to her ears. She had no idea where she'd wear such finery, but she gazed at her aunt in gratitude. "It's gorgeous, Aunt Agatha! You really shouldn't have—"

"Why not?" The little spinster beamed. "While the 'make over and make do' philosophy will get us through these difficult times, I wanted you to have something stylish to replace those gowns you gave Christine. One of these days, you'll have the occasion to wear it."

Still grinning, Mercy fetched the other bulky gift from under the tree. "For you, Christine. Sometimes 'making do' is also making *new*."

Her pulse pounded. She'd warned herself this girl of thirteen might turn her fine nose up at the flour-sack wrapping, even before she considered all the hours and love that had gone into the gift inside.

And indeed, Miss Bristol returned to her guarded, sullen self as she untied the yarn Mercy had used for ribbons. Christine stood up to let the bulky quilt unroll, while Billy hopped up to help her.

"I watched her makin' this!" he crowed. "An' look, Sis! There's pieces from them dresses Mama wore, and the ones Mercy gave ya. And danged if those brown and blue strips ain't made from my old shirt and britches, and some of Judd's."

Mercy spoke cautiously, hoping she wouldn't embarrass or further alienate the girl. "I know our home can't replace the fine one you grew up in, Christine—just as Judd and I will never be the parents you're missing right now. But I chose the Log Cabin pattern, hoping that years from now—when you've grown up and moved on—you'll have fonder thoughts of your time here with us."

"And aren't these sturdy, masculine fabrics the perfect complement to those silks and satins?" Aunt Agatha came over to get a closer look, running an admiring finger over the rectangular pieces that joined at right angles. "What a lovely symbol of the patchwork family you've become. As practical as denim, and as pretty as silk."

"High praise indeed, from the headmistress who used to rip out my messy quilting stitches," Mercy quipped. That her starchy, unmarried aunt had discovered the quilt's intended meaning touched her more than she wanted to let on, with the bristling Miss Bristol looking on. "It seems your lessons about doing my best have carried over into other areas, Aunt Agatha. And you've been a tremendous help to Christine in a very short time. I can't thank you enough."

"Oh, yes. Thank you both *so* very much."

Christine's sarcastic words sent Mercy's joy flying like snowflakes before the north wind. The girl rolled the quilt into a lump and laid it on the end of the table. Then she snatched a box from beneath the tree and shoved it toward Mercy. "I believe these are yours."

Without another word, the girl hurried from the room. Billy scowled and got up to follow his sister, but Judd put a hand on his shoulder.

"She's having a hard time of it today, son. Let's—"

"She's got no call to get snippy, after Mercy worked so hard on this quilt," the boy retorted. He looked ready to cry—or cuss—as his face turned pink with agitation. "Mama would never've made her nothin' that took so much time! She'd've just bought some frilly girl-thing uptown, and Christine would've swooned over it from here to Kingdom Come."

His insight made a single tear slip down Mercy's cheek. "Thank you for understanding that, Billy. But I suspected she might react this way. It's all right. Really it is."

She focused on the gift she was unwrapping, trying desperately to remain positive; remembering the true meaning of Christmas Day, rather than letting her sharp disappointment ruin her holiday spirit. "Besides, this gift your sister wrapped is the prettiest one under the tree. She must think enough of me—of Judd and me both—to at least offer us *something*."

She lifted the lid of the box and nipped her lip. "Monogrammed napkins, Judd. A set of twelve."

"It was my suggestion, but she bought the linen and embroidered them herself," Aunt Agatha said quietly. "After the way she ran off with the ones Mother made, I thought them a fitting gift."

So why didn't Mercy feel better about them? Because she knew Christine had been prompted?

Mercy ran her finger along the top napkin's smooth, satin-stitched M, wishing this gift were more about peace and goodwill than payment and guilt. Small comfort that Judd seemed so pleased with the new pants and shirts she'd made him, and that Billy was ecstatic to receive new clothes just like them. Asa and Nathaniel were grateful for new union-suit underwear, and Aunt Agatha exclaimed over the table runner of fine filet crochet she'd made.

Billy's squeal made them all look up.

He was holding a carved wooden horse, posed in a proud stance—a replica of the Morgans he tended every day. "You made this, didn'tcha?" he quizzed Judd. "I've seen you whittlin' on—"

"That's just the first part of your present, son."

The big man in the butternut shirt and blue denim pants leaned forward, his eyes ablaze with such love that Billy gazed back at him, entranced. The room fell silent around them.

"But—but I owe you for—"

"The preacher returned that horse and saddle he borrowed, remember?" Judd said softly. "And your sister has more than replaced the napkins she took, so—"

"But she stole money! And her schoolin' . . . I told you I'd pay for—"

"You'll do no such thing, young man." Aunt Agatha laid a hand on his shoulder, her smile kind and conspiratorial. "When I inherited a home far too large for any one family and turned it into my academy, I wanted less fortunate girls to receive the same education as those from blue-blooded families back East. I keep my own accounts, so no one's the wiser about who pays full tuition and who does not. It's an honor and a privilege to be teaching your sister, Billy."

The knot in Mercy's throat nearly kept her from responding. "But, Aunt Agatha, I fully intend to use my inheritance to—"

"Use it on your own children, dear. I'm proud of the home you and Judd have made, and the way you've shared it with everyone here," she said, gesturing with open arms. "I love your parents dearly, Mercedes, but they could never open their hearts the way you have."

Mercy blinked at Judd, who reached for her hand. "Thank you, Aunt Agatha," he said, his voice shaking in a way she'd rarely heard it. Then he chuckled, grinning at Billy again.

"As I was saying, young man, that toy's just a place holder. Come spring, when our mares give birth, you can have whichever foal you like for your own. It's the least I can do, for all the help you've given us."

The boy's face lit up and his mouth fell open. "Well, I'll be—well, *dang!* Ain't that a fine how-do-you-do? I got the best present of all!"

He sprang toward Judd, who sat ready to catch him—and who closed his eyes on tears like those dribbling down Mercy's cheeks. Such a fine father he would make, if only she could conceive. Six years of marriage now . . . what if it simply wasn't God's plan for her to bear this strapping man's children?

But then her gaze fell on Mary, Joseph, and the Christ Child, so serene on the sideboard. She swallowed the knot in her throat. The young virgin had learned firsthand that miracles happen in their own good time—when they were least expected, and because Someone Else was in control. Mercy could do no less than wait patiently, faithfully. Pondering these things in her heart.

The soft chords of Nathaniel's guitar brought her out of her musings. The smiles on the two hired men's faces told her there was still a gift waiting to be given . . . a gift that sparkled in Billy's blue eyes as he eased away from Judd, clasping the carved horse.

"Last night when I shot outta here, all upset, Asa and Nathaniel reminded me that I didn't need no store-bought presents," he began, choosing his words with care. "Mama always praised me when I sang in the Christmas pageant at church—which was such a relief, after bein' the Baby Jesus till I was nearly three!"

Mercy chuckled in spite of her heartache, and so did the others.

"So I wanna sing you a couple songs as the rest of my gift," Billy said. "Nathaniel's been teachin' me to play out in the barn, but I ain't nearly good enough to do that part yet."

The tall, muscled colored man eased into the introduction of a carol they'd all sung since childhood, and Mercy knew she was going to cry through the whole thing. How did this redheaded boy reach inside and pull her heartstrings like no one else ever had? How did that huge black man, who could harness six spirited Morgans to a stagecoach in minutes, caress that old guitar so it sang as sweetly as the parlor organ she'd played back home?

How does anything happen? came a still, small voice in her head. *The answers you need are all within you, my child. Seek and ye shall find.*

" 'Silent night, ho-oly night,' " Billy began. His was a sweet, childlike tone that filled the room with a purity, an innocence he wouldn't have much longer. In a year or so, his voice would crack at all the wrong moments and he'd feel too awkward to sing for them this way.

" '. . . all is calm, all is bright . . .' "

Yes, it is. If we allow it to be, came that inner whisper, like an angel's assurance that she had done her best for both these children, and that her best was somehow good enough. Grasping her husband's hand, she smiled at Billy and let him give her the gift of his unsullied soul, from the bottom of his little-boy heart.

It was a moment she'd remember forever.

The next day, after the stagecoach had left with Christine and Aunt Agatha, and the dirty dishes were washed and put away, Mercy ventured upstairs to tidy Christine's room. Why wasn't she surprised to see the patchwork quilt folded on the end of the bed, with a note?

Thank you so very much for this lovely quilt, but I had no room for it in my trunk. Christine, the pretty script said.

"Well, then," she muttered, "perhaps you had no room for a packet of letters from Tucker Trudeau, either."

Her heart ached at the evenings she'd worked so

feverishly to finish this gift, hoping to touch something within the girl. Hoping to show the love she so badly wanted to share. Christine had seemed withdrawn and unapproachable this entire visit, so they hadn't even broached the subject of her mother—not that offering her Tucker's letters would have resolved this situation. The girl would have been upset at her headmistress for withholding her mail, while Aunt Agatha would've been incensed because her authority had been undermined.

Best to tuck those letters away in the bottom drawer of her vanity, where she kept other things of importance. She had a feeling she'd need the letters someday.

As she stripped the sheets from the bed, Mercy felt a presence behind her.

"Sure would like havin' that purty quilt on *my* bed," came Billy's voice. "Just till Sis gets back—if it's all right with you. Soon as she sees I've got it, she'll want it, of course."

How had he gotten so wise so young? She gathered the quilt into her arms and turned to smile at him. "We'll put it on your bed right now, Billy. I hope you got to talk with Christine more than I did. She was keeping her distance, I thought."

He let out a snort. "Daddy always said she was like a cat—purrs and rubs against you when she wants somethin', and then skedaddles when somebody wants somethin' from her. You ain't gonna change that, Mercy. So don't go frettin' over it."

Christine sat squeezed between Miss Vanderbilt and a woman whose bulk spread across half the stagecoach seat—and who, by the smell of it, had worn the same clothes for more than a week. But what a relief to be out of that house, where people tried too hard to make her love them. As though that could ever happen!

Finally, to break the monotony of the clattering coach's sway, she muttered, "Billy's grammar and table manners are atrocious, Miss Vanderbilt, yet you never corrected him. Why, if *I* had talked with food in my mouth, you would've reprimanded me until—"

The woman's tight smile warned Christine not to venture further onto thin conversational ice.

"Yes, your brother's social graces need some correction, but Mercedes will see he gets it," she clucked. "While I was in her home, among family for a rare holiday visit, I thought it better to be kind than to always be right. Once we're back at the academy, however, your headmistress will return to her strict disciplinary ways."

Christine's sigh escaped more loudly than she intended.

"It doesn't hurt that your brother exudes such an honest, unstudied charm," Miss Vanderbilt went on. "Far more effective than confronting others with a prickly-pear expression, and an attitude to match."

Christine now wished she'd kept her comments to herself. The prim little woman beside her had been waiting for just such an opening.

"It wouldn't have hurt you to accept the quilt Mercedes made," the headmistress continued, in a voice so low Christine had to listen carefully. "If you reject her at every turn, Miss Bristol, one of these days—when you need her help the most—she'll be tired of trying to please you. Mercedes will forgive you, but she'll never forget the way you made her feel this week."

"But I worked just as hard making those linen napkins as she—"

"Did you now?" Miss Vanderbilt's single arched eyebrow told her she was really in for it. "You have *no concept* of hard work, Christine. No idea what Mercedes gave up to homestead on the prairie because the man she loved would be happier there. No idea how every sunrise brings another day in which survival takes up her every waking moment.

"Not that you can help that," the little spinster went on more gently. "I understand why you detest that little house, where the wind whistles in and the lamps never burn brightly enough. I couldn't live there, either."

Miss Vanderbilt paused, as though this admission had cost her something; as though her usual fortitude had fallen short. "But I admire their courage. Their faith that they can make a living, and make the land their own. Twenty years ago I might've tried it myself, but I've become too accustomed to my comforts."

Christine watched, horrified, as the headmistress reached over to grip her gloved hand. The other passengers, who'd been following their discourse, looked on with great interest.

"You were blessed with a different destiny, my dear, and Mercedes has recognized that. Study hard. Develop your talents," Miss Vanderbilt said with a glitter in her pale blue eyes. "Your association with our family will open doors to you, Christine . . . introductions to many a prince of industry who needs a wife worthy of the fine home and elevated social station he can provide."

But what about finding Mama? Christine mused. She nodded her agreement, however, so this tiresome lecture would end and these people would stop staring at them.

And what about Tucker Trudeau?

Chapter Eighteen

May 1, 1867

Dear Mother and Father,

We've come through another busy winter, and the prairie is now vibrant again. As I write this, the new leaves on the cottonwood trees shimmer like sequins on the gown of Spring. What a joy, to realize this homestead will be ours in just two short months!

Judd continues to raise fine Morgan horses as part of our contract with the Wells Fargo express company. Several foals now graze the pasture-land alongside their mothers, frisky and sleek when they play.

Our boy, Billy Bristol, is shooting up, too. I've had to let down the hems in his new pants twice now, and he's no longer the skinny little waif who came to us. He's a natural with the horses, *and Judd gave him his pick of the new foals this past Christmas, in exchange for all his hard work. He's very proud of his colt, which he named Mr. Lincoln!*

He was also thrilled when a black-and-white herding dog stayed behind its wagon train to have her puppies last week. He plans to keep one he calls Spot, and find homes for the other three this summer, when they're weaned. One of our hired hands is teaching him to play the guitar, and he's got a good ear for picking up the music.

His sister Christine continues to be an exemplary student at Aunt Agatha's academy. She has designed and created a new school uniform, no less! We've heard no word from their mother after all these months, so we're assuming we never will. A sad situation indeed, because these children are such a blessing.

And, we're not such an isolated outpost anymore! The Kansas Pacific Railroad is now completed through Abilene, a sign of progress and people to come. This means you could ride the train here to visit, rather than getting bumped and shaken on the stagecoach. July 4th marks the date we prove up on our land, and we would love to have you help us celebrate!

Please pass along my love to everyone there, and do consider a visit!

Your loving daughter,
Mercedes

"And what did you tell your parents about our hired hands? And the way your husband makes you slave in the kitchen to feed stagecoach guests?" Judd murmured over her shoulder.

His breath tickled her ear, and she grinned up at him. "I told them only what they need to know, dear. They'd faint dead away before they sat down at a table with two Negroes. I invited them out for our proving up, but I'm guessing our little secrets will stay safe. Unless Aunt Agatha's filled them in."

When he shrugged, his muslin shirt pulled against his powerful shoulders. "And what if she did? There's no shame in treating Asa and Nathaniel well, or in working hard for land that'll soon be ours."

"Certainly not. Refusing to become one of Father's foremen was the best decision you ever made," she whispered. She giggled when his lips met hers in repeated kisses.

"No," he breathed, inhaling her clean, satisfying scent. "Pursuing *you* was my best move, far and away. Not that marrying you six years ago means I intend to stop chasing after you, honey. Happy anniversary. And a happy, happy birthday."

The hand he brought around from behind him held a bouquet of wildflowers in a riot of pinks and yellows. The love in Judd's deep blue eyes made her hold her breath. What had she ever done to deserve such a very special man?

And what if the perils of the prairie—or difficulties with the Bristol children—came between them, in years to come? Mercy took the colorful flowers, inhaling their sweet freshness to clear her head. Did she dare ask him the other question on her mind?

But his was a kind and giving spirit. He knew of her quandary, even if they rarely spoke of it.

"Judd, I love you so much," she murmured. "I'm just so—*disappointed* that I haven't yet given you a child. I hope you won't come to doubt—"

He cut off her worries with a kiss that lingered even after they heard Billy enter the front room. When he raised his head again, Judd remained focused on her, as though no one else in the world existed. He gently brushed a strand of hair from her face.

"From this moment on, Mrs. Monroe," he replied in a low voice, "that's not your responsibility. We'll pray about it, and we'll bring our bodies together with all the joy and passion we've always shared—and the rest is up to Mother Nature and God. They're a potent pair, you know. Between the two of them, they'll give us the answer that's meant to be."

He pulled the red bandana from his pocket. "Now wipe those pretty brown eyes, birthday girl. Let's cut the cake Billy and Asa made for you."

"Today, on this momentous Fourth of July, when so many in our midst prove up on their homesteads," Gregor Larsen spoke out above the crowd, "it seems only fitting to share that joyous psalm we all learned in our youth.

"Stand with me," the circuit rider called out, raising them from the benches with his outstretched arms, "as we say together the One Hundredth Psalm. 'Make a joyful noise unto the Lord, all ye lands. Serve the Lord with gladness: come before his presence with singing. Know ye that the Lord he is God—'"

Billy looked up into Mercy's shining eyes, reciting the familiar words with the chorus around them. It was a day for celebration, all right! On Mercy's other side stood Agatha Vanderbilt, whose confident voice rang out with all the joy the psalmist had intended. Beside him, Christine recited the verse with less fervor, fiddling with the folds of her pretty summer frock.

But her coolness—and the way she looked, at fourteen so very much like Mama—didn't rattle him. What really mattered was that Emma Clark and her family stood directly in front of them—and Emma's cousin Gabriel kept glancing back with a light in his bespectacled eyes Billy hadn't seen before. Surely it was a sign! The mute, orphaned boy was grinning like a *kid* today, instead of turning in on himself like a little old man whose bent shoulders bore the weight of a silent, desperate world.

After the preacher offered a prayer, everyone sat down, eagerly awaiting the announcements of the federal land agent. Billy realized how important this ceremony was to Mercy and Judd, and to Emma's parents and the others he'd come to know at these parties.

But after the ceremony, there was all that fine food covering the long tables. And then, he could take Emma and Gabriel to meet Mr. Lincoln, his colt—and he could show them Spot, his border collie pup! He was so sure his friends would want one—or maybe two!—of Spot's litter mates, he could hardly sit still.

"Mr. and Mrs. Ira Barstow," the agent called out. He was a tall man, barrel-chested, and his voice rolled with a theatrical flair.

Cheers went up as the skinny fiddler and his stout wife went to the platform to claim their deed, with four cotton-headed kids in tow. Iry waved the paper above his head with unaccustomed glee, his ruddy face alight as the crowd clapped long and loud.

"Mr. and Mrs. Judd Monroe," came the next announcement.

As one, everybody stood up, applauding as Mercy

joined Judd on the platform beside the frock-coated land agent. Billy's heart was pounding. He scrambled to stand on the bench so he could see better.

"It's a proud moment for us all," Miss Vanderbilt twittered, clapping just as wildly as the rest of them. "A testimony to hard work, with help from faith, family, and friends."

From his left came his sister's long-suffering sigh. "*Really*, Billy! *Must* you climb around like a circus monkey where everyone can see you? Get down this minute!"

But Billy had caught Gabriel's attention—and the lanky boy started laughing! And then he, too, hopped onto the bench, so he could see the goings-on up front. Judd and Mercy were sidling back between the benches as the land agent called Clyde and Nell Fergus forward, and before Billy sat down, Judd wrapped an arm around each boy's waist.

"You kids can go out to the barn if you'd like," he said beneath the cheering of the crowd. "It'll take a while for folks to witness each other's deeds, and this ceremony stuff isn't nearly as exciting as puppies."

The O of Gabriel's mouth matched the size and shape of his eyeglass lenses.

It was all the excuse Billy needed; he wiggled out of Judd's arm, shot past Mercy and his scowling sister, and grinned widely when Gabriel followed him. *Months* it had been since he'd teased and tussled with another boy! This kid was still way too quiet to be quite right, but he was at least a potential friend. Emma seemed more interested in the proving-up ceremony, and that was fine by him.

"This here's Mr. Lincoln, my colt," Billy said as they stopped beside the nearest corral. The mares and their foals stood to one side, gazing at the boys with curious brown eyes. "He's four months old now. Smaller than the other foals—but that's why I picked him. Just stand here real quiet-like, and maybe he'll come to us. He don't know you yet, so he might get skittish and stay by his mama."

Gabriel stood stock-still, peering between the fence timbers. With a smile spreading slowly over his slender face, he extended a hand toward the colt. Billy did the same, relieved that the boy knew not to jump around and spook the horses.

"Here, Mr. Lincoln . . . come here, little buddy," Billy crooned. "It's just me and my new friend Gabe, okay? Come on over here, now."

With a toss of his head, the colt whickered and walked a few steps away from his mother.

"Attaway, Mr. Lincoln. Lemme scratch behind your ears." Billy held his breath, willing the colt to walk closer. "Good boy, Mr. Lincoln. Come 'ere and see your Billy, now."

The colt's ears flickered and he took another step, and another, until he reached their outstretched hands. He sniffed and snorted at Billy's familiar fingers first, his muzzle like warm velvet. Then he tentatively stretched toward Gabriel's palm.

The boy bided his time, letting the young Morgan make all the moves. When Mr. Lincoln sniffed his fingers, he lightly stroked the colt's nose—grinning as the animal skittered back to his mother on spindly legs.

"He likes you," Billy crowed softly. "He can tell you're a natural around horses, same as me and Nathaniel. You gotta see these puppies, though! Now that they're weaned, you can have one, if ya want."

Into the quiet, musky barn they went, past the stalls

207

to the back corner where straw bales sat in stacks and
harnesses hung from pegs on the wall. With a finger to
his lips, Billy motioned for Gabe to follow quietly.
Sure enough, the puppies were napping in a nest of
straw, a black-and-white heap against their mother.

When her yip of recognition roused the litter, four
little fur-balls leapt to yapping, wiggling, waggling life
around the boys' feet.

"That's more like it!" Billy reached for one with a
white chest and a white spot encircling one eye. "This
here's Spot. He's my other little runt, but if you want
one of his litter mates, you can have—"

He'd turned to let Gabe hold his puppy, but the boy
was already sitting on the straw-strewn floor, letting
the little dogs crawl into his lap. His eyes followed
their movements, while his hands couldn't get enough
of their soft warmth and their little pink bellies when
they rolled onto their backs. Their tiny teeth found his
fingers, and he giggled. When two of the more adventurous pups had clawed their way up the back of his
shirt, he leaned over to accommodate them.

The first one reached his ear, and Gabriel screwed
up his face so suddenly, Billy thought he'd been
nipped. But no, the boy was wheezing as though he
wanted to laugh and cry at the same time. Grabbing
the little fur-ball at his ear, he hugged it fiercely. It
clung to him like a baby, with its stubby front legs on
either side of his neck.

"Puppies," Gabriel rasped.

Billy didn't know what to do. The kid looked ready
to have one of those fits—looked possessed by demons,
grimacing with thoughts he was struggling to express.
And then he soared like a hawk on a current of elation.

"Puppies," he whispered in a voice that sounded

rusty from lack of use. "Oh, puppies! Had puppies . . . at home when those Indians burned our—"

"Easy now, Gabe," Billy said, his arm going around the boy's shaking shoulders. "I know how hard it was to lose your family, but you're gonna make it. This little girl likes the smell of you, so—"

Rapid footfalls entering the barn warned him they weren't alone. Instinct made him turn to stop whoever was coming, so Gabe wouldn't be jarred back into his lonely, silent state. It was Emma, her blond curls bouncing like plump yellow sausages around her flushed face.

"I tried to come sooner, but my folks was gettin' their—"

"Shhh! Gabe's got puppies all over him. And he's *talkin'*!"

Her blue eyes widened, and she inched toward the corner stall. When she saw the four furry pups, however, she immediately joined her cousin on the floor. Her giggles bounced off the barn walls when two puppies hopped into her lap.

"Oh, Billy, they're so cute!" She sat cross-legged, cradling them in her calico skirt. "And you're sayin' we could have one? I can't decide if I like this one with the white head and shoulders—or the one with the four white feet that looks like he's wearin' a black frock coat. I better ask Mama if—"

"This one's mine," came that raspy voice. "Her name's Hattie. Like my dog back home."

Emma's breath came out in a whoosh. "You *are* talkin'!" she gasped. "And would you look at the way that puppy loves you, Gabriel? It's like she's been waitin' for you to come and get her!"

With her lap full of little dogs, all she could reach were Gabriel's knees, and she grabbed them with both hands. "If Hattie's the one you want, then she's the one we'll take home. I can always—"

"You can pick one, too, Emma." Billy joined them on the floor with Spot. "Far out as your place is, it might be better if one puppy had another one around to play with."

"Keeps them out of . . . trouble, too," Gabriel added haltingly. He lowered his puppy so it would quit gnawing on his collar. And when her little brown eyes fixed on his, she went absolutely, adoringly still, supported by his hands and forearms. The barn around them went quiet.

"Can't argue with that," Emma whispered in awe. "And if we've already named 'em, well, Mama can't tell us to leave 'em here, now can she? I'm thinkin' this little fella in the frock coat likes me best, and I'm thinkin' his name's gonna be Boots. 'Cause that's what he's wearin'!"

"Can't argue with that," Billy echoed as they all stood up. "We'd best get us some dinner now, 'fore the good stuff's gone. Let's see how long it takes folks to realize Gabe's talkin' again."

As they left the barn, clusters of men sat on the benches, or on wooden crates in the shade, while the women sat on quilts in the shadow of the house. The three puppies nipped and tussled around their feet, and when they got within sight of the food on the tables, Emma's cousin chuckled.

"Pie," he stated, as though that were all it took to make a complete sentence—or a complete meal. "Pie like I had . . . the first time I was here."

"You are gonna be all right!" Billy crowed as they picked up plates. "Asa made us two gooseberry pies for today, and that big ole pan of peach cobbler there. Won't have no more punkins till September, ya see."

210

The boy gazed solemnly at him from across the laden table, adjusting his spectacles. "You say you won't have any more *pump*kins until September, Mr. Bristol?"

Billy paused with a spoon halfway to the cobbler. Gabriel was only eight and built like a beanpole. Easily pinned to the ground if he needed to be put in his place. But worth humoring, just this once.

"That's right, Mr. Getty," Billy replied in an elevated tone. "We'll have no more *pump*kins before the fall harvest. Thank you, sir, for your *observation*."

Gabe's face split with a grin. "Sorry. Mama was a schoolmarm."

"Daddy was a rancher." Billy lifted a big corner of the cobbler to his plate. "Guess our horses didn't much care how pretty I talked, long as I kept 'em fed and exercised."

"Hmmm," Emma joined in, stabbing the biggest piece of chicken before her cousin could. "Maybe you was better company when you couldn't talk, Gabriel. If you boys're gonna get all uppity, Boots and me'll just go sit with Christine. I sure like that yellow dress she's wearin'."

"She does, too," Billy quipped at her retreating figure. Then he finished filling his plate. "Let's go sit by Judd and Mike Malloy. He always tells good stories 'bout what's goin' on along the stage route."

He started away from the table, and then noticed his new friend staring after Emma. "She didn't mean that part about you not talkin', Gabe. You know how girls can run at the mouth, just to make you suffer for some fool thing you said. Or didn't."

Gabe's lenses flashed in the noonday sun. "Your sister's very pretty."

"Yeah, well don't tell *her* that! Christine spends enough time gawkin' in her mirror without anybody givin' her a reason to."

Careful not to trip over Spot, who was frisking between his feet, Billy headed toward the men sitting on bales in the shade of the barn. Their voices floated to him on the hot breeze, deep and masculine, as they quizzed Mike Malloy about the latest schemes in Abilene.

"You're tellin' me Joseph McCoy's been advertising in Texas? Making our town out to be the best market for their cattle?" Iry Barstow demanded. "Where's he going to pasture 'em? Why does he think for a minute—"

"Must be the railroad," Judd joined in. "Now that it's running through here, McCoy probably thinks those beeves can fatten up on all the prairie land hereabouts, after drovers herd them up from Texas. Then he'll ship them east in cattle cars."

"That's about the size of it," Malloy agreed. "McCoy's invested a bunch of money in this. Already got a hotel going up, and he's bought a lot of land east of town for stockyards."

He was dressed in denim pants and a collarless shirt, much like the fellows around him. But Mike was younger, and Billy thought his slender mustache and sunstreaked hair—which was a little longer than most men's—gave him an air of adventure and derring-do. Almost like an outlaw.

"So what'll happen when those drovers run their herds past our places?" George Clark protested. "How're we supposed to keep that Spanish fever from infecting our own cattle? That's why Missouri's having nothing more to do with those longhorns!"

"I hear tell Missourah's got a new breed of trouble,

212

without steers carryin' the fever," Clyde Fergus chimed in. "Bandits named Frank and Jesse James held up the bank in Richmond a couple months ago. In broad daylight!"

Billy's mouth dropped open. He knew of the James family—why, their daddy was a preacher! He itched to know more particulars, but as the other men scraped the last food from their plates, Mike Malloy was intent on discussing Abilene.

"Maybe McCoy's more of a visionary than we think," he challenged. "If he's smart enough to take advantage of the law that bans Texas cattle from Topeka on east, there might be a way for farmers around here to ship their own herds at more of a profit.

"And I've got to tell you," Malloy went on, his voice rising with his expressive eyebrows, "our stagecoaching days are numbered. Folks're taking the train now—just like Miss Vanderbilt and Christine did this time. You might want to think about other income from your land once Wells Fargo isn't paying you to feed their passengers and provide fresh horses."

"Still sounds half-baked to me," Barstow muttered. "If you've got longhorns on the trail, you've got cowboys driving them. And you know what an ornery lot *they* are! And you know the gamblers and barkeeps and loose women'll follow them. Where does McCoy think all these people're going to stay?"

"Just lookin' to make a buck," Clark groused. "Can't tell me that little hole in the road'll ever be much more than a general store and a train station."

Billy was following the conversation with interest, and he set his plate on the ground for Spot. "You like cows, Gabe?" he asked in a whisper.

"They seem pretty dumb and ugly, compared to horses and dogs."

Nodding at this wisdom, Billy scooped his puppy back into his lap. "Ever met a real live cowboy? Sounds like a fine life, ridin' in the open air all day, ropin' and wranglin' them steers."

The kid sitting next to him closed his eyes in ecstasy when Hattie licked his face. "Right now, I want to catch up with my studies, so I can go on to school somehow. I want to be a lawyer. That's how President Lincoln started out, you know."

Billy's eyebrows shot up. He'd never known of an eight-year-old boy considering such a high-minded profession, yet Gabriel Getty seemed suited to it. And how much different might his own life be, had his daddy's lawyer prevented the bank from foreclosing on their home? There was something to be said for men who studied their lessons—in books and in real life.

He was stroking Spot on his lap, considering these things, when a familiar wail arose from over by the house. Christine leapt to her feet, wiping frantically at her skirt with her napkin.

"Get that ugly mutt away from me!" she screeched. "Lord, I hate this place! I'm never coming back! And you can't make me!"

Billy swallowed hard when Mercy stood up to make amends. But Christine, with her flair for high drama, was running toward the house like a pack of wolves was after her. Everyone had heard every word, of course. And they were speculating about who would win this battle of wills . . . and wondering if the Monroes were sorry they'd taken this ungrateful girl under their wings.

Emma knocked into Billy in her hurry to sit down. Her puppy landed in his lap, which made Spot playfully bare his little teeth, which started Hattie yapping to join in the fray.

"Say there, Billy Bristol! Where'd you get those fine collie dogs?" It was Mike Malloy coming over, grinning like he was truly interested and not just humoring a little kid.

Billy grinned back, lifting his pup from the tangle of black tails and furry bodies. "This here's Spot. His mama hung back from a wagon train to have her litter in our barn!"

"And you and your cousin have pups, too, Miss Emma?" Malloy knelt in front of them to stroke and admire the three wiggling dogs.

"Yessir, this here's my new dog Boots, and he's already got me in trouble," the girl wailed, "on account of how he just peed on Christine's new dress."

Billy patted her hand, noting her valiant effort not to bawl in front of them. He knew firsthand how his sister's wrath could sting. "No harm done, really," he consoled her. "It's a yellow dress, after all."

The cheerful notes of Nathaniel's guitar and Iry Barstow tuning his fiddle announced it was time for the dancing to start. If Mike Malloy was right, these gatherings where friends shared their food and faith might not go on for much longer. The world as he knew it seemed to teeter on the brink of big changes and exciting times—and he hoped to be right in the middle of them!

Billy glanced over to see Gabe hugging his puppy. His glazed-over expression suggested he'd retreated into his own little world again. But thanks to that little fur-ball named Hattie, he knew his new friend was on the road to recovery, and would come to see him whenever he could.

Just as he knew Christine would not.

Chapter Nineteen

October 3, 1867

Dear Sis,

You won't believe Abilene! It's a real town, now that they're starting to drive those long-horns up from Texas. When we went to Doc Moon's store last week, all the talk was about the fancy new Drover's Cottage hotel that fellow Joseph McCoy is building for Eastern cattle buyers. Hundreds of folks've come here to open stores and saloons and such, and by next year they'll be in real buildings—including the Great Western store that'll sell EVERYTHING!

They say more than twenty boxcars of beeves got shipped to market on the first day! And they're still coming in! The new stockyards'll hold 3,000 head, and McCoy's built huge livery stables and a scale that weighs twenty cows at a time! The Clarks are pretty peeved about how

some of their corn crop and garden got trampled
when a herd got out of control, hurrying to the
river to drink. Spot and Snowy earn their keep by
barking and biting, to run those longhorns down
the road instead of through our fields! It's a sight
to see!

Sure wish you'd come for Christmas again.
Now that the train comes through, we don't fix
so many meals for the stagecoaches. So it'd be a
nicer visit—and an easier ride—for you. Mercy
would really love to see her Aunt Agatha again.
You'll be amazed at how much Mr. Lincoln and
Spot and Snowy have grown—and how smart
they are! Both dogs are house-trained and sleep
with me, when I can sneak them upstairs.

I'm sorry about Emma's pup wetting on you.
You were wetting on Mama when you were that
little, too, after all. Please come to see us soon!
Mercy and Judd are really very nice people, who
want us to have a good life.

Love from your brother, Billy
12 today

"Did I spell everything right? Do you think it'll get
her to come?"

Mercy wanted more than anything to assure the
earnest boy at her elbow that his sister couldn't possibly
resist his plea. He kept busy managing the horses, playing with his pets, and helping her serve meals, but she
knew there were times—like his birthday today—that
Billy Bristol was acutely aware of his family's absence.

"Your letter is perfect," she pronounced with an em-
phatic nod. "We'll send it on its way with Mike Malloy
and our prayers."

"Do you s'pose Christine ever thinks about me?"

His voice swooped up a few notches at the end of his question, cracking with emotion and the change that came with his age. He resisted her displays of affection these days, but Mercy framed his face in her hands anyway. It was an open, honest, sturdy face now, tanned and without freckles. His shining blue eyes and auburn hair were going to make the ladies take notice someday.

"Your sister has *always* loved you, Billy, and I'm sure she'd be happy to see you if she didn't have to come out here to do it," she said. "She's different from Emma—"

"*That's* for dang sure!"

"—and she's always had a mind of her own—"

"Amen to that!"

"—so even a starchy old battle-ax like Miss Vanderbilt can't make Christine behave the way we'd like her to. The way she *should*." Mercy patted his hair back from his face, amazed at how thick and soft it was, but not surprised that he flinched a little.

"You're a fine young man, Billy. You could teach your sister a thing or two about what's really important," she said, gazing proudly into his eyes. "But she's a girl, and right now she's caught up in her dressmaking and schoolwork and social activities. Now run on out and help Judd. I have a pumpkin pie to make for somebody's birthday."

November 19, 1867
My dearest Mercedes, Judd, and Billy,
Holiday greetings to all, as I'm not sure how soon this letter will arrive. It's snowy and cold here, and before we know it, Thanksgiving and Christmas will bring us to the end of another year.

I have asked Christine again and again if we couldn't accept your invitations. I have reminded her that seeing her brother is so much more important than her objections to the "isolated wilderness" she calls Kansas. She will be serving holiday meals at the Home for the Friendless, and is sewing new clothing as Christmas gifts at the local orphanage. Honorable, commendable pursuits, but she commits herself to these projects before asking me—and no doubt in defiance of our wishes that she'd visit Billy!

I know, however, that she reads his letters again and again. I don't look over her shoulder as she writes to you, but I suspect Christine's letters express a lot about her various interests and activities, and little in the way of affection. Though I cannot condone this attitude, or the shabby way she has treated you, Mercedes, I attribute her aloofness to the way her mother broke her heart when she abandoned those children. You know—quite well—how I cannot force that willful young lady to do anything!

You can at least be pleased that she has advanced far beyond any student I've ever instructed with her design work and sewing. You have saved that young lady's life, by giving her the opportunity to develop her God-given talents, and to forge a future for herself.

As far as I know, Christine has heard nothing more about her mother. I have, however, enclosed the last of the letters from Mr. Trudeau. I wrote him a brief but firm note insisting he correspond with her no more, and he has kindly complied. I see no honorable purpose in letting him

believe she is receiving his mail, or that it would
be proper for her to reply, anyway.
　　Have a Merry Christmas, my dears, and know
that I wish I could be there to celebrate with you!
　　My love,
　　Aunt Agatha

With a sigh, Mercy glanced at the unopened letters. Two more of them, in thicker envelopes than merely polite correspondence would require. Her fingers stroked the seals, itching to rip them open. What if Tucker Trudeau had written news about the children's mother? What if Virgilia Bristol was trying to contact them, and the Atchison photographer was the only connection she had to her daughter?

It was probably true that Christine's imagination had magnified her girlish feelings toward an older, compassionate man, and had embellished his kindness into an affection she believed was mutual. But who was to say that Tucker's intentions weren't perfectly honorable? The girl had no doubt sneaked letters out to him—probably as she went to help at the orphanage and the soup kitchen. Christine had to be wondering why he didn't reply, just as Mr. Trudeau had probably puzzled over letters that reflected no knowledge of his.

At least Aunt Agatha had informed him of the situation now. It seemed so unfair not to tell Christine what her well-meaning headmistress had done. But again, Mercy didn't want the girl to explode in Aunt Agatha's face and run off—or otherwise jeopardize the bright future she'd have if she graduated from the Academy for Young Ladies with Miss Vanderbilt's blessings. Not to mention her personal and social connections.

Mercy smiled wryly. She couldn't send Trudeau's letters to Christine at school, knowing Aunt Agatha would see them. And since the willful redhead refused to come here, she had no chance to hand them over in person. A dilemma she didn't like, but one she hadn't created, either.

And surely if Mr. Trudeau had urgent information about Mrs. Bristol or that huckster Wyndham she'd run off with, he would be resourceful enough to send his letter here to Abilene. Unless, of course, Christine had told him not to. Another situation of the girl's own making.

So once again Mercy tucked the unopened letters into the bottom drawer of her vanity. And once again she wondered how to tell Billy his sister wouldn't be coming for Christmas.

Chapter Twenty

As the blowing of snowflakes gave way to the greening of trees, it seemed to Mercy that the world was aflutter: birds winging over the sprouted corn rows, cottonwood leaves quivering in the wind, butterflies lighting on wildflowers. It felt so good to be hanging the wash on clotheslines Judd had strung between the trees, watching the garments flap and dance instead of freezing stiff. And then a fluttering inside made her retch so unexpectedly, she almost splattered the shirt she'd just hung.

She sat down hard on the grassy bank. Was her head reeling with the June heat? Or had she eaten something that was taking its revenge? The sunlit diamonds on the river nearly blinded her, yet she couldn't stop staring at them. Her mouth tasted coppery and began to water like she was about to vomit again.

When she gazed anxiously toward the corrals, the motion made her too dizzy to holler for Judd, even if she'd spotted him. The heavy clang of hammer on anvil told her he and Ned McKenzie, the farrier, were still shoeing horses. Billy and the hands were in the barn, too, so no one would hear her if she cried for help.

Somehow, slowly, she got the rest of the clothes hung, and somehow, slowly, she got to the house. Her need for the bread she'd baked that morning couldn't wait for the next meal or even a knife. Judd came inside just as she was stuffing a hunk of it into her mouth as though she hadn't eaten in weeks.

He wiped sweat from his forehead. "You all right, honey? You look a little pale."

Mercy nodded, trying to chew and swallow without choking. She hated to worry him. If he was playing nursemaid, he and the farrier wouldn't finish today, and Ned had other families to work for tomorrow.

Judd filled two cups with water he'd just brought in, setting one on the dry sink in front of her while he downed the other. Watching her. Assessing the possibilities, as she had: In the years they'd lived here, their diet had varied little and she'd shown no inclination to be sickly.

Gently he raised her cup to her lips, but, feeling another sudden urge to regurgitate, she knocked it from his hand. Truly frustrated now, Mercy began to cry. Yet as her husband held her against his warm, solid body, she could feel him laughing. With a towel, he wiped her mouth and then blotted her wet blouse. She wanted to slap that grin right off his face.

"Is there something you want to tell me, sweetheart? Or is your body already doing that?" he crooned.

"What are you . . . how can you laugh at me when I'm trying not to—"

Judd held her fast so she wouldn't struggle out of his

embrace. His deep blue eyes seemed to see inside her very soul—or at least see what was wrong with her.

"I have a feeling Mother Nature and God have finally put their heads—and whatever else—together, Mrs. Monroe. And come next spring, we'll be calling you something besides Mercy."

Why wasn't any of this making sense? Had she lost her mind along with her breakfast? She rested her head against his chest, wondering when she'd be able to get on with her day.

"So now you've got a real decision," he went on, still chuckling softly. "Do you want to be called Ma? Or Mother? Or Mama?"

A baby? Could it really be?

That night Mercy's mind raced with the implications of what Judd had suggested. When she heard his deep, even breathing, her hands went to her abdomen, to feel for any changes that might be taking place inside her.

Nothing.

Thank God she'd stopped vomiting after Judd returned to the barn, so Billy and the two hands had no idea of her supposed *condition* at dinner. They'd been talking about the day's work with the horses, and Billy now sported a huge bruise on his thigh. Mr. Lincoln's mama had kicked him when he found a tender spot while filing her back hoof. So if she seemed pale or different somehow, none of them had mentioned it.

Maybe she wasn't in the family way at all. Wasn't she supposed to look radiant enough that others would notice the change immediately?

Mercy turned on her side, frowning in the darkness. What if she *was* carrying a child? What on God's earth did she know about such things? As the youngest daughter, who'd been sent away to school among other young girls—with a spinster aunt for a headmistress—she'd had no exposure to those mysteries of womanhood. Mother wasn't one to talk about such things. It was Judd who'd taught her the details of intimacy on their wedding night.

What if she did something wrong? How would she know?

What if the baby was malformed or sickly? Though she took no stock in the old beliefs that barren women were being punished for their sins, she had to wonder why—after six anxious years—she now showed signs of being pregnant. Or at least Judd saw it that way.

She sighed, and a tear slithered down each cheek. And this infuriated her. She was *not* a crybaby. Mercedes Monroe was a stalwart, cheerful woman of faith who had adjusted to the rigors of homesteading with few regrets about what she'd left behind in Philadelphia. While she sometimes missed the little luxuries of privileged living, she'd wholeheartedly chosen to homestead with Judd, and she'd never looked back. This was her life now, on land they owned free and clear. And she was proud of that.

But it would be nice to have another woman to talk to. Someone to answer my silly, fearful questions.

There was Elizabeth Barstow, on the next place over. With those four blond children who stood like stair steps, she certainly knew about birthing and babies.

Yet as Mercy recalled that day in Doc Moon's store, when Elizabeth had ridiculed her decision to send Christine to school, she'd felt their friendship slip a notch. And it wasn't as if she could go running over there with every little twinge and concern.

Mercy kicked off the sheet. In a couple of weeks, all the neighbors along the stage line would be here for their annual Fourth of July gathering—not only Elizabeth, but Rachel Clark and Nell Fergus and other women. By then, perhaps she could decide whom to trust with her questions.

Maybe the ladies would have a quilting bee or other gathering to give her gifts for the new baby, as they'd done for Elizabeth. There, they always passed along their wisdom and remedies and advice. How she wished she'd been listening to this chatter, but it hadn't seemed important before. Collectively, those hardy women had experienced nearly every situation or complication she would confront. Out here on the prairie, they relied on each other, for only women really understood how to elevate this isolated life above the level of mere survival.

She sighed. So many things to think about, when she really wanted to rest. Mercy hoped she'd get her cooking done without being sick when the stage came through tomorrow. How humiliating, to be retching behind the house, knowing the passengers could hear her. They'd probably guess at her condition and whisper behind her back.

What if there really is a baby? What if we get snowed in this winter and—

Judd's arm slipped around her from behind. "Our smiles will probably give it away," he murmured against her ear, "but are you going to announce our big news at the party?"

"No! It's too soon," she replied. When she sensed she had burst his balloon, Mercy added, "I want to be *sure* before we say anything. No sense in having everyone congratulate us for a false alarm."

Judd's chuckle told her he would humor her. For now. "Honey, if the Lord has chosen this time to bless us," he whispered in the dimness, "we might as well decide we're along for the ride. God's been the driver all along, and He will change *everything* with this child."

Did she look any different? Would the neighbors *know*, from the way she acted today?

Mercy watched the wagons pulling into the yard and wanted to hide in the house. Even though the little kitchen sweltered from baking prairie chickens and a buffalo roast, it felt more comfortable than subjecting herself to their pointed stares at her pale face or her belly—even though her dress still fit the same.

Billy and Nathaniel unhitched horses and led them into the corral, while Asa carried the food to the long tables. Reverend Larsen was opening his Bible on the podium. Some of the women had faded like flowers in a drying bouquet, and the men had gray in their hair, but these friends were essentially the same solid farmers who'd agreed to work for Ben Holladay and then for the Wells Fargo express lines.

Only her *view* of them was different. Because a baby was on the way.

But no—Emma Clark wasn't jumping down from the wagon today. She was dressed in bright green gingham that looked new, and her hair was pulled back into a matching ribbon at the crown so her golden waves cascaded halfway down her back. When her father helped her to the ground, she turned, and Mercy's jaw dropped.

She had hips. Curves above and below that announced she was no longer a little girl—and a smile that said she *knew* it, too. Now thirteen, Emma Clark exuded a confident charm Mercy couldn't have mustered at that age, and the girl was searching the yard to see what her buddy Billy thought of it. Gabriel and the two dogs bounded down as though they knew they were mere commoners accompanying this queen.

Take note, that little voice inside Mercy teased. *This young lady can remind you of a thing or two about being female. And being pleased about it.*

So Mercy stepped out into the yard, carrying the covered roasting pan of carved buffalo, smiling despite the July heat. Her stomach lurched, but she walked on.

I will not vomit! I will NOT vomit! she vowed with every step.

"Here—let me help you with that."

"Why, thank you, Michael, but I can carry—"

The stage driver stepped in front of her, grinning mischievously as his hands closed over hers. Despite the thick hot pads, Mercy was suddenly aware of the heat her pan gave off as Malloy's hazel eyes sparkled above hers.

"So it's true." His mustache twitched with mirth. "Congratulations, Mercy. Judd told me about your blessed event—but I'm sworn to secrecy."

When her mouth fell open, he relieved her of the pan.

"Now, don't be mad at him! He's just so proud he's going to pop if he doesn't tell *somebody,*" Malloy went on. He set the pan on the table, glancing around to be sure they weren't overheard. "Couldn't happen to nicer folks—you'll be a wonderful mother, Mercy. Now, what'd you cook today? It's always the best food on the—"

When he lifted the lid, the aroma of the buffalo made Mercy gag and grab her mouth. Mike quickly covered the pan again. "Soda crackers. You got any soda crackers?" he asked quietly. "Breathe deep and slow now . . . that's the way. This, too, shall pass, you know."

How did he know? Yet his suggestions, spoken with low assurance, settled her enough that she thought she could make it back to the house without erupting. Mercy walked without meeting anyone else's eye, grateful that Malloy accompanied her to steady her arm.

Once in the kitchen, she grabbed the sack of crackers on the shelf and ate one, then another, praying nobody would come in to ask what was going on between her and Malloy. It didn't seem to bother him that curious neighbors could spread all kinds of rumors—and *then*, when they found out she was *expecting*—why, the speculation—

"Eat another one, honey. Sugar cookies work, too, if those crackers taste stale." He leaned a hip against the dry sink, as though he had no intention of moving until she felt better. "I have six sisters. There's not a lot I haven't seen when it comes to bringing kids into the world."

"Thank you," she gasped. "I was fine while that roast was baking, but when you lifted—"

"Probably the gamey smell set you off." He let her take one more cracker and then folded the bag down. "Stick with potatoes and bread and cake today. You'll be fine in a few weeks, and then you'll be eating everything in sight. Odd combinations, like jelly and pickle sandwiches."

When she grimaced, Malloy's laughter filled the kitchen. He focused those eyes on her one more time, eyes that mellowed with friendly affection. "I'm really happy for you, Mercy," he said. "I know you've been waiting for this a long time, after giving up so much to come out here."

Was that wistfulness in his smile? As though he wished for a family of his own? Michael Malloy was a handsome young man, yet she'd never heard him mention a sweetheart. He stepped back outside, hailing his friends as though nothing unusual had happened.

A few deep breaths later, Mercy rejoined the gathering. She didn't want to be the last one to sit down for the church service. Judd patted the bench beside him, smiling.

"Hope you don't mind my telling Malloy—"

"No, it's fine," she whispered.

And when she looked up at Judd, she saw the pride Michael had been talking about; realized that she wasn't the only one with something at stake here. Something to hope for.

Nor did she have to go through the next several mysterious months—and then endure the somewhat terrifying ordeal of giving birth—alone. For when had Judd Monroe ever fallen short or let her down? When had he ever lost his temper—or his nerve?

The comforting drone of Gregor Larsen's Scripture reading made her breathe deeply and prepare herself to hear his message.

"It's going to be all right," she repeated, lacing her fingers between Judd's. "Everything's going to be fine. I can believe that now."

Chapter Twenty-one

"So what do you think of my new dress, Billy? I've been savin' it 'specially for today."

Emma pivoted to make her skirt billow out over her shoe tops, and when she stopped, that look on her face made him press back against the side of the barn. He could feel the crack where two boards came together, and he was wishing he could squeeze through it and disappear.

"It—it's real purty, Emma."

"So do you know why I wore it for you?"

Now, *there* was a trap if ever he'd heard one. "Can't rightly say," Billy ventured warily, "but I'm guessin' it wasn't so we could catch frogs on the riverbank."

When she rolled those eyes and planted her hands on her hips, he knew he was in for it. His sister had performed this way since she was much younger than Emma Clark.

Billy swallowed hard. With Christine it had been different, because when she'd been here at Christmas he'd noticed right off that his sister had sprouted fronts and she walked with a sway. But she'd looked so much like Mama, and acted so standoffish, those changes hadn't really affected him.

Now, however, he wondered what in tarnation was taking Gabe so long to fetch their pie. And he realized, too, that it was Emma's bright idea to send him after it.

"I was hoping," she hinted, "that you might ask me to dance later, when the music starts up. I *love* to dance, Billy. And now that we're old enough to join in with the adults—"

"I—I don't know how!" he fibbed, wishing that even the dogs would come to his rescue. Never mind that he'd been drafted into dancing lessons when Christine's class had lacked for boys. Those girls had seen him as Christine's pesky little brother once the lesson was over, but Miss Clark obviously had something more . . . private in mind.

"Well, perfect!" she crowed. "I can teach you! Back here, where nobody'll see if you make a mistake or step on my foot. You just put your arm around my waist—"

Emma hadn't given him a chance to step away from the wall. Now she was guiding his hand to the small of her back . . . grinning prettily while those soft, yellow waves of hair teased that hand. She stepped against him, her eyes shining blue with intention.

Yes, he realized, she *was* pretty. Perfume drifted up from the neck of her dress—first time she'd ever worn *that*! And he knew if he said another word, that hard lump pulsing in his throat would make his voice jump like a squirrel the dogs had treed.

And danged if she wasn't leaning in real close, like

she was going to kiss him! It surely couldn't be all bad, kissing her—but she'd have to swear on the Bible not to tell anybody. If Gabe or anyone else walked by right now—

"Billy! You gotta see this!" his friend's voice came from the yard. "Another cattle drive's heading into town. Holy smokes, there must be a million of them!"

Spot and Snowy raced past, followed closely by Hattie and Boots, all barking gleefully at the oncoming excitement. So Billy bolted.

"Sorry about the dancin', Emma," he blurted, "but it's my job to see that those longhorns don't trample anything! Come along, if you want. We've got some ridin' to do!"

With a burst of energy born of extreme relief, Billy sprinted toward the yard. Gabe was standing on a crate gazing south with the other men who'd spotted the oncoming herd, a forgotten plate of pie in his hands.

"Let's saddle up!" Billy called out. "The dogs'll keep the cattle in line, but me 'n' Nathaniel ride along to be sure the cowboys behave themselves. Can't have that herd of cowpokes stampedin' through our party, now, can we?"

Gabe's eyes grew wide behind his spectacles, but he left the pie on the crate and came running around the barn. "But what if the horse you choose doesn't like— doesn't know me—"

"Hop on behind me and just hang on tight!"

His pulse beating for a whole different reason now, Billy rushed into the barn and took a bridle from the back wall. He motioned for Gabe to follow him.

"Hey there, Trojan," he crooned at the huge black gelding Nathaniel was saddling. "We'll be right behind you, fella. Hey there, Mr. Lincoln! If you were a couple years older, buddy, we'd be ridin' out to our glory. Here we go—Pepper's the lady for us, aren'tcha, girl? You're smellin' those longhorns and itchin' to go after 'em."

He bridled the dappled gray as Trojan trotted out first, whickering and tossing his massive head. Blanket, saddle—with an extra slap on her belly so he could tighten the cinch enough—and he was leading Pepper out into the sunlight.

Judd was just entering the barn with a couple other men. "Careful now, boys! Those sharp horns can do some damage—not to mention your mothers blaming us if you get hurt," he called out. "Let the dogs do the job they were born for."

He was right, of course: the fastest way to stampede those cattle was to ride hell-bent-for-leather at them. But their large dust cloud was still half a mile down the road, and Billy itched to run with the wind for a minute. Maybe to blow off the effect of Emma's perfume. And maybe to show off a little, because he *could*.

He vaulted into the saddle and pulled Gabe up behind him. Then he nudged Pepper into a trot. "Hang on, cowpoke!" he cried, and they shot past the corrals at a gallop.

Was there anything as glorious as lying flat against a flying horse's neck? Billy felt like one huge grin, charging full speed through the flattened prairie grass alongside the road. He gave Pepper her head, knowing she'd be easier to control after running off some nervous energy. Gabe's arms tightened around his waist. He suspected the slender boy was holding his breath and clenching his eyes shut. But Gabe didn't make a whimper.

The thunder of Pepper's hoofbeats took control of Billy's pulse. The dust flew wildly behind them, and the wind whistled in his ears at a different pitch when he cocked his head. He wondered if Emma was peeved at him for running off this way, yet he could recall a time when she would've been neck-and-neck on her horse, giving him a real run for it.

How come girls had to change so, anyway? What had possessed her to press him against the barn wall? He'd always enjoyed these parties because tomboy Emma Clark had been his friend, his equal. But now the balance had shifted, and he sensed that things would never be the same between them.

"Whooooa, Pepper," he murmured as they approached Nathaniel and Trojan. "Easy does it now. Gotta stand our ground and look those longhorns in the eye. Show 'em who's boss here."

"Who's *boss?*" Gabe echoed with a chuckle. He sat up to assess the cattle at closer range. "One look at those dogs tells you that, Billy! Far as I'm concerned, there's no finer sight than watching a border collie put a herd in its place."

"Yeah, look at that! Spot and Hattie're not one bit afraid of those big ole beasts," he replied in awe. "They know when to dart in and nip, and when to crouch and just stare 'em down."

Snowy yipped a warning at one unruly steer, jumping back to avoid his long, lethal horn as it shook its bony head. The beast plodded back into the herd, which rumbled forward in a wave three times the width of the road. For as far as the boys could see, the prairie looked like an undulating blanket of dusty hides with horns like handlebars.

Billy returned Judd's wave as he, Clyde Fergus, and

Emma's dad rode along the edge of the procession to let the drovers see them. It never hurt to let those cowboys know that this homestead's owner was watching their every move until they got past his property.

"Call the dogs to the other side," Nathaniel instructed, his eyes never leaving the herd. "Gotta keep these beeves from trompin' through the yard, scarin' folks."

With a nod and a whistle, Billy directed the four dogs across the rutted road. "Come on, pups!" he called out. "Over here, now! Move 'em along!"

Four black-and-white faces turned his way, ears alert. Then the collies shot across in front of the first steers, as though this game was created solely for their delight. Down the edge of the plodding, scrawny-looking beasts they raced, each picking a section to patrol.

"Those cows look tired," Gabe remarked, "like they won't be giving us much trouble. Been a long walk from Texas, I guess."

"Yeah, but soon as we figure they're gonna behave, that's when one'll decide he needs a drink from the river," Billy replied. "Then the rest'll follow him, and that's what we can't have."

He was letting Pepper mosey along, staying within sight of the dogs as he constantly scanned the cattle.

"You seen that new hotel yet? The Drover's Cottage?" Gabe asked. "Three stories high! And they say it's the fanciest place this side of St. Louis."

"Yeah, well, it was the new saloons Mercy took note of," Billy responded with a chuckle. "And shifty-eyed fellas in fine clothes, waitin' to gamble with these cowpokes' wages. And ladies who weren't wearin' nearly enough to be goin' to church.

"But she was excited about the new stores," he went on, "because that means that more merchants and bankers and regular, decent folks will settle here. Which means there'll be churches and schools goin' up soon."

They had almost reached the yard now, and Billy could see the neighbors watching this dusty, shuffling parade from the benches behind the house. Emma's fresh green dress stood out in that crowd of faded calico, but he didn't wave, because the movement might spook the cattle. He pulled Pepper to a halt in front of the house, to give the dogs room to work. Their tongues lolled long and pink, and they were covered with dust, but they wouldn't stop nipping and yipping and darting at stragglers until the last cow was well past the pastureland and corn crop the dogs considered their territory.

Nearly an hour passed before the last tired cowboys brought up the end of the parade. Ira, Clyde, and George trotted up alongside Judd, wiping faces smudged with sweat and dust.

"Well, we got lucky today," Judd said to his nodding neighbors. "I hear things aren't nearly this calm in Abilene. They expect nonstop carousing and trouble in town well into the fall."

"Can't say I'm happy about this so-called *progress*," Iry Barstow groused. "Sure hope I got some crop left when I get home—and by the end of the summer. That McCoy fellow might be doing big things to get Abilene on the map, but us homesteaders are the ones paying for it!"

It was a common complaint among them. And once the riders had washed up and gulped lemonade the ladies brought them, the party broke up. Everyone wanted to go home and assess the damage those Texas steers had done on their places.

Billy held Gabe's eyeglasses while his friend rinsed the grit from his face. Their four dogs sprawled in the shade of the barn, with their tongues hanging long and their breath coming short.

"Now, that's what I call dog-tired," Billy quipped. "Spot and Snowy was real glad your two pups come along to help today. I'd say they all earned their keep."

"And I'd say *you* were the best cowboy of the bunch, Billy Bristol!"

Before he knew what was coming, Emma grabbed him and kissed his gritty cheek. His face went hot, and he hoped nobody had noticed. It was a touch of justice that she had to wipe his sweat and dirt off her mouth, and then brush dust from her new dress. Billy knew better than to laugh at her sour-lemon expression, though.

While her parents packed food into their wagon, Emma leaned closer. "I didn't let on," she murmured, "but while everybody was watchin' those longhorns, there were Injuns in the trees by the river, watchin' us."

Billy scowled, glancing beyond the barn. "Any women or kids with them? Judd says as long as squaws are along, they stay pretty peaceful."

Gabe quickly put his glasses back on and peered warily toward the cottonwoods. He whistled at the dogs as he started toward the wagon. "Come on, Hattie! Boots! Time to get on home now!"

Emma cast a sympathetic gaze his way. "Don't guess poor Gabriel's ever gonna get over that attack on his family. Thought I better let you know about those Injuns, though, 'cause Pa heard they've really been on a rampage farther west."

"Don't guess I'd like it much if a bunch of farmers

took over my tribe's lands and hunters killed my buffalo for sport, neither," Billy remarked quietly. Then he smiled at the girl, for no matter how prissy and prancy she got, he knew Emma Clark had good intentions. Mostly.

"You got a cellar under your house?"

She nodded, lingering even though her parents called from across the yard. "Yup. I can be down that trapdoor in less time than it takes an owl to hoot."

"Good. Take care now, and I'll see ya next time."

Billy watched the last of the neighbors' wagons pull out onto the rutted road, returning Gabe and Emma's waves until they were out of sight. Then he knelt to slip an arm around Spot and Snowy, hugging each one tight.

239

Chapter Twenty-two

The dawn felt hot and prickly, like a wet wool jacket, on this late-September day. Mercy tossed cracked corn for the chickens, chuckling when Spot and Snowy herded them her way for their breakfast. The air felt unnaturally still, as though the breeze had been sucked back to blow in one huge swoop across the prairie. Was this the calm before a storm? Even the birds were silent.

The back of her neck prickled. Was someone at the creek? Or farther up the river's shore? She stopped tossing grain to scan the horizon. Where the cottonwoods and maples curved to follow the Smoky Hill River, she thought she saw movement.

And then it was gone. Absolutely still again. Her hand went to her abdomen, and she chided herself for being so skittish. She should be feeling grateful now that she was no longer sick with this baby.

She wanted butter and eggs from the springhouse

for today's stagecoach meal, yet something kept her from asking Billy to fetch them. Instinctively she looked for the boy, smiling at the way his coppery hair caught the sun as he toted water to the horses' troughs. Judd, Nathaniel, and Ira Barstow were harvesting the corn with a horse-drawn threshing machine at the top of the eastern ridge, and she heard the high, sweet refrain of the hymn Asa was singing in the kitchen.

Everyone was fine and accounted for. Mercy took a deep breath, shaking her head at how every little thing seemed to rattle her these days. It was time to leave off her belts and let her dresses hang loose. Time to announce this child she carried—although she sensed that everyone already suspected it.

A high, shrill cry pierced the air. Then came a chorus of cries just like it, and the thundering of hooves.

Mercy dashed toward the corrals. "Billy! Billy, you get inside now!" she screamed.

Her heart pounded up into her throat. To the west she saw a band of black-haired warriors, brandishing bows and arrows, riding ponies that flew like the wind itself. On the ridge, Judd and his two helpers broke into a run toward the barn, where they kept rifles at the ready for wolves. This was a different beast altogether, though, and Mercy wavered between watching to be sure they were safe and following Billy inside.

"Get in the house, Mercy!" her husband cried. "Take care of yourself—take care of my family—while we fight them off!"

His black hair framed a face bronzed by the summer sun and taut with purpose. His blue shirt strained against his chest as his sturdy legs carried him well ahead of the others. Mercy wavered, assessing their distance from the approaching redskins and the time the men would have to defend themselves.

"Get in here *now!*" Billy ordered, yanking her sleeve. "Asa, move the rug! Open the hidey-hole while I bar the doors!"

Her head began to spin, but she forced herself to focus. The little old man who'd been singing in her kitchen had flour on his dark face, and his eyes registered the same fear that was making her heart beat triple-time, but he was waiting to help her down the ladder into the root cellar.

"Careful now, Miss Mercy," he warned, forcing a brave smile. "Got to keep that bundle of joy safe for Mr. Judd, don't we? Got to keep our wits about us and outsmart those Indians! Step easy now . . . feel your way until Billy can bring us a candle."

Every fiber of her being told her to remain in the kitchen. Perhaps she should grab the shotgun in the corner, to shoot those savages from the shelter of the house. Judd had taught her how to handle a gun because hungry wolves howled too close for comfort some nights.

But Asa's hand rested firmly on her head as she began her descent to the cellar. "Find that next rung, missy," he urged. "Our rope ladder's not the best, but Billy's waitin' on us, and I don't want those redskins to claim a redheaded scalp today."

It was all the incentive she needed. Mercy groped for the next rope rung and the next, until she felt the floor beneath her. Asa scrambled down, and they moved through the darkness to make room for Billy.

"Here comes Spot! Catch 'im, now!" Billy called down. "And Snowy, too!"

She heard Asa grunt with the squirming weight of

the first dog. The light caught Snowy's white face before she, too, hopped down to safety. Billy pulled the trapdoor closed after him, and then there was only total darkness, the panting and pacing of the dogs, the heavy scent of the earthen floor, and the electric tension that kept them quiet, straining to hear what was happening in the yard.

The *pfffft* of a match brought Billy's face into view. He set the lit candle on a shelf, beside jars of green beans Mercy had put up that summer.

Then he knelt to settle the dogs. "Prob'ly too crowded down here, but when they rushed into the house, I couldn't just shove 'em out—"

"It's all right, honey," Mercy said, finding the warmth of his hair with her hand. "Judd said to keep his family safe, and we had no time to argue."

"He was talkin' about the baby, wasn't he?"

"He was talking about you and—how'd you know that?"

Mercy's voice rang more sharply than she intended in the close, dirt-walled cave. Yet she felt immense relief that she didn't have to find some perfectly worded way and the right time to reveal her miracle. She chuckled despite her anxiety. "Some secret, eh?"

"We've known for a while now." Asa's old voice crackled with his laughter, but it was a nervous sound, just as his chatter was a diversion from what they feared was happening above their heads. "Mr. Judd couldn't keep it to himself. By the time he told us, we were just glad you'd quit bein' sick."

She wanted to laugh but was afraid she'd cry.

From above them came the sound of rifle fire and horses' hooves . . . muffled shrieks she chose to interpret as war whoops, for she couldn't allow herself to

243

think anything else. Nathaniel and Ira Barstow and Judd—the man she and this baby simply could not live without—were up there fighting for all their lives. Mercy blocked the image of those oncoming warriors from her mind, so she wouldn't think about how badly their men were outnumbered.

"I shoulda been watchin'," Billy chided himself. "Emma told me the Cheyenne had been attackin'—"

"Son, the way they sneak up and hide themselves, there's no way any of us could've known," Asa insisted. He moved beside them in the flickering candlelight and pulled them both into his embrace.

"Don't blame yourself one bit, Billy," Mercy agreed. "I had a feeling something was odd—ignored the pricklings at the back of my neck. So now Judd and—"

A loud cry rang out above them. A cry that sounded far too triumphant and unfamiliar to be good news.

Mercy's face crumpled and her eyes went wet. The sob she bit back came out as a whimper, and the two men she crushed against herself were shuddering as badly as she was.

But then Billy wiggled loose. "I'm goin' up there!" he whispered fiercely. "I'm gonna grab that shotgun and . . . I got nothin' left to lose if they shoot *me*, but by God, Judd and Nathaniel ain't goin' down to them—"

"You'll do no such thing!"

Asa sprang toward the ladder and grabbed Billy by his pant legs. "It's Miss Mercy who stands to lose, boy! If you go up there and get yourself killed—or those Indians see you movin' in the house—they'll be down this trapdoor in a flash!"

The two dogs began to yap and circle each other in a frenzy. While Mercy tried her best to quiet them, it was Billy they wanted to follow—and Billy who settled them by returning to the dirt floor with a muffled *thump*. He knelt to wrap an arm around each border collie, stifling a sob against Snowy's white shoulder.

Mercy huddled with them, craving their warmth, and the colored cook took them all in his arms again.

"Our Father, who art in Heaven," Asa began in a ragged voice.

Mercy and Billy joined in, desperate for the prayer's familiar promise, in words that welled up without conscious thought. After they whispered the "Amen," their restrained breathing was the only sound in the candlelit cellar.

It was absolutely silent above them.

After what felt like an eternity, Mercy whispered, "We have to go up there. We can drag the men inside and dress their wounds. Elizabeth's got four children. We have to let her know that Iry—"

"We're stayin' right here," Billy stated. "Asa's right. They're up there just *waitin'* for us to show ourselves now! Prob'ly lookin' in the windows, 'cause the curtains ain't shut."

"We can't take that chance," Asa agreed. "I can't let something happen to you like in the horrible stories I've heard. Can't give one good reason to risk you—and that little baby—on the notion we can do any good up there."

"But how long—? How will we know—?"

The old man stood close enough that she could smell flour and yeast on him. His eyes glimmered like dark coals in the candlelight.

"We keep believin' that Judd and Iry and Nathaniel are doing their level best—without having our hides to look out for, too," Asa said softly. "We keep believin' the Lord's got this whole situation in hand. Our faith and our prayers are the best gifts we can offer right now."

"But what if—"

"They know we're in here, Mercy," Billy said, pleading for reason. "They was watchin' us before the attack, and they figure we'll be stupid enough to open that door if they wait us out. Let's just hope they don't break out the windows and come in after us."

She opened her mouth to protest, but Asa overrode it.

"The Lord's the only one we can trust right now," he whispered urgently. "That'll have to be enough, until He sends us a sign."

Chapter Twenty-three

Mike Malloy surveyed the landscape ahead and kept the stagecoach's team to a trot, rather than racing toward the Monroe home with his usual flourish. Something didn't look right. It was way too quiet.

There were no horses in the corrals. No smoke coming from the kitchen chimney.

"Whoa, now," he murmured, and grabbed the field glasses from beneath his seat. The telegraph wires into Topeka had buzzed with the threat of attacks from the Southern Cheyenne and confirmed that this hostile tribe had been on the warpath farther west, along the Solomon River. But he hadn't figured on their coming this close to Abilene. Not when drovers and vast herds of longhorns had become such a common sight this summer.

But then, maybe that was the very reason the Indians were upset.

A sick feeling in the pit of his stomach told him not to take his passengers into the yard. A moment later he spotted three figures spread-eagled in front of the house, left so those traveling the road would see the consequences of homesteading in what had been tribal territory. The wind kicked up in an empty, desolate whisper.

Mike had some quick decisions to make. His first urge was to help the Monroes, because Judd and Mercy had become fast friends, but he was responsible to Wells Fargo for these passengers, and the coach and team.

He hopped down from his bench, grabbed his Winchester, and opened the coach door. The gun got everyone's attention, as he'd planned. Mike kept his voice low.

"Folks, there's been Indian trouble, so I'm sending you back to the previous stop," he announced, looking into their startled faces. He pointed to a man of about thirty, dressed in denim, who'd mentioned he was searching for work on a ranch.

"You, sir—drive the stagecoach back to the Barstow place, and then telegraph Fort Riley that we need their help out here. You two ladies, lend whatever assistance you can to Elizabeth Barstow, and—"

"But we must get to Denver to meet our connecting—"

"Ma'am, I'm sorry, but your inconvenience is *nothing* compared to what these homesteaders have just been through," he replied, his voice rising with his anger. "Did you see those four little Barstow kids? Do you recall Mrs. Barstow's agitation because her man wasn't home from harvesting with the Monroes? Well, this is the Monroe place. There's three men tied to the

248

ground in front of the house. Any guesses as to who they are?"

He hadn't intended to upset them with the gruesome details, but some folks just didn't listen any other way.

"Right now, being a couple days late is pretty small potatoes compared to what Mrs. Barstow has sacrificed—and to what might've happened to Mercy Monroe and the rest of this family. So I'm hoping you folks will be decent enough to stay with Elizabeth, and to tell Reverend Larsen we'll be needing him. Telegraph Wells Fargo so they can send another driver for you. Tell them Mike Malloy's picking up the pieces at their way stations west of Abilene."

Without giving them a chance to protest, he swung down from the doorway and loped up the road toward Judd Monroe's log house. The September sun beat down relentlessly, and he hoped those three men in the yard hadn't suffered long in the heat. Hoped he wouldn't find Mercy and Billy tortured in some other way—or, God forbid, not find them at all.

He entered the yard with his heart in his throat, because even from this distance, his worst fears were confirmed: Judd, Ira Barstow, and Nathaniel lay displayed as grisly reminders that the West hadn't yet been won. He bit back a moan at the way they'd been stripped and mutilated, and then moved on around the house to look for survivors.

A few chickens pecked forlornly at the ground, but the empty corrals and the dead milk cow told him all he needed to know about the livestock. It was pure relief not to find any more bodies—outside, anyway. As he approached the house, Mike was torn about telling Mercy the details.

Mercy. Carrying Judd's baby. She was unaware of her man's fate or she would be out here to—

I can't let her see him this way.

Quietly, he tried the door, knowing she might come out if she heard that someone was here. It was bolted shut.

No windows were broken, so, for reasons only God would ever know, the Indians hadn't gone in after them. Could be the bloodstained ground and flurry of hoofprints back here meant the three men out front had fought hard and well, and the Indians had retreated with their own dead, knowing they'd slaughtered the muscle that kept this place running.

Malloy exhaled, concentrating on survivors. A peek through the back window revealed a bed and simple furnishings, immaculate except for a rug that looked rumpled.

She—they—must be in the cellar. And they weren't going to know he was here until he'd tended to those men. The grisly sight of those bodies would haunt him forever, and he couldn't let Mercy and Billy suffer the same nightmares.

With a strength he didn't know he possessed, Malloy pulled up the stakes and dragged the three bodies into the barn. On his way back to the house, he kicked loose dirt over the trails their weight had made, hoping Mercy wouldn't ask too many questions.

She'd be running the way station alone now—with a baby on the way. And what about the rest of the crops? How could she and a worn-out old colored man and a pint-sized kid hold it all together out here?

He pounded on the door. If they were down there in

that cellar, they had to come out and face the facts. And he was the one who had to help them.

He pounded again. "Mercy? Billy?" he called into the gap under the door. "It's Mike Malloy! Anybody in there?"

Silence. A silence that tore at him.

"Mercy! It's all right to come out now!" he hollered, his voice rising with fear. He pounded on the plank door again, more urgently. "Billy, you in there, boy? Asa? Can you hear me?"

Not a sound.

Heedless of how precious glass was in these parts, he thrust the butt of his gun through the kitchen window. She had to be here—and she had to be alive! He would hunt those Cheyenne down and slaughter them all himself if Mercy Monroe had lived these six years on the plains in vain.

Mercy jerked awake, instinctively wrapping an arm around her belly and then reaching for Billy in the darkness. What was that sound? Had the Cheyenne come back to finish them off?

Asa and Billy moaned, and the dogs stood to shake themselves.

"How long have we—"

"Shhh!" Mercy insisted, afraid to speak loudly enough that their upstairs intruder might find them. The candle had guttered out long ago, and they were drowsy from lack of air and sleep. "I think I hear footsteps. Right above—"

"Mercy? Billy? It's Mike Malloy," came a voice that made her choke with emotion. "You can come out now! Where are you?"

251

"Down here!" she rasped, struggling to her feet.

"Mike! Open the trapdoor—under the rug!" Billy yelled. He was already groping for the rope ladder that dangled in the darkness.

Rapid footfalls—a creak of hinges—and then daylight! And a face they knew framed in the opening above them.

"Come on out of there—"

"Here—take Snowy!" Billy said, thrusting the wiggling dog toward Mike. Spot was handed up next, and then Billy climbed up.

"Praise God, didn't I tell you He'd send us a sign?" Asa rasped. "Now let me steady that ladder while you—"

But Mercy was already halfway up the swaying rope, fighting a stomach that rumbled and a head that spun like a top.

"Michael! Michael Malloy, you're an angel!" she panted as he grabbed her hands and pulled her up. He did appear to have a halo, with the light from the windows shining in his hair. "The Cheyenne attacked before we knew . . . Judd and Iry and Nathaniel ran in from the cornfield to . . . oh, please tell me you've found them! Please tell me they're safe and they'll recover from—"

But his expression said otherwise.

She was still grasping Michael's hands as she stepped onto the puncheon floor . . . the floor Judd had cut and laid himself six years ago when they'd made this their home.

Mercy swallowed hard. She was vaguely aware of the two dogs scurrying past her toward the open door, and Asa faltering as Billy helped him out of the cellar, but all she could see was Malloy's blue-gray eyes. The way they didn't waver as they got wet and shiny. The way his sandy mustache didn't flicker with the grin he always flashed at her. The way his Adam's apple bobbed with words he had to say but couldn't.

She crumpled; her heart and mind and soul shut down before she fell against him. A single sob racked his body—a body that felt shorter and smaller and more compact than she was used to, but she leaned into his embrace anyway. It was better than collapsing.

"What happened?" she asked, needing to know while she could still manage rational thought.

"You don't want to know, Mercy," he rasped. "I drove the stage up the road and—"

"Oh, my Lord, all those people need to eat and use the—"

He grabbed her to keep her from rushing to the kitchen. Hysteria would set in soon unless he stopped it.

"They're fine," he stated, gazing into the depths of eyes already denying what she knew inside. "I sent them back to help Elizabeth, and to tell Reverend Larsen we'd be needing him."

Her mouth fell open but no sound came out. "Elizabeth, too? So—so all three men—?"

"I—I'm so sorry, Mercy, but yes—those damned savages—"

He paused, crushing her closer than he had a right to. But he knew no other way to deal with a grief that already scorched him. Knew no sane way to tell this woman the truth she would be determined to hear.

"What they did was unspeakable," he finally whispered. It was all the voice he could muster as the grisly recollections came rushing back. "I—I put them in the barn, until we can make their coffins and dig the graves—"

"I have to see him, Michael. I have to prepare him for burial."

Her voice sounded firm with purpose, and he pulled away more forcefully than he intended. "No!" he cried. "No one should ever see another human being in such a . . . let alone see her husband that way."

Mike recognized the glassy look in her eyes. It signified the state folks entered when they functioned from need alone, one task drawing them to the next because they couldn't think about the realities they faced. Mercy Monroe had already known her husband was dead—what else did she have to think about, all those hours in that cellar when Judd didn't come for her? So now she was engrossing herself in the practical necessities.

But he couldn't allow her to witness what the savages had done to the magnificent man that had been Judd Monroe. Nor to her friend's husband, nor to the strapping hired hand who'd worked beside them so faithfully.

And, considering that Billy Bristol had watched as his father got shot down and his twin was snatched away, and then watched his mother ride off with a handsome hustler, *he* didn't need to see Judd's remains, either. Monroe had become the kid's idol, his father figure. Even a boy as resilient as Billy had only so much mental fortitude. And considering how long it took Gabe Getty to recover after a similar loss, Mike simply couldn't risk it.

Mercy needed Billy. And Asa.

And right now, they all needed *him* to set their world back on its broken axis again, so they could at least wobble along.

Glancing over at the boy and the old man, seeing tears but determination, Malloy made some quick decisions. "I want you two to stay with Mercy. Figure out where you want to bury Judd and Nathaniel, because this heat's not doing us any favors. And then, Billy, I'll need you to start digging. All right?"

"Yessir, I can do that." He was fighting to remain calm. Already taking on the burdens that came with being the man of the family, as he'd done with his mother.

"I knew I could count on you." He squeezed the boy's shoulder, looking pointedly at Mrs. Monroe. She'd be the most obstinate about following his instructions. "I'll take water out and clean them up as best I can. Meanwhile, Mercy, I'll be needing clothes for all three of them. We don't know whether Elizabeth will want to bury Ira here or take him home, but I can't just leave any of them—"

"Only if I get to see him after you've dressed him. Otherwise I'm coming out there to prepare him myself." Her brown eyes simmered like coffee left for hours in a pot, and her gaze never wavered. "It's my right, Michael. His last words to me were 'take care of my family.' He died protecting us. I need to tell Judd I love him one more time. Need to tell him . . . good-bye."

There would be no arguing with this woman. Even though Mercedes Monroe was shrinking in on herself with this loss, she would have her way—just as she had prevailed through so many other hardships out here. If he was to keep her friendship and respect, so she would accept his help in the months to come, Malloy knew he couldn't completely protect her from the harsh realities of this life she'd chosen.

It would be a challenge to cleanse the dirt and gore

from that thick black hair—yet only by the grace of God had Judd's scalp remained attached. Mike hoped he could wipe the grimace of a horrendous death from those handsome features, just as he would need to dress and arrange the rest of Judd so his disfigurements didn't show.

"I understand," he finally murmured. "I consider it an honor, and I—I'll do my very best to make him look the way he'd want to for you, Mercy. It'll be my final gift to a fine man. My very good friend."

"'I will say of the Lord, He is my refuge and my fortress. My God, in Him will I trust. Surely He shall deliver thee from the snare of the fowler, and from the. . . .'"

Billy stood staring at the coffin Mike Malloy had pieced together from lumber scraps. It rested in the hole Billy had started digging yesterday, until it got too deep for him to throw the dirt out of. The blisters on his hands still hurt, but nothing was as horrible as knowing Judd was in that makeshift box—and that Nathaniel lay in the one a few feet away. It didn't seem fair that these fine men had met such a horrendous end.

And yet Reverend Larsen was reading about how God took care of those who loved Him. Where was God when those Cheyenne attacked?

"'Thou shalt not be afraid for the terror by night, nor for the arrow that flieth by day; nor for the pestilence that walketh in the darkness, nor for the destruction that wasteth at noonday . . .'"

Now, *there* was a sore point! Arrows and destruction were exactly what this burial was all about, yet the circuit rider had chosen those passages to read over the bodies of men who'd fallen to them! Surely other Psalms and chapters would bring better comfort to folks who'd just lost the mainstay of their family. Billy intended to tell the preacher just how he felt about it, too.

Shielding his eyes from the late-summer sun, Billy glanced around him. Asa looked a hundred years old, hunched and hugging himself, while Mike Malloy stood with his feet apart and his head bowed in stoic respect. On the other side of Billy, Mercy cried quietly into her handkerchief, her face shielded by a brown coal scuttle bonnet. Spot and Snowy sat at Billy's feet, panting and alert, yet subdued by the weight of everyone's sorrow.

Mama had been so helpless at Daddy's service, they'd had to hold her on either side while she walked to and from the grave and the church, sniffling loudly and inhaling her smelling salts. Yet he sensed that Mercedes Monroe grieved more deeply. While Malloy had been cleaning up the bodies, it was this woman in loose brown calico who'd finished digging Judd's grave—until Asa wrestled the shovel from her hands, on account of the baby.

" 'For He shall give His angels charge over thee, to keep thee in all thy ways. They shall bear thee up in their hands, lest thou dash thy foot against a stone.' "

He shall give His angels charge over thee? So where were they, these angels?

Billy scowled, scrunching his bare toes in the dirt. Something seemed desperately wrong about services for a man like Judd Monroe, loved and respected by everyone along this stretch of the Smoky Hill River, when only the four of them marked his passing. The heat had forced them to bury Judd and Nathaniel quickly, before neighbors could all be notified. Elizabeth Barstow had asked Reverend Larsen to bring Iry back with him for a service at their own home. Mercy had offered to provide a grave—to share in her friend's sorrow—but the persnickety Elizabeth refused to bury her husband so close to a Negro.

For *that* remark, Billy had suggested they leave Iry in his messy, mangled state. He would miss Nathaniel Horne fiercely, because the dark giant had a wise, gentle hand with horses and had so patiently taught him to play the guitar. But Mercy had insisted on giving Ira the same respect Judd received, since he would still be alive if he hadn't helped them with their harvest.

Billy didn't see it that way. And only his affection for the woman who'd taken him in kept him from lashing out even now. The circuit rider seemed hideously ignorant of their pain as he mouthed the same useless phrases about God's providence that the preacher back home had pronounced over Daddy.

Such sermons hadn't kept the ranch running then, and he saw no future in them now. Would pretty words get the rest of the corn crop harvested? Would poetic phrases feed the stage passengers—or, more importantly, assure Mercy they'd have enough food to survive the winter?

"I'm so sorry," Reverend Larsen was murmuring, holding Mercy's hands between his own. "Judd was a fine man. An example to us all of how to live out the Lord's words and ways."

Mercy nodded, mumbling her thanks.

But when the circuit rider turned to him, Billy refused to meet his eyes. "If you know anybody who can be *real* help, send him our way, will ya?" he challenged. "Seems to me God lets the strongest and the best get killed, leavin' us weak ones tryin' to get by without them."

His arrow hit its mark—he'd actually left the preacher speechless. "Young man, I understand your frustration with—"

"No, sir, you don't understand *nothin'*!" Billy jerked away from the preacher's touch. "After I lost my own folks—when nobody else would take us in—Judd treated me like I mattered! Called me *son*, even! And when Injuns would come around, needin' food or just curious about us white folks, neither he nor Nathaniel *ever* did anything to provoke an attack! So don't *tell* me God was watchin' out for 'em—or for us!"

He bolted then. Couldn't stand the pain he'd increased in Mercy's red-rimmed eyes. Didn't want to hear Malloy's explanations, either, when they both reached out to comfort him. Into the shadowy barn he raced, with the two dogs following, even as he climbed the ladder to the hot, silent hayloft. Spot and Snowy leaned into him, whimpering as they gazed at him with their soft brown eyes.

Only then did his emptiness overwhelm him. Slinging an arm around each dog, Billy shook with his sobs.

"It certainly wasn't my intent to upset the boy," Reverend Larsen mumbled as he stood beside his wagon.

Mercy glanced sadly toward the barn, knowing exactly how Billy felt. She, too, had trouble reconciling scriptural promises of care and protection with the realities she now faced. "He and Judd were close," she said softly. "And Billy's old enough now to be embarrassed by tears."

"And why wouldn't he be upset?" Malloy added. "Only twelve, and already he's watched two fathers die of violence. It *isn't* fair that Judd and Nathaniel died. And no amount of faith or reassurance makes it easier for any of us."

Reverend Larsen's narrowed eyes suggested he was about to launch into a sermon, so Mercy mustered a smile. "Thank you so much for being here when we needed you, Gregor," she said. "And please express my sorrow to Elizabeth. I hate it that Iry died while he was helping with our harvest. I imagine she feels we're partly to blame."

With that, the circuit rider climbed to the seat of his wagon and turned to Mike Malloy. "It was kind of you to prepare Ira's body and build his coffin. I'm sure she'll appreciate that, even if she won't say so."

He clucked to his horse, and as the wagon approached the road, Mercy winced at the crude box containing Ira Barstow's remains. Michael had done his best, but by the time he'd constructed Judd's and Nathaniel's coffins, he was piecing together slats from old crates and their Sunday service benches. Nothing was easy out here.

And it was about to get a lot more difficult.

"You go along and see to Mr. Billy, now." Asa's gentle voice interrupted her thoughts.

She blinked. The kind old man was giving her a reason to leave while he and Mike filled in the two gaping graves. "All right. Thank you—thank you both, for all you've done for me—"

"There's nothing I can do to repay you and Mr. Judd for your kindness," Asa replied with a sad smile. "You'd best be getting out of this hot sun now, Miss Mercy. Mr. Judd knew what he was saying when he told you to take care of yourself, and I intend to see to that."

It felt exceptionally warm for late September, and she couldn't wait to take off her bonnet. On the way to the barn, she dipped up water from the rain barrel and drank deeply, wondering what she could say to set things right for Billy. Pausing inside the door, she listened . . . heard the faint rustling of hay as the two dogs came to peer over the edge of the loft. Very carefully she climbed the ladder, stopping when she caught sight of Billy.

He'd cried himself to sleep. He was curled into a half-sitting position, with his arm on a bale and his head resting on it, his breathing deep and even. A shaft of sunlight came through a crack in the roof to make his coppery hair glow like an ember. His face shone with the radiance of an angel in a sacred painting.

Mercy held her breath, for as she gazed at this fortuitous scene, she knew exactly what she needed to say. Exactly what this burdened young man needed to hear.

She eased herself onto a bale near him, quietly murmuring to the dogs. They were compact black-and-white packages of compassion, aware that the scent of blood in the yard had changed everything while they'd huddled in the cellar. They could love Billy in a way she could not, and for that she was grateful.

He stirred, and she put on a smile. She let him stretch and regain his bearings—which quickly put a frown on his face.

"I s'pose you come up here to get after me for the way I gave Reverend Larsen the what-for," he began, his blue eyes wet and defiant. "But it was true! He had no call to read those verses about not bein' hit by arrows and destruction! About angels takin' such good care of us!"

261

His voice cracked, and Mercy's heart went out to him. No longer the boy who would allow her to hold him, he was not yet a man. Not only had he lost his family, he'd forfeited his childhood.

As he swatted straw from his auburn hair, she made a vow: In the weeks ahead, when she saw no other reason to go on, Billy Bristol would become her purpose. Her reason for going forward, no matter how badly she wanted to retreat into the darkness of her grief.

"You're absolutely right," she said in a low voice. "Everything inside me railed against the words he read. Because, in our situation, they were very hard to draw comfort from. Judd would've chosen better. He had a way of knowing just what people needed to hear, didn't he?"

Billy swallowed so hard, his Adam's apple bobbed. "Yes, ma'am, he did. Now that you mention it, I don't reckon he liked hearin' those passages any better'n we did."

"And I'm sure Gregor chose them to make us stronger. To reassure us of God's love and protection, now that we don't have Judd and Nathaniel looking out for us," she continued. "He's grieving, too, you know. Every time he comes here for services, he'll remember how Judd read aloud with such power and conviction. He feels humbled by that. Confidence isn't Gregor's strong suit."

As she'd hoped, Billy sat staring ahead of him, fondling the dogs as he considered this.

"But the part about giving His angels charge over us?" Mercy took a deep breath, hoping she expressed this part effectively—knowing she would never possess Judd's unstudied eloquence. "I've heard that passage for years, but today I finally realized what it means. It has nothing to do with round-faced cherubs coming down through the clouds with a flutter of their wings. It's about real live people. You and me, Michael and Asa—and even these dogs."

Billy was looking doubtful, so she disregarded the lump in her throat to make her point.

"We are angels for each other, Billy. Just as Judd was the angel who took you and your sister in, and Michael was the one who brought Christine home," she said, her voice barely a whisper now. "And *you* will be the angel who takes charge of me. When I stumble and just can't make it up one more time, Judd will whisper in your ear and you'll know what to do. Am I right?"

His eyes widened in the dimness. And then he nodded. Tears made two shiny trails down his face as comprehension dawned: the promise she and Judd entered into the day he came here had just been enlarged. She had asked Billy to become a man, and he had agreed.

She stood up, brushing her skirt. "Take all the time you need with your sadness, sweetheart. It's going to be a long, hard winter. I have no idea how we'll harvest the rest of that corn, or supply the stagecoaches with fresh horses, but I know we'll get by somehow. We simply must."

Chapter Twenty-four

A few days later Mercy looked out to see horses—half a dozen or more! And they were tethered to a wagon George Clark was driving with Rachel and Emma and Gabriel. Behind them came Clyde and Nell Fergus, with three more Morgans trotting proudly behind their buckboard. Mercy's heart pounded at the sight of the animals, for the empty, silent corrals had been a painful reminder of Judd's death.

But then she clutched herself. Did they know about the attack? Had they survived it themselves?

And what would she say to them? While she'd always enjoyed their company, it was quite a different thing to accept their condolences—especially now that she couldn't hide her swelling belly.

Asa looked up from the turnips he was peeling. "Well, now—there's a sight for sore eyes! We'd best get on out there—"

"But I look frightful," she whimpered. "I'm just getting used to Judd being gone, and now they'll dredge the attack up all over again. Asking questions, and feeling sorry for me—"

"Missy, it's too soon for you to be used to anything." He looked at her with wise old eyes that conveyed a deep sadness. "That's part of the package when somebody dies. You just get the wound to stop bleedin'— just get accustomed to the pain—and then somebody scratches off the scab. They don't mean to make you feel bad again, that's just how it works."

He opened the kitchen door, giving her no chance to hang back as her neighbors climbed down from their wagons. "And as for the baby, well, isn't that just about the happiest thing they've heard in a while? Far as we know, they barely escaped with their own lives, and it's time to hear their stories."

She took a deep breath. She hadn't combed her hair today, and it was too late to remedy her neglect. It took all her energy to step outside behind Asa, who immediately went to open the corral gates.

"Mighty fine to see you folks—and these horses!" he sang out.

Clyde Fergus was untying the tethers, looking around the yard. "Yeah, when we found them grazing along the river, we figured they had to belong here. Guess those Southern Cheyenne found your place, too, eh?"

"Yessir. They killed Mr. Judd and Nathaniel. If Mercy and Billy and I hadn't scrambled into the cellar, we'd be gone, too."

Everything went so quiet, Mercy felt she'd been rendered invisible. The Ferguses and the Clarks slowly looked over to where she was standing, but they didn't seem to *see* her. Billy came around from behind the barn, carrying a crock of butter from the springhouse. He froze when he saw the small flock of neighbors wearing the dazed expressions of mute, confused sheep. When he caught sight of his colt among the horses, however, he ran to grab the lead ropes from George's hand.

In slow motion, George removed his hat and glanced at Clyde. "That explains why Judd didn't come looking for those horses," he mumbled. "We had to fix a hole in the roof where the Cheyenne's fiery arrows landed, and—"

"Had to butcher what hogs we could, after those savages shot 'em up—"

"Oh, would you listen to yourselves!" Nell cried as she rushed forward. "Mercy just lost her husband and you're babbling on about hogs and—oh, honey, I'm so sorry! So very, very sorry."

"And there's a baby!" Emma exclaimed. "She's in the family way, Gabriel! Didn't I betcha?"

Was she suddenly caught up in a three-ringed circus? Nell and Rachel were crying, both talking at once about how awful it must be to lose such a devoted man, while their husbands quietly conferred with Asa at the corral gate. Hattie and Boots had spotted Billy's dogs and were barking gleefully, chasing them across the yard. Emma bounded up beside Mercy to gawk at the way her dress stuck out in front.

Mercy felt like a freak in a side show. Maybe now that they knew about Judd, they'd go home and leave her to her quiet house and her desperate thoughts. And her messy hair.

"We brought dinner," Nell said somberly, "because we suspected you'd had trouble. And, quite frankly, we thought it might be best to cancel the services and party next week, in case those savages are still watching us. Waiting to catch us on the road after dark."

"You're absolutely right," Mercy managed. "Bad enough Iry Barstow was killed here while he was helping Judd harvest the corn."

The women's jaws dropped. "Ira, too? And Elizabeth with four children—"

"Five," Emma piped up. "*She's* got a bun in the oven, too!"

"Where are your manners, young lady?" Scowling, Rachel Clark planted her hands on her daughter's shoulders. "If you're going to act like a child, you can just go play in the caves—you and your smart mouth! Billy's in a bad way, too, with Judd gone. You be kind to that poor boy."

Emma's face crumpled. Then she pivoted and stalked toward the barn.

"It's good those three have each other," Mercy remarked, watching the sway of the girl's calico dress. "They're at an awkward age. Acting like adults one moment, and then saying something childish the next."

Emma's mother nodded, looking pale and exasperated. "I'm sorry about the way she was staring. She's been fascinated by babies and how they're made, of late. It's downright embarrassing."

Nell Fergus, a swarthy, stalwart woman who'd never had children, smiled sympathetically. "And how will you raise this baby all by yourself, Mercy?"

Mercy longed for another of Emma's eruptions of curiosity, or for Billy to come over with that butter—anything to distract them from Nell's pointed question. For as she looked at these two women, who still had husbands and families intact, Mercy suddenly had nothing to say.

* * *

"I better warn you that Emma made the pie we brought," Gabe said as he and Billy sat against the barn, chewing blades of grass. He chuckled as Hattie nipped Spot, which started the dogs tussling in the dust. "The pumpkin filling's not bad, but you might as well toss the crust up in the air to use for target practice. Half an inch thick, I'm thinking."

Billy groaned, and then noticed the cook in question coming their way. "Guess I'm lucky Christine never went through that, since Beulah Mae wanted *nobody* in her kitchen. Maybe I just won't eat no pie today."

"Emma might shove it down your throat, then. She made that pie to remember your birthday next week." Billy's slender friend elbowed him, rolling his eyes. "She's sweet on you, Billy."

"*Sweet* on me?" He spat in the dirt to emphasize his disgust. "Well, I ain't sweet on her! Whatever possessed her to—"

"Yes, you are, Mr. Bristol. You don't realize how moony you act—"

"Do not!"

"Do, too!"

"Do not, not, NOT! Ya hear me?"

Adjusting his eyeglasses, Gabe nodded pointedly at their oncoming intruder. "So how long were you down in that root cellar, Billy? Could you hear the Indian attack going on?"

Billy tried to focus on Emma's swaying blond hair as she walked—or on her big blue eyes when she locked her gaze on him. Anything to forget that one triumphant war whoop, followed by an unearthly silence, when all they could do was wait in the cellar. And wonder.

"Most of a day," he replied. "Not near as long as you hid behind them bins that time, Gabe."

"He wasn't in any hurry to go down in the cellar with us this time," Emma said. She stopped in front of Billy, smugly crossing her arms. "We saw those Injuns coming in time to disappear, just like nobody was home. So they rode on to the next place, I guess. Shot arrows into a few hogs as they passed through, was all."

Billy closed his eyes against this image. In his mind, those arrows felled Judd and Nathaniel—and it was more than he could bear, to think of them writhing in agony while he'd been safe in the cellar. "Yeah, well, Judd and Nathaniel and Iry Barstow was out threshing the corn when them Injuns charged in from outta nowhere. Mercy shooed us into the house 'cause Judd told her to, so—so—"

He swallowed the lump that made his voice jump; separated the two dogs snarling playfully beside him so Emma wouldn't see his wet eyes. He fixed a phony-feeling smile on his face, but then grinned with quick inspiration.

"Gabe says you been makin' pies lately," he remarked in a hopeful tone. "Since the men're lookin' over the rest of the corn crop, and the women're talking to Mercy, I'm thinkin' it's the perfect time to snitch us a little dessert. Slip on out to your wagon and get that pie for us, Emma."

She smiled with the mischief of his idea, but then her brow puckered. Was he trying to get rid of her?

"So how'll we cut it?" Emma looked over her shoulder, to plan her path to the wagon. "Can't just tear into it with—"

"Asa gave me Nathaniel's knife. To remember him by—and in case I ever need to use it."

His two friends went silent with awed respect as he lifted his pant leg to slip the sheathed blade from inside his boot.

"Holy smokes," Gabe breathed. "That's the wickedest thing I ever seen."

The eight-inch blade glinted in the sunlight. Billy gripped its handle, wishing for the power and protection the knife represented. Wishing it hadn't been lying useless in Nathaniel's quarters in the loft on the day of the attack.

"Nope," he countered. "The wickedest thing you and I ever seen was the way men with murderin' hearts tore apart families who did nothin' to deserve it. I promised on Judd's grave that someday I'll make them killers pay for what they've done—to *both* my families. Are you with me on this, Mr. Getty?"

Gabe sat taller, his face somber with thought. He looked older and wiser than his nine years—more like an early version of Abraham Lincoln than a kid. "I'm not much of a fighter, Billy," he murmured. "But by golly, you're right! If we don't halt these predators in their tracks, why—they'll just keep taking advantage of us!"

"We oughta make a pact," Billy whispered. It felt good to hear Gabe's resounding agreement; the fire of a friend's conviction. "Blood brothers?"

The boy beside him hesitated when the knife's edge caught the sunlight, but he rolled up his shirtsleeve. "Blood brothers. Just like the Indians do it."

"I'm not watchin' this." Emma's hair and skirt swirled behind her as she turned to go. "If you cut off your fool arms with that thing, don't come cryin' to me!"

* * *

Mike Malloy saw the wagons in Mercy's yard and brought his horse to a halt, planning his strategy. Though he wasn't surprised that neighbors had come to her aid, he hadn't planned on parading his own assistance in front of folks who would jump to conclusions.

His intentions were perfectly honorable.

He just wasn't crazy about the gossip this might cause, or about making Mercy react to his gift in front of other people. Bad enough that he felt as jittery as a kid at his first dance. Even though he was doing the right thing—helping her because Judd would expect nothing less—he'd be living with the consequences of whatever Mrs. Monroe said or did today. Time was short, before she had to be ready for winter, but people's memories were not.

Thinking he could leave his surprises in a grove east of the yard until the others cleared out, Malloy clucked to his horse. The two cows he'd brought had other ideas, however. When the wagon bumped against the ruts in the road, they began to bawl and balk. Four barking border collies—and the three kids they belonged to—immediately came running out to greet him.

So much for secrets.

"Hey there, Michael Malloy!" Emma called out. "We're just fixin' to eat! Can ya come and join us? Are those cows a present for Mercy?"

The girl looked more grown up every time he saw her, but she still had all the subtlety of a six-year-old. Those blue eyes didn't miss a trick, so he'd better lay his cards on the table. More or less.

"How do you suppose she and Billy will get by without milk and butter?" he asked. He had to drive slowly, with four dogs running in circles around him, nipping at the cows in their excitement. "In a few days, another stagecoach'll come through and . . . well! I see some of the horses are back!"

"Yessir—and Mr. Lincoln, too! The Ferguses and the Clarks brung 'em!" Billy scrambled up onto the moving wagon's seat beside Mike, looking vastly improved by the company of his friends. "George and Clyde're gonna hitch up the threshing machine after we eat and get some more of the corn in—"

Damn. That was why he'd brought this Belgian.

"—and the ladies're gonna help Mercy take care of Judd's clothes and such."

Which meant she'd be in no mood to hear what *he* had to say. Mike flashed a smile at the redhead beside him, and then his eyebrows flew up. "What happened to your arm, Billy? Looks like you fought with a knife and the knife won."

The boy's face, now lengthening with adolescence, set in a defiant smile. "That's where me and Gabe just made a blood-brother pact," he announced proudly. "Someday those Border Ruffians and the Injuns are gonna pay for wipin' out our families. We're gonna see justice done!"

"Better justice than retribution and revenge," Malloy replied pointedly. He waved to the lanky kid walking just ahead of him. Gabe was wiping a similar gash with his spit and then his shirtsleeve as he and Emma headed for the house. "And meanwhile, you'll both have scars the rest of your days to remind you of this decision."

Malloy waited a moment longer so Gabe and Emma would be out of earshot. "Now—before she catches sight of me—how's Mercy doing?"

Billy's expression lost its shine. He speared his fingers through his unruly red hair. "Okay, I guess," he said in a low voice. "She don't say much. I can't think she was real happy to see these folks show up to-day—'cept they brought back some of the horses."

"They had to find out about Judd and Nathaniel sooner or later. But that doesn't mean it's easy."

"You're double-dog right about that part." As they got close to where the other wagons were parked, Billy looked behind them. "Thanks for these cows, Mr. Malloy. We'll pay you for 'em when we get the corn sold."

Billy's face was an open book; a story of fear and grief no boy about to turn thirteen should know. So Mike took his time about wrapping the reins on their hook, while Emma and her cousin entered the house. He sensed this boy needed to talk about things. And he was just the man who wanted to listen—because he cared, and because Billy would fill him in on things he needed to know about Mercy.

"You know . . . it's like Mercy realizes that Judd and Nathaniel—and the cow—got slaughtered the other day, but she doesn't seem to *do* nothin' about it," Billy said in a shaky voice. "Sets on the stoop and stares a lot. I—I'm afraid winter's gonna catch her unawares. Asa and me, we've been gatherin' buffalo chips and gettin' the rest of the garden picked, but with two men gone—"

"That's why I'm here, Billy."

Mike looked into blue eyes that burned bright with concern, and it occurred to him that bringing this abandoned boy to the Monroe place might have been the best thing that could have happened for all of them.

"The way I see it, it's up to you and me to take up that slack," Mike said quietly. "Mercy's still in shock. Still sadder than any of us can imagine. But she's got a

273

baby to think of, and we have to keep her strong and fit, so the birthing goes well."

The boy glanced away, as though the prospect of Mercy growing weak—maybe dying in childbirth—was a whole new weight upon his young shoulders.

"It'll be all right, Billy," Mike said, hoping he sounded convincing. "Now let's get these cows tethered, and we'll pitch in to help these generous neighbors while they're here. What Mercy has to know, though, is that after everyone else goes back to tend their own places and live their own lives, she can depend on us."

Billy's smile crept back, giving a hint of the fine, considerate man he would become. "Double-dog *right* she can," he stated—and he stuck out his hand to shake on their agreement.

Mike smiled, sharing the kid's grip.

If only Mercy would be this easy to convince.

Chapter Twenty-five

Malloy thought the meal would never end. While Emma's flirtation with Billy relieved the heavy atmosphere in Mercy's front room, the other guests at her table kept eyeing him. Fishing for information that had traveled along the telegraph wires and Wells Fargo line, but mostly being just plain nosy.

Well, he'd dealt with contrary passengers for years. He could answer these people's questions—or not.

"Thought you'd be driving today," George Clark said. "Didn't quit your job, did you?"

Mike smiled. That was closer to the truth than they needed to know. "It's like I told you earlier," he hedged, watching Mercy from the corner of his eye. "Now that Abilene's a railhead, and the tracks go most of the way across Kansas, Wells Fargo's not making as many runs. Can't compete against that Iron Horse for speed and convenience when it comes to carrying people."

Mrs. Fergus clucked. "Why would anyone ride that

bumpy road and eat dust when they could *enjoy* watching the countryside from the train?"

"My point exactly. Plus the train provides a way to haul corn, wheat, and cattle to market," Malloy continued. "It's certainly turned Abilene into a boom town."

"Yeah, the paper's saying Hell is in session, what with all those cowpokes carousing in the saloons these days," Clyde joined in. "Not a place to take your wife and children, that's for sure!"

Mercy's brow puckered in thought. When she fixed her red-rimmed eyes on him, Mike badly wanted to take her in his arms and tell her that things would get better. These well-meaning neighbors probably sensed his intentions, the way they were dawdling over coffee and pumpkin pie with a crust too thick to chew.

"Are you saying we'll no longer have the income from providing horses and food for the stage line?" Mercy asked. Worry edged her voice, as though her husband had never mentioned these financial matters.

"That day'll come, yes," Mike said gently. "Which is why Judd planted more corn this year, and has experimented with that new strain of Russian wheat. I've sown several acres of Turkey Red myself, figuring that by this time next year I won't be driving much."

By this time next year, Mercy Monroe, I hope to be your husband.

He wanted to look deep into those mournful brown eyes and tell her that straight out; wanted to clasp those small, strong hands between his own and tell her of his plans. But that would have to wait.

As he got up from the table with the other men, he felt Mercy's gaze on him. Did she want to talk? Was she surprised—or impressed—that he'd become a landowner looking toward a more lucrative future?

Malloy didn't dare say more than a thank-you for the meal. Her neighbor ladies were already bursting with curiosity, ready to swoop like two magpies on the tidbits he'd tossed out—he, a single man, watching out for a good friend's widow.

It was hours later when he, Clyde Fergus, and George Clark finished with a cornfield and called it a day. From the basin in the shade, where they drank and then doused themselves with cool water, Mike saw Mercy coming out the kitchen door to lean against the side of the house. She shuddered with a sob, shaken by the painful task of sorting through Judd's belongings. Probably also smarting from remarks her friends had made without realizing how deep her emotional wounds were.

He wiped his face and bare chest with his shirt. If he couldn't provide the care and compassion she needed, well—he had no business being here, did he? And if these neighbors had their suspicions about him giving her that comfort, well—he couldn't live his life by their opinions, seeking their approval. Mercy Monroe had been dealt a losing hand of late, and he hoped to turn her luck around. That was all that mattered; this brave, hardworking woman needed to *receive* kindness, after years of giving it to everyone else.

So he strode toward her, his heart pounding. He made enough noise and came at her from a visible angle, much like he'd approach a skittish mare. She needed to see he was coming straight on, rather than sneaking up on her at a vulnerable moment.

Mercy looked his way, blinking. Slowly she raised her hand, to brush back the hair that had come loose from its ribbon. Lord, but she was pretty, even in her grief. Graceful, even with Judd's child making her thick in the middle.

He knew the two men were watching him from the barn, just as their wives would listen from inside, near the open window. But he had to state his case. A month from now the snow could be blowing.

He stopped in front of her, drawn in by those doe-like eyes, which hadn't dropped their gaze. "Are you all right?" he whispered.

What a stupid question! She was anything but all right.

Yet her lips lifted in a half-smile of understanding. "No. But Nell and Rachel are helping in the only way they know how, whether I'm ready to pack away Judd's clothes or not," she replied. "It's better than trying to come up with conversation while we wait for you men to finish."

Mike nodded, admiring her honesty. "Your crop's real good. I'll come back tomorrow and finish that last field, so I can haul it into Abilene for you."

"You'll do no such thing, Michael Malloy."

He blinked, aware that she'd just refused his help—and that he was wadding his shirt between his hands rather than wearing it. "Mercy, if you wait much longer, the frost—"

"I see no sense in your going all the way home and coming back, when you could bunk in the barn," she informed him. "And maybe I should hang on to some of that crop. Grind it into cornmeal. It might be what we eat this winter."

A muffled sound came from the house. Oh, but they were clucking in there, and it was Mercy's plainspoken practicality that ruffled their feathers.

But she was listening to him. Making decisions without leaning on her women friends or wallowing in self-pity. Mike knew then that beneath her careworn appearance, this fine woman was stronger than she seemed. Stronger than any of them here, truth be told.

"If you think that'll be all right," he replied, pointedly looking toward the neighbors on either side of their conversation, "then I'd be pleased to stay over. It'd mean Billy and Asa and I would have those extra hours of daylight to finish your fieldwork tomorrow."

"Thank you, Michael. Your help means more than I can say."

She leaned toward him, making his pulse pause as she held her belly. Mercy stood so close, and looked at him so earnestly, Malloy wondered if she was about to steal his thunder and mention marriage. Coming from an influential Eastern family that believed in educating its women, Mercedes Monroe was known for stating opinions and taking actions lesser women considered improper.

He held his breath. Though he wasn't any more exposed than Clyde and George had been at the washbasin, right now he felt downright naked.

"You're a fine young man, Michael. An angel," she murmured.

His stomach kicked like a frisky colt. And coming from her, his full name sounded potent and powerful rather than like a starched collar his mother had buttoned on him when he was born.

"You have my best interests at heart—and your heart's as big as all of Kansas," she went on quietly. "And I know you've always admired the way I made a cozy home for Judd and put good food on his table."

He swallowed. The other shoe was about to drop, and he hadn't gotten a word in edgewise.

"But I won't marry you, Mr. Malloy. Not because these neighbors will be scandalized by your proposing so soon," she said so Nell and Rachel could hear it on the other side of the log wall, "but because right now, I can't give you the love and devotion you're looking for.

"Judd took my very soul to the grave with him. What little energy and ambition I have left, I'm devoting to his baby, and to Billy and Christine," she went on with quiet conviction. "It was his last request, and I'll honor it. An admirable man like you deserves a whole woman, Michael."

Mike's heart thudded in his chest. She'd given the most respectable of reasons, but still—she'd refused him before he could even state his case.

"Mercy, I understand—"

"No, you don't."

Her sad smile wrapped around his heart and squeezed until her pain made him lightheaded. He nodded mutely—because she was right, and because there would be no wheedling or sweet-talking Mercy Monroe into seeing his side.

She was no ordinary woman. Which was why he wanted her. "I'll ask you anyway, you know. My reasons are as right as yours," he replied.

"You're a persistent man. I've always admired the way you live your convictions." Her face softened enough to relieve the etchings of grief around her eyes. "Where would I be if you hadn't insisted we give the Bristol children a home?"

He chuckled, shrugging into his shirt. "The girl's been a hard pill to swallow. I probably brought you more trouble than she's worth."

"She'll come around." Mercy looked off toward the trees along the river where Gabe and Emma and Billy were tossing sticks for the dogs. "Billy's been my mainstay through this ordeal. And with Asa to help me cook for the stage passengers, we'll be fine this winter, Michael. Honestly, I'll ask for your help if I need it."

It sounded fine, as far as it went. Yet when his fingers finished with his shirt buttons, they found the side of Mercy's face and then slipped beneath her warm, silky hair. He knew he should stop there, but he couldn't. Mike kissed her on the lips, his other hand finding the swell of her belly to span it protectively. He wanted to raise this child every bit as badly as he longed to plant his own in its place. And he refused to be ashamed of such desires!

"I want to do more than help, Mercy," he breathed as he broke away. "I love you. And I intend to have the last word on that!"

"I suspect this'll be the last of the longhorns we'll see for the season." Mike shifted in his saddle, ready to ride if any of those rangy beasts turned cantankerous. "They're saying Abilene did such a booming business this year, all the stores are closing for the winter. Going to restock—and even enlarge! Getting ready for a stupendous season next year."

Mercy shielded her eyes from the late-October sun, watching Billy, Gabe, and the four dogs escort the small herd along the road. "I've laid in all the supplies I have room for, so let the stores close. It'll give decent people a rest from all the carousing and lawlessness. At least these cattle were kind enough to leave me a little more fuel."

Malloy smiled. Though the woman beside him on the horse was by no means bubbling over with mirth yet, she could find a silver lining in the clouds of dust—and the cow pies—caused by the cattle drives.

"Sure glad that mama dog had her pups in your barn. Saved you from a lot of damage."

"And I can't imagine those two boys without their constant companions." Mercy chuckled. "I'm not supposed to know it, but Spot and Snowy sleep upstairs. I've told Asa to bunk up there for the winter, too. No sense in him being cold and lonely in the barn."

"You want him nearby to make your breakfast every morning," Malloy teased. "I hear you've become a regular sleepyhead. Never would've believed that about the tireless saint of the stagecoaching table."

Her sigh sounded a little weary even now, and he hoped he hadn't overstepped her threshold for humor.

"It's the baby, I guess. The doctor pronounced me healthy, but warned me that all those hours on my feet would take their toll."

"Now, there's an open invitation." Leaning down, Mike grinned rakishly to make her smile back. "If I were your husband, I could massage those tired legs and rub your aching back . . . right here, where you're going to sway forward when that baby gets bigger."

His hand drifted down to the spot he spoke of, pressing firmly at the base of her spine. When she leaned into his touch, hope ignited inside him.

"If you were my husband, Michael Malloy, I'd keep you awake at night with my tossing and turning," she challenged. "I'd exasperate you with my quicksilver mood changes, and my crying for no apparent reason—"

"And I'd rejoice that it was me you shared it all with." He lowered his face until their noses almost touched. "I'd chase away those moods and tears, so you would rejoice in me, as well. Marry me, Mercy. We'd be happy—"

Her kiss nearly toppled him from his horse.

His hand slipped behind her head, to hold her as he savored her sweet acceptance—and so she couldn't break away until he'd shown her exactly how much he wanted her, how desirable he found her. Mercy's mouth responded so eagerly, his pulse drowned out the shuffling of the last cattle and the possibility that two boys might be watching them. All he knew was the silk of her lips and the warmth of her breath . . . and the sigh that said she'd soon be his wife.

"Well now, Miz Monroe!" a shrill voice called out. "So it's true you didn't waste any time findin' a replacement for Judd."

Mercy jerked away from Mike's embrace to see a surrey coming into the yard—and a very smug smile on Elizabeth Barstow's face. Mercy's cheeks burned with embarrassment, yet she wanted to hurl a fresh cow pie at this obnoxious woman.

"Hello, Elizabeth," she managed, wondering once again why she'd once considered this neighbor a good friend.

And it wasn't as if the widow Barstow was driving that jaunty surrey herself; the man beside her wore a fine vested suit with a wide-brimmed hat that had a huge ruby centered in its band. Between his portly build and her advancing pregnancy, it was a wonder the seat supported them. Mercy felt sorry for that fine-boned pony with the braided mane.

Mike rode forward, his expression as stiff as the arm he extended. "Don't believe we've met," he said, eyeing the driver. "I'm Mike Malloy. And this fine woman is Mercedes Monroe."

"Obadiah Jones," the man crowed with a heavy Texas accent. "Come up here to sell my cattle, and come away with a purty little heifer. Well, a *bred* heifer," he added with a sugary smile at Elizabeth.

"Obie and I got married yesterday," she twittered, displaying another ruby that nearly hid her finger. "And after we left the justice of the peace, why, Obie bought us some furniture to start our new life on his ranch in Texas."

Her eyelashes fluttered with the exhilaration of it all, until she looked down from her surrey seat again. "I just had to come say good-bye, Mercy, and wish you well. Although you've obviously settled for sod busting on the prairie, with this fellow who runs the ruts for a living."

Mercy didn't know whether to slap Elizabeth or spit in her fleshy face. She stepped back, her thoughts spinning like a dog chasing its tail.

"Good-bye, Elizabeth," she replied coolly. "And thank you for coming. I was afraid that Ira's dying here had driven a wedge in our friendship. It's good to see you've recovered so completely—and so very quickly!—from your loss."

Mercy crossed her arms over her bulging belly to signal the end of the conversation—and so she wouldn't cry and cuss, while this insolent woman could witness it. With a nod, Mr. Jones clucked at his pretty pony.

The surrey had barely made it to the road before Mercy cut loose. "Of all the vile—repulsive—disgraceful—"

"That was the most disgusting display of hypocrisy I've ever seen," Mike muttered, dismounting. "If you hadn't sent them packing, I would have."

He pulled the bandana from his pocket and gently wiped her tears, as sorry for the hurt and confusion clouding her huge brown eyes as for the guilt he sensed would plague her for days.

"We've done nothing wrong or dishonorable, honey," he whispered. "Frankly, I could never figure out what Iry saw in that high-toned woman."

"She must've charmed him the same way she latched on to *Obie*," Mercy sputtered.

"And *Obie* will regret this hasty hitching by the time he gets that woman settled in Texas," Malloy said. "Fast as this happened, they neither one know what they've gotten themselves into."

"And what about those four children? Where have *they* been during this whirlwind courtship?" Blowing loudly into Mike's bandana, she composed herself again. "Aunt Agatha always taught us that if you can't wish someone well, you can hope she'll get what she so richly deserves. Politely, of course."

He wanted to laugh with her, but he sensed her retreat into sadness, shadowed by guilt and heartache that had nothing to do with him. It was part of her grieving, dredged up afresh by Elizabeth. Whatever he said would only rekindle her flaring emotions.

"Why don't you rest awhile, Mercy?" he suggested gently. "I'll be back as soon as I've had a little talk with that woman."

Her eyes widened. "You're not going to make her apologize?"

"No. I'm going to buy her land. Before somebody else snatches it up."

Chapter Twenty-six

December 18, 1867

Happy Birthday, Sis!

And Merry Christmas, while I'm at it. It's been a while since we've heard from you, so I'm guessing you've been busy with things at the Academy. Maybe going to parties in those dresses you took along, or new ones you've made since then. Mercy hasn't felt much like writing, so I'll fill you in on some big changes out this way.

First, the Cheyenne attack. A dozen pages can't describe what it was like down in the cellar with Asa, Mercy, and the two dogs while we heard those war whoops overhead. Judd and Nathaniel gave their lives protecting us, and it was a sorry day when we stood over those graves. If it hadn't been for Mike Malloy, I'm not sure what awful things we'd have seen. He took it hard—we all did. He's been helping Mercy keep this place going, which is giving the neighbors a lot to talk about. Asa and I just let them talk. Malloy at least cares enough to DO something.

Then, end of October, Elizabeth Barstow stopped by with her new husband. (Forgot to tell you that Iry died here, in the Cheyenne attack.) Fattest old snake you ever saw: While she was telling about going to Texas with this cattle baron, she was actually hissing about how stupid Mercy was to stay here on the homestead—and how sinful, letting Mike kiss her. But then, I'm sure you remember that woman's forked tongue.

Anyway, Mike went right on over to buy the Barstow land. Did you know he already had a place he was farming? I guess when he wasn't driving these past couple years, he was planting wheat and grazing cattle. Now he's quit Wells Fargo altogether. Says the stagecoaches won't run much longer, on account of the railway goes almost all the way to Denver.

Mercy doesn't know it yet, but he's going to build a white frame house with a picket fence on the parcel of his land nearest Abilene. He showed me the plans for it—ordered them by mail, he did! He's asked her to marry him, so she and the baby (oops, I forgot to tell you about THAT!) will have a nice home.

But Mercy's having a tough time of it. She misses Judd something fierce. I think she really likes Malloy—and I KNOW Judd would want her to take up with a man who cares so much for her. Asa says she's torn between moving ahead, maybe betraying her husband's memory, and keeping Judd alive in her mind. Thank goodness Asa can cook, because when the stagecoaches come through, Mercy can't move fast enough to suit VanBuren.

She's pretty big with that baby, and I'm guessing come spring it'll be here. Maybe then she'll be happy again—and too busy to pine for Judd. This house gets so quiet when she stares into the fire that we can hear the wind whistling through the cracks in the logs. She says she's tired from not sleeping good, but it looks to me like she's listening for the sound of Judd coming in from chores. Or remembering the sound of his voice when he read from the Bible each night. I'm not near as good at that.

Me, I stay busy with the horses, now that Nathaniel's not here to hitch them to the stages or train them. You should see Mr. Lincoln! He's nearly two, and while he might be the littlest fellow in the corral, he's the feistiest, too. Already follows my voice commands—smart as they come. (Sounds a lot like me, don't you think?)

Spot and Snowy are asleep at my feet. Asa's sleeping in your room for the winter—although I'd let him bunk over here in a minute if you'd come to visit! I'd sure like that! The snow's been drifting deep, though, so you'd best wait for winter to blow through.

Your brother,

Billy

P.S. No word from Mama. How about you?

Mercy saw the boy slip his letter into the mailbag that would go out with tomorrow's stagecoach. Such a shame that his sister didn't write him once in a while. Christine was progressing well in her studies, according to Aunt Agatha's occasional notes, but she had a mind of her own when it came to keeping up with correspondence. And at fifteen, she was much more interested in her circle of friends than in a brother she recalled as pesky and pint-sized.

Billy would always be short and compact, a lot like Michael Malloy, she supposed. But his sister would be amazed at the way he'd filled out from working so hard around the homestead. With hair of a deeper rust now, and a face toughened by the sun and the wind, he had lost the pale, freckled look that often plagued red-headed males. When his blue eyes sparkled with mischief, Mercy saw the attractive man he would someday be—a man Emma Clark already considered *hers!*

As Billy opened the Bible for their evening devotional, it was another man's presence that unsettled her, however. At Asa's insistence, they had invited Michael Malloy for dinner. She suspected it was the old cook's excuse for serving pan-fried chicken and mashed potatoes instead of their usual corn cakes, or cornmeal mush, or corn chowder. Supplies were running low, and, as she'd anticipated, they relied upon the corn they'd saved back from the fall crop—the crop Judd had died defending—for a meal or two each day. The man across from her had offered to drive into town for groceries, but she'd deflected his help.

What did it matter what she ate? She had as little taste for food as she had for living these days, although she put up a good front, for Billy's sake.

And as he opened to his passage, Mercy braced herself for another episode in the lives of the Holy Family. Without Judd here, Christmas was a farce. She'd stubbornly refused to put out the crèche or decorate a tree: why pretend she'd find meaning in that age-old story this year?

Yet this morning, the stable and the porcelain figurines had appeared on the sideboard as if by magic, or a miracle of the season. Baby Jesus, of course, was in the drawer, but Mary and Joseph gazed at the manger with a glassy-eyed anticipation that seemed to her as false as her own pretenses this evening.

She felt Michael gazing at her, and found a grease spot on her napkin that required study. Mercy let him place his hand over hers, but she didn't return the pressure of his fingers. No sense in leading the poor man on, she simply wasn't interested. The baby shifting in her oversized belly was the only sign of life she acknowledged these days. It took all her energy to believe her time would come and she would deliver—and live to tell about it.

Billy cleared his throat. "From the Gospel according to Saint Matthew, the first chapter," he began from his place at the head of the table. " 'Now the birth of Jesus Christ was on this wise: When as his mother Mary was espoused to Joseph, before they came together, she was found with child . . .' "

Mercy drifted on the cadence of his voice, letting the words roll by her. What did she need to hear about this woman who carried a child of mysterious origin? Or about the man who agreed to marry her anyway?

" '. . . the angel of the Lord appeared unto him in a dream, saying, Joseph, thou son of David, fear not to take unto thee Mary thy wife; for that which is conceived in her is of the Holy Ghost. And she shall bring forth . . .' "

The hand atop hers tightened. She glanced up. The love she saw in Michael's hazel eyes was so stunning, it scared her to death.

Was Malloy devious enough to play upon this biblical passage to corner her? Ever since Elizabeth's hints at her ruined reputation, Mercy had dodged his affection: She could *not* lower herself, as that woman had, to wed her way out of loneliness! Judd had married her for love, for her strengths and abilities. To cleave to another man for anything less was a betrayal of Judd's faith in her.

" 'Behold a virgin shall be with child, and shall bring forth a son, and they shall call his name Emmanuel, which being interpreted is, God with us. Then Joseph . . .' "

Mercy looked quickly away from Michael. Such a fine man he was, so young and earnest in his affections—and what she wouldn't give for a man's strength and comfort right now!

But it was too soon, and she was too vulnerable to the moods Judd's baby created within her. To give in to Michael now would mean she couldn't survive on her own. And that thought went against everything Mercy wanted to believe about herself.

Or were these pleasant, warm sensations from the touch of his hand actually signs of her love for Michael Malloy? Why did these matters of the heart have to be so confusing? She didn't dare look at him again, for fear she'd do something stupid—something they'd both regret.

So Mercy gazed intently at the Holy Family, trying to

find meaning in the words Billy read to them. Her gaze lingered on the figurine with the dark, wavy hair standing beside Mary at the manger. He suddenly looked so very much like Judd, her heartstrings snapped.

With an agility she hadn't felt for weeks, Mercy leapt up off the bench. Her heart thudded ominously as she strode to the sideboard and grabbed Joseph. He'd been in Judd's family for generations, but she could bear no more of his perfect patience, his faithfulness to Mary—or his unquestioning obedience to God.

"Let's see how *you* like it, Mary! Try raising that child without your man!" she cried.

Even as she threw Joseph, she regretted it. The figurine shattered against their wedding portrait, which had graced the mantel since Judd had built her this home. Then the framed photograph toppled, landing on the stone hearth atop Joseph's china remains.

Mercy stared at the shards that shimmered in the fire's light, feeling extreme sorrow rather than the release she'd sought.

The faces around her froze in horror. As one, Asa and Mike stood up, while Billy slowly set the Bible on the table, never taking his eyes off her. Their stricken expressions told her what she already knew: She was insane. Insane with grief for Judd. Insane with fear about how she'd raise his baby.

"I'm sorry," she rasped. "Please eat your dessert and leave me alone. I can't bear this right now."

Before anyone could protest, Mercy hurried to her bedroom and closed the curtain with a decisive *swish*. They were men—they couldn't possibly understand what she was going through! They would just have to indulge her.

She sat on the edge of her bed, too agitated to lie down; listening to be sure they were eating, while she knew they listened to her, as well. Did they realize how impossible it was to sleep in this bed alone? This little makeshift room could never again be the haven where Judd's embrace had chased away her fears, her doubts.

After the sounds of clearing the table came low conversation, and then the soft strumming of a guitar . . . Billy's voice, lower than last year, singing softly of peace on earth and goodwill—for her benefit, she sensed.

The music lulled her. Mercy closed her eyes . . . stretched out to nap while his lullaby lasted. She was strung too tightly to sleep, so her mind drifted on the words and melodies, which sounded disjointed and out of key because she was so exhausted.

In a restless state between waking and dreaming, Mercy rose and took the scissors from her sewing machine. She opened the trunk in the corner, where she'd stored Judd's clothes that day Rachel and Nell had helped her. The sturdy denims and soft chambray soothed her need to touch her husband again, to see the browns and butternuts and blues he'd worn so well . . . the colors of the earth he'd worked and of the eyes that no longer sparkled with love for her.

Why had God taken him just when she needed him most?

With a keening cry, Mercy slashed the pants in her hand. The scissors seemed to fly of their own accord, dismembering shirts she'd sewn only months before. Muslin and corduroy and cotton fell prey to her exasperated wrath, and she didn't stop until she'd reached the bottom of the trunk. She was panting, holding her belly from her exertions, when Billy's gasp brought her out of her fixated state.

When she saw the boy's fear—heard him mumble something like "crazy and helpless, just like Mama got," Mercy became too horrified to cry. The floor was littered with pieces of Judd's wardrobe, the very fabric of her life with him.

Michael and Asa were beside her then, coaxing her up from the floor. "I've put on water for tea. It'll help you sleep," the old Negro said, while Malloy felt her forehead for fever.

She allowed them to remove her shoes. She made no protest when they plumped her pillow and eased her onto the bed. Asa's tea tasted medicinal and warmed her all the way down. When she'd sipped the last of it, she got under the covers—only so they'd stop fretting and leave her alone.

Mercy closed her eyes, pretending to rest. She heard the three of them slip into the front room, whispering among themselves, but the colored cook's potion was casting its spell.

All she could think as she sank into oblivion was, *My God, my God, why have You forsaken me?*

Chapter Twenty-seven

Mercy awoke from a deep sleep to see the scraps of Judd's clothing stacked neatly beside her sewing machine, with the glassless wedding portrait on top of them. Poor Joseph had been swept up from the hearth, too. As Asa set a plate of mush and stewed apples in front of her, his dark eyes filled with sympathy.

"He was in too many little slivers to glue back together," the old man said sadly. "I know you didn't mean to—"

"I know just how broken Joseph must've felt," she replied with a sigh. "Thanks for taking care of me last night, after I spoiled your nice dinner. I hit bottom, Asa."

"Yes, Miss Mercy, you did. Can't any of us just sweep away our grief like I cleaned up that little statue." He gave her a hopeful grin. "But once you hit bottom, why, the only way to go is *up!* When God's all you've got, He's all you need. You'll figure out how to preserve your life with Judd, now that your heart's on the mend."

Was it? Mercy looked at all those ruined garments—fabric scraps too small and oddly shaped to be of any use—and ached with the sheer waste of it. Had Judd been here to witness her loss of control, he would have been appalled.

No, he would've made the best of it. He wasn't wearing clothes when you conceived his baby, after all.

That intimate thought made her smile—not as brightly as when she was a bride in that photograph, but with the renewed hope of a woman who'd survived her life's most difficult loss.

She set the portrait on the small table beside her bed, as inspiration. And as Mercy fingered the scraps of blue and brown, colors of the earth and sky her husband had loved so much, she knew exactly what she must do. This little curtained-off corner of the house he'd built for her would again become her haven, and by the time her baby came, she'd have a fitting memorial to Judd Monroe's all-encompassing love.

Every spare moment that winter, Mercy focused on the newfound purpose that made the cold, snowy days pass into weeks: The ache for Judd's love became a feverish need to create a permanent picture of their life together. Something grander than she'd ever attempted. From the clothing she'd destroyed, Mercy pieced together their Kansas homestead: the fields her husband had plowed, the rutted road of the stage-coaches, the endless sky above the prairie, where a sunrise parted dark storm clouds.

Once she'd stitched the larger scraps into her quilt's panoramic view, she engrossed herself in the details that would make it so intensely personal. From another trunk she pulled out her embroidery basket and the bright silk and satin scraps left from making the log-cabin quilt on Billy's bed.

During January snowstorms that blew in horizontal sheets of blinding white, Billy and Asa followed a rope they'd stretched between the house and the barn so they could tend the animals. In the corner room of the house, Mercy tended her own needs: This quilt was her lifeline. Except for walking around occasionally to ease her back, and helping with the meals Asa now cooked for the stage passengers, she contentedly spent her hours behind that calico curtain.

More often than not, she awoke with her clothes on, after naps that lasted longer than she intended. She lived by her body's clock, smiling when the baby moved inside her. It was a sign of life to come; a miracle to anticipate while this quilt gave her days a focal point.

With infinite care and patience, she embroidered fields of golden, waving wheat and corn standing proud and green. Near the center, a two-story log house of brown corduroy chinked with muslin appeared. Behind it, she placed a barn and corrals where Morgans with embroidered black manes looked toward the approaching red Wells Fargo wagon. Cottonwood trees shimmered along the bend in the Smoky Hill River, fashioned from scraps of Mrs. Bristol's pretty green evening gown.

Because the fabric pieces reminded her of the people who'd worn them, as she worked, Mercy recalled the occasions the clothes had graced. Sometimes smiling, sometimes wiping away a tear, she relived the best and worst moments of her life as Mrs. Judd Monroe, acknowledging those times—and her feelings about them—as sacred.

Since this project had become an obsession that now required her total attention, Billy and Asa kept their little snowbound world functioning. They called her when meals were ready, respecting her strict order not to look at this quilt yet. They plastered the walls with wet newspaper to block the drafts, and they brought in cow chips for the fire. Both of them understood, after that incident with Joseph, that she needed these weeks to heal in her own way. In her own time.

Cold, wet noses and curious bright eyes made her stop to stroke Snowy and Spot when they came inside after the chores were done. Asa filled her pitcher with fresh water each day, and emptied her chamber pot— that extremely personal chore Mercy would never have expected a male to perform before.

But life was different now. *She* was different.

Mercy had attained the very elemental state of knowing that whether her life continued in the way she'd prayed it would—or not—and whether she lived through her isolated ordeal of childbirth—or not— everything would work out as it was supposed to. Asa was right: All she had was God, and her faith, and her two caretakers, and they were all she needed. It was the way Judd would have expected her to live.

And as February blew in with snow drifting so deep the stagecoaches didn't run, Mercy embraced the isolation as she embraced the baby growing huge in her womb. She knew now that she could not only survive whatever hardships life handed her, she could *triumph* over them. As Billy read one night from the Psalms, his passage resonated within her:

"'Delight thyself in the Lord,'" his voice drifted through her curtain, "'and He shall give thee the desires of thine heart.'"

And what were those desires? She wanted her child to be healthy, of course. And she wanted to raise it as a living memorial to Judd Monroe's love in her life.

But when Mercy looked beyond this birth—beyond the time when Wells Fargo paid her and brought the rest of the world to her doorstep—*what did she want?* She'd been so occupied with day-to-day survival, she hadn't given her future, her inner needs, much thought.

I can raise this child alone. But do I want to?

If Michael Malloy proposes marriage again, what will I say?

The steady dripping of icicles sang to her of warmer days approaching, just as Billy's guitar blessed her nights with its benediction. As Mercy worked on the quilt's final details, she wondered if Elizabeth and Obadiah Jones were still speaking to each other—or if those four little towheads had driven the ostentatious cattle baron crazy by now. *They* couldn't have remained holed up as contentedly as she and Billy and Asa had, that was for sure!

Aren't you glad you chose the wiser path, allowing your heart to heal?

Was that Judd's voice inside her head? There were times when she couldn't recall what he sounded like. But because she saw him in her dreams, alive and potent and whole, Mercy could better accept his absence now.

She could also assume a different perspective about the day Elizabeth humiliated her, insinuating that she'd shamed herself by kissing Michael Malloy. Because, while he had taken that first kiss sooner than she was ready for it, she'd given him the second one without conscious thought. She'd stood on tiptoe when he leaned down from his horse, and her mouth had latched on to his as though she had no intention of letting go.

He tasted different from Judd. He moved his lips differently—*and didn't you linger in that kiss because the silken tickle of Michael's mustache made you laugh when you needed to? There's nothing wrong with that, Mercedes.*

Mercy's fingertips went to her lips as she paused over her embroidery. *That* was Judd speaking to her, so plainly that she glanced around the little room to see if he'd come back. It unsettled her, that her husband *knew* what fascinated her about Michael's kiss.

Yet he was encouraging her to enjoy it. Encouraging her to *feel* again.

The baby kicked and wiggled inside her, and Mercy felt a giggle bubbling up from a place she'd thought had died last September. She laughed out loud, and moments later she noticed the pale glow of sunshine from outside the frosted bedroom window. These omens urged her on—and when she realized that the aroma from the kitchen was roasting *meat* rather than corn or eggs again, her fingers flew. The facial features of her last patchwork family member came to life beneath her needle, and when she snipped the floss, a feeling of exultation washed over her.

"It's finished! It's finished!" she called out. Carefully she folded the large quilt so the design wouldn't show, and then lumbered over to throw the curtain aside.

There stood Billy and Asa with expectant, conspiratorial grins on their faces. And behind them, a very familiar, silken mustache flickered beneath eyes as warm as a midsummer evening.

"Mercy," he murmured, coming toward her with his arms open wide. "It's the first day the road's been clear enough to . . . I've missed you, and wanted to see how you were—"

A strong spasm doubled her over. She looked down to see a pink puddle spreading around her shoes.

Chapter Twenty-eight

"Keep walking, Mercy. Let gravity help you," Mike instructed gently. He hoped his worry wasn't showing, but Mercy's labor was continuing into the wee hours of the next day.

"I'm *tired* of walking around these rooms!" she wailed. "And if I have one more of those awful pains—"

"Here, missy, more of this tea might help."

"Begging your pardon, Asa," she rasped, "but if I can't guzzle some laudanum or whiskey or . . . Lord help us all, here comes another one!"

Mike held her hard against himself, torn by the torment on her face. She was getting weaker with each pain, and if this baby didn't come soon, it meant there were complications he couldn't deal with. The nearest doctor was miles away, in Abilene. There was no riding over to fetch Rachel Clark or Nell Fergus, either, because another snowstorm was keeping them housebound.

"Maybe we should walk you up and down the stairs."

"I'll fall. My legs feel like rubbery noodles." Mercy wiped the sweat from her forehead with the sleeve of her flannel nightgown. Tears dribbled down her pasty face. "I bet you're sorry you showed up, Michael. I just want to lie down and forget this whole thing."

Mike smiled sympathetically, kissing her forehead. "Shall I tell you about our house again? About our bedroom in the back, overlooking the river? And the nursery beside it—and those four bedrooms upstairs?" he said in a quiet sing-song. "And have I told you Gregor Larsen's gotten up the money to build a church in town? It should be finished for Easter services. A good time to christen this baby, I'm thinking."

Grimacing, Mercy began another walk around the front room. "Nice of you to keep believing we'll both make it."

"The first one's the hardest, honey. I can't tell you enough times how much I love you, and how much I want my own children to be yours, too."

"You're not listening, Michael! I refuse to go through this ever again." She sucked air between her teeth until the contraction subsided. "Maybe this is why Judd didn't stick around. Didn't want to go through this with—"

"That's your pain talking, Mercy. Judd was ecstatic about this child." He glanced at tired old Asa, and at Billy, whose eyes were wide with concern. "Let's get her back to bed. See if we've made any progress."

Mercy was growing slower and heavier, just as her

303

talk reflected her long hours without sleep. More than once she'd wanted to put this behind her—to awaken and find her pain was only a nightmare. Mike wished it were that easy.

"Here—I'll sit behind you, with my back to the bedstead." He moved as fast as his own tired limbs allowed. He then felt her weight fall against him, and he prayed this was the right thing to do for her. "Catch your breath, honey. Gather your strength again."

She let out a long sigh. Then she slumped sideways enough to look up at him with red-rimmed eyes. "Why are you doing this, Michael?"

"Because I love you, and—"

"Why?" She sounded out of her head with agony, yet lucid enough to expect a real answer. "You've been saying that ever since Judd died. But I will always love him—"

"I expect you to, Mercy."

"—so I can't understand why you'd settle for another man's child, and a woman who can't give you her whole heart."

She nipped her lip. It wasn't her way, to rail at people and make demands. "It's not like you couldn't have your choice of women, Michael," she went on more gently. "You're young—"

"Old enough to know what I want in a wife."

"—and able to afford a farm and a new house, and—"

"Didn't have time to spend my pay while I was a stage driver."

"—attractive enough that any woman would want you."

A ripple of warmth flowed through him as he focused on her doelike eyes. "Why, thank you, Mercy. I'll take that to include *you?*"

She blinked, and then valiantly gritted her teeth against another contraction. "I still don't understand the fascination," she rasped. "You've fallen for some paragon of your fantasies, but right now you're with the real Mercy Monroe. What do you see in me, Michael?"

Malloy hugged her, amused by her humility—but also aware that she wasn't nearly as strong as she'd been an hour ago. "Who wouldn't love you, Mercy?" he asked softly.

Billy and Asa sat slumped against the wall, but they might as well be his witnesses—in case this poor woman forgot what he was telling her from the bottom of his heart. He couldn't endure many more of her intense questions, but they gave her something besides her pain to concentrate on.

"From the first time I came here, I knew you were different from other homesteading women. Special," he began. He called up his memories from three years ago, hoping to convince her of his sincerity. "It wasn't that I had designs on you, or wanted to steal you away from Judd—"

"He wouldn't have let you."

"—but every time I entered this house, it felt like a *home*," he insisted, his voice going shaky with unexpected emotion. "You didn't put food on the table for strangers as a job, Mercy. You did it because you believed in feeding people, and in being your husband's helpmate. You offered your hospitality and friendship to me—seemed genuinely glad I was here.

"And every time I drove off," Mike said softly, "I

told myself what a lucky, lucky man Judd Monroe was. I spent a lot of my hours in that driver's seat wishing I could find a woman just like you."

Her mouth fell open into an O, so he pressed on.

"My daddy was a pretty fair carpenter. Worked hard to keep us fed and clothed," he said in a faraway voice. "And while my ma did the best she could at raising my sisters and me, I took a lot out of her, just being the seventh one born. I tested her at every turn, and ran off to fight for the Union because I felt cooped up by her rules."

He paused to honor the glimmer of grief he still felt; the guilt for being too arrogant and cocky to understand his mother's sacrifices back then.

"Came home from the war to find she'd died just the week before," he sighed. "My sisters claimed she'd been 'pining for her precious Michael' since the day I left, and my name was the last word she ever spoke. Well, that was a sad way to wake up to how much that woman loved me. How she'd been a guiding light in my life."

Mike repositioned himself beneath Mercy. Was his story making a stronger case, or wearing her out? She looked weaker now. Needed something more to keep her focused on birthing this baby.

"You're by no means old and frail like Ma was," he said with a little laugh, "but you have her spirit of goodness about you. I've known from the moment we met that somehow I had to be with you. You're the shining star who'll take me the way I'm supposed to go, now that Ma's gone."

Her head rested against his shoulder, but her eyes were glazing with another pain. "I—I'm glad you told me about her," she murmured. "And I believe you truly care for me. But why should I love you, Michael? Why should I give up the homestead Judd and I worked so hard for—"

"Who said you'd have to?"

"—to come live in that new house you're building? Why should I become your wife?"

Malloy swallowed. Any man who thought all the fight had gone out of this woman, simply because she was birthing a baby, had a lot to learn about her. And about gumption.

But what a question! "I—"

"I'm being difficult, Michael," she gasped, "but without Judd to look after my best interests, I have to be sure . . . oh, God, this is the worst one yet."

He kept his arms around her loosely, so she could ride it out, much like a bronc buster submitted to the beast he had to tame. When she fell back again, Mercy felt limp and spent. But she deserved his best attempt at an answer.

"If you don't marry me, Mercy," he whispered against her clammy ear, "I'll have no reason to plant more wheat or finish that house. I might as well live in that little dugout I had while I was driving. It was a poor excuse for a life—but I'll be a poor excuse for a man if you don't want me."

A weak smile found her face, but she was losing strength. Malloy held her, glancing anxiously at the old Negro and the boy against the opposite wall. The lamp guttered, like a sign that every light here might soon go out. And he couldn't allow that. "You ever helped with your mares when they foaled, Billy?"

"Why, yessir, but"—the boy sprang up from the floor—"a kid my age ain't supposed to see a woman—"

"But you've been at birthings. The blood won't scare

you when we need you most," Mike insisted. "What do you say, Mercy? Do you think—"

"I can't think," she mumbled, sounding very near defeat. "I just want this baby out of me."

Mike settled her against him again. Her breathing became shallow.

If this woman dies, there'll be no living with yourself, Malloy.

"Spread your legs wide apart, Mercy," he whispered against her sweaty hair. "Bear down as hard as you can, and focus on—"

The woman in his arms stiffened, and her eyes grew wide with renewed purpose. "Here it comes!" she rasped. "I—can feel it—"

"There's it is!" Billy cried, springing onto the bed. He dodged just in time to miss butting her head when Mercy surged forward with all the strength she had left. "Thatta way, Mercy! Oh, Lordy, Asa, here it comes! You gotta help me catch it now!"

The old man was already beside them, his face tight with cautious excitement. "Hold steady, boy . . . I've got the towel around it . . . here's the legs—"

"Clear out the nostrils and eyes," Mike offered quietly, watching from behind Mercy's leaden weight. "Smack that bottom to force air into its lungs."

As a wild cry rang around the log walls, Asa's grin flashed white.

"You've got yourself a baby girl, Miss Mercy. And a fine little lady she is, too!"

Chapter Twenty-nine

Mercy was vaguely aware of voices, but she willed herself to keep floating . . . to remain in this dreamlike state, resting without responsibilities. Light passed through her eyelids . . . a warm weight on her chest shifted slightly . . . her skin felt blessedly clean, and the scent of fresh bedding mingled with the invitation of coffee and bacon from the kitchen. Her stomach rumbled, but she savored this state of relaxation. Had she died and gone to Heaven?

She felt a presence nearby. The weight lifted from her chest, and she snuggled more deeply beneath the covers without opening her eyes. Once she was awake, the real world would return—and if it resembled that place of agony and exhaustion she last recalled, she wanted no part of it. Best to just drift for now . . .

A familiar humming came from beside the bed, soothing in its familiarity, even though she sensed the low, hushed hymn wasn't crooned for her. The baby? Without moving, she took mental inventory, and yes! She had delivered! Curiosity flashed like lightning, and Mercy peeked through the crack of one barely opened eye.

Asa held a blanketed bundle against his chest, smiling as though he, too, were in Heaven. It occurred to her then that angels came in all colors and sizes and ages, and this one with the wrinkled chocolate skin and springy, white-sprigged hair was so enraptured by the baby in his arms—her baby!—that she could watch him and he would never know.

This is what unconditional love looks like.

Mercy gazed at him, memorizing the sweetness of his old smile as she recognized the words to "What a Friend We Have in Jesus." She lay in total contentment, willing this wondrous sensation to linger as long as possible. When she allowed herself to think, she would again realize that Judd would never hold his child, and she would somehow have to raise it in a way that would honor his love for both of them.

"'. . . in His arms he'll take and shield thee,'" the man beside her sang softly. "'Thou wilt find a solace there.'"

His final phrase hovered like a benediction above the bed, and then Asa beamed down at her. "We've got us a fine little girl here, Miss Mercy. Your first job as a mama will be to name her."

When he sat on the edge of the bed so he could tilt the bundle toward her, Mercy scooted up against her pillow. Here was the weight that had wiggled on her chest; here was a puckery little pink face framed by downy hair that already promised to become thick and dark and wavy.

"She—she's her daddy's daughter," Mercy rasped, trying to grasp the magnitude of the new life she was finally holding in her arms.

"Spitting image," concurred a voice from behind the curtain. Michael smiled at her and came to the foot of her bed. "But she's got her mama's way of getting men to do her bidding. And she's informed us that warm cow's milk sucked through a sugar tit is no substitute for a real meal."

Mercy chuckled at the pacifier they'd made by wrapping muslin around wet sugar to resemble a little breast. "Thank you for taking care of her. How long did I sleep?"

Asa looked at Michael, wanting to keep that a secret. "You were in and out for the better part of twenty-four hours—"

"So tired and weak, we dribbled broth and laudanum—"

"Mercy! You're back!" Billy stepped through the curtain, wearing his snowy coat and an apple-cheeked grin. "I thought you was a goner! Got so double-dog upset, I tromped through the snow to give Judd a talkin'-to."

His words tumbled out in a rush, and when he removed his hat, his eyes shone a bright blue—the color of joy replacing anguish. "After we did our dangedest gettin' his baby born, it just wasn't right for him to take you away from us. Guess he musta listened."

The little room got so quiet, Mercy heard herself swallow. Only thirteen-year-old Billy would have railed at a dead man after delivering his baby—and not appeared one bit embarrassed about it.

"Of course he listened," she finally whispered. "Judd always respected those who did their dangedest. I—we both—thank you from the bottom of our hearts for all you've done."

Three heads nodded solemnly, but then Mercy looked into her daughter's face and forgot everything else. A wave of love such as she'd never experienced washed over her, strong as a tidal wave yet gentle as a spring rain. Once again she had the sense that all was well: Her world was already spinning around this new little axis, just as it was supposed to.

"Solace," she whispered, gazing raptly at those closing eyes, the softly rounded cheeks, the little bow-shaped lips. "That's exactly why you've come to us, little girl. I'll find my solace in you."

"Well, I'll be double-dog danged! It's about *time* you showed up!"

Mike shifted the baby into the crook of his elbow, to rub a clear spot in the window glass. Since it wasn't the day for the stagecoach to come through, Billy's excited voice suggested an unexpected guest.

Through the fogged window Mike watched a carriage stop beside the corral. When the driver opened the door, a small, white-haired female stepped down, hugging her woolen coat against the March wind. Next came a thinner, taller woman—and when her red hair caught the morning sun, blowing out from her fur-trimmed coat, Mike turned to Mercy.

"You might want to get dressed real quick," he suggested. "Your Aunt Agatha and Christine just pulled in. And from the trunks I can see, they intend to stay awhile."

Mercy looked torn between excitement and extreme agitation. "But they never sent word about . . . it's not like my prim and proper aunt to—"

"Scoot!" he said, waving her toward the bedroom. "You know darn well what she'll think, seeing me with the baby and you in your nightgown."

Mercy hurried behind the calico curtain, muttering

things he was glad he couldn't understand. But as he looked outside, watching Billy make awkward conversation with his long-absent sister, he heard the curtain swish open again.

"Phooey on what Aunt Agatha thinks! I'm going to sit in the rocking chair with my child," she announced. "If my nightgown doesn't suit her sensibilities, well— she can stay somewhere else!"

Chuckling, Mike kissed the baby's velvet cheek—a habit he'd fallen into without a second thought. "Let's join your mama, Solace," he murmured. "Billy's acting as the official greeting party, so you can be the royalty they've come to worship from afar."

He watched Mercy settle into the chair he'd made her for Christmas. It was a major triumph that she used it, considering how rocky things got that day she threw Joseph across the room, before he could give her the rocking chair. She looked like a Madonna sitting in it, holding Solace, and he could only hope she'd soon be as comfortable with *him*.

The kitchen door flew open. They held their breath, listening.

"You gotta come see the—oops!" Billy lowered his voice to a loud whisper when he remembered that the baby or Mercy might be asleep. "They're doin' pretty good, but we had a hard time of it. It's only been three days since—"

"And who delivered the baby?"

Aunt Agatha's voice cut like a knife, so Malloy was glad to see Mercy's little grin. Billy would set things straight in short order, in a way the headmistress would accept with dignified humor rather than disgust. She and Christine might as well get used to the way things were, now that Judd was gone.

Charlotte Hubbard

"*I* delivered her!" came the boy's proud reply. "But I ain't gonna do that again soon, I can tell ya! Asa was—"

"You did *not* deliver—"

"Did, too!" Billy informed his sister. "Me and Mike and Asa—"

"Mike and Asa and *I*," came Christine's correction.

"No, *you* weren't here! So don't come flittin' back like some social butterfly, tellin' me how things shoulda been!" he countered hotly. "You're just like Mama that way, and it's *aggravatin'*!"

Solace squirmed, blinking at such a rude awakening. And then the entire house rang with the wails of a baby whose lungs seemed nothing short of amazing. Mike jiggled and rocked and cooed, but he was walking toward Mercy as he did. She was opening her arms just as their guests entered the room.

"Well, now. What a cozy scene."

Agatha Vanderbilt watched with pinched lips as Mike handed the squirming, squalling bundle to her mother. Just out of orneriness—and because he was feeling protective—Mike slung an arm across the top of the rocker while he stroked the crying baby's hair.

"Aunt Agatha! What a nice surprise," Mercy said above the racket. She smiled, but Malloy felt the agitation radiating from her in waves.

"You didn't get my letter?" the headmistress asked.

"No, ma'am," Mike replied. "The roads were impassable until yesterday. And with Judd gone, and Mercy in the family way, we thought it best for George Clark—west of here—to handle the mail. They'll be serving the meals for a while, too."

The little woman crossed her arms and lifted her nose slightly, never taking her eyes from the three of them. Studying their faces. Assessing. Speculating. Obviously

314

laced up tighter than she should be about *something*.

"We never got *your* letter, either, Mercedes," she remarked stiffly. "If Billy hadn't written his sister about the Indian attack, and then mentioned how Mr. Malloy had taken such an *interest* in—"

"Oh, my—oh, my goodness, would you look at this little angel!" Christine cut in. She had shed her coat and come over to see the baby, undaunted by her cries. Without blinking an eye she leaned down, scooped Solace from her mother's arms and began to pace with a practiced sway.

The room went quiet, except for the whisper of kid slippers crossing the wooden floor. The girl stopped beside Aunt Agatha, delighted in her triumph with the baby. "Anyone can see this is Judd Monroe's baby," she announced. "Here comes that same dimple, right below the corner of her mouth."

Malloy blinked. Did women always notice that sort of thing? He'd figured Judd's distinctive mark was a small scar.

"And why would anyone think she *wasn't* Judd's?" Mercy sat straighter beside him, her question pointed enough to make her aunt and Christine shift uncomfortably.

Miss Vanderbilt looked Malloy over again. "I didn't *want* to believe—but when we came in and saw the two of you—"

"The way Billy's letter sounded," Christine cut in, "Judd was killed in that Cheyenne attack before the baby was conceived. And since he wrote so much about Mr. Malloy helping out around here, and just mentioned the baby in passing—we thought maybe—"

"Well, you thought wrong!" Billy blurted, his cheeks flushed with anger. "Can I help it if you two had

nothin' better to do than think things was goin' on between Mercy and Mike?" he went on, glaring at his sister. "Here we were, fightin' for our *lives*—dependin'
on each other to *survive*—while you were goin' to
charity balls to catch a man with money! Maybe my
writin's not the best, but it *got* you here, didn't it?"

Malloy couldn't recall when he'd felt prouder of
anybody. His surge of love for this kid came in second
only to his feelings for Solace when he'd washed her
just-born body. He stood staunchly beside Mercy, his
gaze never wavering as he awaited their guests' reply.
Judd Monroe wouldn't have stood for such insinua-
tions about Mercy, and neither would he.

Aunt Agatha sagged like an old balloon. "This is a
horrible way to begin our visit. I'm sorry we inferred
such unseemly details from Billy's letter, Mercedes. I—
I hope you'll accept our apology, and the gift we made
for your baby."

The room rang with a long silence. "Apology accepted," Mercy said.

Mike smiled. She wasn't going to make this easy
for them.

"I was still terribly excited to hear your good news—
and so very sorry to learn of Judd's death at the same
time," the little woman went on. "I expected to hear
such things from *you*, though."

Mercy leveled her gaze at her aunt, breathing deeply
to control her emotions.

"I know how . . . *unseemly* you must find it that I've
spent the past months with a colored hand, an adoles-
cent boy, and a man I'm not married to. And you're
aghast that no women were here to assist with Solace's
birth," she said quietly. "But if it weren't for these
three men, I wouldn't be talking to you right now,

316

Aunt Agatha. I almost lost my mind mourning my Judd, and then I nearly lost my life giving birth to his daughter. It's been a difficult winter."

"But you should see the big ole quilt she made!" Billy piped up. Then he grinned sheepishly at Mercy. "We snuck a peek while you was sleepin'. And it's the purtiest piece of work I've ever seen, Mercy. You poured your whole self into that, all those weeks you was workin' on it. I reckon that's what saved you, before any of *us* did."

"Thank you, Billy," Mercy murmured.

"You're a wise young man to see it for what it is," Mike remarked. He smiled proudly at the boy. "Shall we let these ladies decide for themselves?"

He brushed Mercy's forehead with a kiss, flaunting his affection for her. As he and Billy unrolled the bulky bundle, he sincerely hoped Miss Vanderbilt and Christine would get the message—see the real picture—when they witnessed the love Mercy had lavished upon this work of her heart. It was all Billy could do to keep the quilt from dragging on the floor as its bottom edge unfurled from the center.

Agatha and Christine gasped together. Then the older woman stepped closer, to view the patchwork through eyeglasses on a chain around her neck.

"Look at the ruts from the stagecoaches in this corduroy road," she murmured, "and the corn and wheat fields! Why, every stalk and ear is embroidered with such detail, they look alive! And that sunrise parting those black brocaded storm clouds. And here's your house, Mercedes!"

Mike grinned. High time Mercy received the praise she deserved from her aunt—not to mention vindication for holing up all winter to heal herself with her sewing.

"And look, Christine—it's you and Billy, with your red hair shining in the sun!"

"And that's my colt, Mr. Lincoln," Billy chimed in. "And that's Snowy and Spot herdin' the chickens by the corral. And *you*, of course."

Miss Vanderbilt's smile creased the corners of her eyes. "Yes, I suppose that white, upswept hair has to be mine. And here's Mercy, holding the new baby—"

"And Asa, holdin' one of his pies!"

Mercy chuckled until the chair rocked with her mirth. But she was waiting for the final truth to dawn on her aunt.

"And the detail on this Wells Fargo wagon is stunning! I don't recall you being such an *artist*, Mercedes."

She shrugged, looking pleased. "I stitched whatever felt important on any given day. Or what I could bear to think about in the wake of Judd's death."

"And of course we know who the man with the mustache is, driving the stagecoach." Miss Vanderbilt's grin flickered Mike's way, yet when she stepped back, her expression waxed more cautious. "I don't mean to upset you, dear, but . . . where's Judd?"

Christine let out a long sigh, holding Solace closer.

"Step back here and you'll see him," she murmured, her green eyes bright with tears. "Those dark, parted clouds? They're his hair. And the two birds are his long eyelashes, there in the sunrise. He's wearing a shirt the color of the sky, and his fingers form the ruts in the road."

She blinked rapidly, her voice grown hoarse with emotion. "Judd's watching over us. Holding us all in the palms of his hands."

"Amen to that," Billy whispered.

Chapter Thirty

Just as sunshine brought comfort after a rain—and chased away the winter's snow—Aunt Agatha's and Christine's presence restored a rightness to Mercy's days. They couldn't stay long, as the academy's classes would resume after Easter. But once the clouds of doubt and misinterpretation were cleared away, Solace became the sun they all revolved around.

"Look at that dimple! And those blue, blue eyes," Christine cooed.

That the girl had been enamored of Judd, and missed him terribly, shone through everything she did and said. Yet Mercy took tremendous pleasure in watching the interplay between this stunning young woman—now sixteen—and the baby who openly adored her. Christine had a real talent for talking in just the right tone, swaying and singing just enough, so that Solace never fussed while in her arms.

Glancing at Billy, Mercy considered a subject that

had gone undiscussed long enough. "Forgive me if I sound insensitive or impolite," She began cautiously, "but it's difficult to believe you're the same Christine Bristol who swore she'd never return, and who refused to write to her brother—or me—for a long time. Dare I hope you've grown up, young lady?"

Christine's face flushed a becoming pink, while Aunt Agatha let out a smug chuckle. "So you've noticed that, have you? It seems that once our girl got a glimpse of those less fortunate while working at the orphanage, she gained a whole new perspective on what really matters. She took to those little children from her first day there—perhaps because she, too, was once abandoned."

"Well, isn't *that* progress!" Mercy said, lighting up with a smile. "Though I know you'll never fuss over Billy the way you adore my daughter—"

At this, both Bristols rolled their eyes.

"—at least something positive was going on while we were apart. No doubt the Lord was at work without you suspecting His direction," she continued. "And I'm grateful for your way with babies, believe me!"

Christine grinned. "Who wouldn't love a little sweetheart like Solace?"

"I remember holding you when you were this size," Aunt Agatha remarked wistfully. She gazed into Solace's impish face, tapping that tiny upturned nose with her fingertip. "You shrieked and screamed as though I'd clawed you with my fingernails. As I think back, I was so afraid I'd drop you, I probably held on too tightly."

Mercy smiled. It was an unexpected joy to share her daughter with these two. And a treat to hear how she'd once intimidated the fearless Agatha Vanderbilt without even trying.

"That must be where Solace gets her loud voice," Billy said matter-of-factly. "I tell ya, when she starts squallin', the dogs run for cover. Even the dang horses prick up their ears and start prancin' out in the corral."

"You cuss too much," his sister chided him. "You'll have—"

"You bring it out in me, Miss Priss!"

"—this little girl talking the same way if . . . Billy, how can you say that?" Christine's fist went to her hip, probably the same way their mother's had. "Your mouth's going to send you straight to the devil for bearing false witness against your sister!"

Widening his blue eyes to mock her, the boy shrugged. "Least I ain't worried about his pointy ole pitchfork jabbin' *my* backside—cause yours'll already be on it! Now let me hold her. You've been hoggin' her ever since—"

"You'll drop her sure as—"

"Actually, Billy handles her very well," Mercy said above their sparring. Now it sounded like old times again. "She seems to remember that he brought her into this world. One look at him and Solace stops her crying."

"Yes, well," Christine said with a roll of her eyes, "a face like Billy's would leave anyone speechless. Here—but be careful!"

With the same natural grace he showed around the horses and dogs, the boy slipped his arm beneath Solace's body so her head lay cradled in his hand.

"Yeah, what do they know?" he asked the baby in a shameless sing-songy voice. "Come the time when you're walkin', talkin', and housebroke, Solace, you're gonna be all mine. We'll herd cattle with the dogs, and train horses for competition, and—"

"I hope your plans will allow us a chance to dress Miss Solace in ribbons and lace," said Aunt Agatha. She'd gone upstairs while the Bristols caught up on their bickering, and she handed Mercy a box wrapped in pretty paper with yellow ribbon. "I would love nothing more than to be present when she wears this christening gown."

Mercy fumbled with the ribbons in her excitement. "Oh, Aunt Agatha! You made *my* gown, as I recall!"

"Yes, and I'd have freshened it for Solace," she replied with one arched eyebrow, "but someone we know dressed her mama cat in it, and then wandered away before Tabby had her kittens."

"It looked like a wedding dress!" Mercy countered, imploring Billy and Christine to see her side, "and I thought anyone having babies should be married!"

"An astute observation."

Aunt Agatha looked at her pointedly, but Mercy finished unwrapping her package. This was a favorite topic of Michael's, too, and whatever she said would be repeated to him.

"'To everything there is a season,'" Mercy remarked coyly, and then her joking tone gave way to an exclamation of pure awe. "Aunt Agatha! This is absolutely gorgeous!"

"Yes, it is. Christine designed and sewed the dress—including all those little seed pearls down the front tucks—and I made the lace."

"I don't suppose that circuit rider will be coming around soon?" Christine asked. "Not that he'll want to see *me* again, but I'd be honored to attend Solace's christening."

"He's got him a new church in town now," Billy said.

"The road'll be clear enough if you want to go this Sunday."

"Palm Sunday," Aunt Agatha joined in with a nod. "An auspicious day for a triumphal entry into Abilene."

Mercy let them chatter while she studied the minute details of the ivory gown: row upon row of delicate lace coming up from the hem, and forming a vee from the shoulder seams to the bottom of the tucked, beaded bodice. While she was eager to worship with a congregation in a real church again, what would she wear? What could she wriggle into, so soon after Solace's birth?

"And if the idea of a new dress appeals to you," the little spinster continued slyly, "Christine thought you'd enjoy attending services in a gown from the latest *Godey's Lady's Book*—which she'll make from one of the lengths of fabric we brought along."

Mercy met the girl's green-eyed gaze and saw a plea for something to *do* out here on the snowy plains. And how could she not accept this offering of Christine's obvious talent? The art of graciously giving and receiving came hard for the girl, but it appeared the academy's headmistress was making headway. And Mercy would be the recipient, for a change!

"Easter it is! Truly a time for rebirth," she agreed, crossing the room to hug her aunt and then Christine. "And thank you for understanding my needs as only other women can."

"And what is the Christian name by which you'd like this child baptized?"

Gregor Larsen's accent carried over the congregation gathered in this new sanctuary, and for a moment

Mercy was transported back to the services she attended before she married Judd. What a joy to have an organ playing the Easter hymns! And to have polished wooden pews with backs on them!

"Solace," she replied. "Solace Monroe."

"What a splendid name for this lamb of God. She will bring comfort and joy to everyone she meets." The pastor gazed into the baby's face as though he couldn't get enough of her wispy dark waves, distinctive little eyebrows, and long, curving lashes. "She's the image of her father. Just as we are every one created in the image of God, the Father of us all."

As he gently touched her scalp with water, Mercy couldn't swallow the lump in her throat. Although Aunt Agatha and the Bristol children stood to her right, while Michael and Asa completed this arc of love and support on her other side, the man she longed for wasn't here.

When Reverend Larsen charged her to raise this child in the ways of Christ, she realized anew what an overwhelming responsibility she faced. She took Solace into her arms with a tear dribbling down each cheek, crying for the solemn joy of this occasion, but also out of desperation.

Who did she think she was, assuming she could handle a homestead and provide for this child? How would the fields get planted? And without the income from her cooking, how would she get by?

What if the Indians come again? Who will they murder this time?

Mercy blinked, aware that the pastor was smiling at her, prompting her to sit down.

"Thank you," she murmured, grateful for the hand Michael placed on her elbow and the grin Billy flashed her.

The rest of the service went by in a blur as Mercy gazed into the sweet, sleeping face of her baby. Oh, to feel so utterly confident that all was right with the world! To know that all needs would be met, and all matters were in the hands of the Lord. Judd had always believed these things without a second thought or a glance backward. Why couldn't she? Why did her faith waver?

A triumphal chorus on the organ announced the last hymn, and then the benediction rang in the rafters—and then Michael Malloy's hazel eyes were gazing into hers as music swelled around them in a majestic postlude.

"Those vows about raising Solace? I took them right along with you," he said beneath the chatter around them.

Mercy's mouth fell open. The intensity of his expression—the utter sincerity of his remark—wiped away all rational thought. "You don't have to—"

"Yes, I do, sweetheart." His lips curved with elation. "I don't know how it'll all work out, but I still intend to be the man in your family, Mercy. And on the way home, you'll see how I've built upon my best intentions."

She'd heard his proposals before. She'd always admired Michael Malloy, for being a man of his word and a man of action. She'd always *liked* him, for his open smile and his enthusiasm. Today, he looked extremely handsome in a suit of dark fawn wool. And then there was the way that mustache curved around those lips . . . just one of the things that made him so very different from the husband she'd loved.

"You gonna let us out of this pew? Or do we have to stand here all day gawkin' atcha?"

The impish grin on Billy's face made her laugh despite the way everyone in the pew had been watching her talk quietly to Michael. As though no one else existed.

She stepped into the aisle, cradling Solace in the crook of her arm, and felt his hand at the small of her back. As though it belonged there. As though it were the most natural of gestures for them to share. Mercy felt Christine's curious gaze, too—not to mention the way her aunt sidled up beside her, acting as a chaperone without even thinking about it.

Exasperated at their snail's pace, Billy stepped around them. "Why don't you two just get hitched?" he teased. "Then we wouldn't have to watch those cow-eyed looks you're givin' him."

"I do not give him—"

But the boy was already slipping through the crowd, toward the door.

"Do, too," Aunt Agatha murmured.

Mercy let out an exasperated sigh. Why did everyone else see things she swore she wasn't feeling? She again thanked Reverend Larsen at the door, and then stepped outside. What a relief to feel the spring air, and to have safer subjects to talk about.

Even on this Easter Sunday, merchants were pounding nails and putting up new signs for the businesses they'd expanded over the winter. A sense of great anticipation seemed to drive them, and many called to Michael from upper windows and rooftops.

"Didn't recognize you in those fancy duds, Malloy!"

"Hey, we've got a hammer to fit your hand!"

"That your little lady? The one you've been braggin' on?"

Michael waved back as though he'd known them for

years; as though he played an important part in up-and-coming Abilene.

Mercy's cheeks went hot. It felt different, being hailed as another man's woman. Especially since she hadn't said yes yet. She wondered if Michael had parked his new carriage so far from the church to show her off . . . which wasn't a bad thing. Just something she wasn't used to, after her years on the homestead with Judd.

She noticed then, standing beneath a sign that said Texas Street, a dark-haired woman holding her little boy. He was kicking to get down, fussing in a torrent of baby talk that made his sandy curls shimmy around his head.

"Must be about two," Christine remarked. "No telling what he'll do if she gives him his way."

Mercy smiled, seeing herself in that situation with Solace someday.

And yet, as they got closer, she had the distinct impression this woman hadn't come from Sunday services. Her shawl was draped low over exposed shoulders. She wore a bright blue gown that displayed her bosom to best advantage as she lowered her son to the street. She smiled at Michael as though she knew him—or certainly wanted to.

"Good morning, Michael. And don't you look dashing on this fine Easter morning!" she called out.

"Good morning to you, Miss Lucy. And how's Joel today?" He crouched to the little boy's level, holding out his arms.

Joel's face lit up and he lunged joyfully. "Papa! Mama!" he crowed. "Papa come see Joel! Go for walk now!"

"Yes, it's a fine day for a walk, little man." Scooping

the boy up, Mike turned to them, grinning. "Joel and Lucinda Greene, this is Mercy Monroe holding Solace, and her Aunt Agatha Vanderbilt, and Christine Bristol—whose brother Billy has run ahead to the carriage—and Asa Thomas. We're on our way back from baptizing Solace, so it's a fine day all around."

"Well, how nice for you." Lucinda studied them with dark, speculative eyes. "And what a sweet little angel in her lacy gown. You must be very happy, Mrs. Monroe."

Mercy caught a whiff of—was that liquor on Lucinda's breath? It took all her strength not to jerk away when the woman stepped close enough to admire her daughter. This woman whose little boy called Michael his papa.

"It's been a lovely occasion, indeed," Aunt Agatha filled in with a crisp nod. "And what a handsome young man you have here."

The lines on the woman's face softened and she looked ten years younger. "Oh, yes—Joel's my pride and joy, he is. Come to Mama now, sweetie. These folks need to go—"

"*No!* Go with Papa!" The boy's face contorted, and he began to wail as Michael handed him back to his mother.

"We'll see you again, Joel." He reached into his pocket for his money clip. "Take care of your mother, now."

"We'll be fine." Lucinda gripped the folded bills he slipped her, and then wrapped her arms around her toddler as though she anticipated a struggle. "He gets so excited when he's out and about. He doesn't mean anything by it."

"A pleasure meeting you," Aunt Agatha called in her most elegant voice.

But the woman had already started down Texas Street—and it couldn't happen soon enough to suit Mercy. Her aunt's gentility amazed her, but then, the headmistress of Miss Vanderbilt's Academy for Young Ladies had devoted her life to the handling of such situations. She was no doubt in high form as an example to Christine, leading the way to the carriage as though nothing unseemly had just happened.

And, since Mercy had no way to express the assumptions and fears spinning in her head, she, too, reverted to that ultimate hallmark of decorum: She would say nothing if she couldn't say anything nice. As they walked at a brisker pace, she felt the inquisitive gaze of green eyes. She covered her agitation by gawking at merchandise displayed in one big window after another.

"Quite a change from the time we took you to Doc Moon's log cabin, isn't it?" she asked Christine cheerfully. "Just look at these new stores and hotels!"

"And the saloons and bawdy houses," her aunt remarked drily. "It's a wonder they all expect to stay in business."

"A month from now these streets'll be crowded with Texas cowpokes and cattle barons," Michael remarked with a sweep of his arm. "Nonstop commerce, whether it be trading in longhorns, or providing food and rooms, or selling supplies. All because the railroad came through—and because Joseph McCoy wouldn't let government regulations limit his ambitions."

"And will *you* be taking up residence here?"

Mercy winced. Aunt Agatha sounded like a father

quizzing his daughter's prospective fiancé. Why was everyone so determined to bring them together? Especially now that they'd met Lucy Greene?

"No, ma'am," he answered with a shake of his head. "I was lucky enough to latch onto land the railroad first sold to pay its way. Then I bought the Barstow homestead when Elizabeth took off with that Texas cattle baron. I planted eighty acres of Turkey Red last September, and I plan to sow more this fall."

"As opposed to wild oats."

Mercy's jaw dropped. Her aunt had made this remark nicely, but there was no mistaking her insinuation.

Michael kept walking toward the carriage as though it were an everyday thing to discuss his personal pleasures with a spinster headmistress.

"Wild oats grow like weeds, Miss Vanderbilt," he replied in a philosophical tone. "I'm no saint, mind you. But I'd rather plow a furrow that belongs to me than use a . . . hoe, someplace else. If you see my meaning."

"Quite clearly, Mr. Malloy."

Aunt Agatha paused as he lowered the steps of the carriage. Then she gripped his hand for more than mere assistance. "Thank you for your candor, Michael. Mercedes needs—and deserves—a man of courage and conviction. You'll do."

Malloy was chuckling as his matched grays trotted out of Abilene.

"What's so funny?" Mercy demanded. He'd invited her to share the driver's seat, suggesting that Christine keep Solace inside the carriage, out of the wind. But now being alone with this man seemed more difficult than having the others watch them. Questions whirled in her mind, and she wasn't sure she wanted the answers.

"Aunt Agatha. She didn't want to like me," he explained. "Wanted to believe I was taking advantage of her bereaved niece, like a fox slipping into a hen's nest—"

"Thank you so much for comparing me to a chicken, Michael."

"—but I won her over," he finished with a boyish grin. "And now I have you all to myself, with no one to protect you from my sly, beguiling ways."

"Sounds like a melodrama. But I own my land, so roping me to the railroad tracks for nonpayment doesn't fit."

"'Nope. And I have no use for desperate, clingy women." Mike let his gaze linger on her. He knew nothing about fabrics, but Mercy's new suit, the color of the springtime sky, followed curves she hadn't displayed in loose calico. "For me, only a woman of substance and independent means will do."

She pretended to study the hills on her side of the road. How could he say this, when he'd given Lucinda money? "So you've noticed I now wear a larger size, and you have designs on my land because it adjoins yours. Not very flattering, Michael."

Why wasn't this going the way he'd imagined? Where was the Mercy whose brown eyes sparkled during word play like this?

He understood her tears during Solace's christening, and her exasperation with her sanctimonious maiden aunt. But she was with *him* now! She had to know he loved her, or he wouldn't be taking her to the house he was building—for her. That, after helping her survive the winter and the birthing of her baby.

Mercedes Monroe was nobody's fool, and it wasn't as if he'd kept his intentions a secret. She'd been married, after all: she *knew* how a man valued a well-kept home and good cooking. Not to mention how males responded to inviting smiles, which led to laughter and love and kisses.

He stopped the carriage. Right there in the middle of the road.

"Mercy."

She looked at him with doelike eyes that made him melt. And in those eyes he saw not affection or confidence, but confusion. Uncertainty. Fear. Of him, mostly. Was he moving too fast, even after all this time?

He slipped his hand over hers. "I've never seen you look so pretty, Mercy. I was a proud man standing beside you in that church. Pleased that you wanted me there, at such an important but difficult time."

"Thank you for driving us in your new carriage—"

"No! I'm not just a means for you to get from one place to another," he insisted in a lower voice. "You'd find a way without me. Just as you survived being snowed in this winter. It's humbling, to meet a woman every bit as strong as I am, in her way."

Her eyes widened at that, so he pressed on.

"Humbling without being humiliating. I couldn't tolerate a woman who drove a man to do her bidding with the whip of her tongue. Or who became her man's doormat, and had no opinions of her own."

He wrapped the reins around the hook in front of him, giving himself another moment to think. "I saw a lot of marriages on display during my stage driving days, and the only man I ever envied was Judd Monroe," he said softly. "And though I know I can never love you *more* than he did, I love you completely, Mercy. Everything I do is already for you."

She trembled. Looked as skittish as a filly ready to bolt. So he cupped her face in his hand and kissed her, rekindling the oneness they'd felt when *she* initiated the kiss that had kept him warm and hopeful all winter.

Her soft sigh encouraged him. Mike moved closer, still kissing her tenderly—aware that these stolen moments couldn't last long. He released her so his heart could whisper what she needed to hear.

"Please tell me I have a chance," he pleaded. "I love you so much, Mercy. If I could know you might someday love me, too, I—"

The baby wailed in the carriage below them, drowning him out. The woman he'd held captive with a blissful kiss broke away then. The wife he wanted became a mother again, attuned to a more immediate need.

As she tended a wet, soiled Solace at the side of the road, Mercy knew just how her howling baby felt: helpless, without the words to express herself. It wasn't a seemly thing to do, but she couldn't worry about what her aunt and Christine might think, and when Michael helped her back into the driver's seat, she fed Solace as discreetly as she could. He had, after all, seen her in a more exposed state. And he deserved an answer.

But what could she say, now that she'd seen Lucinda? Where was the sense of rejuvenation she'd felt when Christine finished this new dress?

She felt like a woman again, ready to be seen. Ready to rejoin the living. Michael Malloy's plea came as no surprise, just as his intentions were as respectable as the babe she cradled at her breast—or at least she'd assumed so, until Joel exposed him. She wasn't one to back down from a challenge, yet her pulse was pounding so frantically she couldn't think of a thing to say.

"I—I wish I could give you a resounding *yes*, Michael—"

"And that's the only answer I'll accept."

She nodded mutely, focusing on Solace so she wouldn't see his disappointment. The sway of the carriage lulled her little girl into a dreamy-eyed state, and as she fastened her jacket, Mercy longed for that same sense of contentment.

Why couldn't she decide? Was her independent nature rearing its head, now that she'd regained her strength? Or was her heart telling her Michael Malloy simply wasn't the right man, and this wasn't the right time? If only she had the nerve to ask him—

"There it is," he said, halting the horses. "Thanks to the neighbors, I got it enclosed before the first snowfall. Worked inside all winter."

Mercy looked over at a white frame house she'd admired on the way into town. It rose two stories above mud that was sprouting grass, and behind that the skeletons of a large barn and a stable awaited completion. Beyond these buildings, bright green wheat fields rolled as far as she could see.

"I built it on enough of a rise to catch the breeze and see the river," Michael went on, pointing past her. "We'll have a porch there on the front, and that window has beveled glass that makes a rainbow on the parlor walls when the sunrise hits it. A picket fence will keep the livestock out of the yard, and give the kids a place to play. We can go inside, if you want."

*We'll have a porch . . . beveled glass that makes a
rainbow . . . a picket fence will give the kids a place
to play.*

Mercy hung on his words, hugging Solace. What
woman on these plains wouldn't jump at the chance
for such a house—such a *home?* Yet she closed her
eyes and shook her head.

Michael sighed. "Well, it'll be here whenever you're
ready."

For the rest of the ride she chided herself. How long
would he tolerate her ambivalence? How long before
that other woman made herself welcome in that
house—and in his heart?

Mercy noticed how small and plain the log house
looked as they pulled into the yard. Though she'd
never forget how Judd had told her to take care of herself and his family, she wasn't ready to leave this place:
a simple home, yet sacred because they'd made it together. Just beyond the corrals, a little iron fence enclosed two large stones from the riverbank that
marked where Judd and Nathaniel would rest forever.

When the carriage rolled to a stop, Michael placed
his hand over hers. "I know how much you loved him,
Mercy," he murmured. "And it's your loyalty and devotion that makes me wait. I hope it won't be for much
longer, though."

Mercy nodded, aware that the door had opened below them and everyone was getting out. There was
Easter dinner to prepare, and chores awaited them—
valid activities, yet surely he felt she was hiding behind
them. She looked into hazel eyes shining in a face that
was handsome in its own right—smooth and youthful,
with a hint of mischief in that slender mustache.

"Michael, I—"

"Mercy! Mercy, we got somethin' on the stoop! Looky here!"

Billy's excited cry drew their attention to the kitchen door. Asa, Christine, and Aunt Agatha were hurrying over to where Spot and Snowy sat like sentinels, guarding a large basket.

From her high seat, Mercy saw a big pink ribbon tied on its handle. "What on earth can *that* be? Someone must've stopped while we were—"

"It's a baby!" Christine exclaimed. "She's dressed all in pink, and she's *beautiful!*"

Chapter Thirty-one

"There's a note! What's it say?"

Aunt Agatha was taking the single sheet of vellum from its envelope as Mercy approached the doorway, where Christine was already holding a child with features as fine as a china doll's. Her blond hair framed a face of velvet cream, with pale brows and lips like tiny, dew-kissed petals. Dressed in pink, from her gown of ribbons and lace to her miniature kid slippers, this little visitor realized she was holding court—as though it were her rightful role to be the Queen of Easter.

"'My name is Lily, and I am eight months old,'" Aunt Agatha read. "'My mama has died, and my papa can't take me where he needs to go. He has visited you before, and he believes you are an angel of mercy who will care for me until he can return. He's a man of great wealth and influence, and will repay you a thousandfold for your kindness. God bless you for opening your heart and home to me.'"

"Well, what do you think of that?" Asa sang out. He tenderly touched one rosebud cheek, grinning as the baby looked up at him. "An Easter lily, indeed! Even Solomon in all his glory wasn't arrayed like *this* little angel."

"Do you s'pose it's true, what the note says?" Billy asked as he gazed at her. "I mean, if he's so rich, why don't he hire somebody to travel with him and take care of his little girl?"

"An excellent point," Mercy replied. "And he could be any one of hundreds who've stopped in during their stagecoach trip west. Impossible to recall, and—"

"And how could anyone just *leave* such a perfect little princess?" Christine said. "If she were deformed, or sick, or—"

"Maybe he's still around, watching." Michael surveyed the yard and corrals. "Mighty strange that he happened by on the first day Mercy's been away from home since last September."

She frowned. "Do you think it's a trap?"

"I think you ladies should wait here while I check the house, and then go on inside while Asa, Billy, and I check the barn and the riverbank. More than one thing about that note just doesn't add up."

Holding Solace closer, Mercy nodded, gazing around the yard but noticing nothing out of the ordinary. Billy was already sprinting off toward the river, with the two dogs scampering alongside him, while Asa headed for the barn. Inside, she heard the trapdoor thumping shut, but when Michael returned he was shrugging.

"Nothing so far. No sign that anyone's been inside, but I'll go upstairs. Just to be safe."

Mercy went in first, instinctively glancing around

her kitchen, the front room, and her bedroom. Solace was drowsy from the ride, so she laid the baby in her cradle—the beautiful cradle Judd had begun making out in the barn, and which Michael had finished during the winter. It was getting harder to tell where one man left off and the other began, they were alike in so many ways. Almost as though Judd was gradually slipping away, taking the pain of his passing with him, to allow Michael Malloy a chance to win her.

Or so she'd thought, until Lucinda Greene burst her bubble.

A little howl from the front room brought her out of such thoughts. As she closed the calico curtain, she watched Christine stroll the parameters of the front parlor, with Lily slung on her hip as though she'd done this a hundred times.

"You certainly have a way with babies," Mercy said quietly. "At times, I still wonder if I'm holding Solace wrong, or perhaps dressing her too warmly. And more than once, I've reached my wit's end, trying to stop her crying."

Christine looked up with such a striking smile that Mercy was taken aback: The slender redhead was only sixteen, yet poised and pretty. Mature in a most attractive way.

"When I started spending time at the orphanage, the littlest children just took to me," she said in a soothing voice. She was cheek to cheek with Lily, obviously smitten. "My mission project for this semester has been sewing clothes for them. I can't help noticing that Lily's dress is very well made, from expensive watered silk and lace that looks imported."

"She's a mystery in many ways," Mercy agreed, stepping up for a closer look at the little girl. "I hope this isn't just one of many times her father has dropped her someplace, to retrieve her when it suits his schedule—"

"Just when the family has come to love her."

Mercy smiled, caressing one of the golden curls that framed Lily's face. "We'll take her, of course. But I'm tucking that note away for safekeeping. When her father shows up, I certainly have some questions for him!"

Christine's complexion took on the glow of a sun-ripened peach as she swayed from side to side, gazing at the little princess in her arms. "What if I . . . well, how will you manage this place and take care of two babies?" she asked in a rush. "Instead of going back tomorrow, I'll stay here and help you!"

Christine might as well have slapped her. Who would have dreamed she would want to stay here, for any reason at all?

"Why, thank you, dear! But after two more months at the academy, you can graduate—or continue your studies," Mercy reminded her. "I'd never want you to give up—"

"Oh, it would be no sacrifice," she replied, her green eyes alight with the idea. "Abilene's a bustling town now. I can take in sewing and dressmaking."

"What about your apprenticeship with Madame Deveraux?" Aunt Agatha asked pointedly. She'd come from the kitchen with a stack of plates, to set the table. "While it's admirable to offer your assistance, Mercy's right. In only two months, you'll complete your studies, and you'll then be working with the most sought-after couturiere in St. Louis."

"Well, congratulations!" Mercy hugged the girl, and they both laughed when Lily gleefully clapped her little hands. "You'd be silly to pass up such a chance, Christine. It could open doors to some very lucrative work, when the most I can give you here is a room—and a double bunch of dirty diapers!"

The subject wasn't closed, however: When Christine held Lily closer, the little cherub snuggled as contentedly as if she'd found her long-lost mama.

Yet as she put potatoes on to boil, Mercy realized the young woman had a point: How *would* she handle two babies? Lily would be learning to walk soon—and she had nothing for this little newcomer to wear. Billy would be planting crops with Asa, in addition to tending the horses for Wells Fargo. She'd considered preparing meals again, because she could certainly use that income until they sold the corn crop they hadn't yet planted. But with a second little mouth to feed, and another bottom to wipe—

"Best we can tell, Miss Lily's father left her basket and went on his way. Probably so we couldn't corner him," Michael said as he stepped inside. "Everything looks fine out there."

And everything in here's looking very, very complicated.

So he wouldn't notice the strain on her face, Mercy leaned down to toss cow chips into the oven's fire box. "He must've stopped here before Judd's death," she remarked tersely, "or he'd realize how many irons I already have in my fire! That little girl's going to be—"

"A blessing, just as Solace is," Michael reminded her quietly. "Just as the Bristols have become. It's not as if you have to assume this added responsibility alone, you know."

There it was again: his talent for turning her own words—every little circumstance—into another reason she should marry him. She should have seen it coming.

"Billy's bringing in cream and butter, and Asa's cutting down a ham in the smokehouse," he continued. "What may I do to help you, Mercy?"

You can stop being so damn helpful! she wanted to scream. *You can show me a side that isn't so patient, and—and you can tell me about Lucinda Greene and that boy who resembles you!*

His kiss made her sigh in a way that sounded far too needful. The silk of his inner lips felt warm and moist as he slipped his arm around her waist. She tried to pull away when her aunt entered the kitchen, but Michael held her head.

So Mercy had no choice but to endure—no, to enjoy—the way his mouth moved over hers. And the way that silky-soft mustache tickled her, in spite of her anxieties.

"We—we would be honored if you gave the devotional reading after dinner," she suggested when he let her up for air.

That should make him think twice about being the solution to her every problem! And it would encourage any *honorable* suitor to clarify his other relationships, too. While Michael Malloy was a decent, hardworking man, she'd never once seen him with a Bible at their gatherings with Reverend Larsen, nor had he ever led them in prayer or the evening's devotional.

"I'd be happy to," Michael said with a nod. "I know a passage that speaks perfectly to this day we've had."

Mercy sighed. Why did it sound as if she'd just given him the keys to this little kingdom?

Chapter Thirty-two

"Therefore I tell you, Don't worry about your life, what you'll eat or drink," Malloy paraphrased. "Nor about your body, what you'll wear. Is not life more than food, and the body more than clothing?"

He looked up from the well-thumbed Bible to see if Miss Vanderbilt would protest his simplification of these verses. The King James version made things more complicated than they needed to be—which was why his mother had taught him to look beyond its archaic phrasing for the meat of each message.

Aunt Agatha's little grin said she knew what he was doing by choosing this passage. Billy was resting his head on his elbow to listen—which meant the headmistress was more concerned about Mercy getting his point than about correcting the boy's table manners. Christine sat in the rocking chair from the bedroom, with both little girls nestled against her.

But Mercy . . . the poor woman looked too preoccupied to even hear his voice. She was staring at her hands, apparently lost in her own scary little world. Mike wanted to stroke the loose hair back from her face, but he'd already made too many moves today. He'd said too many things that made her feel like a cornered cat.

He found his place again.

"Behold the birds of the air, they don't sow or reap; yet your heavenly Father feeds them. Are you not much better than they?" He rephrased the familiar passage from memory, hoping his sincerity would convince her. "And why do you worry about clothes? Consider the lilies of the field, how they grow; they don't toil or spin, but even Solomon in all his glory wasn't arrayed like one of these."

Asa was nodding, smiling at the angelic child who'd reminded him of these verses earlier.

"So, if God clothes the grass of the field, which today is alive and tomorrow is cast into the fire, won't He clothe you, too—O ye of little faith?" he went on tenderly. "So don't worry, saying What shall we eat? or What shall we drink? or How shall we be clothed? But seek first the kingdom of God and His righteousness, and all these things shall be given to you. Don't worry about tomorrow."

Mike sighed. Mercy wouldn't look at him.

He closed the Bible, contemplating the magnificent quilt she'd made to celebrate this family and Judd's love. He and Billy had put up a pole to hang it above the sideboard, where guests could marvel over it. Mercy had sewn *him* into her patchwork picture, too, yet she still hadn't taken him into her heart.

What else could he do to convince her of his love?

Looking around the room in its evening shadows,

where Asa and the two Bristol children sat—and where Lily, their most recent refugee, now watched him from Christine's lap—Malloy thought of one more thing.

"It means more than I can say, that you've included me in this special day for Solace, and in your daily lives," he said quietly. "From the first time I walked into this room, where the table was spread to welcome every wayfaring stranger, I knew the Monroes believed in Christ's commandment, 'Feed my sheep.' I had no idea then that I, too, would be gathered into this fold."

Mike gazed sadly at Mercy, knowing better than to proclaim himself again. He would have to follow the Bible's advice himself, and not worry about his tomorrows with her.

"I'll be here whenever any of you needs me. Right now, though, I'm going to hit the hay," he said quietly. "We'll be leaving early so you ladies can make your train. Good night, now."

"Good night, Michael," Agatha replied with a sweet smile. "Thank you for selecting such an appropriate devotional passage, and for making it more understandable."

"Well—it's time to put these babies to bed so I can pack," Christine said quietly. She rose from the rocking chair without rousing the baby on either shoulder, and went behind the calico curtain.

"We should finish the horse chores and get our shut-eye as well, Mister Billy." Asa stood up slowly. He looked stiff from sitting on the bench, but he didn't grouse about sleeping out in the barn.

"It was kind of you gentlemen to give up your room for me," Aunt Agatha remarked. "I hope you'll continue to sleep upstairs after we leave, Asa. I like knowing someone's here with Mercy after dark. This house gets very quiet at night."

Mercy could feel it in the way her aunt rose from the table with a restrained grace, to stand before the quilt that hung above the sideboard: Agatha Vanderbilt was about to impart her wisdom, whether it was appreciated or not.

"This is the most wonderful, original piece I've ever seen, Mercedes," she murmured, touching the people enfolded in Judd's strong, earth-colored hands. "You'll be adding a basket with a pink bow, I imagine. There's more to that story, but we might not know those details for years. I hope you'll accept Miss Lily for who she is, without worrying over who dropped her here and why."

Aunt Agatha shifted sideways, to look more closely at the Wells Fargo wagon approaching from the right-hand corner.

"And we also have the mystery of Mike Malloy, don't we, dear? You've stitched him into this patchwork of your life, and he's all but stood on his head naked to prove his devotion to you." She turned, gazing directly at her niece. "So what's holding you back? Until today, I thought you intended to marry him."

After hours of gritting her teeth, Mercy released the rage she'd been holding in. It sounded a lot like the wind that whipped this little house in the winter, chilling all in its path. "That woman was a—a soiled dove, Aunt Agatha!"

"Was she?"

Her tone sounded innocent, but that single raised eyebrow suggested she knew the truth. "Though I don't condone that business, I believe most women fall into it because their other choices have run out—or their men have. Maybe I'm going soft in my advancing years, but I wonder if we're so busy scowling at the *soil*, we don't see the dove beneath it."

Mercy gripped the edge of the table. How could her aunt play word games at a time like this? "Let's get to the real question, then! What if that boy is Michael's son?"

"What if he is?"

The woman who'd always been such a stickler for decency—living life without need for repentance—sat down beside her again. Her wry smile only exasperated Mercy more.

"Mercedes, let's discuss a very important . . . point. If a man's got lead in his pencil, he's going to write to somebody. It's the way males are made," she said with an utterly straight face. "Again, I'm not condoning those who frequent the brothels. But we should consider some circumstances before we accuse Michael Malloy of hiding a very important detail—or just plain lying about it.

"Joel looks to be two or three, which means he was probably born before either Michael or Lucinda Greene came to town. Say, around Sixty-six or Sixty-seven."

Protesting this woman's long-winded logic would do no good, so Mercy played along. "All right. Back then, Abilene was only a few huts and log cabins."

Aunt Agatha nodded. "Do you know what Michael was doing before he drove stagecoaches? Before you met him?"

"Well . . . no. I had Judd then, so it really didn't matter."

"Then don't be fooled by appearances," she shot back. "Maybe that poor boy calls every man he sees his papa, and we just happened by at the right time. Maybe his father died or ran off before—"

"But he *knew* Michael! And so did that—woman!"

"And so did nearly every person we passed on the street," her aunt insisted. "Mr. Malloy is not only a skilled driver and carpenter and farmer, he's a progressive thinker who's involved in his community, as well."

She reached for Mercy's hand. "So again, until you know the rest of this story, don't let your imagination run away with you—as mine did when I read Billy's letter months ago. I assumed the worst, and when I saw how—*intimate* you were with this new man, it only confirmed my false beliefs."

Mercy's mouth clapped shut. Where had this less-critical version of the academy's formidable headmistress come from? "So why are you defending Michael now? Why are you telling me all this?"

The white-haired woman, still ramrod straight, glanced away as though composing thoughts she'd never expressed before. "I let a man get away once, Mercedes. Because of my own naive notions about how he—and his love—had to be perfect before I could marry him."

Now, *here* was something she'd never heard! Mercy had always believed that Agatha Vanderbilt was far too independent to consider marriage. "What happened? Was he after the family fortune?"

"Oh, he got some of that anyway," she replied with a chuckle. "Because after five years of courting me, and five years of my expecting him to prove himself at every turn, he . . . Robert married your mother instead."

Aunt Agatha's face took on a faraway sadness Mercedes had never seen there. Indeed, she'd never believed that this pillar of decorum and morality ever *needed* regret.

"It took me several years to forgive my little sister. I accused her of seeing him behind my back, and other duplicitous activities which happened only in my imagination," she went on with a sigh. "I was consumed by my envy over Violet's happiness, and the family she delighted in.

"But it was my own fault. While he was courting me, Robert turned himself inside out trying to please me, until he realized he would never measure up. He saw that I would never be satisfied, or love him for the fine man he was."

Mercy considered this. She refused to believe that the intrepid Agatha Vanderbilt had lived her life in vain—or perceived it that way now. "But think of how many girls you've guided over the years. If you'd married instead of establishing the academy—"

"I might've had a fine daughter like you, Mercedes."

The words, spoken so eloquently, echoed in the silence. Like the ticking of the mantel clock, they marked the minutes passing away; they warned of a life wasted on false assumptions and unmet desires.

"If you want the truth about Michael's situation, you'll have to ask him," her aunt said quietly. "You'll have to watch his face, and listen to his replies, and judge their validity for yourself. No more second-guessing."

Aunt Agatha rose from the table, one last matter on her mind. "As you consider your questions about Lucinda Greene and Joel," she went on, "you might remember that Christ spent His time with harlots and tax collectors, and that He ate with traitors and forgave a thief on the cross beside Him. Imperfect human beings, all of them—in direct conflict with His message. But He accepted them. He forgave.

"And He loved children most of all," Aunt Agatha added with a wistful smile. "I was moved nearly to tears today when Michael opened his arms and Joel leapt into them. We witnessed unconditional love, Mercedes—from a man who didn't care what we might think of him! And who receives enough of that?"

Chapter Thirty-three

Mercy wondered, just before dawn, if Aunt Agatha recalled her remark about how quiet the house was: Solace was howling for her breakfast, and when Lily awoke in a strange place—sharing a cradle with a dark-haired stranger, because there was nowhere else for her to sleep—she wailed as though the devil himself were chasing her.

And of course all this racket rose through that open grating into the bedrooms upstairs.

With her daughter at her breast, Mercy slipped her arm beneath Lily, but Sunday's cherub had become Monday's screaming demon. The little blonde's face contorted with rage as she squirmed to avoid Mercy's touch. Solace, in turn, became agitated by this newcomer's squalling and began to cry again.

How on earth had Elizabeth Barstow managed? If her neighbor had borne a child nearly every year since they'd come to Kansas, surely *she* could handle these two girls. But when she maneuvered her arm beneath Lily and lifted the child onto her lap, the little fiend kicked Solace with both feet.

"Enough of *that*, young lady!"

Mercy clutched the child against her. No stranger's baby was going to hurt her little girl. She might just squeeze Lily into submission, burying her crimson face in the folds of her nightgown until this insane wailing stopped.

And what if she quits breathing?

Mercy released the little girl as though she had bitten her. Her lack of experience with babies, her recent loss of sleep with Solace, and her doubts about Michael were driving her to dangerous depths, after only one day. What would she be like after Christine and Aunt Agatha left? When Billy and Asa were outside working?

Lily's frightened whimpers drove her own doubts home. Maybe God had denied her Judd's children for good reason. Maybe she was unfit to be a mother. Maybe she should beg Christine to stay, after all.

Yet moments later when Christine came in, beautifully dressed in her traveling suit of periwinkle blue, Mercy couldn't deny this young woman the chance to graduate and pursue her promising future.

Lily immediately quieted in Christine's embrace.

"How do you *do* that?" Mercy murmured.

The young woman smiled, swaying with the baby before she answered. "I'm not sure," she confessed. "At the orphanage, it helps when I concentrate on one child at a time. Every girl wants to believe she's a queen—if only for a few moments. Some of us never outgrow that, you know."

Christine's wry expression made Mercy laugh, which had a relaxing effect on Solace. Her baby began feeding again, closing her little eyes so those long, dark lashes brushed the tops of her velvet cheeks.

It was a sight Mercy never tired of, and it affirmed Christine's wisdom: one child at a time. One task at a time. One day at a time.

"Are you sure you don't want me to stay?"

Glancing up at that fresh, eager face, alight with eyes of shimmering green, Mercy was tempted to give in. It was Aunt Agatha's purposeful footsteps that made her sit straighter, with firmer resolve.

"Thank you so much for asking, Christine—and for your help since you've been here," she added as the bedroom curtain was drawn back. "You have your studies—your upcoming apprenticeship—and I have Billy and Asa. The three of us have weathered storms much worse than these little girls can stir up."

"Don't forget how badly Michael wants to help you, too," her aunt reminded her. She kissed Mercy's cheek and stroked the down on Solace's head. "Right now, however, he and Billy are loading our trunks so we can catch our train. We'll come back this summer, dear—if you'd like us to."

"Oh, yes, please do!"

Why did she feel the weight of this woman's leaving? Was it because her mother hadn't been here for Solace's birth? Or because Aunt Agatha had become more of a mainstay than she'd ever imagined possible? While this white-haired headmistress had seemed unspeakably old and set in her ways when Mercy was Christine's age, Agatha Vanderbilt had acquired a youthful sense of adventure and confidence over the years.

Or was *she* the one who'd changed? Mostly because of the unconditional love this woman had lavished upon her when she'd needed it most.

Mercy walked outside with them, delighted by the spring sunrise. A warm breeze stirred her hair as she shifted Solace to her shoulder. Her eyes followed Michael Malloy's lithe body as he hefted the last of the luggage into the carriage boot. He felt her gaze and returned it, pausing to let the moment have its full due—as though he, too, needed her complete attention.

Mercy's heart thudded as she said her good-byes. Billy took Lily from his sister's arms as though it were the natural thing for a boy of thirteen to do, while Asa checked the horses' hitchings. Michael Malloy closed the carriage door, ready to spring into the driver's seat—until he looked her way again.

He swiftly covered the distance between them, to catch her up in a kiss. One arm held her firmly against him while his other hand cradled Solace's little head, and Mercy felt a surge of sublime happiness.

He showed his affection so freely—in front of everyone—without reservation or apology. Surely this man had a clear conscience and a heart set only on her! As his lips lingered on hers, Mercy saw brief visions of how this man had changed her life by bringing the Bristol children here, and burying Judd and Nathaniel, and birthing Solace, and building a home intended for them all.

Feed my sheep, he'd said. And Michael Malloy was the embodiment of that commandment. Yet when his hazel eyes read her unspoken question, they dimmed with regret.

"I'll be back soon," he murmured. "Your eyes are the windows of your soul, Mercy Monroe, and I see a festering wound I never meant to inflict. Be ready to talk about it when I return. Be ready to say yes or no."

Chapter Thirty-four

Malloy clucked to the horses. Then he turned to look at the woman who'd confounded him at every turn.

First she'd been married to a man who made her blissfully happy, even though she worked like a slave to support his dreams. Then, when Judd died, she'd let him patch her life back together and allowed him to help deliver and baptize her child. She had worked him into the patchwork of her daily life—not to mention that magnificent quilt hanging on her wall.

He'd professed his love. He'd given up his job and his freewheeling ways. He'd built her a new home. He'd bared his soul. He'd even won the support of her unflappable Aunt Agatha.

Yet Mercy resisted him.

Everything about her felt like a yes, but her troubled brown eyes were telling him no. There she stood beside Billy and Lily, holding Solace, watching him drive away. Acting like she didn't need his help, while he

355

wondered how long it'd be before those two babies raised the roof with their wailing again. He'd seen Lily as a stroke of luck at first, a final straw to convince her she needed a man again.

But just as Easter lilies made a lot of people sneeze, this temperamental little flower turned Mercy watery-eyed for a whole different reason. Driving her away from him by demanding constant attention.

Stop blaming that baby. You know what changed Mercy's mind.

Mike kicked at the front of the carriage the way he wanted to kick himself. Not his doing, that Lucy Greene appeared after he'd stood up with Mercy in church. Not his doing, that Joel looked desperately for a daddy in every man he met. Was it?

The truth about Lucy would've sounded a lot better right after the two women met. Now Mercy knows you're hiding something. Arranging the details for when you finally tell her about it. Better be ready for a refusal, after that ultimatum you just gave her, idiot.

He got Miss Vanderbilt and Christine to the Abilene station in record time. But it wasn't gratitude he saw in the spinster's face as the porter loaded their trunks.

"Tell her the truth, Mr. Malloy," the little woman said with an unwavering gaze. "Mercedes will see right through a lie and leave you behind. And rightfully so."

So it was "Mr. Malloy" again, was it?

Mike saw them wave from their window and he waved back, but then he left. The horns of his dilemma jabbed him more sharply than a Texas steer's, so seeing them off seemed trivial compared to the situation he had to set straight with Lucy Greene. She would be asleep now—hopefully alone. It was the best time to make his move.

He drove through an awakening Abilene, aware that for every store and business establishment in the respectable section of town, three or four bawdy houses and saloons had sprung up. A savvy young madam named Mattie Silks had constructed an elegant, two-story mansion to house prettier, younger girls. Rumor had it she served only champagne and catered to an elite clientele—but Mike didn't stop at her place. He parked nearby, however, because the sharps and bawds farther down might spot his new carriage and think they needed it more than he did.

He walked down Texas Street lost in his thoughts. How would he tell Lucy he couldn't help her anymore—even to buy a few groceries? She'd insisted he shouldn't worry about her or feel responsible for Joel, but that had never set right with him. Though he'd only bedded her once, under unfortunate circumstances, it seemed providential that Lucy had shown up in Abilene about a year after he did, with a baby boy who stole his heart at first sight.

She understood that his new, adult life didn't include her. She tried to spare him the sordid details of a trade she'd entered into out of sheer desperation.

But what sort of life would Joel have if someone didn't help his mother out of the gutter?

Loud voices drew him from his musings. It seemed early for a barroom brawl to spill out into the street, yet four men circled each other like suspicious vultures. They didn't sound drunk, they sounded outraged, over some sort of investment venture. As they backed away from each other, their pistols flickered in the sunlight.

"You lousy, cheatin' son of a—"

"Hey! I'm going by what the contract said!"

Malloy walked faster. Lucy's room was upstairs in the saloon behind them, and he wanted to arrive in one piece.

He had not figured on seeing her in a doorway, obviously taking shelter from the four-way fight. And the last thing he needed was for Joel to spot him right now.

"You owe me a thousand bucks, you no-good—"

"He paid you half of that! I was there when—"

"Papa! *Papaaa!*"

Malloy's heart flew up into his throat as the little boy squirmed out of his mother's arms. For a toddler, Joel had amazing strength and agility—so he ran right through the middle of the squared-off men brandishing their pistols.

"Joel! Joel, *no!*" Lucy cried. And she followed him, as any mother would.

Mike was too scared to see what happened next. As he ran hell-bent toward the little boy, he heard startled exclamations and at least two shots. Followed by a scream that could only be female.

By the time Lucy hit the ground in a puddle of blue satin and blood, all four men were disappearing in different directions. Abilene still had no organized law enforcement, but none of the men wanted to be seen near this woman of dubious repute, let alone assist her, with a smoking pistol in his hand.

"Lucy? *Lucy?*" Mike called out as he grabbed her little boy.

A groan escaped her. "Michael," she gasped. "Michael—Joel—"

"I've got him right here. He's all right, but we've got to get you—" He knelt beside her to assess her wounds, his arm firmly around the terrified little boy, who was starting to cry.

"Doctor!" he shouted at the top of his lungs. "Somebody get a doctor!"

She was gut-shot and losing blood at an alarming rate. And as Mike pressed his palm against the nearest crimson stain in her blue dress, he saw his promises to Mercy Monroe growing as pale and lifeless as the woman lying beside him.

Chapter Thirty-five

Mercy clambered down from the wagon with Asa's help, and then took Lily and Solace as Billy handed them to her in their baskets. Thank goodness for Hattie and Boots, who barked an eager greeting to their two dogs, and for Emma's delighted cry at seeing the boy she was sweet on. It was May Day: her first birthday without Judd, and the anniversary of a marriage that had kept the promise of "'til death do us part." She needed every possible distraction to keep from sagging like a soggy handkerchief.

And why had Michael not returned? She didn't want to think about that, either.

She put on a smile for lanky, bespectacled Gabriel, who came running up behind his pretty cousin. "Did you bring us a pie, Asa?" he asked. "Wouldn't be a party without that!"

"Yessir, I did myself proud," the old Negro replied

with a wide grin. "Not only cherry and apple raisin, but a buttermilk custard one, too. It's not pumpkin, but I think you boys'll eat it anyway."

"Yeah, we can probably choke some down," Billy teased. "C'mon, Gabe! Let's get these benches outta the back. Folks'll be gettin' here soon."

Mercy glanced around the neat little yard, situated between the corrals and a small log house. It felt strange, having their gathering here, yet she was grateful for the Clarks' hospitality today. When Emma crouched between the two baby baskets, she smiled at how this blond tomboy had undoubtedly worn her newest dress, of sky-blue calico with ribbon trim, to impress Billy.

The girl lifted Lily to her shoulder. "So here's that little bundle of joy somebody dropped on your doorstep. Why, she looks just like a doll!"

"Miss Lily's a charmer when she wants to be," Mercy agreed. "Once she starts walking, the rest of us'll be going at a trot to keep up with her."

Lily giggled, making the golden curls shimmy around her head, as though she knew what a princess she was.

"And what a pretty red dress, Mercy!" Emma gushed. "You're gussied up like it's a special occasion."

Mercy decided not to say how old she felt today. "My Aunt Agatha gave me this gown for Christmas a couple years ago, and I'm celebrating the fact that I can get into it," she said in the steadiest voice she could manage.

"And that color becomes you like nothing I've ever seen." Rachel Clark came up beside them, eyeing her new dress with envy. "All of us admire how you refused to dye everything black, and the way you've kept Judd's memory alive by keeping *yourself* that way. Takes a special kind of woman to do that."

Well, now! She'd never heard this slender, soft-spoken woman string so many sentences together. Mercy was thinking of how to respond when Nell Fergus scooped up her daughter with a grin as big as Kansas.

"And look at Solace, how she's grown! No doubt who this one's daddy is!"

Yes, I see him each time I look at her. Depending on how lonely she felt at any given moment, her daughter's resemblance to Judd could be a boon or a bane. Mercy blinked rapidly, determined not to put a damper on everyone's day.

"It's so nice of you to host the party this time," she remarked. "What with the two babies and—"

"Well, it's high time the rest of us took a turn," Rachel replied. "Lord knows you have your hands full these days. And now that Reverend Larsen has a church in town, and the stages aren't running but once a week, who knows how much longer we'll meet this way?"

"We've seen a lot of progress since we settled here." Waving at George Clark, who was helping the boys arrange the benches, Mercy fought a pang of envy. Being a woman alone wasn't one of the better changes this life on the prairie had brought her.

"Without the help of all my neighbors, the corn wouldn't be planted and I'd have to consider going back East," she continued softly. "Even though I miss some of the conveniences, I'm not sure I'd fit in again."

"We've gotten used to doing things our own way," Nell agreed. "Nothing like life in a log house to teach you how resourceful you can be."

Now *there* was a thought.

And as other wagons rolled in, with the friends who'd seen her through the valley of the shadow, Mercy felt a deep sense of satisfaction. Yes, she missed her parents and the rest of her family. Yes, her days felt impossibly full with these two little girls demanding so much of her time. But she *belonged* here now. To return to that privileged niche of acquiring gowns and jewelry, just to rival her friends at parties, would be a denial of the life she and Judd had forged for themselves.

It would be an admission of defeat, too. Her parents would smugly remind her of that as they went about finding her a suitable match.

No, thank you! that voice in her head cried out. *Happy birthday to me!*

With a smile on her face—a real one this time—Mercy greeted Gregor Larsen and the other families, who made much of the two girls and complimented her new dress. Never mind that she was twenty-nine! Though she'd realized her dream of motherhood only to lose Judd in the process, hers was still a life blessed with fertile land, and a family she'd never anticipated, and friends who would see her through the coming years.

With her girls on either side of her, Mercy took her seat as Reverend Larsen called everyone to worship. The sun felt warm on her face. The spring breeze whispered its promise in her ear—

And Billy was up to something.

He stood beside the preacher now, shifting from one foot to the other. "You prob'ly don't know it," he said over the noise of the crowd, "but we need to start this party with a special surprise—'cause it's Mercy's birthday! Come on out here, Asa!"

Her face went hot. Applause began as a slow ripple, until everyone stood up to congratulate her. And here came her faithful friend, carrying a tall, decorated cake he'd stashed in the wagon without her knowing it.

"Happy birthday, Miss Mercy!" he crowed. "We're glad to help you celebrate this day."

The colored cook pulled a match from his pocket and struck it against the bench, to light the single candle that rose like a steeple from his creation. "Now make a wish! And make it a good one!"

Flustered—for everyone was watching—Mercy closed her eyes. What on earth should she ask for? What wish did she most want to come true?

"Well, hey there, Michael Malloy! High time you showed up!" Billy cried.

Mercy's eyes flew open. A murmur rose from the crowd, like the purr of a curious cat. Despite these past weeks of doubt and disappointment in this man, she turned to watch him ride in on his horse.

He wasn't alone.

Knowing her face matched her crimson dress—and knowing everyone was watching—she whispered to Asa to mind the girls for a moment. Then she strode toward the horseman whose hazel eyes burned into hers as though he had a *right* to gaze at her that way.

"Mercy!" he said with a big grin. "If I'd known today was your—"

"I thought you were ready for my yes or no," she began in a low voice.

She crossed her arms to glare at him. If he thought he could just show up with that loose woman's little boy in his lap, well—she'd let him know different! She felt no inclination to be quiet and polite about it anymore.

"For *weeks* I've been ready to talk—like you wanted," she added in a sharp whisper, "and you were the last man I'd figured for a coward, Mister Malloy. You could have at least—"

"I was tending to Lucy. Had to get her buried and—"

"Is this boy your son, Michael?"

His arm tightened protectively around Joel, who sat listlessly against him. Mike knew she'd tolerate no hesitation on his part, nor any embellishment of the truth. Telling her how gorgeous she looked in that red dress wouldn't help him any, either.

"He is now," Michael replied. "His mama got caught in the crossfire of—"

"Mama?" the little boy chirped sadly. "Mama?"

When Joel raised his head to look at her, Mercy's heart stopped. A more forlorn little creature she'd never seen. His sandy waves dangled past his eyebrows, and his frown looked so melancholy, she knew Michael was telling the truth about Lucinda Greene's death. But that still didn't explain—

"Mama?" Joel asked more loudly.

The sun peeked out in that cloudy little face as he studied Mercy with the profound eyes of a child whom life had tossed aside. Then his arms shot out, and before Michael could catch him, he lunged at her.

"Mama!" he shouted. "Papa, it's Mama!"

Mercy caught him, of course. What else could she do? Her eyes closed and her heart thudded, and she held on to him for dear life. To keep him from falling and hurting himself, of course. But also because she'd never known how very, very sweet it sounded when somebody called her *Mama*.

Michael dismounted, knowing an opportune moment when he saw one. "You see how it is?" he whispered. "I couldn't just leave him at an orphanage. Couldn't trust somebody else to care for him, so—"

"Is Joel your son, Michael?"

Mercy looked into his eyes for signs that he'd orchestrated this little drama to play upon her sympathies. But she saw only a wondrous love as Michael laid his hand on Joel's back while she held the boy.

Well, really the boy was holding *her*. Not much way to refuse him, when his arms were wound around her neck and his head rested blissfully against her shoulder.

"He could be," Malloy admitted, praying Mercy wouldn't be repelled by a regrettable moment in his past. "When I came home from the war, to find Ma dead and buried, I was so upset I got liquored up with a couple buddies I'd soldiered with. We went to visit Lucy in her upstairs room at the tavern," he continued, closing his eyes against memories of that distorted day. "We three heroes were so glad to see a pretty girl, and so full of ourselves at seventeen, that we—"

"You were only seventeen and you'd been to war?"

"Yes, ma'am," he murmured. "And we'd handled our Henry rifles with more respect than we showed for Miss Greene that day. Not long after that, I hired on as an overland stage driver. Lucy showed up in Abilene about a year later, thinking ladies of her profession could make out pretty well in our up-and-coming town. But she had a *baby*. That's no kind of life for a mother and her child."

Mercy considered these details, swaying from side

to side when Joel got restless. "This little boy could belong to any number of men who—"

"After the way I'd treated her, I felt responsible," he stated, his hazel eyes alight with conviction. "Which is why I looked in on her occasionally, even though I never bedded her again. Her life and mine were separate, Mercy. She took that money for groceries and for Joel's sake."

Malloy pressed on, despite how tawdry things must look to this virtuous woman. She was his best chance for happiness. It wasn't particularly an advantage that he was bringing her yet another child . . . one more child than she had hands to manage now.

"I meant it every time I said I loved you," he murmured. "I'm sorry I didn't tell you about Lucy when you needed to hear it most. I should've sent word, I know, but I've been pretty busy."

The crowd behind them had gone silent, probably straining to hear his every word. It would be so easy to accuse this handsome man of manipulating her, perhaps as he himself had been manipulated. Yet Mercy sensed he was playing the hand fate had dealt him as best he could. Just like she was.

Joel relaxed into a deep, contented sleep on her shoulder.

"So nobody will ever know whose boy he is?" she asked. Stalling, mostly, because now that Michael had answered her questions, he deserved the same of her. Lord knows he'd been waiting for an answer longer than she had.

"Well, he's *somebody's* son," Malloy insisted. "I consider him mine, because I believe Joel was God's way of telling me to grow up. I—I can understand if you don't want—"

"Hey, is ever'thing all right over here?"

They turned to see Billy approaching, watching them with intense blue eyes. When he stopped beside her, Mercy sensed he was defending her honor—or making sure Michael Malloy wasn't talking her into something.

Which, of course, he was.

"Well, Billy, Michael's been taking care of Joel because his mother got shot," she said, dipping down so he could see who slept against her shoulder.

Billy gazed warily into the boy's face. "This is the kid who called Michael his daddy, ain't it? After we baptized Solace and that lady in the . . . showy blue dress come out to talk to him."

"Yes. And—knowing how Michael has always looked after children—you're not surprised he's claiming Joel, are you?"

He speared his fingers through his auburn hair. "You was awful aggravated at him after you met that other woman."

"Yes, but I understand the circumstances now." With an apologetic glance at Michael, she added, "If I'd asked him about her that day instead of stewing in my assumptions, I wouldn't have spent so much time and energy being *aggravated.*"

Billy gently lifted Joel's hair for a better look at him. A smile dawned on his face.

"Little kids're cute when they're sleepin', ain't they?" Billy murmured. "And when you're a kid, you love your mother no matter what she does. And you miss her somethin' fierce when she's gone."

Mercy sensed that Billy Bristol had just given his blessing. And though the matter between her and Michael Malloy wasn't his to resolve, he *had* come over to see that she was all right. Just as he'd probably pass along the details to those who sat watching from the benches.

They'd talk about her and Michael anyway. She might as well make it worth their time.

"I was ready to make my birthday wish when you rode in," Mercy reminded Mike. "But I couldn't decide what I wanted."

He heard the shift in her voice, saw the new mood lighting up her pretty face. Malloy's heartbeat thundered like stampeding cattle. "And?"

"I wish you'd kiss me, Michael."

He blinked. "Right here in front of God and everybody?"

"*Especially* in front of God and everybody."

His eyebrows raised playfully. He slipped his arms around her, holding her so Joel wouldn't wake up and ruin his big moment. "Don't toy with me, Mercy," he breathed. "Is this a yes?"

She laughed—no, she giggled! The light shining in his blue-gray eyes warmed her entire being, after so many months of wondering if she'd ever laugh—and love—again.

Mercy nodded. "In front of God and everybody."

"She said *yes!*" Billy yelled. "Mike and Mercy're gonna get hitched!"

The friends behind them jumped up, clapping and whistling, while Joel raised his head with a questioning, sleepy frown.

"Don't cry, little man," Michael said, bussing his temple with a kiss. "It's working out just like we hoped! We're going to be a family, Joel. We're going to be just fine!"

"Fine," Joel echoed. "Just fine, Papa! Mama fine, too!"

The boy extended an arm toward Michael, giggling when his papa moved in to make Mercy's wish come true. Joel wrapped an arm around each of their necks, as though he wanted to make very sure this kiss sealed the deal.

With the first brush of his mustache and the silk of his warm inner lips, Mercy tasted heaven; a new flavor of happiness for the life that would soon be hers. Their friends were coming over to congratulate them, but she refused to shorten this moment for the sake of propriety. She was, after all, honoring her final promise to her husband: taking care of herself and his family—with a few extras thrown in for good measure.

Judd would have wanted it that way.

After a spirited worship service, a meal seasoned by hearty best wishes, and a ride home that rocked the three little ones to sleep, Mercy sat down on the stoop beside Michael. Billy and Asa had tended the horses and slipped upstairs—although she'd heard the old cook coax a redheaded eavesdropper away from the open window.

Above them, the stars sparkled like diamonds in the canopy of the night, each gleaming in its ordained place. Mercy felt a profound sense of rightness as the full moon bestowed its special benediction.

"Thanks for a wonderful day," Michael whispered. "I love you, Mercy. Even though you had me worried there for a while."

"Oh, I'm not finished with that. I'm a woman, you know," she replied. "Born to ask too many questions and expect way too much of my man. So let's review, shall we?"

He wrapped an arm around her, reveling in the

sleek feel of her red dress and grateful for the lilt in her voice. This woman had weathered some tough times, and he admired her resilient spirit. "All right. Let's review."

"Well, if I recall correctly," she began, "you fought in the war, and then you drove a stagecoach and brought us two abandoned Bristols. Meanwhile, you'd latched onto railroad land, and then bought the Barstow place—probably with an eye toward acquiring mine all along—and you've had the foresight to plant winter wheat, and compassion enough to claim a son. And you built a home for a family you didn't even have yet. All this, and you're only twenty-one?"

"Yes, ma'am. Twenty-two in June," he added.

She brushed a lock of his hair aside, to better see his face. Michael still wore his hair longer than was the fashion, but it fit him. He'd never be a slave to convention, and she admired that in a man.

"So you're saying you can manage nearly five hundred acres, and our corrals full of horses, plus three little children and Billy? Not to mention me?"

"Yes, ma'am. More than three children, though," he corrected softly. "Lord willing, we'll have our own, you know."

Something wonderful fluttered inside her, but it was too soon to give in to mere kissing—his favorite way to sidetrack her. There was a lot more she wanted to know about Michael Malloy while she was alone with him, and she hoped for many, many years of sharing this kind of quiet talk.

"So how will you keep this little empire running, young man?" she quizzed. "I'm quite a lot older than you—"

"No, you're not."

"—yet I stand in awe of all you've accomplished."

"Good."

He kissed her, because that's what moonlight was for—and because he knew she loved kissing him more than she let on. "It'll all work out, Mercy. I'll hire good help, and I'll work very hard. And I'll say, 'Yes, ma'am, you're absolutely right,' every chance I get."

When she swatted him, he grabbed her hand and held it against his heart. Its beat felt strong and steady, much like Michael himself.

"I don't talk about such things too often," he whispered, his eyes alight like the stars, "but I believe that goodness—and Mercy—will follow me all my days. Ma taught me at a tender age, using that verse from the sampler in your front room, about what the Lord requires of us."

"To do justice . . . to love mercy . . . to walk humbly with your God," she breathed.

Her heart quivered. For a moment, she was standing beside Judd on a very hot July day three years ago. A dusty driver, Mike Malloy, was asking if they'd look after the Bristol children while he hunted for their mother—and she'd balked, until her husband reminded her of this verse. Her gaze went up the hill to the large river rock marking Judd's grave. The stone glowed serenely in its own patch of moonlight.

"Honey, have I said something wrong?"

Mercy blinked. The love that radiated from his handsome face warmed her like a love she'd known before. "Not at all, Michael. I just . . . once again, I've been reminded that you and Judd are very much alike."

"Well, now," he murmured, "*there's* a compliment worth living up to. Seems to me Judd was as simple and straightforward—yet as deceptively complex—as that Bible verse. Doing justice means—"

"Taking in helpless children, like Christine and Billy and Joel. To give them a good life when their families can't."

Michael paused to kiss her solemnly. "Just as you took Lily and the rest of them into your heart and home. You're a model of mercy, Mercedes—which is only one reason I love you. But I guess Judd must've used that line, too. Long before I had the pleasure."

"I'll never tire of hearing it." She ran a fingertip along the mustache that had just tickled her with its silk, aware of some very sensual differences between Michael Malloy and Judd Monroe. "I don't want you to live in his shadow, constantly comparing yourself to him, sweetheart. I love you for many wonderful, fascinating traits you do *not* share with him."

"Such as?" He arched one eyebrow.

Mercy laughed. "Walking humbly, for one. That's never been your style."

"Ah. Humility. You think I need to work on that?"

"Nope. I think your swagger suits you just fine. It gives me something nice to watch when you walk."

He chuckled. Serious discussion had its place, but so did this playful give-and-take. And who was he to deny her the delight she'd done without for so long?

"Want to know the *real* secret to my success, pretty lady?" he murmured.

Mercy nodded, her eyes wide with anticipation. He hoped he could put that look of excitement on her face every single day.

"Ma also favored that verse about 'Blessed are the merciful, for they shall obtain mercy.' She was reminding me to go easy on my sisters, because—although I was faster and stronger—the six of them together could put me in my place."

His mustache flickered pensively. "It works that way in life. You usually get paid back with the same things you've given out."

Michael gazed toward the heavens then, his face aglow with moonlight. "See there, Ma?" he crowed quietly. "I really was paying attention. And I've latched onto the best Mercy of all—just like you said!"

Her eyes went wet as a tingle rushed up her spine. Not only was Michael more spiritual than he claimed, but his little prayer bespoke the peace he'd made with his mother's untimely passing. Any man who confided in his ma while complimenting his wife knew how to appreciate women!

"Blessed are the merciful," Mercy echoed. "I think that deserves its own sampler for the wall of our new home, don't you, Michael?"

He kissed her again, deeply this time. "Yes, ma'am," he whispered. "You're absolutely right."